SHADOW OF THE SWAN

The *Bel*. Another straying memory. He knew the little ship, could even pilot her himself, and had once long ago. Long ago in that other time, that other life.

He was approaching another nexus of timelines, and perhaps it was an error, the decision that brought him to it. Ben would regard it as an error, even a betrayal. But it wasn't his decision. Alex faced him, seeing his downcast eyes, his rough-hewn features rigid.

'Ben, be careful. And keep an eye on Erica.' He put his hand out, and the pressure of Ben's handclasp revealed more than his tense features. 'Don't worry about us. We can stay on top of things here. For a while, at least. Alex . . .' His breath came out in a long sigh. 'Just take care of yourself, damn it.'

'A new classic! Has the sweep and power of Asimov's Foundation Trilogy.'

Jeans M. Auel, bestselling
author of
Clan of the Cave Bear

By M. K. Wren
and published by New English Library:

THE PHOENIX LEGACY BOOK 1:
   SWORD OF THE LAMB
THE PHOENIX LEGACY BOOK 2:
   SHADOW OF THE SWAN

Shadow of the Swan
Book Two of the Phoenix Legacy

M. K. Wren

NEW ENGLISH LIBRARY

First published in the USA in 1981 by
Berkley Publishing Corporation

A New English Library Original Publication, 1986

First NEL Paperback Edition August 1986

NEL Books are published by
New English Library,
Mill Road, Dunton Green,
Sevenoaks, Kent.
Editorial office: 47 Bedford Square, London WC1B 3DP

Printed and bound in Great Britain by
Cox & Wyman Ltd, Reading

British Library C.I.P.

Wren, M. K.
    Shadow of the swan.——(The Phoenix legacy
M. K. Wren; bk. 2)
    Rn: Martha Kay Renfroe   I. Title   II. Series
    813'.54   PS3573.R43

    ISBN 0–450–05868–9

Synopsis

PART 1: APPRENTICESHIP
Octov 3244 to July 3253 A.D.

The Lord Alexand DeKoven Woolf is destined by birth to occupy a unique position of power in the Concord of the Loyal Houses, the monolithic and essentially feudalistic government that is the matrix for all human civilization in the thirty-third century. The Concord, despite its outward appearances of stability and prosperity, is suffering severe internal stresses, primarily manifested by chronic "uprisings" among the Bonds, its serf/slave class. The Concord is, in fact, threatened with the specter of a third dark age.

The Elite, the Concord's ruling class, however, remains myopically oblivious to that threat. Alexand does not, and he accepts as an obligation, not a privilege, the power to which he is heir. He is the first born of Lord Phillip, member of the Concord's Directorate and First Lord of the House of DeKoven Woolf. Alexand is also the grandson of Lord Mathis Daro Galinin, Chairman of the Directorate and the most powerful man in the Concord, and at the age of seventeen Alexand becomes indirect heir to the Chairmanship when Galinin's only direct heirs are assassinated. Those assassinations precipitate a political crisis, and Alexand is not alone in suspecting Lord Orin Badir Selasis, whose ambition for the Chairmanship and antagonism toward Phillip Woolf make him a bitter enemy of the Houses of Woolf and Galinin.

In the highest echelons of power there is little room for love, but Alexand finds it in Lady Adrien Camine Eliseer. He loves her from the moment they meet, as she does him, but political necessity comes between them; both are committed to marriages—but not to each other. Four years pass before an unexpected chain of events alters the political situation, and Alexand and Adrien are at length betrothed.

Yet before the wedding takes place, Alexand makes a decision whereby he forfeits not only his heritage of power, but all hope for marrying Adrien.

Alexand is near the end of his traditional tour of duty with Confleet, during which he has been involved in quelling fourteen major Bond uprisings, each a searing nightmare in his memory. The catalyst of his decision is his brother, Richard, victim of a crippling neurological disease that will inevitably kill him before his twenty-fifth year. Rich becomes a recluse while still in his teens and devotes himself to the study of sociology, his principal subject the Bonds and Bond religion. Using the Fesh pseudonym of Richard Lamb, he earns a University degree in sociotheology before he is twenty. The Bonds with whom he works in his research regard him as a holy man and call him Richard the Lamb.

As a sociologist, Rich recognizes the critical instability of the Concord. By chance he discovers what he considers the only hope for its survival: the Society of the Phoenix, founded in the Centauri System by survivors of the Peladeen Republic, which was crushed by the Concord. Little is known about the Phoenix in the Concord, and the few who are even aware of its existence generally dismiss it as a pirate clan with revolutionary overtones, but Rich learns its true purpose: evolution, not revolution; to *save* the Concord by forcing on it a long-term process of social evolution toward a representational government providing "a maximum of individual choice, opportunity, and judicial equality within the limits of a stable system." Rich becomes a member, well aware that this makes him a traitor in the eyes of the Concord, and the penalty for treason is death.

Phillip Woolf has loved his two sons passionately, as he loved little else in life, but he proves incapable of acceptance or tolerance when at length he learns that Rich is a Phoenix member. It is Rich himself who reveals his "treason" to his father. His disease is only days or weeks from its lethal culmination, and he has two missions to accomplish before he dies. First, to act as an envoy of the Phoenix to Woolf and Mathis Galinin, to give them a true accounting of the Phoenix and its aims. Second, as Richard the Lamb, to become a saint in the Bond pantheon by offering himself as a martyr in a public execution. His purpose in this is to prolong the life of the Concord by sacrificing what little life is left to him. As a saint, he will have profound influence on the Bonds after his death, a pacific influence he hopes will mitigate the emotional chain reactions that precipitate the bloody uprisings plaguing the Concord and contributing to its instability.

But Woolf angrily renounces his son; he cannot believe Rich's purpose in becoming a martyr is anything other than to instigate a disastrous revolt. When Alexand comes to Rich's defense, Woolf turns against him, too, calling him as much a traitor as his brother. It is then that Alexand makes his decision to follow Rich into the Phoenix. He realizes that he is only heir to power, not yet in possession of it, and by rejecting him, his father renders him politically impotent and incapable of altering to any degree the ruinous course upon which the Concord is embarked. He chooses to sacrifice his marriage to Adrien and his very existence as the Lord Alexand to the cause for which Rich offers his last precious scrap of life and for the hope that the ultimate catastrophe of another dark age can be averted.

Rich has his apotheosis, and Richard the Lamb becomes a saint. On the following day the Lord Alexand "dies" in the crash of a Confleet Scout on Pollux.

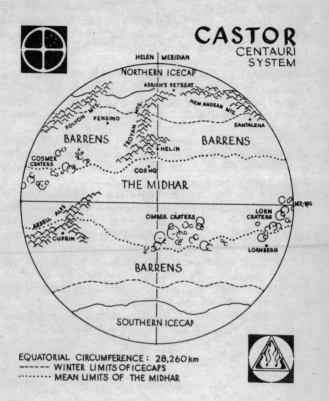

CASTOR
CENTAURI
SYSTEM

HELEN MERIDIAN

NORTHERN ICECAP

ADRIEN'S RETREAT

NEW ANDEAN MTS.

POLYON MTS.

PENDINO

SANTALENA

BARRENS

TROJAN MTS.

BARRENS

HELIN

COSMER
CRATERS

COS HQ

THE MIDHAR

MKR-106

LORN
CRATERS

OMBER CRATERS

ARDEIL ALPS

CUPRIN

LORNBERG

BARRENS

SOUTHERN ICECAP

EQUATORIAL CIRCUMFERENCE : 28,260 km
------ WINTER LIMITS OF ICECAPS
········ MEAN LIMITS OF THE MIDHAR

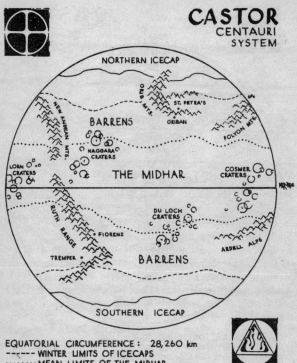

CASTOR
CENTAURI
SYSTEM

NORTHERN ICECAP

OISO MTS.

ST. PETRA'S

ORIBAN

NEW ANNAN MTS.

BARRENS

POLYON MTS.

NAGGARA CRATERS

LORN CRATERS

THE MIDHAR

COSMER CRATERS

DU LOCH CRATERS

RUTH RANGE

FIORENZ

ARDELL ALPS

TREMPER

BARRENS

SOUTHERN ICECAP

EQUATORIAL CIRCUMFERENCE : 28,260 km
----- WINTER LIMITS OF ICECAPS
········ MEAN LIMITS OF THE MIDHAR

Synopsis

PART 2: METAMORPHOSIS
July–Augus 3253 A.D.

The Lord Alexand dies and Alex Ransom is born. At Phoenix headquarters on the island of Fina on Pollux in the Centauri System, he meets its governing Council, including three friends of Rich's: Dr. Erica Radek, Chief of Human Sciences; Ben Venturi, Commander of Security and Intelligence; and Dr. Andreas Riis, founder of the Phoenix, chairman of the Council, and creator of the Society's ultimate secret weapon the matter transmitter.

Alex also meets an enemy: Councilor Predis Ussher.

Phase II of the Phoenix's General Plan hinges on establishing a member in the Concord's ruling hierarchy through whom the social reforms vital to the Concord's survival can be initiated. Before Alex's arrival only one member is likely to be recognized as a Lord by the Concord: Predis Ussher, who claims to be the son of Elor, last Lord of the House of Peladeen. But Alex offers a better alternative if the Lord Alexand—an heir to the Chairmanship—can be resurrected, and Ussher does not welcome him. There is no immediate confrontation, however; Phase II will be achieved only by forcing the Directorate to the bargaining table with a show of military force. The Phoenix isn't yet prepared for that encounter, and beyond that, its primary offering—and threat—is not yet operational: the *long-range* matter transmitter (LR-MT). At present the MT functions only within Einsteinian limits and is not feasible for interstellar distances.

Alex's real identity remains the secret of the Council pending a breakthrough on the LR-MT, and he is assigned to Fleet Operations, the Phoenix's military branch. But his identity is guessed by one member who is not on the Council: Jael the Outsider, who joins the Phoenix shortly after Alex. Before Jael leaves Fina for duty with Security and Intelligence on Castor, he warns Alex to beware of Ussher because he is not only a threat to the future of the Phoenix, but, quite literally, a killer.

Characters

CAST OF CHARACTERS:

ALEXAND DEKOVEN WOOLF (Alex Ransom)	First born and heir to the First Lordship of the House of DeKoven Woolf, indirect heir to the Chairmanship of the Directorate
RICHARD DEKOVEN WOOLF (Richard Lamb)	Alexand's younger brother
PHILLIP DEKOVEN WOOLF	Alexand's father, First Lord of the House of DeKoven Woolf and member of the Directorate
ELISE GALININ WOOLF	Alexand's mother, the daughter of Mathis Galinin
OLIVET OMER WOOLF	Daughter of Lord Sandro Omer, married to Phillip Woolf after the death of his first wife, Elise, in 3253
THERON ROVERE	Lector; Alexand's and Rich's tutor
FENN LACROY	SportsMaster in the House of DeKoven Woolf and Phoenix agent

MATHIS DARO GALININ	First Lord of the House of Daro Galinin and Chairman of the Directorate
ORIN BADIR SELASIS	First Lord of the House of Badir Selasis, member of the Directorate, and bitter antagonist to Woolf and Galinin
KARLIS SELASIS	First born of Lord Orin Selasis
ADRIEN CAMINE ELISEER	Daughter of Lord Loren Camine Eliseer of Castor, and Alexand's Promised
LECTRIS AND MARIET	Adrien's Bond servants

SOCIETY OF THE PHOENIX:

DR. ANDREAS RIIS	Founder of the Phoenix, chairman of its Council, and creator of the matter transmitter
DR. ERICA RADEK	Council member, head of the Human Sciences Department
BEN VENTURI	Council member and commander of Security and Intelligence
PREDIS USSHER	Council member, head of Communications, who claims to be the son of Elor, last Lord of the House of Peladeen
EMERIC GARRIS	Council member, commander of Fleet Operations until his retirement in 3255
JOHN M'KIM	Council member, head of Supply and Maintenance
MARIEN DYCE	Council member, head of Computer Systems

JAN BARRET   Officer in Fleet Operations

VALENTIN SEVERIN   Assistant to Erica Radek

JAEL   First Outsider to join the Phoenix, SI agent in Helen on Castor

PART 3: GAUNTLET

●‖

PHOENIX MEMFILES: DEPT HUMAN SCIENCES: BASIC SCHOOL
                   (HS/BS)
SUBFILE: LECTURE, BASIC SCHOOL 1 FEBUAR 3252
                 GUEST LECTURER: RICHARD LAMB
                 SUBJECT: POST-DISASTERS HISTORY:
                 WARS OF CONFEDERATION (2876–2903)
DOC LOC #819/219–1253/1812–1648–123252

The "Sudafrikan Union" was the Holy Confederation's term. The name the Minister-Keffe Tsane Valstaad used is translated as the "Tsanian Empire." (Or, as some historiolinguists prefer, "Commonwealth.") It was not an alliance put together in the face of the threat of the Confederation, which even the Allienza Salvador was, although it predated the initiation of the Wars. The Sudafrikan Union was forged in a series of wars comparable to Even Pilgram's, and Tsane Valstaad was the third in a dynasty of rulers who held his diverse and scattered subjects in thrall of a centralized, imperialistic government that should have appealed to Lord Patric Eyre Ballarat. Certainly it impressed him in a tactical sense during the seven-year Sudafrikan campaign, the most difficult and most costly of the Wars.

Tsane himself was a fascinating man. ("Tsane" was a surname—his family name—despite its placement; "Valstaad" was actually his forename.) Had his domains been a little more advanced historically and technologically, Tsane might easily have taken Ballarat's role in history as the first conqueror of an entire world. As it was, Sudafrika had advanced little past the iron age, although it made great strides after its initial contacts with the Holy Confederation in its period of expansion by trade; the Tsanians were apt learners and excellent imitators. Still, they didn't have facilities for any kind of heavy manufacturing. Tsane sought to offset that disadvantage while Ballarat was still occupied with conquering the rest of Terra by stockpiling weapons

1

and machines of war, most of which were actually produced in Conta Austrail, but reached him through covert and circuitous channels. Tsane also fortified his territories and trained his armed forces during this preparatory period, and beyond that instilled in his subjects a patriotic fervor that can only arise when people are fighting for their homeland. Further, Tsane, like Ballarat, recognized the efficacy of religion as a motivating force and in essence prepared to cross swords with Bishop Almbert as well as with Ballarat. His was also a holy war, although a battle to preserve, rather than to disseminate, a religion. Oddly enough, the religion sanctioned by the Minister-Keffe and imposed two generations earlier on his subjects was also based, like Mezionism, on Pre-Disasters Christianity, although it had changed almost beyond recognition in its evolution.

Tsane's preparations for his encounter with Ballarat included learning his enemy's language, which I think gives us a measure of the man. I've always been intrigued with the accounts of his first personal meeting with Ballarat, which occurred after the Battle of Capeton, where Ballarat's forces made their first landfall in Sudafrika. Tsane sent a messenger to Ballarat in bivouac asking for a meeting under truce. In an open plain, where every movement could be observed by both sides, Tsane's soldiers erected an open-sided tent luxuriously fitted with carpets of animal skins, furniture of carved ebony embellished with gold, tables laden with wines, fruits, and epicurean viands in serving pieces of silver and gold, the servants in attendance all comely young women decked in silk and jewels. Tsane allowed none of his soldiers within the agreed-upon three-hundred-meter neutral area, although he accepted the ten-man "honor guard" Ballarat brought with him. Tsane entered the neutral area entirely alone, except for the two leashed leopards flanking him. He was an exceptionally tall man, and he dressed himself on this occasion in flowing robes of red silk edged in gold embroidery, with a leopard skin draped over one shoulder, and a plumed crown adding to his imposing height. An impressive sight, no doubt, and his leopard "guards" must have been particularly astonishing, since the animals were thought at that time to be extinct.

Ballarat and Tsane met in those exotic surroundings in the wake of the first battle of what both knew would be a desperately fought campaign and played a game of chess.

It sounds like the fancy of a romantically inclined historian, except that the event was so well documented; there are even photograms of that fateful game, but they're all rather fuzzy since they were taken from outside the neutral zone. Tsane informed his guest upon his arrival in the tent that his sole purpose was to meet the famed Lord Ballarat and to play a game of chess with him. Ballarat was apparently amused at this and willingly acquiesced, even offering to play by Tsane's rules. (Slight differences in the rules of this venerable game developed in different parts of Terra during the isolation of the Second Dark Age, although the basic principles changed remarkably little.) Tsane, however, insisted that a host must always accede to his guest's rules, and so the game was played. It lasted for three and a half hours and ended in a draw. No doubt both men found it enlightening.

It has always seemed strange to me that Ballarat and Tsane didn't become friends, which has happened more than once in history between commanders of opposing forces. I think Tsane could have regarded Ballarat as a friend; certainly we have ample evidence that he held him in high esteem. But Ballarat couldn't regard Tsane as a friend, and not because they were at war. The real reason was far less rational. It was because of Tsane's race. He was negroid, as were all his subjects. The caucasian population that had once inhabited Sudafrika had been entirely absorbed by the negroid, leaving almost no trace of their existence. The opposite was true in Conta Austrail, where the native aborigine population was absorbed by the more numerous caucasian intruders. Ballarat grew up in a essentially caucasian world, and there is ample evidence in his writings and responses to other racial groups that he harbored a deep-seated bias against noncaucasians that was particularly virulent when it came to negroids. Unfortunately, he wasn't alone in that among the Lords of the Holy Confederation, and it was only in the later years of the PanTerran Confederation that the racial barriers Ballarat raised finally gave way.

I should put in a good word for Almbert here. The Bishop did not share Ballarat's aversion for other races, perhaps convinced that all of them were potential converts and therefore worthy of consideration.

Ballarat's next attempt at a landfall at Dares Salma was a disaster, the first of many. His second-in-command, Lord Aram Barth Andrasy, attempting a simultaneous invasion at Luanda, was also roundly defeated. But Ballarat had a firm foothold in the south in Capeton, plus a navy strong enough to blockade every Tsanian port. He also had Sahrafrika in thrall. However, the vast overland distances involved, through desert and jungle, delayed the arrival of supporting forces from the north for months, so that Tsane could concentrate on fending off the assault from the south as well as protecting his flanks. Ballarat made good use of his airships, but their range was short, and Tsane's holds were well fortified and armed with heavy artillery that made air assaults very costly. Ballarat maintained the southern front while continuing to nibble at the eastern and western coasts, and finally Andrasy was successful in another assault at Luanda and drove the Tsanians inland along a strip a thousand kilometers long. This was the Holy Confederation's first major victory in the Sudafrikan campaign, but it cost Lord Aram Andrasy his life. Ballarat was personally grieved at the loss, and it had lasting adverse effects for him in Conta Austrail; Andrasy had become almost as much a hero there as Ballarat himself.

Ballarat took time from the Sudafrikan battlefields to return to Sidny for Andrasy's funeral, where he gave a moving eulogy, and if he had been wise he would have stayed longer, or at least made himself more aware of the changing temper of the Lords. The Sudafrikan campaign was in its second year and proving extremely costly. As one influential Lord complained, "It empties our coffers and brings nothing in; it takes the lives of our young men by the tens of thousands and offers no salve for our grief."

Ballarat did take time to assemble the Directorate and the Council to assure them that Sudafrika *would* bring something into their coffers and salve their grief, but he didn't stay long enough to see how effective his assurances were, nor to notice how *in*effective his brother Hugh was as VisChairman. (Bryan, incidentally, after the Quador disaster, retired to the House's Estate in Ballarat to tend its business affairs.) Perhaps the Holy Confederation had simply, after more than twenty years, grown tired of war, and its Lords were satisfied to reap the tribute of the domains already subdued and leave one part of the planet unconquered.

Patric Ballarat, of course, would not be satisfied with that, and his imperial ambition was bolstered now with personal frustration and grief. He wanted vengeance, as well as victory, and he returned to Sudafrika determined to have it.

In the end, of course, he did have both, but not before another five years had passed, and not before his armies suffered nearly a million casualties. Tsane's casualties can only be estimated, but it's doubtful they were any less appalling. The monetary cost of the campaign came very close to literally emptying the Holy Confederation's coffers. Ballarat saw in Sudafrika's plentiful resources the means for financial recovery, and he was right, but the immediate fiscal strain on the Holy Confederation's Lords, who had so quickly grown accustomed to overflowing coffers, had a strong influence on their thinking and future reactions.

It should be noted that Ballarat was not immoderate in his vengeance. Any reprisals against the Tsanians that occurred were carried out in defiance of his orders. Once conquered, Sudafrika was treated exactly like the other defeated domains. The ceremonies of surrender took place in Tsane's palace in his capital of Pratoria, which Ballarat had occupied and where Tsane was a prisoner, but treated with the respect due an emperor, conquered or not. Before the actual signing of the surrender, Ballarat invited Tsane to meet with him, and the two of them sat down together in a garden pavilion. And played a game of chess. The second game also ended in a draw.

CHAPTER VIII: Decem 3257

1.

On the fourth level of the Hall of the Directorate in the Office of the Chairman, Lord Mathis Galinin stood at the windowall gazing down into the Plaza of the Concord. The atmobubbles were on against the midsummer heat, but the white pavement was a searing glare in the noon sunlight. The Plaza had the look of a desert. The Fountain was off. Perhaps that was it.

The Fountain of Victory was stilled as it always was for a public execution.

Galinin clasped his hands behind his back when he realized he'd been absently pulling at his beard. He despised such nervous mannerisms. An old man's quirk, so Camma used to chide him. But no more. No more chiding, no more laughing reminders that they were both growing old and might as well make the best of it. And no more pain for Camma. Two years ago on a summer day like this she had at last accepted the peace of death. She had borne him three children, three fine children, and outlived them all, and even *their* children, except for Evin's daughter, Camila. At least there was something left, someone to give proof in her ready smile of Camma Nordreth Galinin's passage through this world.

The long sigh was just as much an old man's quirk. His gaze moved to the steps below him, to the black monolith of the execution stand. He had always experienced an inward shock at that light-swallowing mass of black. It was worse since Rich's death. Four and a half years wasn't time enough to dull the pain of reminder, and the reminders came all too frequently now.

There were three execution mechanisms on the stand today, not just one. A bitter economy of his own devising. He had tried to put an end to these barbaric displays, but the Directors, except for Phillip and Honoria, balked. Even Trevor Robek. Examples, they called them; object lessons. There was a crowd of perhaps a thousand gathered to study this lesson—there always was—and he wondered what they came to learn from these deaths.

And he wondered why it never seemed to occur to the Directorate majority of seven that these executions were signals of piecemeal surrender. Galinin had only succeeded, by the expedient of multiple executions, in reducing the number of occasions on which the Fountain was stilled.

The chime of the pager roused him. He returned to his desk, which like everything around him—or so it seemed lately— was heavy with history and tradition, designed by a famous artisan of a bygone century, whose name he had made every effort to forget, displaying the Concord crest in panels of inlaid woods from every part of Terra and even Pollux. Its imposing array of screens and consoles, all of which hid themselves discreetly under polished wood covers at an electronic command, were becoming increasingly intimidating. Or perhaps only annoying. Like the chair, large and deep, soberly carved in ebony, its high back, despite the cushions, offering no comfort for *his* back. It was only a surrogate for that chair in the Directorate Chamber, and neither were designed for ordinary human beings with elderly spines.

He sank into the chair with another long sigh, touched a button, and watched Master Selig's face materialize on the intercom screen. He wondered if Selig ever sighed.

"Yes, Selig?"

"My lord, Dr. Gilcris is here."

"Good. Send him in, please."

Galinin leaned back, waiting for the double doors to slide open and for Dr. Avery Gilcris, lector emeritus, Academicians GuildMaster, and head of the Concord University System sociotheology department, to step gingerly onto the golden carpet.

A peculiarly colorless man, Galinin was thinking; white lector's robes, edged in black, enveloping his frail, stooped figure; wispy gray hair and beard. He fluttered across the room, the handle of a slim case locked in his bony hands.

"Dr. Gilcris—" Galinin gestured toward the chair across the desk from him. "—please, be seated. I was delighted to hear you'd completed the research project."

"I must apologize again for the delays, my lord, but it proved more of an undertaking than I envisioned at first."

"My concern is for insight, not haste. Tell me, did you find the project interesting?"

Gilcris pursed his lips, considering the question, but Galinin wasn't impatient. The professor was honest in his plodding way. That's why he'd been chosen for this task.

"Quite interesting, my lord. I've done very little research on Bond religion, and a certain amount of that was necessary, of course, to establish a background for Saint Richard the Lamb. I was rather amazed more sociotheologians hadn't been attracted to it."

"I gather you found the available material scant. Did you read the theses of Richard Lamb himself?"

"Oh, yes, my lord. I had a Priority-Two clearance since the project was done at your behest."

Galinin stiffened. "Priority-Two?"

"Why, yes. All Lamb's theses are now classified Pri-Two."

"*All* of them? For the God's sake—" Galinin paused to control his annoyance. He should have expected this, should have checked with the Board of Censors.

"My lord?"

"Never mind, Doctor. I was only wondering why those theses were given a Pri-Two rating. I've read them and found nothing at all subversive or inflammatory, whatever Lamb's ultimate political choices."

Gilcris nodded soberly. "I quite agree, my lord. All his works were meticulously scholarly, and not in the least tainted by his political views."

"At any rate, I'm anxious to hear the results of your study."

"Yes, of course, my lord." He rested the case on his knees and opened it. "I have here various recordings and statistical correlations if you'd care to—"

"Please, I'd prefer not to get mired in mathematics at the moment." Then, at Gilcris's stricken look, he softened his tone. "I'll study the material later, if you'll leave it with me, but now I'd like a summation in your own words."

"Oh. Yes, my lord." He closed the case and put it on the desk, pausing for Galinin's nod of permission. Then he cleared his throat, seeming uncertain about what to do with his empty hands.

"Well, then, to summarize... well, first my staff and I sampled compounds on every planet and satellite in the Two Systems and ascertained that Saint Richard the Lamb is a well established member of the Bond pantheon. He's especially revered in the compounds where he made frequent appearances."

"I assume you and your staff interviewed some of the Shepherds who knew Lamb personally. Did you ask them about his connection with the Phoenix?"

"Yes, we did, and it's really quite odd, but none of them seemed at all aware of his association with the Phoenix, or of the fact that he was executed for that reason."

Galinin gave him a suitably puzzled look. "That's strange. How do you explain it?"

"I can't explain it factually. However, I might note that few Bonds are aware of the existence of the Phoenix."

"I see. But don't they wonder why Lamb was executed?"

"They explain it as a Testing, my lord, which is—"

"Yes, I'm familiar with the term."

"Oh. Well, apparently a Testing needs no logical cause. None of the Bonds interviewed showed the slightest interest in the reason for Lamb's execution. They simply dismissed it as the Mezion's will. And perhaps..." He paused, looking down at his folded hands.

"Please don't hesitate to voice any speculations, Doctor. If I wanted bare facts, I wouldn't ask a man of your stature to waste his time gathering them."

A wan flush came to his sunken cheeks, and the compliment gave him courage to go on.

"Well, my lord, it occurred to me that perhaps the Bonds are closer to the truth than one might think. You see, I checked with Commander Quintin Bary of the Concordia SSB as you suggested. It seems that Lamb was arrested solely on the basis of an anonymous tip, and his trial was only a formality; nothing was actually proven against him because he confessed freely to all charges."

Galinin nodded, regarding him with attentive interest.

"And what conclusions have you drawn from this?"

"No conclusions, my lord, actually; speculations, perhaps. I was also considering Lamb's long-standing and close association with Bonds, particularly the Shepherds. He made frequent sojourns into the compounds for years before his death, and his first thesis was published when he was only seventeen. It wasn't what one would call a normal pursuit for a young person. And he was ill; badly crippled, in fact." Gilcris glanced almost furtively at Galinin. "Well, it occurred to me that Lamb might have been somewhat unstable emotionally, that he became obsessed with the Bonds and their religion, that perhaps he *wasn't* a member of the Phoenix. Perhaps he saw his arrest and execution as the Bonds did—as a Testing and the will of the Mezion. He might have confessed to *any* charge brought against him."

Galinin leaned back, reining the ironic laughter that was his first impulse. Phillip Woolf had been afraid the Bonds would be led to the Phoenix's banner by Richard Lamb. It was a paradox that not only did the Bonds show no awareness of a link between Lamb and the Phoenix, but this learned man had come to the conclusion that no link had ever existed.

"Dr. Gilcris, that's an interesting theory, and you may have hit on the truth. I always found it difficult to resolve Lamb's scholarly treatises with membership in what is accepted as a revolutionary organization. Very interesting. And I'm gratified that you've discovered no link between Lamb and the Phoenix in the minds of the Bonds."

"We certainly found no hint of it, and Saint Richard's dictums are notably pacific, condemning violence for any cause. That would hardly seem consistent with membership in a group like the Phoenix."

"No, it wouldn't. Now, the main purpose of your study was to learn what influence, if any, Saint Richard has had on the Bonds, especially in regard to violent revolts or uprisings."

Gilcris nodded, pursing his lined lips. "Well, my lord, our first task was to determine the range of his influence, benign or otherwise, and we discovered that Saint Richard is all but universally known among the Bonds. We were even able, to some degree, to follow the spread of the cult, or rather his acceptance into the Bond pantheon, both in terms of time and distance. For instance, we know that news of his execution— or martyrdom, as the Bonds would have it—reached Helen on Castor approximately a year afterward along with the reliquary ashes."

"The reliquary ashes?"

"Yes, my lord. Lamb was considered a holy man, almost a saint, even before his death. Sainthood is bestowed rather informally, apparently, more by mutual agreement among the Shepherds than anything else. At any rate, it's customary on the death of a holy man or saint to divide his ashes into small containers, which are distributed as opportunity permits to chapels throughout both Systems. They're considered holy relics."

Galinin smiled faintly. It seemed fitting that Rich's ashes should be thus scattered among his believers across planets and satellites and light years.

"Please continue, Dr. Gilcris."

Gilcris glanced longingly at the case, then, "Well, my lord, we have statistical evidence indicating that Lamb has, in fact, had a markedly beneficial influence in counteracting violent reactions among the Bonds. We also have testimony from over-seers and guards that nine minor disturbances were unquestionably quelled by Shepherds quoting the dictums of Saint Richard. In these cases, the witnesses remembered hearing particular phrases or the name of Saint Richard. These are rare instances, to be sure; however, they suggest that others of a similar nature have occurred, but none of the witnesses were aware of the use of the dictums."

Galinin paused, one eyebrow lifted. "You said you had statistical evidence."

Gilcris nodded. "We made stat correlations of all reported Bond Uprisings in the last ten years. We assigned them an intensity rate based on duration, number of Bonds taking part, financial loss, and casualties. We also drew curves based on incidence and correlated both incidence and intensity on other sequences. All curves showed an upward trend from the date of beginning—that is, July 3247. The curve gradually becomes sharper, in fact, and this trend continues well past July '53, when Lamb died, and into the early months of '54."

Galinin frowned. "It continues?"

"Yes, my lord, but that's the data for the entire Concord. We made similar studies of individual planets and satellites, and various subareas on Terra. In eastern Conta Austrail, for instance, both incidence and intensity curves begin to level off by Septem '53; that would be three months after Lamb's death. Luna and Mars show a similar leveling a few months later, although the curves on the Cameroodo compounds tend to be . . . well, rather erratic."

Galinin nodded absently; he was all too well aware of Lord James Cameroodo's high incidence of uprisings and the repressive measures that fostered them.

"Dr. Gilcris, does this leveling coincide with the spread of the cult of Saint Richard?"

"Yes, it does; at least, where we have sufficient data to pinpoint the time at which Bonds in a particular area accepted Saint Richard into their pantheon."

"I see. Go on, Doctor."

"Well, the general curves for the entire Concord don't show a leveling until after the first months of '55, and then there's a marked downward curve that extends into May of this year. Our studies end two months later in July on the fourth anniversary of Lamb's death."

"But there was definitely a downward trend in the general curves for the last two years?"

"Without a doubt, my lord. However, in the latter part of May and into June of this year, they began to level off. I might note this coincides with certain symptoms of unrest among the Fesh."

Galinin found himself venting another sigh and frowned.

"What conclusions have you drawn from these statistics as a whole, Dr. Gilcris?"

His wispy eyebrows lifted in unison with his shoulders.

"There's a definite correlation between the downturn of the incidence and intensity curves and the spread of the cult of Saint Richard. We've looked for other factors to explain the phenomenon, but none seem to fit the data."

Galinin gazed out the windowall a moment, then turned away; the Fountain was still off.

"It would seem that Richard Lamb, whoever he was, and whatever his reasons, has done the Concord a great service. Doctor, I appreciate the fine work you've done on this project."

"Thank you, my lord. It was my pleasure to be of service." He paused, shifting his weight toward the edge of his chair. "My lord . . . uh, there *was* another item I encountered on this project that you might find of interest. You see, in the process of interviewing the various Shepherds, my staff and I came across another—well, would-be saint, I suppose; one associated with Saint Richard. I don't know the actual relationship, but this person calls himself the Brother of the Lamb, referring to Saint Richard, of course."

"The Brother—" Galinin stared at Gilcris, and it was a moment before he remembered to bring his features under rein. "What did you find out about this new saint?"

"Nothing in the way of factual data, and apparently he isn't yet classified as a saint, but as a holy man. He's most influential in Centauri, but he was also mentioned by Shepherds in the Solar System."

"What did they say about him?"

"Very little, actually; no hint of his real identity. None of them know him by any name except the Brother."

"Does that indicate an actual blood relationship?"

"I doubt that. It's a matter of record that Lamb was an orphan, raised by the Sisters of Faith. Of course, this man may have told the Bonds a blood relationship existed if it served his purpose."

"And what *is* his purpose?"

Gilcris shrugged helplessly. "It would seem it's simply to reinforce Lamb's message. The Shepherds say he speaks of peace and often quotes Saint Richard."

"Is he seen frequently?"

"Apparently not. I gather he simply appears in the chapels at odd intervals and speaks only to the Shepherds."

Galinin sagged back into his chair and consciously stopped his hand from going to his beard. Perhaps the Phoenix had found a way of maintaining their indirect influence over the Bonds, and that was disturbing. With Rich, he knew what he was dealing with.

The Brother. Why that? Why not the acolyte? Or the disciple?

Galinin sighed again and looked across at Gilcris.

"Doctor, you'll recognize the need to investigate this Brother more thoroughly. Someone might try to take advantage of Lamb's influence, but with less benign intent. I want you to look into it further, and report to me as soon as you have conclusive data. And I want the work you've done in corre-lating data on Bond uprisings continued. However, I realize that would be too much of a burden for you along with your regular duties. I'd like you to set up a permanent research facility. You may choose the staff and organize it as you see fit, and I'll make sure you have adequate funding. I'll have Master Selig draw up the necessary authorizations today."

"Thank you, my lord." Gilcris beamed proudly. "I'll do my best to carry out your wishes to your satisfaction."

"I'm sure you will, and I'm sure I'll be more than satisfied." He rose, and Gilcris all but hopped to his feet. "I'll look over the material in the case as soon as possible and let you know if I have any further questions."

"Call on me at any time. Good day, my lord." He bowed, then fluttered away across the golden carpet. Galinin touched the doorcon on the desk, catching a glimpse of Selig at his desk and a cluster of waiting Concord officials and House liaisons.

Galinin closed the doors, leaving the intercom on no-call status, then walked slowly to the windowall. The Fountain was on now, and the execution stand was already being dismantled. That called up another sigh. Three human lives had been snuffed out while he talked to Avery Gilcris.

But that conversation took the edge from that realization. Rich had had his apotheosis, and now his ashes were scattered throughout the Two Systems, and his words—those fragile, intangible, powerful abstractions—had done more to maintain peace in the Concord than all Conpol's and Confleet's lethal and very tangible machines.

At length, he turned and walked back to his desk, a frown drawing his white brows together.

The Brother.

He wondered why he felt an irrational chill at that.

2.

First Commander Alex Ransom surveyed the scene, the wake of catastrophe, from the comcenter deck in Hangar 1. He gripped the railing with both hands, and a weaker material would have snapped under the pressure.

The Solar Fleet had taken a devastating blow, and the beaten survivors were limping home to Fina. The Rhea base didn't have the facilities to deal with a disaster of this magnitude.

The steady pulse of the pumps was an insistent undercurrent in the welter of sound—the rumbling of nulgrav generators, the blasts of guidance jets from the ships, the whining hum of towcars, the hiss and thud of magnetic hooks shooting out on their tensteel cables—but the floor of the hangar was still awash with sea water carried in by the ships, making unsteady footing for the swarming ground crews and medsquads. They moved with frantic urgency, and the timbre of their shouted questions and orders verged on panic.

And perhaps it was time, Alex thought grimly, that they felt the goad of panic. Three years of small triumphs bought at small cost because of the cautious tactics that the crews complained of so bitterly, and they'd learned nothing from those triumphs but overconfidence.

Alex stared at the seared and broken hulls. Thirteen Falcons and six Corvets lost or damaged. The Solar Fleet that had cost so much in time and effort was in one encounter crippled. It would be months in recovering. And some things were beyond recovery. Lives. Nearly fifty lives lost.

His gaze moved to his right, fixing on the hulking leviathan painted brown and glaring green with the sleeping-bear crest of Badir Selasis like an eye near the bow. It occupied nearly a quarter of the length of the hangar and loomed too large to be moved through the tunnel into Hangar 2. A First Line freighter carrying a valuable cargo; a prize, indeed. But its price had been high.

The echoing clank of the lock gates brought his attention into focus on the entry tunnel. Another Corvet was moving into the hangar, water sheeting off her hull. *Gamin*. Her port side was ripped with a crumpled gash, the port steering vanes crushed. Towcars and crews and red-suited medsquads scurried out to meet her, while she staggered, then slewed to an abrupt halt, canted over on her side.

Alex listened to the voices emerging from the earpiece of his headset. He was on the ADCon frequency—Approach and Docking Control—and what he was hearing pulled his brows together in a frown; what he was seeing pleased him no more. There were only two towcars working unsuccessfully at trying to right *Gamin*.

He switched on his headset mike. "Lanc, give me an interconn with *Gamin*."

A faint click, then, "Simon on line."

"Captain, this is Ransom. What's your stat?"

"Ground guidance is out, sir. We can't—"

"All right, stand by. Lanc?"

"Yes, sir?"

"Where the hell is Camron?"

"Major Camron's in Hangar 2 berthing the *Hopewell*."

"Connect me. And tell *Loriel* there'll be an entry delay." Another click. "Major Camron?"

"Yes, sir, this is—"

"Get two more towcars to the entry tunnel. *Gamin*'s disabled."

"But I won't have a crew avail——"

"Clear the entry area, Major. *Loriel*'s coming through with a damaged hull; she may not be able to hold against the water pressure."

Alex touched the mike switch and cut Camron off, staring fixedly at the stretcher-laden medsquads. At least *Loriel* was the last of the Solar Fleet ships. Then he turned and strode into the comcenter, barely giving the door time to open. His entrance produced a hush among the techs at their screens and consoles.

Captain Lanc looked up from his comconsole, then turned away, but not before a faint sigh escaped him. There wasn't a trace of expression in Commander Ransom's face. It was that lack of outward evidence of anger that brought Lanc's sigh. When Ransom frowned, there was nothing to worry about.

"Mistra Bayrd."

"Yes, Commander?" A young woman turned from her intent study of the radar projection chamber.

"Is the splash-down area still clear?"

"Yes, sir. There's a three-ship Second Line freighter fleet clearing the Comarg IP. They'll be over the screened field in seven minutes."

"A scheduled flight?"

"Yes, sir. On time and no extra escort."

"Captain Lanc, are you on line with *Loriel*?"

"She's holding. Wait—" He listened to his earspeaker, then turned a frequency dial. "Tunnel area's open, sir. *Loriel*, PNX ADCon on line. You're clear for entry."

Alex turned, looking out into the hangar until he saw the black, shark-like bow of the Corvet emerging from the lock tunnel.

"Lanc, tell Commander Barret to report to me in my office as soon as he turns *Loriel* over to the ground crews." He spun on his heel and left the comcenter.

"Yes, sir." Lanc sighed again. He wouldn't relish being in Jan Barret's shoes right now.

Alex stood behind his desk, facing the screens mounted on the wall. All of them were focused on the hangars; the mirrored walls of the small room reflected distorted images of disaster. He wasn't wearing his headset, but his desk comconsole was on receive.

Finally, he turned and studied Jan Barret, who stood on the other side of the desk at grim, haggard attention. Alex regarded him with purposeful detachment. He felt no anger; he was past that. What he felt at the moment was closer to sympathy, but Barret would see no hint of that.

"Commander Barret, would you care to tell me what happened?" His tone was flat, as was Barret's when he replied.

"Yes, sir. I took a fleet of ten Corvets and thirty Falcons out, our objective a Selasid First Line freighter carrying arms and commutronics equipment for the Confleet base on Charon. We had their SynchShift emergence coordinates, but what we—what I didn't know was that the Charon base was sending out twenty Falcons to meet the freighter."

"When did you find out about them?"

"When they lifted off Charon. At that point, we were only five minutes from the emergence rendezvous."

"I see. And you proceeded with the original plan?"

"Yes, sir. Our navcomp calculations gave us forty-five minutes before the Falcons would be in range."

"Forty-five minutes," Alex repeated with no inflection. "And how long did your navcomp calculations indicate it would take to accelerate back to SS speed after you emerged?"

"I . . . eighteen minutes, sir."

"Which gave you a grand total of twenty-seven minutes to accomplish your mission."

"Yes, sir, but the freighter only had a six-Falcon escort."

"Since they were expecting twenty Falcons from the Charon base, that shouldn't have surprised you."

"It didn't. I meant that I thought it feasible to take the freighter in that time, considering how small their escort was, and we did . . ." He finally averted his eyes. "We did take it."

Alex let that ride for perhaps three seconds, then, "I assume something disrupted your twenty-seven-minute schedule."

"The escort Falcons were carrying heavier guns than usual. I'd estimate X^8s. That's way out of line for Falcons. They're too light for anything over an X^6." Barret's hands began an unconscious clenching movement at his sides. "When we captured the freighter, three of our Corvets and six Falcons were disabled, and it took longer than I expected to disengage. I realized the Charon fleet would be in range before we could reach SS speed, so I sent Captain Straas with the *Magna* and three Falcons to draw off the Confleet ships while the rest of our fleet retreated." His hands closed and stayed in tight fists. "I hoped Straas could distract the Falcons without engaging them, that he could continue acceleration into SS."

"But only two of his Falcons managed to get into SS. The maneuver bought you perhaps a minute of time; enough to save part of your fleet, but not enough for you to avoid engagement with the Confleet Falcons." Alex gave a short, bitter laugh. "*Engagement*. You were in full retreat. All you could do was take the losses and keep accelerating."

Barret made no response, his eyes unfocused, unblinking.

Alex said slowly, "Twenty-seven minutes. Commander, didn't it occur to you that was a very narrow time limit?"

"I . . . knew it would be close."

"Obviously. But I'll concede that it fell within the limits of feasibility. You left no margin for error or the unexpected, but still you might have carried it off, and if you had, you'd be enjoying a hero's welcome now."

Barret's eyes came into focus on Alex. "Would you be offering me any medals?" There was no bitterness in the question, nor did it need an answer.

Alex's response was equally rhetorical. "Why not? Isn't success all that counts?"

"I might have thought that once."

Alex walked around to the front of the desk and leaned back against it, feeling Barret's despair like a tangible weight.

"So. The lesson comes home at last. Conservative tactics lack drama, but we can't afford unnecessary risks. At least you handled the situation well *after* attempting the capture within that narrow time limit."

Barret said dully, "I doubt Captain Straas and his men would be impressed with that."

"Jan, the decision to send Straas to divert the Charon fleet was perfectly sound under the circumstances."

"But *I* created the circumstances." He was silent for the space of half a minute, then his hand went to the double-starred insignia pinned to his collar, the insignia of Second Commander that he had for the last three years worn so proudly. Then, with it held in his hand, he said, "Sir, I'm well aware that I am solely responsible for this disaster, and in view of that, I'm tendering my resignation from FO."

Alex ignored the offered insignia and straightened, frowning irritably.

"Holy God, Jan, don't be—" He stopped abruptly as the S/V doorscreens clicked off, and his first response was only surprise and annoyance. His second was a sudden, almost uncontrollable anger.

Predis Ussher.

He strode into the room as if he belonged here, ignoring Alex entirely, turning on Barret with unmasked hostility.

"Jan, what the hell *happened*? You lost half the Solar Fleet in one day!"

Barret stared at him in bewilderment, and Alex silenced the rebuff that came to his lips, watching Barret's reaction.

"Predis, I . . . I know—"

"You *know*! I should *hope* you know what you've done! You've thrown away two years' work, damn it! You've put us so far back, the God knows *when* we'll catch up!"

Barret was visibly trembling. "Predis, I know exactly what I've done, and I've already ten——"

"Fer Ussher, you're out of bounds," Alex cut in, his incisive tone bringing Ussher's head around with a quick snap; he seemed to become aware of Alex for the first time.

"I'm a Council member, Commander, and nothing pertaining to the welfare of the Society is out of bounds to me."

"Until the Council decides otherwise, this falls under the jurisdiction of FO. Under any circumstances, it isn't your prerogative to place the blame."

"The placement of blame is clear. Jan was in command—"

"If blame is placed on that basis, it's entirely mine; I'm First Commander of FO. As for Jan, he handled an unexpected and disastrous situation very well. He's served the Phoenix all his life with courage and dedication. He doesn't deserve your contempt, Predis, and I won't tolerate it!"

Ussher glanced at Barret, finally recognizing his chagrin. The mental shift of gears was ludicrously obvious.

"Perhaps I *was* hasty, but the shock of seeing—"

"You were more than *hasty*," Alex said tightly. "First, you have no right to be in this room; second, no right to interfere in my command; third, no right to accuse unjustly a man you *call* a friend."

For a moment Ussher didn't respond, his mouth a thin white line. Then he looked at Barret again and seemed to capitulate. But it was only for Barret's benefit; Alex hoped he had some faint realization of that.

"You're quite right, Commander. I *am* out of bounds. Jan, I can only beg your forgiveness. I have the highest regard for your ability; you know that. Please, I hope you'll accept my apologies."

Barret managed an uncertain smile. "It's . . . all right, Predis. I understand."

Alex's jaw clamped tight. Barret understood nothing. But apparently he found Ussher's contrition convincing. Alex watched numbly as Ussher turned and made his exit without so much as glancing in his direction.

In the silence that followed, Barret stared at the dark haze of the doorscreens, and perhaps he wasn't entirely convinced; he was frowning uneasily. Alex motioned toward the chair near the desk.

"Sit down, Jan. You aren't on the firing line now." He waited until Barret sagged tiredly into the chair. "Before that untimely interruption, you made some thoughtless remark about resigning. But I won't accept a resignation. You made a costly error, Jan. If in the future you repeat that error, I'll reconsider my refusal, but I don't think that contingency will arise. You may as well put that insignia back on."

Barret stared at him, then looked down at his own hand; he seemed to have forgotten he was holding the insignia.

"I'm not sure I deserve your faith."

"You wouldn't have it if you didn't. Jan, FO can't afford to lose you. It's as simple as that."

Barret seemed to consider that, then sighed his acceptance and replaced the insignia, his hands trembling slightly.

"Alex, why did you defend me against Predis? You could've let me take the blame; it's mine to take."

"It isn't Predis's to give."

Jan paused, again staring at the door. "I've never . . . seen him like that."

Alex smiled faintly. Ussher's temper might be his undoing one day. He wondered if the Phoenix had time enough to wait for that day.

"Jan, you're exhausted. You've been on duty with the Solar Fleet for—what? Three months? You need some time off. Leftant Commander Gavin's in command at Rhea now. I'll tell him to stay under cover; Confleet will be out in force, and we'll need time for repairs. I want you to take a week's leave, beginning tomorrow morning. And I believe Nina's saved a few free days for your return."

Barret smiled wistfully at his wife's name and came to his feet; it was obviously an effort.

"Thanks, Alex. But right now I should be in the hangars."

Alex nodded. "I'll join you in a few minutes." He accompanied Barret to the door, watching him as he set off down the hall, weariness in the angle of his shoulders and in every step. A hard lesson, Alex thought bleakly, learned the hardest way. Then his eyes narrowed. Predis Ussher had just turned into the hall. He stopped when he met Barrett, and they talked briefly, then walked on together and disappeared around the first corner. When a black-clothed figure approached Alex, he was still so preoccupied it was a moment before he recognized him.

Ben Venturi. Apparently, he was recently returned from the Cliff in Leda; he was still in his SSB uniform.

"Ben, you have the prisoners lined up?"

"Yes. One of Erica's crews is working on them now. There's a couple of Grade 6 comtechs in the bunch."

Alex's eyebrow came up. "Selasid?"

"No, Confleet. They were hitching a ride to the Charon base aboard the freighter."

"Too bad you didn't turn up some gunnery officers. Jan thinks they have some new guns on the Falcons; possibly X⁸s. Ben, I'll have to get back to the hangars."

"I'll tag along." Then, as they started down the corridor, "Have you talked to Andreas today?"

Alex nearly stopped, his frown returning.

"Damn. I had a call message from him, but I was on the SynchCom monitors at the time." He noted the suspicious eye Ben turned on a pair of FO crewmembers as they passed. The suspicion wasn't for these particular men. Ben had something on his mind; something private. "What's this about?"

"I'm not sure. I just transed in from Leda an hour ago.

Andreas left a call message for me, too, but when I returned it, he was out of the lab. In the infirmary."

Alex paused as they reached the main corridor, numbed by the soft sounds of pain-born moans nearly lost in rushing footsteps, mechanical clatterings, urgent voices. They turned down the corridor toward the hangar, and there was a paradoxical privacy in the confusion; no one had time or inclination to listen to them. Ben's jaw muscles were bunched as he watched the stretchers moving out of the hangar.

"Damn, what a mess. Alex, I talked to Erica, and she saw Andreas earlier today. She said we'd better get together. We'll meet in HS 1 at 18:00."

"All right. I'll be—" He quickened his pace as they approached the hangar doors. A loader piled with plasifoam cartons loomed in the opening, blocking the flow of traffic.

"Leftant Spense, what in the God's name do you think you're doing?"

The man driving the loader brought it to a jerking halt.

"Uh—well, this stuff's from the freighter, sir. I'm taking it up to SM."

"At whose order?"

Spense licked his lips uneasily. "Well, Fer M'Kim said he wanted his techs to check—"

"Fer M'Kim? Am I to understand you've been transferred to Supply and Maintenance?"

"Well, no, but—"

Alex cut in coldly, "The crews come first, Spense. If you don't know that by now, you don't belong in FO. The cargo stays until the last of the casualties are evacuated. Clear the corridor!"

"Yes, sir." Resentment slipped through in Spense's eyes, then he turned to look backward as he guided the loader into the hangar.

Alex said under his breath, "Damn fool."

Ben laughed. "Maybe, but you'd better watch him."

"Yes, I know. He's one of Ussher's loyals." He started into the hangar with Ben close at his side.

"And he talks a lot."

Alex glanced at him, then moved to one side of the doors and stopped, distracted by the harried activity. The statistics of catastrophe were all too tangible here.

"What do you mean, he talks a lot?"

"Just that Predis is up to his old tricks again: the gossip routine."

"Which of us has he chosen to defame now? Me?"

"Yes."

Alex gave a short, mirthless laugh. "Well, I'll give him credit, he's tenacious. And intelligent to a point. He has yet to launch an innuendo campaign against Andreas. When he's confident enough for that, we're in trouble. Is Spense carrying the word in FO?"

"Right. And Sargent Hicks."

"Tom Hicks? He won't be doing any talking in the future. He was aboard the *Magna*. She took a direct broadside and exploded."

For a while both were silent, Alex concentrating on the berthing and evacuation crews. The pumps hadn't yet succeeded in clearing all the sea water; the floor was an abstracted glare of reflected lights. Finally, the last of the casualties and medsquads passed on their way to the infirmary.

Alex asked absently, "What word is Spense carrying, by the way?"

Ben sighed. "That you barely escaped a court-martial when you were in Confleet. For cowardice, the way it's being told; refusal to fire under orders."

Alex felt every muscle tightening, and there was that mental shift that always accompanied any memory of his past, an inward jar like an MT trans. He was here and now, then suddenly he was elsewhere and elsewhen, in that other world that seemed so remote; a play remembered from an old vidicom screening. And like a waking dream, an image was in his mind: the smoke-shrouded fields of Alber.

"Predis is hitting a little close to home."

"And below the belt—as usual."

"Ben, have you any idea what Andreas wants to talk to us about?"

Ben's tone was low, pitched for Alex's ears only.

"Erica does. Andreas thinks he may be close to a breakthrough on the LR-MT."

A breakthrough.

Alex didn't move, the physical stricture only reflecting a mental process, one familiar and practiced: holding back a hope. They had all hoped too many times, and the hopes had died in mathematic dead ends.

"Did Andreas use that term—a breakthrough?"

Ben laughed. "No. According to Erica, he said he's working on a 'promising approach.' But *he* asked for this meeting. That must mean something."

Alex's breath came out in a sigh. The hope wouldn't be put down; he could only contain it within tolerable limits. It must come soon, an end to these long months of waiting that slowly ground into years. For the Concord, for the Phoenix, for his own sanity, it must come soon.

But his voice was level, and he managed a brief smile. "I guess we'll just have to wait until this evening." Then he stiffened, watching two figures emerging from the captured freighter. Predis Ussher and John M'Kim. "I wish to hell Predis would keep his nose out of FO."

Ben nodded. "I could say the same about SI. What's he so damned interested in now?"

"Weapons, no doubt. Half the cargo on that ship is Confleet armament. Last week when we took those new Falcons, he was talking about a 'real offensive.' And I call *Spense* a damn fool."

"Commander?" The voice came from the comcenter deck. "Captain Dolf wants to see you in Hangar 3, sir."

"Thank you." Alex paused only long enough to glance back at Ben. "I'll talk to you this evening."

3.

Occasionally, Alex Ransom considered the meaning of words like "home."

He paused inside the doorway of Erica Radek's office, noting the spray of yellow orchids on the deck. Twelve levels below, adjoining his office in FO, there was an apartment where he lived, or at least slept. But he didn't call it home. Home didn't exist for Alex Ransom, and his thoughts seldom strayed into such blind alleys except when he was tired.

"Hello, Alex." Erica turned off the reading screen on her desk and leaned back, her smile warming her gray eyes.

"How are you, Erica?"

"Better than you are, probably. Have you had supper?"

"No, I haven't had time." He had started for one of the

chairs in front of her desk, but detoured to the 'spenser, then with a chilled vaccup of concentrate in hand, continued to the chair and sank into it. "I saw Andreas in the infirmary. He'll be delayed for a while. What about Ben?"

"I don't know. He'll get here when he can. And I'm glad you arrived early; it's been a long time since we've had a chance to talk together."

"I've missed that, Erica. By the way, any recent reports on our Bond project?"

"Yes, I had some reports from the Terran chapters today. I'll have a tape capsule for you tomorrow, but in general the news is encouraging on that front."

"Good." He tasted the concentrate, frowning slightly. "But I've been letting it slip lately, and it's too important. Especially now." He paused, wondering why he'd added that. "What else was in the Terran reports?"

"There were several items. For one, the House of DeKoven Woolf is celebrating the birth of a son today. Justin DeKoven Woolf."

Again, that inward jar. Then a feeling of relief that had no personal overtones. There were never any personal reactions after that initial, fleeting disorientation.

Justin DeKoven Woolf. Son of Lord Phillip and Lady Olivet Omer Woolf; first born of the House. This was the second child born to the Woolfs; the first was a daughter. Alexandra. He didn't dwell on the irony in that name.

"Well, that's definitely cause for celebration," he said. "Justin. That would be in honor of Lady Olivet's grandfather. Very politic." He laughed curtly. "But Selasis certainly won't be celebrating. The lack of a male heir was his only weapon against Woolf, since the Directors are standing pat on his succession to the Chairmanship."

"Alex, I have another piece of news from Concordia, and it isn't so good."

She paused, and he had to ask, "What is it?"

"There's a rumor circulating that Orin Selasis is negotiating a marriage with Eliseer."

"Karlis and the Lady Adrien?"

She nodded silently, eyes clouded, and he understood now why she was glad he'd come early. She thought it would be easier for him if he heard this news in private.

But there was more pain in her eyes than he felt. She

couldn't seem to believe there was no pain for him in that name. There was nothing: a state beyond indifference. He recognized the ominous political implications in a Selasis-Eliseer match, but he could muster no personal response to it. Yet Erica didn't understand that; she expected him to still grieve that loss, years old now. Nothing he said convinced her that it was buried with the other old griefs. Except for Rich. He still felt that sometimes.

"Lord Orin works fast," he commented. "Janeel Shang Selasis is only eight months in her grave."

"Yes." Erica was still watching him closely. "I'm sure Karlis will wait the customary year of mourning before he takes another wife, at least for appearance sake."

"And to avoid further alienating Sato Shang. He seemed inclined to believe the stories about Janeel's second pregnancy. Well, we'll have to find out as soon as possible if there's more than rumor to the Selasis-Eliseer match."

She nodded, her expression resolutely noncommittal.

"Ben has alerted his agents in both Houses. At least we can be sure of knowing as soon as Lady Adrien does. Dr. Perralt is very close to her." She sighed, leaning back in her chair. "I'm afraid there *is* more than rumor to this. It's a logical move for Selasis, and I suppose it looks like a good match from Eliseer's point of view."

"Or an inescapable match." He glanced at his watch, frowning. He'd have to get back to the hangars soon. "Erica, did you have a report on the Directorate meeting today?"

She nodded. "Yes. It was mostly concerned with House politics; nothing new or unexpected, except the Phoenix came up for discussion again."

He rose and began pacing out a circle. "We seem to be coming up frequently lately. What did the Directors have to say about us today?"

"Oh, the usual diatribes from Selasis about our making the spaceways unsafe. He seems to have forgotten about Amik the Thief and his friends. Anyway, he proposed a special task force to ferret out this menace—that's us—and a twenty percent Confleet expansion."

"Yes, he'd like that. It would mean another fat construction contract for Badir Selasis."

"He could use it. Selasis does have a valid complaint about our raids; they've been rather costly for him, along with all those inexplicable mechanical breakdowns."

Alex smiled at that. "That program does seem to be progressing well. What did the Directors do about his proposals?"

"After a great deal of bickering and complaining about rising taxes, a compromise was reached. They authorized the special task force, but vetoed the Confleet expansion."

"Good. Well, the task force will present no problems; Ben will have their strat plans for me. We'll have to lie low for a while, anyway. Maybe I can get M'Kim organized on the MTs for the Corvets during the hiatus, and we have repairs to—" He tensed at the sound of the door chime, and Erica's quick reaction as she leaned forward to check the vis-screen on her desk revealed her tension.

"Andreas," she said, touching the doorcon button.

"Finally." Alex turned as the doorscreens went off, his words of greeting dying on his lips. Andreas had come straight from the infirmary, and his dark eyes were haunted.

"Ben hasn't arrived yet?" Andreas asked.

Alex shook his head. "Not yet. How are you, Andreas?"

"I doubt I should answer that honestly." He sagged into a chair. "It's been a day of shocks, and I had another one a couple of hours ago. I must talk to Ben about—about arrangements."

Alex frowned. The word didn't make sense. Erica voiced the question. "Arrangements? What do you mean?"

Andreas took a deep breath. "I mean arrangements for a short trip. It's . . . Amelia, my sister. I've just learned that she's ill, Erica." A pause, then, "Dying."

"Oh, Andreas, I'm sorry."

He nodded. "It's a heart attack; she's in the convent hospital." Another long pause, then he said flatly, "I'm going to see her. I owe her that much."

Alex felt a constricting chill, and his tone was unintentionally sharp. "You're going to see her?"

"Yes, Alex, but perhaps I should explain the situation." Andreas folded his hands, frowning down at them. "Amelia's my only living relative. Actually, she was a charter member of the Phoenix, but after the Fall she chose the Sisters of Solace instead. The Order maintains hospitals for those who can't afford, or are barred for some reason from Conmed hospitals; the Sisters believe in traditional Church sanctuary. They specialize in mental illness, but they accept any kind of illness or injury and ask no questions." He smiled fleetingly. "Amelia decided she could do more good with the Sisters than the Phoenix. Perhaps she was right."

"You've maintained contact with her?"

"No. We both knew that would be too dangerous, and Amelia Riis was officially a victim of the Purge. Unfortunately, my name was linked with the Phoenix in the beginning; if it were known she was my sister, she'd have suffered for it. But I made her a promise, Alex, that if I died, she'd know, and she'd have some way of letting me know if..."

Alex hesitated, realizing Andreas was close to weeping. "How was she to contact you?"

Erica relieved Andreas of the necessity of answering. "She was given a transceiver in the form of a holy medallion, Alex. It's tuned to a frequency that goes through one of our relay stations for double idents."

Alex made no comment, but he read in her eyes an understanding of a fact neither of them would voice now: the double ident relay system was under the aegis of Communications; Predis Ussher's department.

Then he looked at Andreas's haggard face; all his nearly eighty years were evident now. A few words with his sister before she died was little enough to ask. Andreas had given his life to the Phoenix. How could he be denied this?

"Where is your sister, Andreas? What convent?"

"Holy Carma. It's in the Coris Mountains near Hallicourt about a thousand kilometers east of Hamidropolis. I suppose Ben will worry about my leaving Fina, but there's really no danger. The SSB certainly won't be looking for me in a convent, and it's quite remote."

Erica asked, "When are you planning to go?"

"I should go tonight."

"*Tonight*? Andreas, please don't attempt it now. For once, take my advice as a physician."

He nodded. "I wouldn't feel right about leaving Fina now, with the Solar Fleet disaster and.... Early tomorrow morning. I only hope it—it won't be too late."

Erica looked up at Alex as if seeking guidance, but he had none to offer. He gave himself up to aimless pacing, trying to silence the alarms ringing in his mind. Finally, he stopped and faced Andreas.

"I'm going with you to Holy Carma."

"But why? Alex, you're as bad as Ben sometimes. Really, there's no cause for concern."

"Andreas, you can't go alone, and there's no one in Fina or all the worlds I'd trust with your life."

"Not even Ben?"

Alex laughed. "He's an exception. He's also in a vital position in the SSB. We can't jeopardize that. Anyway, if anything goes wrong, we'll need him to extricate us. Besides, I'd enjoy the trip. Considering how long I've been on Pollux, I've seen damned little of it."

Andreas managed a smile at that, but Erica was on the verge of protesting when the door chime distracted her. She checked the vis-screen.

"It's Ben."

Their eyes shifted in unison to the door as Ben Venturi came in, sparing them a brief, abstracted smile.

"Sorry I'm late; couldn't get loose any sooner. How are you, Andreas?"

"I'm all right. And you?"

Ben laughed. "My ulcers are on the rampage again, but that isn't surprising. Alex, you have everything organized in the hangars?"

"Not entirely, but I called a break for supper." He paused, then turned to Andreas. "Well, now that we're all here, I understand you have something to tell us."

Andreas looked up, and it seemed to take a moment for him to realign his thoughts.

"I've been so distracted, I nearly forgot about it. It's the LR-MT. I've been working on a new approach. A modification of an old one, actually, but a vital modification. I had a readout on the final equations today."

Alex folded his arms, trying to read behind the veneer of practiced objectivity. And there *was* hope there. Andreas might try to rein it, as he did, but it was there.

"A vital modification? What does that mean?"

"Alex, we have our breakthrough."

Alex felt the chill of pallor in his cheeks. *Breakthrough.* For Andreas to use that word—

"Please, Andreas, put that in terms I can deal with."

"I don't know exactly what that means. All I can tell you is that I'm sure of the general principles. The problem now will be to translate the equations into mechanisms; designing and setting up equipment for experimentation."

Alex closed his eyes and the words slipped out, "Thank the God. We're running out of time."

Andreas frowned at that. "We're a long way from working models capable of practical loads. It'll be two to four years before we can offer it to the Concord."

Alex's jaw tightened, the tension taking on a sharper edge now. "Is there any way you can speed that timetable?"

"I can't say. I don't know what problems we'll encounter. Alex, we've waited over fifty years for this—we can wait a few more."

"I'm not so sure of that. There are too many crisis factors in existence in the Concord to consider, and still others within the Phoenix. You're aware of them."

Andreas sighed. "Yes."

There was a short silence. It was Ben who broke it.

"Andreas, you haven't said anything about this breakthrough to anyone except Dr. Lyden and Dr. Bruce?"

"Of course not." He frowned with a hint of annoyance. "I've been very careful to observe your security procedures, Ben, and I've run all the computer sequences myself with an automatic erase. There's no record of the full equations."

Ben nodded, his anxiety unalleviated. Andreas honestly believed he observed the security procedures to the letter, but he was all too prone to carelessness in periods of intense concentration.

"All right, but remember, we're in trouble if Predis finds out about this. He's been biding his time all these years, but he'll *have* to make his move once he knows we have the LR-MT."

"Yes, I . . . realize that, Ben."

Alex knew the cost of that admission; he felt the same resigned weariness. But Andreas wasn't capable of Alex's consuming contempt for the man who would jeopardize the Phoenix to make himself a Lord. Nor was Andreas capable of imagining how far Ussher might go to effect his dreams of glory.

Alex frowned at his watch. "Andreas, I have to get back to the hangars. You can tell Ben about our excursion to Holy Carma."

Ben came alert at that. "Your what?"

"Andreas will explain it. Ben, will you be in your Leda

apartment tonight? I'd like to use your MT terminal."

"Don't tell me you're off on one of your sociological research trips tonight?"

"Yes. It's too important to neglect." *Especially now*. And now he understood that qualification.

"I'll switch off the alarms. You can use it even if I'm not there."

"Thanks. Erica, is the corridor clear?"

She checked her screen. "Yes."

He paused at the door. "Andreas, the Shepherds say every gift has its price. We've been given a gift of new hope. We'll have to accept the cost."

4.

A warm rain rattled at the roof. The hour was late, past the compound curfew, and the chapel was nearly empty. At a small altar along the side wall, a hooded, bent old woman knelt, arms crossed, work-worn hands resting on her shoulders, her face illuminated by the votive candles.

Alex studied her from the shadows at the back of the chapel. A beautiful face, open and guileless as a child's, yet seared with a lifetime of births and deaths. Her lips moved in prayer, her curiously innocent eyes gazed out of sunken sockets at the image of the saint above the altar.

Saint Thea, regarded as a midwife of sorts; she assisted the passage of the faithful from this world into the next.

He always felt a certain time/space disorientation in these chapels, but it wasn't an uncomfortable sensation. It was due in part to their uniformity. This chapel could be anywhere in the Two Systems. Even in Montril, another remote experience from that other world. They were all built on the same simple design: rectangular spaces walled and floored in plasment with barrel-vaulted ceilings, and tall, narrow windows serving more to let light out of the chapels than into them. Even in the style of the ikons decorating the walls there was a high degree of consistency.

The only light now was that of candles, amber-warm, casting rich brown shadows, a light that gave flickering life to the ikons over the side altars and lent an equivocal depth to the grim, omniscient image of the Mezion above the main altar. There the only other worshiper in the chapel knelt; Esaph, Elder Shepherd of Eliseer's Leda smelter Compound B.

Alex's gaze moved back to the old woman. On the sleeve of her cape was the blue-and-silver winged-horse crest of Eliseer. He closed his eyes.

He was standing at the rear of the chapel, a shadow among shadows, the hood of his cloak drawn up. He listened in the darkness behind his eyes to the thrum of the rain. Autumn. A stir of remembrances that never became recognizable images; autumn rains on another world where seasons had more meaning. He was waiting for the old woman to leave, but he wasn't impatient. This place stilled impatience. It was a place outside time, or a little pocket of time dragging behind, collecting the residue of centuries.

He'd come here so exhausted walking was an effort, come with his mind teeming with hectic memories. The hours in the hangars and the comcenter, the decisions and demands, the press and pressure of people, the whines and cracks of machinery shrieking and hammering against the stone-bound vaults. And the oppressive, whispering quiet of the infirmary, the haunted, haunting eyes of survivors facing a vacuum in their lives.

But all that was remote here; more remote than distance or hours. He was wondering if some of these candles were lighted for Saint Richard the Lamb. There was a sense of Rich's presence here that was almost tangible. The Bonds wouldn't be surprised if Rich appeared in the flesh here, and Alex doubted he'd be, either.

The old woman came to her feet, a slow, cautious process, then shuffled to the back of the chapel, past Alex, and out the door. He didn't move, and she seemed unaware of him. The door closed with a gust of rain-scented wind.

Esaph still knelt at the main altar, so much a part of his surroundings, he seemed carved or painted. Alex reached under his cloak and unfastened the medallion, then walked down the center aisle toward the altar. The soft-soled shoes silenced his footsteps; the Shepherd didn't hear him. Alex stopped two meters behind him and waited. Esaph was extraordinarily sensitive; he would sense his presence.

It was less than a minute. Esaph's grizzled head came up, then he rose and slowly turned. His wrinkle-webbed features were the color of mahogany. There was no fear in them; he was only momentarily surprised.

Alex extended his hand, the medallion exposed in his palm, the lamb uppermost. He never showed them the wolf.

"I come in the Name of the Lamb."

Esaph sighed. "It's the Brother."

"Yes, Esaph."

The Shepherd sank to one knee, and Alex closed his hand around the medallion, turning the back of his hand out as Esaph pressed it against his forehead. He still found that gesture of respect hard to accept. But it wasn't only for him; it was also for the Lamb.

Esaph rose, studying him. "Are you well, my lord?"

That form of address was also hard to accept, but—again— it was only an expression of respect.

"Yes, Esaph, I'm well. And you?"

"The Holy Mezion still blesses my long years. Can I bring you some refreshment, my lord?"

"No, thank you." He bowed to the stern-eyed image of the Mezion, then sat down on the dais step, waiting for the Shepherd to sit down beside him. "I find refreshment enough in simply being here."

Esaph's tone was faintly puzzled. "I'd think you'd find refreshment where you come from."

"Where do you think I come from?"

"I . . . don't know. Perhaps the Beyond Realm."

Alex shook his head. "I've told you, I'm as human as you. Aren't you a man, Esaph? A human being?"

"Yes, but not to be spoken of with the Brother."

"All men are brothers in the Mezion's eyes, so you and I are brothers. I don't come from the Beyond, only a different place. Still, it's part of this world."

Esaph nodded, more in acceptance than understanding. "Saint Richard, your brother, said much the same thing."

Alex turned away, gazing at the flame-lighted image of Saint Thea. Midwife of death. There was a brief silence, then he said, "Esaph, we've spoken together often, and I've had a great deal to say to you. You remember my brother's words?"

"Of course. He was a wise man and a saint."

"If I should die, will my words be remembered as my brother's are?"

The Shepherd pulled in a quick breath. "Your words will be remembered."

"I trust you and your fellow Shepherds to see to that."

"We won't fail you. But why do you speak of death? Are you under the Shadow?"

Alex's eyes moved again to the image of Saint Thea. "Sometimes I think that's where I live."

"You're troubled tonight, my lord."

"Yes, but less troubled than when I came here." He smiled at the Shepherd, but it slipped away from him. "Esaph, if you remember nothing else I've said, remember this: There may be a time of war coming, but the Bonds must take no part in it, no matter who tempts or threatens them. The way of the Blessed is peace. That is the will of the Mezion. If this time of war comes and any of your people so much as raise a hand, the Mezion will punish them. The Purge after the Fall of Peladeen will seem a children's game in comparison."

Esaph was old enough to remember the Purge; there was fear in his eyes.

"Have you seen this in a vision, my lord?"

Alex hesitated, and an image came unbidden into his mind— the fields of Alber.

"Yes," he said, "I've seen a vision."

"Will this . . . this time of war come soon?"

"I don't know. I told you I'm not a saint; my visions are imperfect. But if it comes, remember my brother, and remember me. Remember one word: peace."

Esaph's answer was nearly a whisper. "I'll remember."

Alex pulled himself to his feet, feeling the dull ache of exhaustion in every muscle now.

"Tell your flock, Esaph."

The Shepherd also rose, gazing somberly at him.

"I'll tell them, my lord." Then he bowed, again making that hand-to-forehead obeisance. When he straightened, Alex rested a hand on his shoulder.

"Good night, my friend. We'll talk again."

"Good night. May the Holy Mezion send you comfort, my lord."

"Thank you, Esaph." He bowed to the ikon of the Mezion, then turned and walked silently down the aisle to the door. It was still raining outside.

5.

The SSB Administration and Detention Center in Leda was popularly known as the Cliff—even among some of its lower-echelon personnel—an appellation derived only in part from its architectural style. It was one of the tallest buildings in Leda, and from his office on the top level, Commander Hubert Benin had a spectacular view of this largest city in the Centauri System and to the south, the Selamin Sea, and to the east, across the Pangaean Straits, the cloud-veiled ramparts of the Coris Mountains.

Commander Benin was standing at the windowall, but the view from the top of the Cliff held no interest for him. His lips were compressed, his hands, clasped behind his back, worked spasmodically. Leftant Altin's tone was even more restrained than usual.

"Commander Benin, sir, the prisoner."

He didn't turn. "Have him brought in, Altin. I may as well have a look at this—this *prize* Haver's sent me."

"Yes, sir."

Benin wasn't aware of Altin's quiet voice as he relayed the order via the office intercom.

"Damn his soul!" He turned, fixing the hapless leftant with a cold glare. "Hallicourt gets Riis, and what do *I* get? His *chauffeur*, for the God's sake. If Cornel Haver had any sense of—of propriety, he'd have called me in on this. Damn it, *I'm* his senior officer."

"Yes, sir."

"He'll pay for this. He thinks it'll put another chevron on his shoulder, but he just may end up with *none!*"

"Yes, sir."

"And why the hell did that tip go to the Hallicourt unit? Why—" He stopped, frowning. "Did Haver send a VP ident on the tip?"

"Yes, sir. I'm afraid it won't help much, though."

Benin scowled at him. "Larynx alteration? No record, as usual?"

"There was a record, sir, but apparently the Phoenix has devised some means of disrupting the VP computers."

"Impossible!"

"Yes, sir. However, the voice on that tip was identified as belonging to someone now deceased; that's direct from Concordia Central Control. The recording was also determined to be a probable patch, but a very good one."

"Holy God, patched tapes made by *ghosts!*" Benin turned as the door opened, finding a new focus for his indignation.

The prisoner was flanked by two face-screened guards, each with a hand locked around one of his arms, each carrying a charged lash. Benin crossed the room slowly, his lead-colored eyes fixed on him. The man was definitely Phoenix.

Hubert Benin wasted little time speculating on the mental processes of his prisoners; he left that to the psychocontrollers. But occasionally, he wondered what it must be like for these Phoenix agents with the amnesia block.

Damn them! If he could ever break *one* of them . . .

"So, this is Cornel Haver's offering to me. Altin, didn't he have *any* information on him?"

"Only his name, sir. The one given in the tip."

"*That* doesn't mean a damn thing."

Benin studied the prisoner, finding nothing in his face or attitude to calm his choler. The man *had* to be afraid; the amnesia block didn't make them forget how to be afraid.

Phoenix. Madmen, all of them.

Then he paused. There was something familiar about this man, particularly around the eyes. Cold blue; arched, black brows; a gaze that was disturbingly direct.

"Altin, are you sure we have no records on this man?"

"Not under the name given us, sir."

"I suppose he's had print removal." Benin reached for the man's hand to check for the telltale smoothness of fingers and palm. "They always—*damn!*" He stumbled backward as the prisoner's fist shot out, nearly smashing into his face.

"Sir, are you—"

"*Yes*, I'm all right, Altin!" He drew himself up, tugging impatiently at his uniform, lips curling in distaste as the guards brought the prisoner under control. It was incredible. The man was giving them a hard run. Obviously, he had training; such things were reflexive and didn't require memory on a conscious level. It was futile, of course, but what boggled his mind was *why* the man would resist. He didn't even know who he was. It was insane.

Benin glared at the prisoner, but he was unconscious now, sagging between the guards.

"Sir, I'm sorry." One of the guards, his tone fearfully apologetic. "He was so fast—"

"And you were so *slow*! Altin, call Psychocontrol."

"Yes, sir. Will you send him directly to them?"

"Yes." Benin dismissed the guards with a wave of his hand. "Take him to Level 6."

He didn't respond to their salutes as they departed; his back was to them. He went to the windowall and scowled at the vista of Leda.

"Altin, I want that man classified terminal."

The leftant nodded absently. "Yes, sir. I'll—uh, pass the word."

6.

"Val, call that last report from the Concordia PS research unit, please." Erica Radek was studying Valentin Severin closely, even though her gaze was turned on the reading screen on her desk.

Val was at the memfile console. "That would be last week's report?"

"Yes."

Val checked the 'file index, and punched the document locator sequence, then turned to Erica.

"It's ready for your screen."

"Thank you, Val." She switched her screen to the report, frowning over the lines of fine print and columns of statistics, but the activities of certain Fesh students at the University in Concordia didn't occupy her full attention.

She was thinking about Val, sifting the data of posture, vocal nuances, facial expressions, and trying to remember when she'd first become aware of the change in Val, a restraint in her attitude, a sensed antagonism. And Erica was wondering about her own objectivity. Perhaps she was getting a little paranoid lately.

Val came to look over her shoulder, and Erica leaned back and gestured toward the screen.

"I'm afraid we have a serious problem on our hands with the University students."

"The radical liberal movement?" Then, at Erica's nod, "Is it confined to Concordia, or are the other Universities showing any symptoms?"

Erica smiled faintly at that term. "Well, I'm sure there are symptoms, but so far they've only manifested themselves in diagnosable form in Concordia." Then she sighed. "Freedom. What a word. Humankind would be better off if it had never been invented; it's so misleading. I have no doubt that within the year the radical liberals among the students in Concordia will be united under a common banner. This young man—" She touched the controls, the screen blurring until she stopped at an imagraph of a thin-faced, dark-haired youth. "Damon Kamp. Sociophilosophy student, family upper-class Independent Fesh, intelligence index near genius level. But he's a very dangerous young man. An evangelist, and a skilled one. He also has a taste for power, and beyond that, he's highly unstable emotionally."

Val studied the face on the screen. "A dangerous combination in one man, Dr. Radek."

That was one of the things that was bothering her, Erica realized. Lately, Val showed a tendency to address her as "Dr. Radek," even in private, yet they'd been on first-name terms for years.

But Erica didn't comment on that. "Yes, but it's not an unusual combination. Kamp is an archetype, really, so true to form, one can predict his behavior with some accuracy."

"An archetype?"

"A messiah. The species is ubiquitous in any social stratum, any historical period, any*where*, and they're particularly effective in relatively closed systems. They're attractive to youthful idealists, of course, and capable of inspiring classic fanaticism and inducing their followers to deny entrenched moral codes even to the point of betraying family and friends."

She happened to be looking up at Val at that moment, and what she saw stopped her. Val's muscles seemed to go rigid, and her face reddened; a strong emotional reaction that she was obviously trying to conceal. Yet it was so anomalous. What was there about those comments on Damon Kamp that . . .

. . . *betraying family and friends.*

Those were the catalytic words. But why? Val had never suffered serious guilt reactions toward her family as a result of joining the Phoenix, and there was nothing else in her history that could be considered a betrayal of them.

Friends. Betraying *friends*.

Erica concentrated on the screen to mask her own emotional reaction. Perhaps the subject of Damon Kamp was worth pursuing. She touched the controls, stopping at another imagraph: Kamp addressing a crowd of students.

She said, "I'm sure Kamp will cmerge as a leader for the radicals. He has a talent for leadership. He speaks well and offers simplistic solutions with powerful emotional appeal, and believes what he says so thoroughly, he can turn even skeptics into believers. *Active* believers." Even without looking directly at Val, she could feel her increasing tension. "If there were any way he could be silenced, I'd recommend it, but the Concordia unit is convinced it can't be done short of harming him in one way or another."

Val's voice was oddly flat. "If he's so dangerous, I'm surprised you'd hesitate at that."

The statement was so out of character, Erica couldn't entirely contain her astonishment. A comment like that would be far more typical of—

She froze. She had the answer, but for the moment she could only think, *Not Val—not Val Severin*. Perhaps the numbness of shock helped her maintain her self-control. She frowned up at Val, but only with mild annoyance.

"When have we ever condoned causing harm of any sort unless it's unavoidable? And Kamp is a leader. In negating a leader, one must first consider his followers. They believe in him, however false or distorted his statements, however selfish his motives. Leaders become martyrs all too easily, and then the damage is usually irreversible."

Val was staring fixedly at the screen, tension drawing harsh lines around her mouth.

"What do you intend to do about him?"

"What can we do, Val, except investigate him thoroughly and try to accelerate the normal process of disillusionment among his followers?"

"You seem quite sure an investigation will turn up the material you need for disillusionment."

Erica saw the color in Val's cheeks deepening, the defiant

lift of her jaw. She thought Erica was purposely drawing a parallel between Damon Kamp and Predis Ussher. No one else in Val's acquaintance was close enough to Kamp's psychic type for a parallel to be drawn, and her responses obviously weren't for Kamp himself; they were too strong.

Ussher had reached Val somehow, converted her, but she was still capable of guilt on some level; Ussher hadn't yet convinced her that betraying friends was something she could do with impunity. And, more important, she was still capable of recognizing that a parallel *could* be drawn between Ussher and Kamp if she thought Erica was drawing one. Perhaps she considered it a subtle test or challenge.

Erica looked up at her, keeping her voice level.

"We have tapes of Kamp's speeches, Val. You should listen to them. He shows himself incapable of honesty or objectivity; he only uses facts when they serve his purpose, and his purpose is to forward his own ambitions. Couple that with his emotional instability, and it's almost inevitable that we'll find the means for disillusionment."

Val shrugged, putting on an expression of disinterest, but her hand went to her hair in a smoothing gesture Erica was familiar with as an index of uneasiness.

"Well, I suppose if the means aren't there, you can always manufacture them."

You. Not *we.* That cut as deep as the accusation, but Erica even managed a tolerant smile as she replied, "That will be neither necessary nor advisable. Have you read the Lampre treatise on the psychopathology of dominance? He did a series of studies on personalities of Damon Kamp's psychic group. The process of disillusionment needs no artificial encouragement. Given enough time, it's generally inevitable. I'd like to be sure Kamp isn't a localized phenomenon, however. How's your schedule, Val? Are you swamped?"

That shift of direction seemed to throw her off balance.

"I—well, no, not at the moment."

Erica leaned back, smiling at her. "I've been putting so much on your shoulders lately, but that's the price of competence. Or, rather, faith."

Val paled at that, but mustered a weak smile. "Thank you."

"I'd like you to check through all the research unit reports from the Universities. I doubt Damon Kamp, as a phenomenon, is limited to Concordia. We must be able to pinpoint the next

Kamp if we're to deal with—" She stopped abruptly, staring past the open door of the office into the work room, and both Val and Kamp were forgotten.

The corridor entrance had opened, and Ben Venturi was striding toward her. She read disaster in every line of his face, and her skin crawled with a premonitory chill. He stopped inside the office doorway, the defensive barriers coming up when he saw Val.

"Good morning, Val."

She smiled politely. "Good morning, Commander."

Erica rose. "Val, perhaps you should talk to Dr. Herron; he's done some studies on the student liberal groups."

Val seemed distracted; she nodded and started toward the doorway. "I'll see if Dr. Herron's free now."

Ben waited until the hall doorscreens closed behind her, then crossed to the desk and slapped a jambler down.

"I'll have to trust to this. I don't have time to check for plants now."

Erica stared at the small, flat box. "Ben, what's wrong?"

"Think of the worst thing that could happen to us now," he said grimly, "and that's what's wrong."

She shivered, almost afraid to ask or hear more. "Is—is it Andreas?"

"*And* Alex. The SSB picked them up a few kilometers south of Hallicourt about an hour ago."

She sank into her chair, her knees giving way, too stunned to think clearly and incapable of speech.

Ben went on tautly, "The man on the MT said he didn't get a call from Alex until the SSB 'cars had their shock screens out and it was too late to attempt a trans."

"That's impossible. Alex would see the 'cars soon enough to call for a trans. That's open country and he'd—"

"I know. The MT tech must be one of Predis's loyals. Bayly. I had my doubts about him. And he didn't even bother to notify SI when he got the call."

She frowned. "That doesn't matter now. How did the SSB know where to find them?"

"I'm not sure yet." He folded his arms, his jaw muscles working. "Alex and Andreas picked up the airtaxi in Leda as planned. I stayed on the monitors until they were clear of the city. I figured if they had any trouble, it'd be in Leda, and that was *my* error. Anyway, they were taken by the Hallicourt unit, *not* Leda, and we don't have any agents in Hallicourt. Three SSB 'cars. And one of Ussher's men was on the MT."

Erica clutched the arms of her chair, swallowing against the constriction in her throat that threatened to cut off her breath. "This means Predis knows about the LR-MT."

"Yes, and he's made his move."

"Where are they now?"

"I don't know yet. My guess is they'll be taken to Leda; to the Cliff. Hallicourt's just a mining town; they don't have anything but temporary detention facilities." He paused, looking down at her. "We'll pull them out somehow, Erica. But Andreas will be a problem; they know who he is."

"They may know who Alex Ransom is, too, by now."

"Maybe. I'll have more information on that later. I'll put in some overtime in Leda today."

She pressed her hands to her forehead. "Ben, it's—do you realize what will happen here in Fina if—"

"I realize, but don't give up this early in the game. I'm going to set up some life insurance for Andreas."

"What do you mean?"

"The MT. The word will go to SSB Central Control in Concordia. They won't classify him terminal if they know he has the MT in his head. That'll give us some time."

She frowned, then after a moment nodded. "Yes, and the SSB psychocontrollers won't use their usual methods on Andreas. His age is in his favor there; they'll want to keep him alive. But what about Alex?"

"I'll find out how much they know about him. We'll just have to get him out as soon as possible."

"Out of the Cliff?"

"We've done it before."

"And we've failed before."

"I know." He looked at his watch. "I'll get a few wheels turning in SI, then I'm going to Leda."

"Wait, Ben." She stared at the jambler, knowing the answer to her question. "Why this?"

"I sent Haral Wills to the physics lab as soon as I heard about Alex and Andreas. Damn it, we checked it two days ago, and I told Andreas not to let anybody but Lyden and Bruce into his lab. Dr. Bruce said he's sure at least three techs have been in on various errands in the last couple of days."

"Willie found a monitor?"

"Yes, and I'll lay you odds he'll find more."

She closed her eyes, holding back the tears. "He'll find some here."

Ben stared at her. "How do you—Erica, only one person has access to this office when you aren't here."

She only nodded. She couldn't explain now.

Ben said flatly, "That'll have to wait until I get back from Leda. Just keep that jambler handy."

"Be careful, Ben." ·

"Sure. That goes for you, too. Later, Erica."

In the silence he left behind him, Erica stared blindly at the calendar-clock on her desk. 17 Decem 3257. The numbers and letters were limned in red light against black. Connotative colors; blood and death. They were also the colors of the eagle crest of DeKoven Woolf and symbolized the hope embodied in the Ransom Alternative.

Her hands curled into futile fists; she pressed them into her burning eyes. The enormity of this disaster overwhelmed her capacity to encompass its true proportions. She only knew it was a disaster from which the Phoenix might never recover.

And Andreas and Alex—she wondered if she could recover from the personal disaster of losing them.

7.

Predis Ussher seated himself in Andreas Riis's chair, as he had at every Council meeting since Andreas and Alex had been captured. None of the councilors objected, and Erica found that revealing. At first, shock had made them indifferent; now it was indicative of acceptance.

She watched Ussher, noting the hectic light in his eyes. This would be the day. Ironic that he needed formalized sanction; a salve for a brittle ego.

Her gaze moved to Jan Barret, seated on Ussher's left. Jan still wasn't comfortable in Alex Ransom's chair, or with the triple-starred insignia of First Commander on his collar. Then John M'Kim, almost disinterested, his accountant's mind occupied with other matters. Marien Dyce was watching Ussher intently, and Erica thought to herself that she must be slated to make the nomination.

Erica looked to her left, scanning Ben's closed, granitic features, then beyond to Dr. Robert Hendrick, who fittingly enough sat at Ussher's right hand. He was a dark, handsome man not yet forty, one of the first Second Gens born in Fina, and perhaps a little spoiled as a child for that reason. His father had been a close friend of Andreas and held the same position Rob did now, Physical Science research coordinator. But Rob Hendrick wasn't the man his father had been, and his loyalty wasn't to Andreas Riis.

Erica sighed. She had advised Andreas to move Hendrick into a position where he wouldn't be heir apparent to Physical Science's seat on the Council, but Andreas had procrastinated, insisting he was the best man for the job, and he had admittedly inherited or acquired his father's administrative ability, if nothing else. And now Hendrick sat on the Council at the right hand of Predis Ussher. If the contempt she felt for him was evident, she didn't care. He deserved it for many reasons, not the least of them his arrogant estimation of his personal appeal to women.

She turned her attention to Ussher as he touched the "record" button on the console in front of him.

"The Council is now in session on 31 Decem 3257." He surveyed the councilors, then, "We'll begin with a report from Commander Venturi." Ben became the immediate center of attention, but he was intent on Ussher. "Commander, have you more information on the fate of Dr. Riis and Commander Ransom since our last meeting?"

"Not much new on Andreas. I know he was taken off Pollux, and I have evidence he may still be on Castor."

"But you aren't sure of that?"

"I'm sure he was taken to Castor," Ben replied, meeting his skeptical gaze coldly.

"I see. Have you any evidence that he's still alive?"

"I don't have any evidence that he's dead."

Ussher smiled tolerantly. "Of course. In other words, you have nothing new to offer."

"No. The security lid on Andreas is airtight."

"Well, then, perhaps you've had better luck with Commander Ransom?" The question was clearly rhetorical.

"Alex is still in the Cliff, and he's still alive."

"You've actually seen him?"

"Me? No. I can't go around looking at the prisoners without

authorization. But I've checked the files. He's there."

"But can you be *sure* he's still alive? After all, it's been fifteen days. That's a long time on Level 6."

Ben was finding it difficult to keep his temper in rein. "Predis, I *had* an agent on Level 6, and she saw Alex there. But she was arrested four days ago."

"That *is* unfortunate. Your only agent on Level 6?"

"Yes, but you know that, don't you? And you know damn well she was killed 'resisting arrest.'"

Ussher raised an eyebrow. "I most certainly did *not* know. I'm sorry, of course, but that only makes it all the more doubtful that Commander Ransom is still alive. SSB records aren't always dependable when it comes to prisoners who don't survive interrogation. Now, have you anything *concrete* to offer since our last meeting?"

"No, but our agents in Concordia are working through SSB Central Control to free Alex. We'll have to get transfer orders to Benin through CC."

"Yes. Well, let us know when you have something definite." He glanced around the table at the other councilors. "We'll all continue to hope both Dr. Riis and Commander Ransom *are* alive, of course. Meanwhile, the work of the Phoenix must go on; we can't let our grief blind us to the necessity of continuing to strive for the goals for which our comrades have—that is, *may* have given their lives."

"Damn it," Ben interjected, "you have no reason to assume they're dead."

"Ben, don't bother," Erica put in. "We may as well get to the real purpose of this meeting."

Ussher eyed her suspiciously, then nodded. "Yes, you're quite right, Dr. Radek. It's been fifteen days since Dr. Riis's arrest, and the Phoenix and the Council have been without a—a director. In the interests of—"

"In the interests of saving time," Erica said, "*I'll* make the nomination and we can get that formality out of the way without further explanation or rhetoric."

That elicited responses ranging from surprise to chagrin among the other councilors, and Ussher's face went red.

"*Doctor* Radek—"

"Predis, you've already assumed Andreas's chair and prerogatives. If you want to make it official by a vote, well and good, but I have work to do, and I see no reason to waste time satisfying your ego. For the record, I nominate Predis Ussher as chairman of the Council." She paused, then added, "Interim chairman, of course, until Andreas returns."

He glared at her, then said caustically, "Thank you, Dr. Radek. A nomination for chairman of the Council—"

"Interim chairman," Erica reminded him.

"*Interim* chairman," he amended, sending her a scathing glance, "has been made. Are there any other nominations?" Silence answered that, and he went on, "Very well, we will now hear the votes."

Erica leaned back, and Ben caught her eye, a hint of a smile curving his lips. She waited her turn as the votes were cast. Ussher would have a majority, but it wouldn't be unanimous. The fact that she'd nominated him didn't obligate her to vote for him.

The final count was five in favor, two opposed.

When the last vote was tallied, Ussher looked at her, and his message needed no words. Her time would come. He didn't yet have enough support among the members to risk an open confrontation, but the day would come when he'd be strong enough to dispose of her and Ben, and anyone loyal to them or to Andreas and Alex, without a qualm.

Not yet, she reminded herself. That day hadn't come yet.

8.

It was the coughing that wakened him again. He came out of a dream of a place with trees whose long, narrow leaves rustled in a cold wind. He wondered if it were a place he'd ever seen.

He turned on the bare ledge that served as a bed, his body heaving. Sometimes the coughing ended in unconsciousness lately, but it didn't come now. The spasms subsided, and he pulled himself up into a sitting position, curling in the corner where the bed-ledge met the walls. The loose shirt and trousers were soaked with the sweat of his fever and added to the chill that set his teeth chattering.

The cell was probably cold; they kept it cold. He knew that, just as he knew they were letting him die, and he wondered how he knew, how he knew so many things about this place, and yet there were so many things he didn't know.

He didn't know his own name.

He didn't know what he looked like, how old he was, where he had lived, if he'd had family or wife or children. He didn't even know if he were guilty of the things they accused him of: subversive activities, destruction of Concord property, homicide, piracy, treason.

It might be true. But he didn't know. He wouldn't recognize his own face in a mirror.

He felt the passage of every breath as a searing ache. If he didn't breathe deeply, there was less pain. He had learned to take slow, shallow breaths, learned to keep his body still so it wouldn't demand more air.

The food-tray slot by the door was empty. He noted that only because it was a vague measure of time; the food was of no interest to him. He knew, in the intuitive manner in which he understood anything here, that the food trays didn't appear at regular intervals. Prisoners were denied a measure of time that precise; it was part of the reduction process. But when he'd last fallen asleep a full tray had been in the slot. He knew some span of time beyond twenty to thirty minutes had passed. It took that long for the tray and utensils to disintegrate into a fine powder to be sucked up into the slot with any food remains. But even that time span was an estimate. All time was an estimate here.

He stared up at the glowing white ceiling. The light never faded, never changed. The whole cubicle was white; no breaks in the walls, no fixtures that weren't necessary. He wondered sometimes if he'd been born into this cell.

His pulse quickened. A sound. The beat of booted feet and the soft slap of naked ones.

His gaze shifted down, blurred and unfocused, until he was looking straight ahead to the open door, the door that *seemed* open. The faint shimmer of a shock screen made that empty space as impenetrable as tensteel.

The booted cadence induced a sudden tension in every muscle and a demand for oxygen. He closed his eyes, pulling for air, listening to the footsteps fading. They weren't coming for him; the slap of those bare feet told him that. They already had their victim.

There was little sound here; they left almost nothing for the senses to fix on. But they left the sound of boots, and every time he heard it, he cringed inwardly. That was also part of the reduction process.

He'd learned to listen for the sound of boots after the first interrogation. The lesson was quickly learned. And if they stopped outside his door, those black-uniformed, faceless, shadow-men, the terror began in earnest. It was a ritual, and that was purposeful, too. The victim knew exactly what to dread.

There were always two of them, and all these men were so nearly alike in physical conformation that, with the face-screens and uniforms, it was impossible to differentiate them except by voice. And they spoke few words.

They gave the order to stand and strip. Two words. Initially, it had taken more, but their charged lashes and gloves were compelling. Resistance was inevitably agonizing and futile. Even unconsciousness only delayed the ritual; it never stopped it. Finally, obedience became reflexive.

Everything in the ritual had its purpose. Nakedness added to vulnerability, and cold added to muscular tension, and both made the pulsed electrodes more effective. And the long walks down the white, bleached corridors served to heighten dread and in their labyrinthine windings to disorient the victim spatially. The goal of those passages was always the same: the interrogation room. There were many of them. That was something he *knew*. But they were all identical; for the prisoner, there was only one.

An empty dome; a hemisphere of satiny metal with no seam, no slightest imperfection for the eye to focus on. Voices echoed, space became equivocal, and the metal was always cold.

There was ritual here, too. It began when the guards delivered the victim into the hands of the men uniformed in white; all white, even to their boots and gloves. Except for the dark shadows of their face-screens. The psychocontrollers. Their part in the ritual began with the preparation of the victim for the inquisition.

The victim might struggle at this point, but again it was futile. He was usually laid on his back, flat on the chill floor, limbs spread; the vulnerability quotient was enhanced by the position. The shock cuffs next on wrists and ankles. Sensitive mechanisms; the flexing of a muscle would activate them. Then the electrodes were attached to his body with purposeful deliberation to allow him time to anticipate the pain each would inflict. They could be activated individually or in combination. The victim could not anticipate the amount or source of pain at any given time once the interrogation began.

But not yet. The preparatory ritual continued with the insertion of needles trailing fine tubes—he never saw the other end of the tubes or knew where they came from—into the veins inside his elbows, his thighs, sometimes even into the jugular. Each was strapped in place ready to mete out inhibition-reducing or hallucinogenic drugs on remote-controlled command.

Then the sensitizing injection, always administered with such skill that he never felt the injection itself, only a few seconds later the quivering sensation of having been flayed, every nerve exposed and raw to the slightest stimulus. It was at this point that the white-garbed acolytes left him, and the door closed behind them with a reverberating clang, leaving no hint of a seam in the flawless dome, nothing to suggest it had ever existed. The sound had the finality of the closing seal of a tomb.

They left him alone, splayed on the cold floor, the electronic leeches and the needle-fanged vipers poised on his shivering flesh; left him alone to stare up into the dimensionless dome, waiting. The controls, the controllers, even the questioners were outside. The victim was denied any focus for resentment and hatred; such emotions tended to reinforce resistance.

Then the interrogation began. The questions echoed, sourceless, emotionless, incessant, interminable. The electrodes came into play now in constantly varying combinations and intensities, with the drugs to add mental agonies to the physical agonies. It was a calculated assault on the mind designed to reduce the victim to total malleability, to something less than human. There was no hint of sadism. The questioning voices never displayed anger, impatience, or contempt, and that was the ultimate contempt. He existed in a limbo of pain and terror where there was no point of reference.

Finally, his only hold on sanity was to assign himself a task, or rather a challenge. And he wondered why he did it. What made him resist, made him *want* to hold on to his sanity?

But he set the challenge for himself every time. It was a grim game he played against an opponent as nameless and insubstantial as himself. The object of the game was to endure an entire interrogation session without screaming.

He never won the game.

And the sardonic irony in the whole ritual was that he didn't know the answers to the questions. If he did, he had no doubt that sooner or later they'd have them from him. But he didn't *know* the answers.

His eyes came open and he shuddered, staring at the white walls. Then his breath came out in a long, rattling sigh. He'd been dreaming.

He was hot again, pulse pounding under his burning skin. His head rolled back against the wall, his eyes closed. Sleep had been impossible when he first came here, but with the illness he moved in and out of it easily. Not a restful sleep, but better than wakefulness, except when he was assaulted by those terrifying, meaningless nightmares. He wondered if they were born in the drug-induced horrors of the interrogations or out of real memories. Sometimes he woke with the smell of smoke in his nostrils.

His body was that of a young man, and his physical condition was good—at least, it had been when he came here—but there was no comfort in that. It only meant it would take that much longer to die.

And that was the only way out of this place.

PHOENIX MEMFILES: DEPT HUMAN SCIENCES: BASIC SCHOOL
(HS/BS)
SUBFILE: LECTURE, BASIC SCHOOL 7 FEBUAR 3252
      GUEST LECTURER: RICHARD LAMB
      SUBJECT: POST-DISASTERS HISTORY:
      WARS OF CONFEDERATION (2876–2903)
DOC LOC #819/219–1253/1812–1648–723252

Throughout the twenty-seven years of the Wars of Confederation, Lord Patric Eyre Ballarat devoted most of his scant free time to a document he called "The Articles of the PanTerran Empire." This is the first use of the term "PanTerran," or of "Terra" instead of "Earth," but although the "PanTerran" was retained, the planet was generally called by its old name until the extraterrestrial colonization phase in the thirty-first and thirty-second centuries.

Ballarat's Articles codified minutely the centralized, imperial government so pivotal to his ambitions. At the apex of his power hierarchy was an hereditary emperor, the first of whom was to be elected by a "senate" of Lords, and no doubt he expected to be the one so favored. If it had been put to a vote of all the citizens of the Holy Confederation immediately after Tsane Valstaad's surrender, Ballarat probably *would* have been made an emperor, but it's unlikely the concept of a popular election occurred to him; that was a concept even he would have called radical.

In the wake of Tsane's surrender, Ballarat returned to Conta Austrail and a hero's welcome. The celebration of the successful end of the long campaign lasted a full week, and Ballarat obligingly spent it traveling from one city to another to accept personally the public acclaim and answer it with eloquent addresses expressing his gratitude and optimism. Perhaps he forgot that it was the Bonds and Fesh who were doing all the cheering, not the Lords. No doubt they also considered him a hero, and certainly they had ample reason to be grateful to him; he had made them Lords of an entire planet. But it soon became apparent that their

51

gratitude and esteem were not strong enough to induce them to make him their emperor.

Ballarat in his *Autobiography* displays a poignant surprise at that, which later turned to bitterness. His error, he asserts, was in waiting until after the victory celebrations to assemble the Council and Directorate in order to present his Articles of Empire. He should have done it immediately upon his return to Conta Austrail before the "reactionary" Lords had a chance to rally against him. In actuality, the Lords were rallied long before Tsane's surrender, and Ballarat's empire was doomed from the beginning to be rejected by a senate composed of the Holy Confederation's Lords. He underestimated the inertia of power, the tendency of those in possession of it to retain it. Power can only be wrested from the powerful by the application of greater power, and in that feudal society, virtually all power was concentrated in the hands of the Lords. Ballarat had only one option open to him for the needed greater power—a military coup.

And that would have been entirely feasible. His troops remained solidly loyal to him despite the rigors and heavy casualties of the Sudafrikan campaign, but at this point Ballarat paid for his neglect of the Directorate and particularly of his brother Hugh, who still held the title of VisChairman of the Directorate. At the urging of a coalition of influential conservative Lords, Hugh, on the fifth day after Ballarat's return to Conta Austrail, ordered the decommissioning of all conscript troops, which constituted nearly half the Holy Confederation's armed forces. The order could only be overridden by a Directorate majority, and even if Ballarat could have managed that, by the time he learned of the order—he was in Perthhold in the midst of his victory tour—it was too late to attempt it. The conscript soldiers, of course, were all too happy to throw off their uniforms and return to their homes and families, and those stationed in Conta Austrail did so immediately, while garrisons in occupied territories struggled with the problem of manning their posts adequately while the conscripts crowded into every available vessel and airship in a jubilant exodus. Some of the remaining volunteer troops and officers might have been willing to attempt a coup in Ballarat's behalf, but their numbers were too small, and the decommissioning order created chaos in the ranks of Ballarat's vaunted military machine.

The crucial moment passed and left Ballarat standing by helplessly. His Articles of Empire were never presented to the Council or Directorate. He wasn't given an opportunity for that, even if he'd been naive enough at that point to try. He sent Hugh packing to the Home Estate and exercised his prerogatives as Chairman to call the Directorate into session, but at their first meeting he was unanimously voted into the newly created position of Chairman of the Dominions (that is, the conquered territories) Council, and voted *out* of the Chairmanship of the Directorate.

His successor was the Lord Paul Adalay, once one of his staunchest supporters, and apparently Adalay was chosen as a compromise candidate; Ballarat still had adherents among the Lords. The Directors could have done far worse, and although Ballarat retired to embittered isolation in the House's Tasman estate and never came to terms with Adalay—or his own brothers, or even his wife and children—Adalay proved a far wiser Chairman than Ballarat ever gave him credit for.

It was Paul Adalay who drafted the Articles of the PanTerran Confederation (the appellation "Holy" was dropped with its acceptance), which retained many of the centralizing measures in Ballarat's Articles of Union. The division of power between Houses and Confederation was precisely delineated, and the Houses retained unchallenged authority over their internal affairs, but the Confederation retained the rights of taxation and conscription based on House revenues, and the right to maintain armed forces as well as a civil police. The University system was taken out of the hands of the Church and made a part of the Confederation administration, with a separate medical research and practice division that later developed into Conmed. The Directorate was retained as the governing body of the Confederation, its members elected by a majority of the Council of Lords *or*—and that ultimately became a fateful alternative—by the Lords of the Directorate itself.

In comparison to the pre-Ballarat Holy Confederation, the PanTerran was highly centralized and a far more stable structure. That stability, as well as its new prosperity and the wider geographical and intellectual horizons opened to it, was a product of Ballarat's twenty-seven-year campaign, and made possible the further technological advances that opened humankind's way to the stars.

But Ballarat remained unimpressed. His lifespan of

eighty-one years was too short for him to see a man set foot
on Luna again after an interregnum of more than a thousand
years. He only knew that Patric Eyre Ballarat had conquered
a world only to end his years in impotent self-exile, his
imperial vision smashed by what he called the "stubborn
myopia of niggardly men who hoard personal power at the
expense of the future of civilization."

One wonders what the future of civilization would have
been if Ballarat's vision had been realized, and I can't share
his faith in it. On the other hand, I *can* share his antipathy
for those shortsighted and "niggardly" men. Such men are
always with us, of course, and conservatism serves a meaningful purpose in social equations. It's a stabilizing factor,
a check on uncontrolled change. But, like so many things,
it can be regarded as "good" only in moderation. It's unfortunate that conservative factors have throughout our history since Pilgram seemed to outweigh the innovative factors that admittedly can be dangerous, but that—also in
moderation—are so necessary to social evolution.

CHAPTER IX: Januar 3258

●||●||●||●||●||●||●||●||●||●||●||●||●||●||●||●||●||●||●||●||●||●||●||●||●||

1.

The dream wasn't a pleasant one. Predis Ussher stirred, then came awake, frowning at the glowing digits of the clock on the bedside table: 02:33. He jerked the thermblanket up over his shoulders and settled back again. He couldn't even remember the dream, only its emotional feel.

It was just a dream, damn it, whatever it was about. He lay still, concentrating on clearing his mind for sleep. He would need a good night's sleep. The Council meeting tomorrow. He must be at his best—

The room was suddenly flooded with light.

He cried out, thrashing to free himself from the blanket, reaching blindly for the table. The drawer; the X^2 in the drawer.

A hand closed on his wrist, forcing his arm against the sharp edge of the table. The pain shot up to his shoulder.

Venturi.

Ussher's eyes were coming into focus now. Ben Venturi still in his SSB black.

Ussher hissed, *"Damn you!"*

The rage was as blinding as the light, and the low, mocking laugh that answered the expletive added fuel to it. The pain was excruciating.

Then suddenly it stopped. His arm was free.

He lunged for the drawer, fumbling, only asking himself why he'd been freed when he had the answer. The X^2 was gone.

"Relax, Predis. Nobody's going to hurt you."

Ussher squinted up into the light, expecting to see the laser in Venturi's hand. It wasn't there, and his SSB gun was holstered at his side; his hands were empty.

A movement at the end of the bed distracted Ussher, and a moment later renewed the rage.

Erica Radek. Like a shadow somehow, even dressed in pale, light-catching blue, her silver hair glinting. Her eyes, those steel-colored eyes—they *made* shadows.

And she was relishing his confusion, his—yes, *fear*. It was normal enough, that fear. But she was enjoying it. Her face was expressionless, but he knew she was enjoying it, and he wouldn't give her more satisfaction. He had himself under control now, and his eyes were adjusting to the light. He looked up at Venturi.

"How the hell did you get in here?"

"Through the door," he replied, smiling faintly.

Ussher felt a chill. Hendrick had told him no one could even touch that door without setting off alarms. The fool; the stupid fool. Not only had the 'screens been unlocked, but Venturi and Radek were inside the room, his gun was gone. They could've killed him.

And that was exactly the point, obviously. They *could* have killed him. But they didn't, and that was revealing.

Ussher started to throw the blanket back preparatory to rising, but Venturi's flat, cold tone stopped him.

"Just stay put, Predis." He didn't make a threatening move; no move at all. "There are ways to immobilize you so you can still hear and talk. Save me the trouble and you a drug headache."

Ussher smiled. Hear and talk. It was beginning to make sense. He propped the pillows behind him and sat up against the headboard, arms folded.

"Very well, Commander. Now, to what do I owe this unexpected pleasure?"

Venturi gave a short laugh as he drew up a chair by the bed and seated himself, perfectly relaxed, it would seem, but there was a ready tension in the curl of his big hands. It was Radek, still standing at the end of the bed, who answered the question.

"We thought it time the three of us had a private talk, simply to clarify the existing situation."

Ussher glanced at Venturi. He was silent now, and his stony expression said he would remain silent. As usual, he'd let Radek do the talking while he waited like some sort of lackey, a trained guard jumping to the orders of a—a woman.

Radek walked slowly to the other side of the bed, drawing his eye away from Venturi.

"First of all," she said, "we know your plans for tomorrow's Council meeting. We know you intend to present your 'evidence' and charge Alex Ransom in absentia—or, rather, behind his back—with betraying Andreas to the SSB."

Ussher frowned in spite of himself. He'd discussed that with no one but Rob Hendrick.

Radek gave a short laugh that set his teeth on edge.

"Don't be concerned that you've been betrayed. It's an obvious move, and I've been listening to the gossip. It's a very effective ploy, Predis, but it has a disadvantage. It signals your moves well ahead of time."

He said stiffly, "I don't know what you're talking about."

A laugh from Venturi. Ussher glared at him, then back to Radek as she said, "The gossip making the rounds lately has it that Alex never did signal the Fina MT terminal for a trans when those SSB 'cars appeared so conveniently near Hallicourt, and that he was never arrested, that he is not now, and never has been in the Cliff." Those eyes turned even colder and harder. "But you know he *is* there. Of course, that doesn't worry you too much. He's been there for twenty days, and we've never had anyone survive that long on Level 6. At this point you've had time to establish yourself as a leader in the minds of the members, and you've assumed you can safely consider Alex dead. But you still have a problem. You know who Alex Ransom really is, and you know the potentials he offers for Phase I would dwarf the Peladeen Alternative."

She paused as if waiting for him to respond to that, but he only offered her a mocking smile. She was purposely trying to make him angry—did she think he didn't know that?—and he wouldn't let her manipulate him.

"It wouldn't be such a problem," she went on, finally, "if you and Ben and I were the only ones in Fina who knew Alex's identity, but John M'Kim, Marien Dyce, and Emeric Garris also know it, and you must also deal with the possibility that other members—all of them, conceivably—might learn Alex's identity and its potential, and that they might resent the fact that you threw away that potential to protect yourself and the Peladeen Alternative. So your problem is to negate Alex. You're confident he's been negated literally by the SSB, but you still have to negate the Ransom Alternative for those who know his identity already or might learn of it in the future. Your course of action is obvious. You must make him a traitor, which will also provide a scapegoat for Andreas's betrayal so you won't have to worry about anyone considering *you* as his Judas."

Ussher straightened, feeling acutely the awkwardness of his physical position, but saying with as much dignity as he could muster, "Dr. Radek! That accusation is patently absurd. How could you—"

She laughed. "Spare me, Predis. Save that for your faithful sycophants. As I said, branding Alex a traitor is an obvious move; essential, in fact. Branding Ben and me accomplices to his treason is equally obvious. We're a constant threat to you because we're not only well aware of the Ransom Alternative, but we also know you betrayed Alex and Andreas, that you betrayed the Phoenix, and will continue to do so in order to fulfill your own ambitions."

"Spare *me*, Dr. Radek," Ussher said hotly. "Take your own advice and save that for *your* sycophants!"

"If necessary I will, Predis."

Somehow she'd turned the thrust on him; her quiet rejoinder came back at him as a threat. Again, he started to rise, but at that Venturi leaned toward him. His hands were still empty, but Ussher, after a brief pause, sank back against the pillows.

She went on as if nothing had happened, "You intended to make a clean sweep at the Council meeting by including Ben and me in a conspiracy to betray Andreas. But now I'm sure you'll admit that ploy might be rather risky, since we're prepared for it."

"Ah. And you're preparing me for your counterthrust?"

"Warning you of it."

"That's rather an unusual approach, isn't it?"

She raised an eyebrow, but ignored the question. "Predis, are you aware of how the members stand now where you're concerned? I've been sampling and analyzing member reactions in Fina. I can't get enough dependable data from the outside chapters, but I assume the data from Fina is applicable to the entire membership. Approximately fifty percent of them support you and your grandiose plans wholeheartedly, primarily because in Andreas and Alex's absence they see no other alternative. Another twenty-five percent is undecided,

and the remaining twenty-five percent is loyal to Andreas and
Alex and totally opposed to you."

He considered the figures, then gave a short laugh. "Very
interesting."

She glanced at Venturi with a knowing smile.

"We thought you'd find that interesting. But before you
congratulate yourself too heartily on the fifty percent you can
claim as converts, remember the remaining half that's either
undecided or totally opposed to you. At the present time, the
members are still united simply because the rift hasn't been
brought out into the open. But if it is, if a true schism occurs,
then both sides will lose because the Phoenix will disintegrate.
You know the old axiom, divide and conquer; you use it constantly. But if it's carried too far in this situation, the result
will be divide and *destroy*."

He studied her for a moment and almost laughed. He found
all those statistics interesting primarily because she did. They
had her scared. *He* had her scared.

"I assume, Dr. Radek, there's a point to all this."

Those cold, steel-colored eyes flickered briefly.

"Why else would Ben and I be losing sleep talking to you?
The point is that all of us can agree that destroying the Phoenix
is not desirable—for our own reasons."

He shrugged. "That we can agree on."

"Then this is the situation: if you try to dispose of Ben and
me by branding us traitors or by killing us outright, then you'll
precipitate an open schism that will destroy the Phoenix."

"Is that a prediction or a threat?"

"Both. A prediction because Ben and I have loyal followings
of our own, and we also serve as surrogates for Alex and
Andreas among their loyals. It's a threat because Ben has
provided us with a sort of insurance which is also designed to
stop you from branding Alex a traitor and making him the
scapegoat for Andreas's betrayal. It consistes of microspeakers
that are presently hidden not only in every part of Fina, but
in every chapter HQ in both Systems. They number in the
thousands, and it would be futile for you to try to find them
all." She walked around behind Venturi to the bedside table.
"They can be activated by any one of several hundred loyal
members, and it would be equally futile for you to try to
identify and kill all of them."

"And why am I supposed to be so concerned about these

'speakers, that I'd bother to search them out, much less kill to keep them from being activated?" Hendrick; he'd have to talk to Hendrick. There must be some way to detect microspeakers, even when they weren't activated.

She opened her hand and let him see the tape spool in her palm, then dropped it on the table.

"This will answer your question, Predis. Listen to it. This is what the members will hear from those 'speakers: an outline of the Ransom Alternative—including Alex Ransom's identity, of course—along with excerpts from recordings we've acquired in our little war of monitors, primarily conversations between you and Rob Hendrick, which will explain certain recent arrests of members, as well as several 'accidental' deaths. If any member hearing one of these tapes can still maintain any faith in you, then the Phoenix is made up of fools, and you aren't fool enough to believe that."

Ussher felt the rush of blood to his face, the pounding behind his eyes. His fists thumped impotently into the bed.

"Lies! You think you can—all *lies*! It's—"

"Predis, be quiet and listen!" Venturi was on his feet, slitted eyes glittering.

Ussher subsided. He couldn't lose control. That's what they wanted, and he had to think this out. It could be a bluff, a bluff he might be willing to call. And, given enough time, he could make the name of Alex Ransom so despised, those microspeakers wouldn't mean a damn thing. He didn't need to bring it up in the Council, either. Gossip. Yes, Radek was right; it *was* an effective ploy. It had always worked. Time was the important thing. All he needed was enough time.

"Very well, Commander, I'm listening."

It was Radek who replied, "We're well aware that you may not take our predictions or threats seriously, but I'd advise you to do so. If you don't, you'll risk destroying the Phoenix, and you need it."

"And what about you? Aren't you taking that risk with those microspeakers?"

"True, but they won't be activated unless something happens to Ben or me, or unless you carry out your plans to make Alex your scapegoat."

"I see. In other words, you don't care what happens to the Phoenix if you're not around to try to run it your way."

Her chin came up slightly. "Yes, Predis, we do care; that's

why we'll see the Phoenix destroyed rather than leave it to
you."

He only smiled at that. She might talk about saving the
Phoenix, but the real issue here was clear. She was afraid, and
she was here to bargain—to bargain for her life, hers and her
trained lackey's. Ussher leaned back, crossing one leg over the
other.

"All right, Dr. Radek, I'll bargain with you. I'll give you
and Venturi your lives. And Ransom. You can have his good
name untarnished. For now, anyway."

"What do you mean by 'for now'?"

He laughed, enjoying it. "What do you expect? A date
written into a contract? For *now*. For as long as I feel like
standing by the bargain."

She smiled, and there was something incomprehensible
about it, an incredible *satisfaction*.

"Then we'll also stand by the bargain . . . for now."

She reached into the pocket of her slacsuit and took out an
X^2 and handed it to him. It was his own gun.

"Sleep well, Predis."

Then she turned and left the room, with Venturi following
silently behind her.

Ussher looked down at the gun. It was at full charge with
the safety off.

Sleep well. . . .

Damn her!

2.

The sun in Helen wasn't yet at zenith, but the pavement
sent up shimmers of heat. Adrien Eliseer wore a wide-brimmed
hat to augment her eyeshades, but both were as much to hide
her face as to protect it. She was too preoccupied to control
her expression now.

Lectris followed her across the baking pavement from the
'car to the compound gate. Their shadows angled ahead, merg-
ing in a shifting, black pool. She didn't pause as she passed
the gate, and she was surprised when one of the guards took
a tentative step toward her.

"Uh—you're going to see the old Shepherd, my lady?"

"Yes, Cam. Why? Is something wrong?"

The guard glanced toward the neatly arrayed, multileveled dormitories, his brow furrowed under the shadow of his helmet.

"Nothing's wrong, my lady. I just thought maybe I should . . . well, go along with you to the chapel."

It was too much. Sargent Cambridge, who had blithely waved her in and out of this compound for years, muttering about "going along." *Guarding* her. It was yet another symptom, a sign of the times, and on some level she recognized its seriousness, but at the moment all she could feel was anger. But even that left her as suddenly as it came. Despair is stronger, she thought numbly, stronger than any other emotion.

She said lightly, "Oh, really, Cam, this isn't Toramil or a Selasid compound, thank the God. Besides," she added, glancing up at Lectris, "I'm very well guarded."

She set off for the pedway ramps, ignoring Cambridge's dissatisfied, "But, my lady . . ."

Lectris went into the chapel, but Adrien didn't accompany him; she never entered the chapel except on a direct invitation from Malaki. At least in their prayers the Bonds should be free of the shadow of their Lords.

Lectris left her at the walled garden behind the chapel and sought the solace offered him by the candle-lit ikons. She entered the garden for another kind of solace.

A space no more than five meters square with an open area in the center paved with stone, the periphery was crowded with miniature terraces supporting a varied array of plants. But there was little color here; it wasn't a flower garden. It was an herb garden, its hues subtle, its scents tangy. Adrien took a deep breath. Solace. In these earthy scents, in the shade of these walls, she always found solace. She couldn't turn to her father now, she'd ceased to look to her mother years ago, and Dr. Perralt couldn't yet be told of this possibility. No. This probability.

Karlis Selasis. She would be his bride.

"Oh—my lady!"

Malaki came erect from his kneeling position near the chapel door, unfolding his spare, blue-robed body stiffly. She had startled him, but now his lined face came alive with a smile, and that gratified her. There were Bonds outside the chapel lately with no inclination to smile on recognizing their Lord's daughter.

"Hello, Malaki." She removed her hat and eyeshades, then, noting the spindly sprigs he'd been pressing into the damp earth, asked, "What's this?"

He wiped his muddied hands on the apron at his waist, seeming to find them embarrassing.

"Hemus, my lady, from Pollux. My third cousin, Haldan, is Bonded to the Lord Selasis and he came with the Lord on his tour of the Centauran ports and brought these seedlings from Leda."

And all the latest news from Terra and every stop along the way, she added to herself with a private smile. Then Malaki's eyes widened with a remembrance that apparently pleased him.

"Oh, Haldan also brought me some sassassa tea. Perhaps you'd like some. It's a bit hard come by, but my niece, Dorit, who works in Lord Loren's Leda smelter—"

"I'd be delighted," Adrien said, laughing, "to partake of this rarity with you, Malaki."

He smiled and started for the open door into his quarters. "I'll only need a few minutes to prepare it."

Adrien crossed to a bench by the garden wall. She sat down and leaned back against the cool, shaded plasment. It would be cool inside the chapel, too, and beautifully quiet. Lectris would be kneeling, lips moving in prayer, at one of the side altars under the ikon of Saint Boras, the limbless Shepherd of Mosk, who was said to have been a friend of Lionar Mankeen, and who became the guardian saint of the crippled and infirm. Lectris would be lighting a candle not for Boras, but for another saint regarded as one of his spiritual protégés, a candle lighted at Adrien's request for Saint Richard the Lamb.

Adrien knew who Richard the Lamb was, and perhaps that was why she found a comfort here even Malaki's presence couldn't entirely explain. But it had been nearly two years after Rich's death before she finally put all the pieces of the puzzle together.

After that devastating double grief, she'd been a frequent visitor to Malaki's garden. It had been on the first anniversary of those deaths that Malaki had mentioned Saint Richard the Lamb. He was preparing for a special ceremony: the Reliquary Rite, the investiture of a new saint.

Curiosity made her question him initially, then insight. He

described the Lamb in detail—he'd spoken with him often—
and quoted him endlessly, verbatim, she was sure. From Malaki, her curiosity led her to the Archives, where she pieced
together the short history of Richard Lamb, sociotheologist.
The Priority-Two rating on Lamb's theses was no impediment
to a Lord's daughter. Then she had only to compare those
theses with the ones Rich had sent her years ago under another
pseudonym.

Rich had become a saint, and that seemed fitting.

The Archives also told her of the manner of Richard Lamb's
death: he had been publicly executed as an agent of the Society
of the Phoenix.

That sent her into another Pri-Two, or more often Pri-One,
area, and most of the latter 'files were closed to her. A frus-
trating inquiry, even in the information accessible to her, which
was revealing primarily in the dearth of concrete facts and the
multiplicity of its contradictions. Above all, she could not
resolve the Concord's attitudes toward the Phoenix with the
fact that Rich had been one of its members. She remembered
well the man who called himself Richard Lamb.

She asked Malaki about Saint Richard's death. His Testing,
the Shepherd called it—the term "Phoenix" was meaningless
to him—and although he'd never set foot out of Helen, he
described the execution minutely, his account in perfect agreement with the official accounts. With one exception.

He described the miraculous intervention of Lord Alexand
DeKoven Woolf, who ordered the body of the Lamb given to
the Elder Shepherd Zekiel so he might have the Rites of Passing. Adrien had wept at that, but Malaki assumed it was only
her grief for Alexand. But even now the thought of Alexand
at Rich's execution brought the threat of tears.

She looked down at her right hand. The sapphire and ruby
ring glinted in the shadows. She'd moved it to her right hand,
but she could never bring herself to stop wearing it. A life
vow.

And she'd be taking another life vow soon and wearing
another ring. Sapphire and emerald. Eliseer and Selasis. She
had left her father only minutes ago after he haltingly explained
the results of his meeting with Orin Selasis two days before.

There was no choice for the House. The alternatives spelled
ruin for Eliseer. For one thing, Lazar Hamid's eldest daughter
was of marriageable age. An alliance between Selasis and

Hamid would threaten the smelter sites and mineral leases on Pollux so vital to the survival of Eliseer, and between that and constantly increasing freight rates, Orin Selasis could squeeze Eliseer into bankruptcy.

The despair engulfed her, and it was all she could do to hold back the tears. To be bound for the rest of her life to Karlis Selasis, that cruel, contemptible half man. She should have sought the safety of the cloisters after Alexand's death. A false vow in some senses, but not so false or so dreaded as this one.

Safety.

Perhaps it was the calm aura of this garden. The despair suddenly ebbed.

Safety—a hollow word. Why was she concerned with safety? What had she to lose? Her life?

For a long time she didn't move, barely breathing, a stillness within her; a resolution. Potentials tooks shape in her mind like figures moving out of shadows into light.

She had *nothing* to lose; nothing meaningful to her. The corollary to that was that she had nothing to *fear*.

The House. She must protect the House, but she had no reason to protect her own life. The Selasids lived and fed on fear. Without it, they'd be helpless. She curbed the urge to laugh aloud, remembering Malaki busy beyond the open door. But the laughter made her lips curl sardonically. The Selasids made an error if they expected another docile granddaughter of Shang like Janeel.

When her father told her about the marriage, she had been too shocked to feel anything but dread, too numbed to think through the possibilities. It hadn't occurred to her to see it as an opportunity. A bride of Karlis Selasis who wasn't afraid could destroy—

"Here we are, my lady."

She was startled out of her reverie, remembering belatedly to order her features. Malaki was approaching, carrying a tray laden with a proceleen tea service.

Adrien smiled and moved to the end of the bench while he put the tray down beside her.

"The tea has a delicious fragrance," she said.

"So it does. They say it makes for quiet sleep, taken at bedtime." He filled one cup, his hands scrubbed pinkly clean now, and he handled the pot as if it were infinitely precious.

The tea service had been a gift from her: white porceleen decorated with painstaking representations of herbal plants. She'd had it made expressly for Malaki because he enjoyed sharing his herb teas with her and was always embarrassed with his plain, plasex mugs.

He counted out three drops of sucros, gave the mixture a turn with a silver stirring rod, and handed her the cup. She took it, then paused.

"Am I to enjoy this alone?" There was ample room for him on the bench and an empty cup on the tray, but he waited for the invitation. "Please, join me. You've probably been working in your garden all morning without a rest."

"Only since morning matins, my lady." He seated himself and filled the other cup, pausing to add the sucros. "And I can't call my garden work; I enjoy it too much."

"Even pleasure can be tiring." She tasted the tea, and her brows went up. It had a faint citrus tang and a hint of Castorian comaris. "This is delightful. Mother would never admit it, but it's quite an improvement over Black Shang."

He smiled politely. "I'm glad you like it. I have a packet for you to take home with you, if you wish."

"Thank you. And am I to take some at bedtime for quiet sleep?"

"If you think it needful." He studiously sipped at his tea, the creases between his brows deepening. "You're troubled, my lady."

She almost expected him to say, "my child," as he would to one of his flock. She nodded, but remained silent for a while, knowing he'd wait patiently and ask no questions of her. And it was ironic that she could tell Malaki the whole truth with no concern. What couldn't yet be spoken aloud in the Estate, except in the monitor-proof privacy of her father's office, could be spoken freely here. No one would monitor this garden; it would be inconceivable to anyone that she would trust anything of importance to a Bond.

Finally, she said, "I *am* troubled, Malaki, and it might seem odd, the reason for it. You see, I've learned I'm not to end my days as an unmarried matron after all."

He seemed surprised, almost unnerved. She wondered if he connected her marriage with Lord Orin's recent visit, but his reply didn't suggest that.

"You're to be married, my lady? That's . . . strange."

She couldn't repress her laugh. "My friend, it's far stranger that I've reached the ripe old age of twenty-eight and managed to maintain my blessed vir——" She stopped and amended herself, "—single state. But why do you say its strange, my marrying?"

His narrow shoulders rose in a quick shrug. "Perhaps I meant I was surprised, my lady."

He never lied to her; he added the "perhaps" to make that statement less than a lie.

"No doubt you *were* surprised, but I don't think that's what you meant."

"Well, perhaps I was thinking of the spirit weft between you and the Lord Alexand. Such things can't be broken." He looked down at the ring on her right hand, then with a sigh admitted, "I thought it strange because I . . . I had a vision once. You might think it only a dream." He glanced at her, as if expecting a doubting response, but she only studied him soberly. "It was right after the Brother first came to me. The same night, in fact. It was on Saint Richard the Lamb's day, two years ago, and it was the Lamb who spoke to me in the vision, or . . . dream."

Adrien wondered at the term "the Brother," but Richard the Lamb distracted her from that.

"What did he say to you?"

Malaki's eyes narrowed in concentration, and she knew the words would be exactly those heard in his dream.

"The Lamb said to me, 'Comfort your Lady, Malaki. She will never be the bride of any man but her Promised.'" He saw that Adrien had paled at that and added, "I didn't tell you because even then the wounds of grief were too fresh. I took it as a prophecy. That's why when you told me now that you're to be married, I thought it strange. It seems to go against the prophecy."

"Prophecies can be interpreted in many ways."

"True, and now I don't know what this one may mean."

"No doubt the meaning will be clear in time. Malaki, who's this 'Brother' you mentioned?" Then, when he paused uncertainly, "Is it something you'd rather not tell me about?"

"Oh, no, my lady. It's just that the Brother is a mystery to me. He says he's a mortal man and not a saint. But he's a holy man. He first came to me, as I said, on Saint Richard's day two years ago."

"Came to you? In a vision?"

"Oh, no. He came to the chapel. He always does."

"Does he come to you often?"

"No, I wouldn't say often. But I've talked with him many times. The last was on Saint Ruth's day in levenmonth."

That would be in late Novem. Adrien maintained her attentive expression, but she was wondering how a mortal man, however "holy," managed to slip into the compound "many times" without attracting the attention of the guards.

"*How* does he come to you?"

"Well, it's always late at night when I'm in the chapel alone. He never comes when anyone else is with me, but he asks me to tell my flock about him and his words."

She took time to taste her tea and assess the fact that this holy man appeared only to Malaki. His mind had always seemed clear, but still, he was at least ninety. His next words embarrassed her, as if he'd read her thoughts.

"I say he appears only when I'm alone, my lady, but I don't mean he appears to me alone." He smiled as her eyes met his. "I've talked to other Shepherds here in Helen who've seen the Brother, and I've heard of him from Shepherds even in the Solar System."

"Well, he seems to be quite mobile." She made a mental note to ask her father if he'd had any reports from his intelligence section on this mortal holy man. "You say he talks to you, Malaki. What about?"

"Many things. Peace and humility. He says true victory is only in submission to the Mezion's will. Even if many suffer, they're Blessed, for the humble will say the Rites of Passing for the last of the prideful. He says humility turns the sword like water; a sword can't cut water."

"He seems a man of peaceful purpose."

"So he is, my lady, as his brother was."

She was confused. "*His* brother?"

"The Lamb. He's the Brother of Saint Richard the Lamb."

She grasped her cup with both hands, numbed and trembling, and at first all she could think was what an unforgivably cruel hoax this was.

But the necessity of maintaining control in Malaki's presence brought her thoughts into focus. It wasn't cruel; it only seemed so to her because she knew Richard Lamb's real identity and still grieved the man who had actually been his brother.

It wasn't cruel, but it was purposeful.

The Phoenix. Who else could provide a "brother" for Richard the Lamb to maintain and reinforce his influence over the Bonds?

She asked casually, "Who does the Brother speak for? Does he belong to any Order or religious brotherhood? Any kind of organization?"

"I don't think so, my lady. He doesn't wear a monk's habit or sign. I asked him once why he came to me and the other Shepherds. He said, 'I come to finish my brother's work.' The Lamb had no master but the Holy Mezion. I think the Brother is sent by Him, too."

And not by the Phoenix; not as far as Malaki was concerned. Adrien considered this and found herself amazed. An extraordinary organization, whatever its real purposes.

"Has he no other name than the Brother?"

"No. I mean, he's given me none, nor any of the other Shepherds."

"What does he look like?"

"Well, he's a young man and well favored like his brother. But his body is sound. He's tall, a head taller than I, and very much like the Lamb, really. His hair is the same color, and his eyes."

Adrien didn't realize at first that she was holding her breath; she found the shadowed garden suddenly cold. But this was ridiculous. She was beginning to believe in Malaki's spirits and Beyond Souls. Or perhaps her nerves were in a worse state than she realized.

"Is that how you know he's the Lamb's brother? Because of the resemblance?"

"Yes, and things he's told me about the Lamb. And he has a sign."

"What kind of sign, Malaki?"

"A medallion. He wears it on a chain around his neck."

She felt the chill in the air again. "A medallion?"

"Yes. It's small; perhaps half again as wide as your thumbnail, my lady. And very fine; of gold, I think."

"Is there something on the medallion?"

"Yes, my lady. The image of a Lamb."

Her cup crashed to the stones, exploding into thin shards of ruin.

She was on the verge of fainting, and in one sense grateful

for that startling explosion. It served to bring her to her senses, to dispel the ghostly shadows called up by Malaki's words. And it silenced the question in her mind: What is on the other side of that medallion? A wolf?

But she couldn't be grateful for the cause of the distraction. Malaki seemed shattered with the cup, the dismay in his eyes cut to her heart, and she felt the tears coming.

"Oh, Malaki—I'm so sorry." She reached out for his hand, and at that he recovered himself, gazing in bewilderment at the tears moving down her cheeks. "Forgive me, please. It was so careless of me. But I know the craftsman who made the set. He's in Leda. I'll have another cup made, I promise you—"

"My lady, please." He smiled now. "You mustn't worry about it. It was dear to me only because it was a gift from you. But it is said, who loves things of substance more than things of the soul is a fool. It was the soul in the cup that was important. Your soul, my lady; your kindness."

She said softly, "You're an extraordinary man, Malaki." Then she looked down at the broken cup, her uneasiness returning as she remembered the words that made her lose her grip on it.

Enough. Enough of saints and Brothers and ghosts, products of Malaki's faith and the Phoenix's purpose. She had the future to think about; to plan.

She frowned. Could anyone ever be truly free of fear of death? She'd felt free only minutes ago, but now—

"My lady, I hope you aren't still worried about the cup."

"No, I . . . I was only thinking of other things." She glanced at her watch and rose. "And among them is a luncheon for Lady Almiret Shang. My aunt; she's visiting us, you know."

He had risen with her, and now he started for the chapel. "I'll tell Lectris you're ready to leave. And I have some sassassa tea for you. Don't let me forget."

"I won't; I enjoyed it very much. And I *will* have the cup replaced."

He paused at the chapel door. "Thank you, but your concern is a greater gift."

"So is yours for me, Malaki. My solace."

His cheeks went red. "In that I'm only an instrument of the Holy Mezion, my lady."

She smiled as he hurried on his way, wondering if she could

ever regard herself, as Malaki did, as an instrument of anything but her own will.

Perhaps that would be enough. Enough to see her through her coming Testing.

3.

He came awake suddenly, wracked by violent chills, his eyes closing as soon as they opened, reacting to the stabbing ache of the eternal white light.

He'd been dreaming again. Nightmares. For a moment, he tried to recapture the images; however terrifying, they might be the memories of his past. If he had a past. But they slipped away before he could grasp them.

He pushed himself up into the corner of the bed-ledge, body curled into a foetal position against the walls. It was only then that he recognized the sound of footsteps. The cadenced beat was so far away it was almost inaudible, but that was what had awakened him, not the nightmares.

The terror gripped him, and with it came another spasm of coughing. Even when that subsided, it was still some time before hc could stop gasping for air so he could hear.

Booted feet. No sound of naked feet.

A new chill enveloped him; he clenched his teeth to stop their chattering, and stared out the doorway through the shimmer of the shock screen at the blank segment of corridor. The booted feet were almost at the door. But something was different. He held his breath, concentrating on that ominous cadence.

There were more than two pairs of footsteps.

He was afraid to close his eyes. He pressed back against the converging walls, listening with every cell, hope giving the terror a cutting edge. Hope that they weren't coming for him, that they would move like shadows past his door.

Three pairs of footsteps. But there were always two when they came for him. Only two. Perhaps they weren't coming for him. Perhaps . . .

The black shadow-figures filled the doorway, and his vision

dimmed under the pressure of his pulse.

The sound of footsteps had ceased. In the silence, he let his breath out in a searing sigh. Perhaps he wouldn't survive another interrogation.

He didn't move. He waited, hearing the click as the shock screens went off, watching two of them respectfully step aside while the other entered the cell. Then a second followed the first, while the third waited outside the door.

"This the one, Sargent?" The first shadow-man loomed over him, turning his faceless head to the second.

"Yeh: 17–073. That's him, Major."

"He's in bad shape," the major commented, as if it were a matter of inconvenience to him.

The sargent shrugged. "Well, we thought he was . . . uh, terminal, sir. That's the word we had."

"Central Control says otherwise. Can he walk?"

"I can walk."

He wondered even as he spoke why he said that. He wasn't entirely sure he *could* walk, and what drove him to make that assertion of his existence, his humanity? It would make no difference in the end.

The major hesitated, then gave a curt laugh. "He talks, too. Did he break?"

"Him? No. He's Phoenix."

"Maybe they'll have better luck where he's going." His tone turned clipped and flat. "All right, you. If you can walk, you've got some walking to do. On your feet."

It must be pride, he thought, as he swung his legs over the side of the ledge and levered himself to his feet. What else would make him defy the contempt beyond contempt in that cold, indifferent voice? What else would make him set his mind to the game again, the game of holding back the screams through another interrogation?

But the major had said, *Where he's going. . . .*

He flinched as the major's hand closed on his arm, expecting the jolt of a charged glove, but there was nothing except the hard grip of his hand.

The sargent asked, "You want cuffs, Major?"

He laughed. "I think I can handle this one without cuffs."

They started down the corridor, the beat of boots echoing around him. The ritual had been changed, and he didn't know what to expect or dread. He was only sure there was something to dread.

The major was his only attendant as the door opened onto the landing roof. It was night beyond the white glare of helions lighting the roof. The sound—a pervading, undefined, rumbling hum—was an assault on his ears so accustomed to sterile silence. He felt the beginnings of a coughing spasm and swallowed hard, his throat aching, his breath coming in burning gasps. The price of pride.

The major stopped as another shadow-man approached. "Where's my 'car, Leftant? Damn it, I 'commed from the sec-station."

"Just a moment, sir. I'll check."

"Hurry it up. I've got a ship to catch."

.The leftant disappeared somewhere. The air seemed damp and chill. The shivering set in again, and he felt himself swaying, but the major's firm grip on his arm kept him upright. And that irrational pride. He looked out beyond the roof. A city; lights stretching in all directions, motes of 'cars darting above against the dim stars of an unfamiliar night sky.

How did he knew it was unfamiliar? What sky would be familiar?

"Hold on." The major's voice, his hand guiding him forward, toward the open center of the roof. "Just hold on a little longer."

He turned to stare into the major's screened face. There was no hard edge in his tone; it was oddly solicitous. It didn't make sense. . . .

The sound of the approaching 'car startled him. He couldn't locate it at first. Above him. He looked up and saw it hurtling toward the roof on a crash trajectory.

"*Hey!* Damn it, what—" The major's chagrined exclamation was drowned in the rushing whine of the 'car, the explosion of jet brakes.

He was falling, the hard, white surface coming up at him; he couldn't breathe. Footsteps tumbled around him, he heard a cry of pain. It wasn't his. Shouts and meaningless thuds. The shriek of sirens. His vision was too blurred to tell him what the shifting patterns of light and dark meant.

Hands clutched at him, pulling him into the 'car. The door

snapped shut; he fell into the cushions as the 'car lurched into the air. Then the coughing began again and ended this time in that welcome oblivion.

4.

Predis Ussher frowned from behind his desk as the doorscreens clicked off. Ferra Regon knew better than to let anyone past that door without notifying him. Then he sighed with disgust. Rob Hendrick.

"For the God's sake, Rob, you might at least—"

"Predis, he's *here!*" The doorscreens clicked on behind him, and he glanced back as if it startled him, then crossed to the desk, his dark features pasty. "*Ransom* is here in Fina!"

"He's what?" Ussher came to his feet, his face as pale as Hendrick's. "That's impossible."

"I just heard from Bridger down in the pharmacy—"

"Wait! Just be quiet!" He reached for the comconsole, his hands shaking as he switched on the jambler circuit. "Damn it, Rob, will you ever learn to watch your mouth? Now, what about Ransom?"

Hendrick licked his lips nervously. "He's in the infirmary. Venturi pulled him out of the Cliff somehow. Holy God, he must've been here for hours, but we don't have anybody in the infirmary on the night shift *or* on the MT."

"You're sure it's Ransom?"

"Of course I'm sure! Bridger talked to one of the medtechs. I guess he's in bad shape, but he's here—and alive."

"Damn!" Ussher sank into his chair, his hands curled into fists. "Twenty-six days, Rob! He was on Level 6 for twenty-six days. We've never had anyone survive interrogation that long. Where's Venturi now?"

"He was in SI a few minutes ago. I checked with Mills."

"And Radek?"

"She's in the infirmary with Ransom."

"Playing nursemaid, I suppose. Who do we have on the day shift in the infirmary?"

"One medtech, but she got a special assignment in the prisoner ward this morning; direct order from Dr. Calder."

"Then they know she's with us. That order came from Radek." He consciously relaxed his hands, frowning speculatively. "You say Ransom's in bad shape? How bad?"

"Viral infection, malnutrition; the usual. But he's in no danger of dying. Not now, anyway."

"Mm. Still, after twenty-six days on Level 6, a relapse wouldn't be unreasonable."

"But we can't get anyone into the infirmary until—"

"Relax, Rob. Let me worry about that. I suppose the news of his return is common knowledge by now."

"Hell, it went out with the shift change."

Ussher nodded absently. "We aren't done yet. We've had nearly a month, and Riis is still—" He paused. "Unless Venturi's turned up something on him, too."

Hendrick shook his head. "I don't think so."

"Well, then, that still gives me a majority on the Council, and perhaps Ransom won't be..." He didn't finish the sentence, his lips drawn in a faint smile.

Hendrick waited a few seconds, then asked, "What about Barret? Ransom had him programmed like a robot."

Ussher laughed. "Don't worry about Jan. *Or* Ransom." He was still smiling as he reached for the intercom. "Ferra Regon?"

A brief pause, then Caren Regon's plain, squarish face appeared on the screen. "Yes, sirra?"

"Contact the councilors. Tell them I'm calling a meeting at—" He checked his watch; it was 12:10, "—at 13:00."

She hesitated. "Very well, but Commander Barret is out on a mission, you know; his scheduled arrival time is... let me check. 13:30. And Fer M'Kim is in Helen arranging for some electronic components for the new MTs."

"Oh. Yes, I'd forgotten." His fingers began an impatient tattoo on the desk. "The meeting will be at 14:00, then. Dr. Hendrick will contact M'Kim and Barret via SynchCom. The other councilors are all here in Fina, I believe. And make it clear that this is an important meeting."

"Yes, sirra. Oh—have you heard the good news? Commander Ransom is—"

"I know. Take care of this immediately, Ferra Regon, so the councilors can make their plans for the meeting."

She blinked at his sharp tone, then nodded. "Yes, Fer Ussher, I will."

He cut off the intercom and leaned back, the muscles of his jaw working.

"Good news! You'd think the Phoenix couldn't function without Ransom to punch the keys. Fools—all of them! Rob, you'd better get over to the SynchCom transmi——no, wait." He frowned, then, "No. First, I want you to talk to Val Severin. Radek's probably still in the infirmary, so Val won't have any trouble slipping out. When you get it set up, come back here. I'll have instructions for you."

Hendrick sighed and started for the door. "All right."

"And don't waste any time."

He cast a brief, resentful glance over his shoulder. "Don't worry, Predis."

"I'm *not* worried, Rob." Ussher smiled. "There's nothing to worry about."

5.

"For all intents and purposes, Predis is in control of the Phoenix."

Erica spoke calmly, sitting on the bed beside him, her hands folded in her lap, but the grief was there behind her cloud-gray eyes; grief for hope, for the Phoenix. Alex reached out and touched her hand, noting the deepened lines striating her forehead. Scars of anxiety. She had aged more in the last month than in all the years he'd known her.

Ben Venturi was standing on the other side of the bed, his narrowed eyes fixed on a passing medtech. The cubicle was walled with S/V screens set on one-way opaque, but every time someone passed he watched them suspiciously. On his forehead was another kind of scar—or, rather, a wound. It was covered with a bandage and had been received by *Major* Venturi in the line of duty while attempting to prevent the escape of a prisoner from the SSB DC in Leda. Commander Benin was putting his name in for a special service citation.

Alex closed his eyes, knowing neither Ben nor Erica would make any demands of him, nor be surprised at his silence. He had a great deal to assimilate in the short span of time since he'd awakened and Erica had spoken the personal code word that brought him out of the TAB, another and more profound awakening.

He had been a prisoner for twenty-six days, and Andreas was still in SSB hands, and Predis Ussher had stepped into the vacuum he had himself created, firing the members with dreams of glory that transformed shock and despair into hope. It wasn't surprising that they accepted him so readily. They didn't know how the vacuum came about; they were only grateful that someone was there to fill it, to give them purpose and direction, and they were especially grateful when the rumors began circulating that Ussher was the son of Elor Peladeen.

It was all inevitable and predictable; basic politics.

Alex frowned and took a slow, testing breath. The searing edge was gone, but he hadn't yet attempted to stand, and he was acutely aware of the weakness in every muscle. A Polluxian variant of a Terran virus, Erica said. Nothing serious, if properly treated; a few antivirals would have stopped it. But without treatment . . .

He consciously shut off the memories. They were all too clear, even the memory of not remembering.

Ussher hadn't quite succeeded in killing him, but that was scant consolation. He'd had nearly a month to establish himself as a leader in the eyes of the members, and Andreas Riis, the only person who could conceivably challenge his leadership without precipitating a disastrous schism, was in SSB hands somewhere. Castor, probably. Ben couldn't be sure.

And Alex lay in Fina's infirmary, every breath a relief because of the absence of pain. Full recovery was only a matter of a few days' rest. Yet he wondered if he'd be allowed that.

He looked at the clock on the bedside table: 12:40.

"Ben, when's that Council meeting?"

"14:00. It'd be sooner, but Jan's out on a mission and M'Kim's in Helen. Predis wants a solid majority on hand."

"No, just a full audience." Alex touched the controls and tipped the bed up further, absently noting the bandages on his wrists; burns from the shock cuffs. "I'm afraid Predis will consider his bargain with you no longer binding. Alive, I'm more of a threat to him than those microspeakers. He'll call your bluff on that now and hope he can discredit me thoroughly enough to negate them if you *do* activate them. And that's a last-ditch measure; we can't use it now. You know that, and

Predis knows it. What he doesn't know is that I intend to be at that Council meeting to defend myself. I think I can at least cast some doubt on his 'evidence' and convince him that it's in his best interest to confine our differences of opinion to the Council room—'for now.' And for us, that means until we get Andreas back to Fina."

Ben considered that and finally gave a caustic laugh.

"Well, if you can make it to the meeting, you won't have to say a damn word. Anybody who takes one look at you will know you haven't been on vacation. Who's going to believe this was the SSB's reward to you for giving them Andreas?" Then he sobered, his eyes going to slits. "But Predis has another option you haven't mentioned for dealing with you."

Alex nodded. "Yes. He can kill me." He pressed his hands to his eyes. His skin still had the hot, dry feel of fever. "He might be desperate enough to try it, too, although it would be a hell of a risk for him." Then he let his head fall back against the pillows, and the constriction in his chest was more than illness. "Ben, the important thing now is to find Andreas. We *must* find him. Everything hinges on that. You've had no luck through Central Control?"

Ben shook his head. "Every lead we've had ran into a blank wall. But as long as he's alive, he'll leave tracks of some kind. We just haven't found them yet."

"Was there a public announcement about his arrest?"

"Of course. You didn't expect them to sit on *that*? But there's been nothing on him since then, and that's the surest sign we have that he's still alive. They won't execute *him* without plenty of fanfare."

"No. Erica, can they break his conditioning?"

She shrugged uneasily. "It might be done through stimulus response patterns, but it would be a long, exacting process. They've never had the patience for it. But they can't use their usual methods on Andreas without running the risk of killing him, so they might be forced into patience."

"Still, it gives us some time. What's Predis doing about the LR-MT?"

Ben responded bitterly, "What *can* he do? I don't think he had that one figured; he probably thought all the equations were in the memfiles. Lyden and Bruce are still working on it, but even they admit there's not much hope without Andreas."

"I assume Rob Hendrick took Andreas's Council seat."

Ben slumped down on the end of the bed. "Of course. We warned Andreas about Rob, damn it."

Alex didn't comment on that. "Erica, have you any idea how Predis managed to bring Val Severin into his camp?"

"Yes." Her eyes had a stony sheen now. "We monitored a conversation between Predis and Rob. It's despicable, really. Val's so vulnerable in some areas."

"What do you mean?"

"Predis commissioned Rob to get Val—well, romantically involved. Rob thinks himself quite a blessing to women, and she's capable of very intense emotional responses. Rob's taken full advantage of that. She's totally converted; she'll believe anything he tells her. If she knew how he really feels about her..." Erica sighed wearily. "As I said, we monitored a conversation. Rob was telling Predis about the...fringe benefits of his 'assignment' in very graphic terms."

Alex was silent. Despicable, indeed. Val Severin didn't deserve that.

"Erica, have you a recording of that conversation? Perhaps Val should have her eyes opened."

"But she has to be ready for it, Alex, or we'll lose her entirely."

"Does she know you're aware of her divided loyalties?"

"No. Ben and I thought it best not to unmask her. For one thing, we know she's involved with the monitoring and can watch her. And I don't consider her a lost cause."

"I hope you're right—for her sake. Ben, how is Jan doing in FO?"

"Damned well. He's already recouped most of the losses from the Solar Fleet disaster, and FO's running full rev. Predis is concentrating on a military buildup."

"Of course." Again, inevitable and predictable, but that didn't dull the edge of anger and disgust. "Exactly what does he hope to accomplish with a military campaign, Ben?"

"Well, he never really comes out with any detailed plans, but the general idea seems to be common knowledge. It isn't so far off the Peladeen Alternative and General Plan ex seqs except on a few crucial points. He isn't planning on just forcing the Concord to the bargaining table with a limited, controlled military campaign, he plans to force the Concord out of the Centauri System, and the prime objective isn't anything so modest as the Directorate reestablishing the House of Peladeen with him as First Lord. He's talking about reestablishing the *Republic*, too."

Alex concentrated on slowing his breathing to ease the ache in his chest. His pulse rate was going up.

"I wonder what kind of 'republic' he really has in mind. And he expects to accomplish all that with a military campaign—and without the LR-MT?"

"He's ignoring that; he hasn't much choice. And without it, we don't have much to bargain with."

"So he's also ignoring the bargaining phase?"

"Oh, he talks about offering the Concord 'terms.' That's after we bring them to their knees with our overwhelming military might. Then it gets even more grandiose. Something about using the Centauri System as a power base for future expansion into the Solar System."

"Damn. He's *insane*."

"I know," Erica said quietly. "Literally."

"Erica, the members don't accept that nonsense, do they? I mean, except for his loyals?"

"If he handed it to them straight and in total, they wouldn't, but he feeds them one piece at a time, all in terms of possibilities, and he makes it sound not only feasible, but nearly inevitable. He has an extraordinary talent for that, and we can't prick his bubbles too openly because of the risk of schism." Her mouth tightened, white-lined. "Since you and Andreas have been gone, he's come into full flower as the resident Lord of the Phoenix; he plays the role to the hilt. It's ludicrous, really—Predis swaggering about with a cloak draped over his shoulders, surrounded by his awed sycophants. And we have sycophants in Fina, too."

Ben said grimly, "There's one more little item our resident Lord has in mind, Alex. He plans to 'rally the citizens of Centauri to our banner.' Open revolt."

"Including the Bonds?"

"Nothing specific has been said about the Bonds—yet."

Alex let his breath out slowly. This was also inevitable and predictable, but averting a Bond revolt was a basic tenet of the Phoenix from its inception. The members weren't ready to accept that. At least, as Ben said, not yet. Alex met Erica's haunted eyes and called up a smile.

"I'll have to step up my 'sociological research.'"

"Thank the God you've already laid a strong foundation for it."

"Thank Rich." He paused, then, "Do any of the members know Predis betrayed Andreas?"

Ben replied, "We've kept it quiet. As far as most of them know, you and Andreas were picked up on a fluke. We've lined up a few solid loyals, though, and told them the whole story."

"How much did you tell them about me?"

"Only that you offer another alternative for Phase I."

Alex nodded, and through the short silence, that followed, he was aware that they were both waiting. Erica finally put it into words.

"Alex, what are you going to do?"

He laughed at that. All he *wanted* to do was sleep.

"In long-range terms I don't know, but for now you'll have to dig deeper into your medical kit. I intend to be at that Council meeting, but I want to be sure I can stay on my feet."

"I can give you a drenaline injection, but I warn you, it'll slow your recovery. It will last about two hours. Four at the most."

"That isn't much time." He glanced around him, wondering at the sense of confinement induced by the shadowy walls. "Another thing, I'd prefer to convalesce elsewhere."

Ben nodded. "You're moving into the guest room in HS 1 as soon as possible—by MT. No use advertising your change of quarters. Oh—you'll need an MT fix."

"I might need some clothes, too."

Erica laughed. "I'll take care of that, Ben, and the fix for him."

"Good. Well, I'd better get it set up now." Ben paused as if he were reluctant to leave. "Alex, will you be—"

"I'll be safe here for a while, at least. You said Predis has no loyals on this shift."

"Only one we know about, and she's busy elsewhere. Erica has you on a no-visitors stat, but we can't seal off the infirmary." Ben's right arm came down with a quick snap that brought a small X^1 into his palm from the spring sheath on his wrist. "Here—keep this handy."

Alex took it and put on the bedside table, thinking how indicative it was that Ben was carrying a gun in Fina. He wondered if Erica was armed, too.

"There's a pocketcom and a jambler in the drawer under the table," Ben continued. "The 'com's set for an emergency frequency; hit the switch and I'm on."

Alex nodded. "Thanks. By the way, any news from the outside world I should know about?"

The question produced a tense silence that brought Alex's attention into immediate focus on Ben. He was the source of the silence. Erica was only vaguely curious as she looked up, waiting for his answer.

Ben managed a quick shrug. "Nothing important. I'll send down some tape capsules when you get settled in HS 1."

It was an evasion, but Alex let it stand. "All right, Ben."

Ben turned to leave, then stopped and said a little too casually, "Erica, why don't you walk with me to the hall."

Alex studied him a moment, then nodded to Erica. "Go ahead. I need a few minutes to sort things out."

She rose and followed Ben through the screens and along the aisle between the cubicles. As they turned out of sight, Alex closed his eyes, considering Ben's constrained attitude. It had nothing to do with Predis Ussher.

News from the outside world.

When Erica returned a few minutes later, Alex was sitting on the edge of the bed, frowning down at his legs and arms, at the bones too close under the skin, the laxness of the muscles. It would be a long time before he was fully recovered from the last twenty-six days.

Erica stepped through the screens, then paused. "You're getting rather ambitious, aren't you?" She came over to him and pressed her hand to his forehead. "You shouldn't even have to be awake now, much less—"

"Erica, I've had ten hours of sleep and medication. Now, please, sit down and tell me why Ben was holding back on me."

She hesitated, then with a sigh sank down on the bed. "His concern was partly medical. He thought I should decide whether you're up to dealing with it now. I'm not sure you are, but I'd rather take the risk of telling you myself than have you find out from a newscast. Alex, it's the . . . Selasis-Eliseer match."

No doubt she'd chosen the words carefully. The Selasis-Eliseer match. That put it in objective, political-economic terms. Equations. Calculations.

At first he didn't understand the dizziness, the palpable pain that struck so abruptly, choking off his breath.

Adrien . . .

The illness. It must be the illness.

There was no pain for him in that name, not even when it was linked with Selasis. He could never make Erica understand that. There was no pain. No pain . . .

Yet something doubled him in breathless agony.

He shut his eyes against it and heard what seemed a cry of anguish. No. Laughter; sardonic laughter, and a rattling. The black angel, the beast he had wrestled into its steel-barred cage in that equivocal other time that was suddenly now. And now he understood.

He understood that it wasn't Erica who had been deluded all these years. It was he who deluded himself in thinking there was no pain. It had only been caged, locked in with the black angel, the immortal beast waiting within him.

Adrien, what have I done to you?

Eyes still closed, hands gripping the edge of the bed, he searched desperately for a touchstone, a focus for his own identity.

Alex Ransom. The Ransom Alternative. Methodically, he considered every aspect of it, past, present, and future, and its every implication and potential. Equations. Calculations.

I came to finish my brother's work.

Finally, he could even remind himself that there were more imminent threats to the Ransom Alternative now than the Selasis-Eliseer match.

Still, he had made a decision that had no bearing on the Ransom Alternative, or Alex Ransom, or even Rich.

I owe her something—at least she must know the truth.

He wouldn't verbalize the decision, not even to Erica, who was capable of understanding it. But it was made.

It was rooted in his pain-born understanding of two truths. First, he understood now that the Lord Alexand wasn't a tool of Alex Ransom existing in frozen suspension on some mental life-support system, waiting to be called back to life by the command of equated necessity. Alex Ransom was only a mask to be tossed aside, and the Lord Alexand wore that mask, and the Lord Alexand had never given up that hope that had no bearing on anyone's calculations but his own: the hope that he might one day fulfill the life vow he had made to Adrien Eliseer.

The second truth was Adrien herself. A Selaneen with bones of steel. How would she respond to the factor of the Selasis-Eliseer match? That was something Alex Ransom had never considered, but the Lord Alexand could not ignore. The Lord Alexand knew Adrien Eliseer would not accept marriage to Karlis Selasis submissively, and in that equation was the cipher of death.

"It's past the rumor stage, then?" Alex didn't try to meet Erica's eyes yet, but his voice was under control, his tone level.

"Yes. Ben had a report from Lile Perralt a few hours ago." Her tone was as contained as his, her face stringently expressionless. "Lord Loren and Lady Adrien are in Leda now. Perralt says she'll return to Helen on her private planethopper this afternoon, but her father has chartered a ship for Concordia. Perralt's sure he has the Contracts of Marriage with him. The Lady Adrien has already signed them."

He was silent for a moment; the control was slipping.

Then he frowned. "You said she—Lady Adrien and Lord Loren are in Leda now. Why?"

Erica replied, finally, "Lord Loren is meeting with Lazar Hamid. Business, for public consumption, but no doubt it has to do with the marriage. It will give Eliseer something of an advantage over Hamid. Business is also the reason he's giving for his trip to Concordia. The marriage negotiations have been kept entirely secret."

Alex nodded absently. There was still more.

"Why did Lady Adrien accompany him to Leda?"

"Ostensibly to see Aron Luxe, who was a professor of hers. She visits him quite often. But the real reason was an appointment at the . . . University Medschool Hospital. The reporters have been laying siege to the hospitals in Helen for weeks. Rumors have been flying about the marriage, of course, and they all want to be first with—with confirming evidence."

He frowned, feeling as if he'd missed something. Then with comprehension came an acid surge of anger.

"Of course! Lord Orin wants medical verification of the Lady's *virginity*. Holy God, even DeKoven Woolf didn't subject her to that humiliation!"

"I know, Alex, but it's an old custom in Elite marriages. Many of the Houses still—"

"I'm well aware of the customs of Elite marriages!" The words came out cold and slashing, a voice he didn't recognize as his own. He closed his eyes, reaching blindly for Erica's hand, holding on until he had himself under control again.

"Erica, forgive me."

"There's nothing to forgive," she said softly.

He pulled in a long breath, consciously relaxing his tense muscles. "Lord Loren is leaving for Concordia this afternoon? When will he return?"

"Perralt wasn't sure, but probably Friday. Lady Galia is planning a banquet that evening. It's been assumed that the announcement will be made then."

Friday. Four days.

"Erica, there's no hope of stopping this marriage now?"

"You know the odds are against it at this late date."

He nodded, wondering why he'd bothered to ask.

"What about Adrien? Has she given Perralt any hint of what she might do?"

"Do? What do you mean? She wouldn't try to avoid this marriage; she knows she can't without jeopardizing the House."

He laughed bitterly. "And has she no other options open to her? Did we enter Adrien Eliseer into our calculations? Did we assign a factor value to her loathing for the Selasids and all they stand for? Did we equate the potentials of her courage and intelligence against—" He stopped; it was getting out of control again.

"Alex, what is it you think she might do?"

"I don't know." It was true, but he doubted that was what silenced her. He looked at the clock. "Erica, perhaps you should get my clothes and the MT fix now."

She didn't respond for some time, studying him, a mute question in her eyes. Then she rose, glancing at Ben's gun on the table.

"All right, Alex. By the way, the medallion is in the safety box in my office. Ben found it in your apartment after you were arrested."

"Thank you. Erica . . . what about Amelia?"

Her breath caught on a brief sigh. "She died. The same day you and Andreas were arrested." She broke the short, aching silence that followed with, "I'll bring your clothes and a fix, then you can rest until the MT's clear."

"And the drenaline injection?"

"Not now. I'll give it to you later. I told you, it'll only last a few hours, and I won't give you another; not in your state of health. I might be doing Predis a favor." Then she touched his hand and smiled. "Alex, thank the God you're safe. We need you."

He could find no adequate answer to that.

6.

He slumped down on the bed, the slacsuit trousers in his hands, inwardly rebelling at the weakness that forced him to rest after the grand achievement of putting on his underclothing and taking a few steps to test his legs. Then he looked up, his eyes drawn by a movement outside the cubicle.

Valentin Severin.

She was questioning a medtech, a short exchange ending with the medtech's nod, a finger pointing toward Alex's cubicle. Then Val's smile, a few words of thanks.

His surprise at seeing her was brief; he could guess her purpose. Ussher had no loyals in the infirmary on this shift, and he wanted a firsthand report on Alex's condition.

He watched her curiously as she stopped at the signal console outside. She was carrying something in one hand, but he couldn't identify it. And she was uneasy, despite the confident expression she wore. She touched a button, and a chime sounded from the bedside console, but Alex didn't respond to it. Instead, he folded his slacsuit and stuffed it under the pillows, swept the gun and 'com into the drawer, then lay back in the bed and pulled the covers up. He didn't intend to let Ussher know he was well enough to be on his feet yet.

The chime sounded again. Val glanced around the ward, one hand moving to her hair to arrange what needed no arrangement. He wondered what she'd do if he didn't respond at all. Finally, he reached for the intercom.

"Come in, Val."

She jumped at the sound, glancing at the console, then put

on a smile and stepped through the screens.

"I hope I didn't . . . wake you . . ." The smile faded.

He hadn't had access to a mirror, but no doubt his appearance *was* a shock.

"No, Val, I was just resting."

She recovered her smile and approached the bed.

"I—I know I shouldn't bother you, but I was so relieved to find out you're back safe and . . . sound." She was nervously toying with the object—no, objects—she was carrying: three pill bottles. Her eyes shifted from his bandaged wrists to the burns visible on his chest and arms. "I guess they—they gave you a hard time."

He smiled faintly. "I wouldn't care to enjoy their hospitality again, but fortunately it's all over now."

"Yes." She looked down at her hands and seemed to become aware of the pill bottles for the first time. She put them on the bedside table. "These are for you. Dr. Radek asked me to bring them over from the pharmacy. She said you're going to need all the help medical science can offer." It was meant to be humorous, and Alex laughed, but Val couldn't quite manage it.

She asked hesitantly, "Are you . . . really all right?"

He glanced at her, then picked up one of the bottles, noting that Erica was listed as the prescribing physician.

"I can't say I'm feeling too well, but I understand I'll be up and about within a week." *Acetyhistine: one every hour as needed.* "It's nothing serious, actually. The SSB is just a little lax about medical care for some of their guests." He leavened that with a laugh, intent on her reaction, even as he picked up the second bottle. *Trimycin: one every four hours.* And the third—

It nearly slipped from his hand.

Doricaine: one at night for sleep.

"Alex? Are you—Alex?"

He masked his shock with coughing, and it wasn't entirely a subterfuge. The physical response to what he read on that bottle choked off his breath. Ussher obviously had a loyal in the pharmacy. Erica would never prescribe a sedative for him; she knew his aversion to them and knew he would never take one of his own volition. But Predis Ussher wouldn't know that.

And Val Severin—

He couldn't believe Val knew the real purpose of these pills. "Alex? Should I call a medtech?"

It was ironic, the concern in her eyes.

"No, I'm all right," he said, mustering a smile. He glanced at the bottles. "Erica may be right about my need for aid from medical science. When am I to start on these?"

Val frowned distractedly, then, "She—she said I was to see that you started on the antiviral immediately. You can take the acetyhistine whenever you need it." She checked the labels, then uncapped the one marked trimycin.

He watched her as she filled a cup with water from the dispenser on the table. Her hands were trembling. He picked up the third bottle.

"Doricaine. That's rather a strong sedative, isn't it?"

She didn't look at him. "I don't know. I mean, I . . . I don't know much about sedatives, really."

That was a lie and an error, but Val Severin was out of her depth. She proffered the cup and a tablet. "Here, you'd better get this down."

He didn't move; he only looked up at her with a direct gaze and asked, "Val, are you sure you want me to take that?"

She went pale. "What?"

He put the doricaine bottle down beside the others.

"Take a fresh cup and empty half the pills from each of these bottles into it." His tone was still quiet but carried an undertone of command, and she responded automatically, putting down the water, reaching for another cup. Then she stopped and stared at him.

"Put the—Alex, I don't understand."

"I won't argue that now. Half the pills from each bottle."

She complied without further protest, her hands shaking, her breathing shallow and fast. When she finished, he said, "Take those pills to ChemAnalysis and have them run through the analyzer. When you have a read-out, bring it to me."

She turned even paler. "Why do you want them analyzed?"

"Is there any reason you *don't* want them analyzed?"

"No—no, of course not. I . . . I just don't understand why you're suspicious of them. Dr. Radek prescribed them."

"Did she? Val, I want your word that you'll say nothing to anyone about this until you've brought me the read-out."

A grim spark of defiance flashed in her eyes. "Why not?"

"Val, you think you know what an analysis will reveal about

those pills, but you're wrong. At least, I hope to the God you don't know the truth. If I've judge you well, I doubt you'll *want* to discuss the read-out with anyonē else."

She swallowed hard. "I don't know what you're talking about."

His tone was sharper. "Val, give me your word."

She stared down at the cupful of pills as if it held an answer, then finally her chin came up. "You have my word."

"Thank you."

She didn't respond or even look at him again. She moved stiffly, mechanically, away, through the screens and down the aisle, clutching the cup.

Alex reached into the drawer for the pocketcom, relieved when his call got an immediate answer.

"Ben, are you clear?"

"Yes, what's—"

"Do you have Val Severin under surveillance?"

"Yes, and I just heard about her foray to the infirm——"

"She should be on her way to ChemAnal now. I want to know if she speaks to anyone or makes any detours on the way, and if she returns to the infirmary, have your agent tell her I'll talk to her in HS 1. That's if the trans is set up."

"It's set up. I was about to 'com you. And I'll get your message through to her without exposing my agent, if you don't mind. Hold on a minute."

The 'com clicked off. Alex put it on the table, took his slacsuit out from under the pillows, and pulled himself to his feet, pausing until the dizziness passed. It was hard to remember to move slowly.

"Alex—"

He grabbed the 'com. "Yes, Ben."

"Val's under watch. Now, what the hell's going on?"

"I'll explain when I get to HS 1."

Alex finished dressing, his trembling hands fumbling at the fasteners. He put the 'com and Ben's gun in one pocket, then paused before putting the pill bottles in another.

Doricaine. That was carelessness. But setting up loyal followers as scapegoats was more than carelessness, even more than cowardice. It was an act of a man who could only see people as tools.

7.

"Cyanase."

The word came hard. If he had any doubts about Val Severin, they were stilled by her ravaged face and the choking effort of pronouncing that word. She hadn't known what she was carrying in those pills.

Alex sat in one of the chairs in HS 1's work room. He remained seated simply because it was necessary to hoard his strength, but the flash of heat under his skin wasn't a product of illness. Rage. Ussher had used Val, and used her badly.

"Val, please—sit down."

She was so white he was afraid she might faint, but she shook her head.

"No, I . . ." She couldn't explain her refusal, and he let it pass. Perhaps she found it difficult to sit down with someone she'd come so close to poisoning.

Cyanase. An expert choice; extremely fast-acting, its initial symptom a paralysis that made it impossible for the victim to call for help. And Ussher would have let Val carry that on her conscience.

"You needn't explain yourself to me," he said. "I'm sure you didn't know the actual content of those pills. You were probably told it was a sedative to preclude my attendance at the Council meeting." Her lips parted, but no sound emerged. After a pause, he added, "Val, I want you to remember one thing: Erica has known you were working for Ussher since you planted the first monitor, but she's never lost faith in you. Talk to her, Val. Please."

She turned away, one hand pressed to her mouth.

"*No*. I can't . . . talk to her. I can't—oh, God, I don't believe it. It *can't* be true!"

He rose, watching her. She swayed against the back of a chair, her hair falling forward over her downcast face. "For the God's sake *why?* And why—oh, Rob . . ."

"I can't answer for Dr. Hendrick, but I can explain Ussher's motives. I'm a threat to him, Val. My identity has inherent in it another alternative for Phase I, and he knows who I am."

He took a few steps toward her, reaching up to unfasten the medallion. "This was given to me by my brother. He preceded me into the Phoenix; led me to it. You knew him, Val. He died in Concordia the day before I arrived in Fina."

She frowned at the medallion as if she found it difficult to focus on it.

"A . . . lamb?"

"My brother's called a saint now."

Her eyes flashed up to his, wide with bewilderment. "*Rich?*"

Alex turned the medallion, leaving the wolf uppermost, drawing her eye back to it with the movement.

"His name wasn't Lamb any more than mine is Ransom."

She stared at the medallion, still bewildered. She didn't understand yet, but she would. He reached into his pocket with his other hand and took out a tape spool.

"Val, this is a product of the war of monitors. I haven't heard it, nor has anyone except Ben and Erica. There are no other copies of it. It's yours to dispose of as you see fit." She took the tape, gazing blankly at it as he added, "Listen to it privately. It may seem cruel to give it to you, but you've been cruelly used, and if you're to deal with that, you must understand it fully."

"Understand? How can I understand *any* of this?"

The only answer he could offer to that, and to the anguish behind it, was, "Give yourself some time; you'll understand. Now, you'd better go. And, Val, please be careful what you say and do. You're a witness to an attempted murder; that puts you in a very dangerous position."

She stared at him, unimpressed by her vulnerability. He doubted she'd be any more impressed if she fully comprehended it.

"What are you going to do, Alex? I mean, about . . . me."

"I've done all I can, Val. What do you expect me to do? Call you before a Society tribunal? The tool isn't responsible for the man who wields it."

She shivered uncontrollably and looked away.

"Alex, I didn't know. The pills—I didn't *know*."

"I believe you."

She looked at him, then turned abruptly and stumbled to the doorway. She didn't look back or speak, but Alex wasn't surprised at her sudden leavetaking, or at her silence.

He went to Erica's door, pausing before he touched the

control. His hands were shaking. He stood for a moment with his eyes closed, his arm braced against the wall. He was cold, but that would pass, and the sickness he harbored within his body would vanish with a few days' rest. But the sickness the Phoenix harbored might be past curing.

And how long would it take Valentin Severin to recover, not from a sickness, but from a wound that cut to her soul?

"What was it, Alex?"

Ben was standing near Erica's desk, hands on his hips, eyes narrowed to slits.

Alex eased himself into a chair by the desk where Erica was opening her medical case and frowning absently over its contents. She said nothing, but she was waiting as tensely as Ben for his answer.

"Cyanase."

"Holy God!" Ben's hands knotted into fists.

Erica was still frowning as she looked around at Alex.

"Yes, it *would* be cyanase. Alex, what about Val?"

"To hell with Val!" Ben exploded. "Alex, this makes twice he's tried to kill you. Don't you—"

"I know, Ben." He let his head fall back into the cushions. "But Predis is desperate; he didn't think this out very well, and it may prove a costly error for him. He misjudged his tool. I want you to keep Val under close surveillance from now on. And I mean *protective* surveillance. She didn't know what was in those pills. She thought it was only a sedative."

Ben nodded, lips compressed. "I'll 'com Willie."

Erica glanced at him as he started the call, then looked down at Alex, her scrutiny partly clinical.

"I'm sorry you had to be the one to disillusion her."

"Save your sympathy for Val. I asked her to talk to you."

"I hope she will. Did you give her the tape?"

He nodded slowly. "Yes."

"It's a painful cure, but better than having a murder on her conscience. And Val *does* have a conscience." She looked at Ben, whose soft-toned conversation with Haral Wills was still in progress, then took a pressyringe from her case, leaned over Alex, and pushed up his sleeve. "I'll give you the drenaline injection now, then you'll have an hour to rest before the meeting."

"I doubt I'll have much time to rest. We have some plans to make."

She finished the injection, then swabbed his arm with antiseptic and tossed the pressyringe into the syntegrator. "This will keep you going for a few hours. After that, you'd better be close to a bed."

Ben snapped his 'com shut and put it in his pants pocket. "It's set up. We're short-handed—at least, with anybody we can trust—but we'll look after her." He paused, then said soberly, "Alex, you know Predis won't give up with two tries, and you're an open target here in Fina."

"I know. It means a change in plans. I haven't time to waste looking over my shoulder all the time. I'll have to remove the target from the field. The Cormoroi Tactic; expedient retreat into SynchShift with subsequent reemergence and attack at the flanks. For the maneuver to be successful, Cormoroi advised leaving a minimum of half your forces on the field as decoys. So I'll leave you and Erica to engage the enemy while I make my expedient retreat." He frowned irritably. "And it galls me, this retreat, expedient or not, but that's only pride talking. I'll find it necessary to swallow a lot of pride for Andreas."

Ben asked, "Exactly what do you intend to do while you're chewing on your pride?"

Alex gave a short laugh. "Find Andreas. No, that's your job. I intend to free him once you've found him." He paused, taking a careful breath. His pulse rate was up, but the overwhelming weakness was leaving him. "Ben, we can't set up a rescue operation out of Fina. We can't risk Predis learning where Andreas is once you've found him. He'll kill him if he can get to him first."

Ben folded his arms across his chest, the flexing of his jaw muscles clearly visible. "So your idea is to set up an independent base of operations somewhere?"

"Yes."

Erica stared at him. "But where, Alex? How?"

He shrugged. "I don't know how at this point, but the where has to be Castor. Ben said the best evidence points to Castor, so we'll work on the assumption that Andreas is still somewhere on the planet. Any escape operation will undoubtedly involve MT transing, so the closer we can get to him the better; that will minimize our power needs. Besides, there are loyals in the Helen chapter we can depend on. Harv Vandyne, for instance; SI chief for the chapter. And Jael." He smiled to himself. "He told me once he was on stand-by if it came to a face-off with the tooth-gimmer. And Dr. Perralt and Kahn Telman in the House of Eliseer, both charter members and friends of Andreas. I'll have to play it as it comes, Erica, but I'll start with the loyals in Helen."

She went around the desk to her chair, seeming on the verge of protest, but after a moment she nodded.

"Well, at least it will put you out of Predis's reach. It might keep you alive."

"True. We must conserve our forces; that's one of the purposes of the Cormoroi Tactic." He smiled faintly at her frown of annoyance. "It has the further advantage of demoralizing the enemy. He won't know where I am, what I'm doing, or when I might reemerge and strike. It should give him something to think about, anyway." He folded his hands, noting that there was no hint of trembling now. "I won't be going to the Council meeting, by the way, but it'll keep Predis occupied while I make my retreat."

Erica asked, "You're *not* going to the meeting?"

"You'll have to defend me there. This will be my last chance to make my presence known in Fina for some time. I can't waste it on the Council. I need a larger audience."

"For what?"

"A reminder, I suppose; particularly a reminder of Andreas. At any rate, it shouldn't seem unreasonable for a commander embarking on a special mission to bid farewell to his troops."

Ben raised an eyebrow. "You're going to call a general assembly in FO?"

"Yes. As soon as Jan returns from his mission, which will be about half an hour before the Council meeting. I'd like to be ready to leave Fina as soon as I dismiss the assembly. Can you set something up with Vandyne in Helen by then?"

"Yes. I'll go up to my office and take care of it now."

"What's the best way for me to get there?"

Ben looked at him levelly and laughed.

"The *best* way? Alex, there's only *one* way. FO is out; Predis has too many friends there. And we can't trans you, not until we're sure of the MT techs on the Helen controls. We might end up transing you into a laser beam. That leaves the good old Selasid InterPlan System. You'll have to take the regular passenger shuttle, and that's risky enough. I only hope we get you safe in Helen before Predis can give the SSB another helpful hint."

"Alex," Erica put in, "you also have the problem of your health to consider. I told you that injection will only last a few hours, and—"

"All right, Erica. Ben, tell Vandyne I may need a bed, damn it."

Ben started for the door. "I'll tell him. And I'll put together your escape kit: tickets, ident, that sort of thing."

"Not *escape*," Alex said with an oblique smile. "Expedient retreat."

"Whatever you call it, it's a damn good idea to get you out of Fina."

"It's a better idea," he replied grimly, "to get Andreas *back* to Fina."

8.

Erica had insisted on accompanying Alex to FO on the pretext that she was still worried about his reactions to the drenaline. He probably didn't swallow that, but he didn't object. She stood in the corner of the comcenter where the windowall met the stone, watching the berthing processes in the hangar. Jan Barret would be arriving in the *Demond* in a few minutes, the last of the raiding fleet. The fleet was nearly half an hour past its scheduled lock arrival time, but it had been a successful mission, apparently. Three new Confleet Falcons were berthed in the hangar, and only two of Barret's ships had been damaged. Six crewmembers were injured, but none seriously.

She turned her attention to the comcenter now, and to Alex Ransom. Her real reason for being here was curiosity; she wanted to see how the members responded to him. Still, the medical concern was real enough. Even from a distance, the fevered flush against his pale skin was obvious, but he was moving well, and there had been no coughing.

She watched him now in an intent exchange with Major Eton of TacComm, thinking of the contrast between Alex's approach to leadership and Predis Ussher's. Alex didn't underestimate the importance of emotional responses, but he wasted no effort on stirring verbiage or displays of camaraderie, and certainly not on studied affectations of Lordship. It would be interesting, she thought, if Alex allowed himself to play the Lord. He'd make Ussher look like the posturing pretender he was, because for Alex it wouldn't be a role; it would be a reversion to what he was.

Her frown deepened at the thought of reversion. She was remembering his reaction to Adrien Eliseer's marriage. Something had happened; the defenses had broken. And she was remembering in the same context that when he had first regained consciousness and she gave him the code word that brought him out of the TAB—his was, almost inevitably, "lamb"—her first question had been, "What is your name?" He had answered dazedly, "Alexand . . ." Then, after a moment, he amended himself, "Ransom. My name is Alex Ransom."

She knew he had been right the first time.

Now she studied him as he joined two GroundComm officers at the holojector. He'd been in the comcenter less than half an hour, but it was all business as usual. When he first arrived, there had been a flurry of eager greetings, and his responses had been warm, if a little reserved, but the reserve was expected of him and made the warmth more telling than all Ussher's facile ebullience. Nor did he play on the emotional impact of his appearance as Ussher would, instead passing off expressions of concern with an easy smile that said he appreciated them, but didn't consider his physical state important.

He had them all in the palm of his hand now. Ussher's weeks-long rumor campaign of innuendo and character assassination was totally negated. If the outcome of the power struggle within the Phoenix depended on an open confrontation between Alex and Ussher, she wouldn't be at all concerned. But it would never come to that. All Alex could do now was renew their faith in him; he couldn't attack their faith in Ussher. Schism. The specter that haunted all their decisions.

Demond was coming through the lock tunnel. Alex walked over to the windowall, accompanied by a cluster of techs and officers. Outside, crewmembers were gathering around the deck, talking excitedly among themselves. The news of Alex's return went out the moment he set foot in the hangars. When

Demond's crew began to emerge, he turned to Captain Lanc on the comconsole.

"Captain, call a general assembly in Hangar 1, please."

"Yes, sir." There was a lively snap in that.

Alex went out onto the deck, responding to the enthusiastic greetings of the crewmembers outside, while the ampspeakers boomed with Lanc's assembly call. When Jan Barret left the *Demond* and strode toward the deck, his broad smile making his face seem even more boyish than usual, Erica took advantage of the distraction to slip out to the deck, still staying in the background.

"Alex!" Barret was nearly running by the time he reached the deck. "You're back! Thank the God, you're back!"

Alex was less reserved with Barret. He laughed, his hand going out to meet Barret's in a warm handshake.

"Jan, it's good to see you."

"Holy God, it's good to see *you*." Then his smile faltered. "Are you—are you all right?"

"I will be with a little rest."

Jan's exhilaration returned. He looked out into the hangar, where every available space around the ships and machines was filling with members drawn by curiosity as much as by Lanc's amplified command.

"Damn, what a day! Three Falcons picked off like they were meant for us, and now to have you back. Hey, there's Commander Garris!"

Erica smiled to herself. No mere handshakes for Emeric; he locked Alex in a hearty embrace, his words of jubilant welcome lost in the mounting babble of voices as the hangar filled and more officers gathered on the deck.

"This calls for a celebration," Barret was saying, "and it looks like everybody's here."

Almost literally everybody, Erica thought, noting a high ratio of faces that didn't actually belong in FO; news traveled fast in Fina.

Alex said, "We *should* be celebrating your obvious success in the last month." He looked at the rows of berthed ships, then smiled. "My faith wasn't misplaced, was it?"

Barret flushed. "I—I hope not."

"You know it wasn't. But any celebration will have to be postponed. You have a Council meeting in a few minutes, and I have . . . other plans."

"Damn, I forgot about that meeting." Barret frowned at his watch. "I'll 'com Predis and tell him—" Then he looked up at Alex. "But you'll be going instead of me."

"No, Jan. You're still First Commander." Before Barret could question him, he turned to Captain Lanc, who had left his post at the comconsole to a subordinate. "Captain, I need a mike, and put me on the ampsystem, please."

Lanc hurried back into the comcenter, and Erica studied Alex closely. The acoustics in the cavern-hangar were excellent; normally, he wouldn't need a mike, but he wasn't sure of his voice. Still, it was steady enough, even if there was a hint of huskiness.

Lanc brought a handmike. "You're on the speakers, sir."

"Thank you." Alex went to the railing, surveying the crowded hangar, then spoke into the mike. "May I have your attention—" He was forced to stop as a cheer reverberated in the vault. At that he raised a hand and quieted them, saying, "I'm glad to be back in Fina, and that can only be an understatement. I've heard the word 'miracle' several times in the last half hour, and I'd be the first to agree that my safe return *is* a miracle. But it was one achieved through the faith, perseverance, and courage of members of the Phoenix. Had everyone given up hope for me, I doubt I'd be alive now, and to say I'm grateful is another understatement. There's only one way I can adequately express my gratitude to those who didn't give up hope for me, and that is not to give up hope for another of us who is still imprisoned."

There was a stirring. Erica studied the faces, watched the covert glances passing from one to another. They knew whom he meant, and their expressions reflected a kindling hope, but underlying it a hint of guilt.

"I was freed from the Cliff," Alex went on, "when by all odds I should already have been dead. From some of the remarks made to me here, I had the impression it was assumed in some quarters that I *was* already dead. Obviously, that isn't the case." A ripple of self-conscious laughter, but Alex's intent expression quickly renewed the silence.

"Andreas Riis isn't dead, either," he said flatly. "The man you justly revere as the founder of the Society and your leader waits as I did in the hands of the SSB. The Phoenix didn't surrender me for lack of faith or hope, and I won't surrender Andreas Riis. He's been my friend, and if I call myself his friend, I can't forsake him. But more than his life is at stake. The day before our arrest, Andreas told me he had made a breakthrough on the long-range matter transmitter, and none of you need to be reminded how vital that is to Phase I and the future of the Phoenix."

This was the first open reference to the LR-MT, and it elicited a murmur of surprised speculation.

"In more than one sense, we can be grateful for the MT. The SSB knows Andreas has the equations for it, and he's alive now because they hope to break his conditioning and force him to reveal them. We can also, in a sense, be grateful that he isn't a young man. The psychocontrollers can't use their usual methods of interrogation on him; they want to keep him alive. This gives us time; time to find and free him. But I'm sure you're aware that the SSB has taken extraordinary precautions to prevent his escape, and our task will be difficult at best. It may be impossible. I don't know. But I won't believe that until I have irrefutable evidence of his death."

A long pause while he surveyed the faces turned toward him, unanimously intent.

"The primary concern of the Phoenix at this time must be finding and freeing Andreas Riis, and, in light of this, I've decided to take a temporary leave of absence from FO in order to devote all my time and energies to this mission. It will mean leaving Fina, but I know the fleets will be in good hands. Jan Barret will continue in his capacity as First Commander until I return. I don't know when that will be. I can only tell you this: When I return, it will be with Andreas Riis."

A few voices sounded the beginnings of a cheer of affirmation, but Alex again quieted them with an upraised hand.

"I have something more to say, something I want you to consider carefully. I ask you to remember who you are." That seemed to intensify the silence, as if no one were even breathing. "You are the Society of the Phoenix. You are the hope for the future of civilization. Remember that. And remember the half century of effort and sacrifice that lies behind you, and the *generations* of effort and sacrifice that lie ahead. And remember that the Phoenix has but one enemy: anarchy. The Phoenix was born out of disaster, a symbol of light and hope; hope for the future, light to stave off the third dark age that threatens us. That's our purpose, our goal—to avert the coming dark age. Remember that."

No one presumed to voice even approval. Erica listened to the silence, feeling out the awed, sober quality of it. Ussher would have let them cheer, but something in Alex's attitude denied any inclination to an emotional outburst. And they would remember these words. For a while, at least. Perhaps it would be long enough.

A stir at the hangar doors broke the silence, providing a focus for all eyes. And Erica almost laughed.

Predis Ussher. She'd been expecting him.

He pushed his way toward the deck, his features flushed with suspicious anger. But that was exchanged for a sick pallor when he recognized Alex, and he was too distracted to take full cognizance of the crowd.

He shouldn't have spoken a word; anything he said at this time and in his emotional state could only seem anticlimactic and petulant, but he was beyond realizing that. He mounted the steps to the deck, then stopped short.

"What is this?" In the silence, his voice echoed.

Barret answered, "A general assembly, Predis. Commander Ran——"

"Assembly?" Then he seemed to hear the echo of his own voice and glanced uneasily at the members, who watched in patent bewilderment. He lowered his voice, but not enough. "Jan, I scheduled a Council meeting for 14:00. It's 14:10, and the other councilors are waiting."

Erica moved then, only the turning of her head and a faint smile; a reminder that *all* the councilors weren't waiting. That unnerved him further, but Barret saved him from making the error of saying anything to her.

"Predis, I'm sorry about the meeting, but this assembly was too important to interrupt."

Alex still didn't acknowledge Ussher; his next words, spoken into the mike, were addressed to the members.

"Assembly dismissed. You may return to your duties now. Thank you." As the crowd began dispersing, he turned to Ussher. "My apologies to the councilors, Predis. I'll offer no further delay to your deliberations." He paused for a few parting words with Barret and Garris, then glanced at Erica, an ironic light reflected fleetingly in his eyes.

She stayed a pace behind him, anticipating with some relish the encounter that must occur when Alex reached the steps where Ussher stood. A small incident few people would consciously remember, and yet it would be telling, because Ussher would be the one to give way.

Alex walked toward the steps at a steady pace, and Ussher found himself in the awkward position of seeming to block his exit. Alex didn't pause, and finally Ussher stepped back, so intent on him that his foot slipped off the top stair. He lurched against the railing, clutching at it to avoid falling, while Alex passed him without even recognizing his embarrassment.

But Erica saw the seething rage behind the embarrassment. He'd tried twice to kill Alex Ransom, she thought, feeling a chill as she passed Ussher. And he'd failed twice.

But he wouldn't give up.

9.

The small suitcase was slightly worn at the seams. Alex smiled at that. Ben had a fine eye for detail.

"Wigs, hair color, plasimask . . ." Ben had the suitcase open on the bed, the verbal inventory continuing as he filled it.

Alex went to the mirror by the closet door and waved on the light. They were in Ben's Leda apartment, and the windowalls were on opaque to assure their privacy. He shrugged into the borasil vest and pressed the fasteners closed, then pulled on a knit shirt. Next the cloak: dark gray, conservative, and typically Fesh.

The pills. His hand went to his pocket, encountering the hard cylinder. He was still too weak, and a deep breath would start the coughing. Erica had supplied him with antivirals, and he had added a few drenaline tablets from his own supply.

Ben's inventory went on. "House badges for Hamid, Drakonis, and Eliseer. You have your choice. I've got three alternate idents for you."

Alex nodded. "Let me have the Eliseer badge."

That called up a brief, questioning look, then Ben gave him the cloth disk, and Alex attached it to the shoulder of his cloak. When the edges were smoothed down, it looked exactly as if it had been sewn in place.

"Stun darts, con-rads, ear 'ceivers, minicorders, jamblers, montector, conditioning aids, aural and visual . . ."

"I'd better have one of the visual mod-stims, Ben. The ring. The light beam works faster for me."

Ben gave him the ring, with its milky, cabochon lens/stone, then searched through the items on the bed and handed him a small, flat case.

"Iris lenses, Alex. Use the brown ones. I put brown on all your ident. They'll be looking for blue."

Alex took the case and went to the mirror. He inserted the lenses, blinking them into place, then returned to look over Ben's shoulder.

"Extra MT fixes, wallet and ident cards..." Ben handed him the wallet, checked the plasex ident cards, and gave him one of them. "Here, that's your Eliseer ident."

The wallet, suitably worn, was filled with the kind of odds and ends a man forgets to throw out, and two hundred 'cords. Alex put the ident card in its slot, wondering if he'd ever have an opportunity to make use of it. Not today. The ident, the tickets, everything, would pass the closest SSB inspection, yet it was a waste of effort on Ben's part. But Alex couldn't explain that to him now.

Ben asked, "You have the contact info on Vandyne memorized?"

"Yes. 'Com seq, 5-396-342. Code opening, 'You must be busy,' etc. Have you contacted Jael?"

"I told Harv to fill him in, and I've alerted Dr. Perralt and Kahn Telman."

Alex nodded, studying the contents of the case critically. Ben took another item from the bed and handed it to him, an X^1 laser in a spring sleeve sheath.

"It doesn't have a hell of a lot of power, Alex, but at close range it's enough." Then, as Alex strapped the sheath on his left wrist, he frowned. "When did you become a left-hander?"

"Whenever I use a gun, Ben. Fenn Lacroy's tutelage."

Protect your right hand, Ser Alex.... Learn to use your whole body, Ser Alex.... You're too strongly right-handed, Ser—

His mind kept wandering. He hadn't thought of Fenn for years, hadn't thought of...

"Anything else?" Ben was frowning at the suitcase.

"No, it looks good."

Ben slid the lid of the false bottom into place, then filled the remaining space with clothing—from his own closet—and finally closed the suitcase and set the locks.

"Alex, you press this hinge here to activate the destruct mechanism on the false bottom. There's an airtaxi waiting on the roof to take you to the IP port. Loren Eliseer is due there just before your ship lifts off, so the terminal will be jammed with Conpol and Eliseer guards, but there'll be plenty of crowd—reporters and oglers. That'll give you an advantage in spite of the extra uniforms. They'll be busy with his Lordship."

Alex looked at his watch and picked up the suitcase. "I'd better be going."

"Sure. Don't miss your ship. And that's no joke. Pollux won't be exactly healthy for you with both the SSB and Predis after you. The shuttle is your only way off."

Alex nodded. Ben was wrong, but he didn't correct him. There *was* another way, another ship that would leave Leda and arrive in Helen at approximately the same time as the passenger shuttle: Adrien Eliseer's private planethopper.

The *Bel*. Another straying memory. He knew the little ship, could even pilot her himself, and had once long ago. Long ago in that other time, that other life.

He was approaching another nexus of timelines, and perhaps it was an error, the decision that brought him to it. Ben would regard it as an error, even a betrayal. But it wasn't his decision. Alex faced him, seeing his downcast eyes, his rough-hewn features rigid.

"Ben, be careful. And keep an eye on Erica." He put his hand out, and the pressure of Ben's handclasp revealed more than his tense features.

"Don't worry about us. We can stay on top of things here. For a while, at least. Alex . . ." His breath came out in a long sigh. "Just take care of yourself, damn it."

PHOENIX MEMFILES: DEPT HUMAN SCIENCES: BASIC SCHOOL
(HS/BS)
SUBFILE: LECTURE, BASIC SCHOOL 15 FEBUAR 3252
GUEST LECTURER: RICHARD LAMB
SUBJECT: POST-DISASTERS HISTORY:
PANTERRAN CONFEDERATION (2903–3104)
DOC LOC #819/219–1253/1812–1648–1523252

I wonder sometimes why historians are so enamored of
"golden ages." Almost every textape on Post-Disasters history delights in telling us when our Golden Age occurred,
bracketing it neatly with the dates 2903 and 3104. It is,
unlike so many historical periods that shade indeterminately
from one era to the next, beautifully demarked with the
founding of the PanTerran Confederation at the beginning,
and the Mankeen Revolt at the end. Perhaps it *was* a Golden
Age, but it is also simply the lifespan of the PanTerran
Confederation. (That was always its formal title, although
after the establishment of the extraterrestrial colonies, it
became simply the Confederation in general usage. Only
historians and teachers or students of history have to worry
about differentiating it from its predecessor, the Holy Confederation.)

"Golden" or not, it was certainly an age of great change,
but again most of the changes were technological, not social. The Confederation in 2903 was a planet-bound culture
moving in slow, cumbersome vessels and machines powered by surface-collected solar energy stored and concentrated in Darwin cells, its airships bound to an altitude of
a kilometer, and its marine vessels dependent for part of
their motive power on sails. Yet within a century—in the
year 3000, to celebrate the Trimillennium—the initial step
toward the stars had been made. It was made, incidentally,

in almost exactly the same type of ship, with the same type of chemically fueled rocket propulsion system that carried the first man to Luna before the Disasters.

The twin inventions of MAM-An and nulgrav made museum pieces of the first Lunar ships within half a century and provided the mechanics and power for voyages to the more remote stepping stones of the Solar planets and satellites. Then Orabu Drakon made his entrance upon the stage of history with his principles of synchronilal metathesis and chrono-spatial eversion, tongue- and mind-muddlers that meant little to the average person of his time until they were translated into SynchShift, and the Confederation made the leap to the stars.

If Lord Patric Eyre Ballarat in the year of his death, 2920, could have been transported into the future, say to the year 3084, when the first colony was established in the Centauri System (that would be a time-leap of 164 years), he wouldn't have recognized this world as the same one in which he had lived.

Or would he?

To be sure, these inventions I've mentioned, plus the many others that grew out of them or developed simultaneously, had drastically altered architecture, transportation, communication—almost every aspect of everyday life. Human population had doubled, and cities burgeoned in every inhabitable area of Terra, not to mention the colonies on Luna, Mars, Ganymede, Callisto, Titan, and Triton. The number of landed Houses had also doubled and industrial Houses tripled, and the Confederation—that is, the administrative entity—had become a power unto itself with its own Bonds and Fesh born into allegience to it. It had built a new capital on beautiful Phillip Bay, and the major industrial Houses made it a megacity with their estate/factory complexes crowding the periphery of the administrative hub. The city was called Victoria, then; it was renamed Concordia after the Mankeen Revolt precipitated the formation of the Concord.

An incidental historical sidelight is that the city of Melborn, on whose ruins Victoria was built, had been the capital of a Pre-Disasters "state" named Victoria. But Adalay and the early Confederation Lords were oblivious to the site's history; they chose the name to commemorate the Confederation's victory in subduing the rest of Terra.

But back to Ballarat, magically transported to the Confederation of 3084. Would it all seem so strange to him? He knew about Victoria—the construction began in 2905—and we know he left his self-imposed exile to see it two years before his death. No doubt it changed a great deal in over a century and a half, but he would certainly recognize the Plaza, the Hall of the Directorate, and the Cathedron. And he'd have no trouble recognizing a Bond compound, and he would know exactly what to expect of any individual on the basis of his class. Bonds were still very much Bonds, and Fesh were Fesh, and, although the term "Elite" was just coming into vogue in 3084, he would know a Lord when he met one and understand entirely his position and function in this new world. Even more telling, Ballarat would recognize the House names of almost every Lord then sitting on the Directorate.

And what if one of you were to make a similar chrono-shift a little more than 160 years *backward* to the year 3084?

In many ways you'd find yourself very much at home. The shape and style of everyday objects would be different, but the function would be generally similar. You'd find some conveniences missing. Like the pocketcom. Modern trimensional vidicom was in the early stages of development, and the miniaturization requisite for devices like the common 'com was beyond the scope of commutronics at that time. However, any vidicom you did see would have been manufactured by the house of DeKoven Woolf. And you would find the names on the Directorate as familiar as Ballarat would. More so, in a sense. Those names would be familiar to him as House names, not necessarily as Directors, although an heir of Adalay was on the Directorate in 3084. You would be familiar with seven out of the ten *not* just as House names, but as present-day Directors. That seems beyond belief when you consider that a shattering civil war stands between you and 3084. It would seem more reasonable that Ballarat would find the Directorate occupied by virtually the same Houses, not you. Yet our Directorate is the one that has remained nearly unchanged.

Think about that. Think about the underlying *un*changes it implies. I find it not only incredible, but frightening. It's like a geologically active fault zone. If tension is released in small, continuous movements and tremors, there is, from a human standpoint, little danger. The dangerous faults are those that remain fixed for long periods with the subterranean pressures contantly mounting, but finding no release. The earth *will* move eventually; the pressures *will* be released. And the results can only be catastrophe.

CHAPTER X: Januar 3258

▌●▌

1.

"My lady, give us a smile!"

"...a white suède overtunic with..."

"Look at that pelisse. What kind of fur..."

"...Lord Loren intends to talk to Lord Selasis about..."

"My lady, when will your lord father return with the good news?"

The Lady Adrien Camine Eliseer was halfway across the central lobby of the InterPlan port terminal, and the remaining distance to the private hangar corridor seemed endless. She was feeling Pollux's gravity, a physical burden that seemed to accentuate the mental one that oppressed her thoughts. But neither was evident in her posture or pace.

"...deny the rumors that a wedding is upcoming?"

"My lady, when will the announcement be made?"

The white fur pelisse moved with the rhythm of her long strides. The island of space that moved with her, isolating her from the bristling wall of mikes and imagraph lenses and vidicams, she owed to the six House guards surrounding her. Within the island, Lectris loomed on her right, half a pace back, and Mariet fluttered along at an equal distance on her left.

"...the banquet at the Eliseer Estate this Friday?"

The smile was as much a shield as the guards; a smile that would come across on vidicom and in imagraphs as direct and warm, but was entirely reflexive.

"...comment on the rumors that Lord Karlis intends to give you the Pink Selasid diamond as a betrothal gift?"

"Is it true your cousin, Lady Janeel Selasis, told you..."

The distance seemed to be stretching, but she wouldn't hurry her pace. She moved steadily forward in her island of space, shielded by the guards, the reflexive smile, and a numbing indifference to the whole scene.

Only one aspect of her surroundings held her attention, and that only fleetingly: the long queues at the main entrance, and the unusual number of SSB officers in the terminal. She wondered what vital drama lay behind that.

". . . ceremony take place in Helen according to tradition, or in Concordia?"

"Where will you go on the nuptial trip, my lady?"

The corridor was close, and it was off-limits to all but sanctioned personnel; off-limits to reporters. She noted the DeKoven Woolf badges they all wore as she reminded herself not to quicken her pace. She glanced at her watch. Only a minute and a half had passed since she left her father at the SS boarding ramp. 16:40. She should be home in Helen by now.

Two hours, she thought bitterly; two hours' delay while Lazar Hamid made his lingering, fawning peace with her father now that the marriage was a certainty; two hours while she endured being "entertained" by Lady Falda Hamid.

As she approached the corridor, the port guards turned off the S/V and shock screens for her, eyeing the noisy mob of reporters warily. Their clamor became increasingly insistent. They were worried; she might slip out of reach of their vidicams and mikes. Which was exactly what she intended.

When she reached the corridor, she nodded to one of the port guards, and as the S/V screens went on behind her, putting a silencing haze across the corridor, she looked back and saw two SSB officers passing, their very presence serving to disperse the reporters.

"Captain Hamit?"

The House guardsman came to attention briskly. "Yes, my lady?"

"Why are there so many SSB men in the terminal today?"

"A gate check, my lady. I made a point of ascertaining their purpose in case it might have a bearing on your safety."

"Very commendable of you. But why a gate check?"

"It seems the SSB had an anonymous tip that they might find an escaped felon here, an escapee from the Leda SSB DC, my lady."

"From the Cliff? Well, good luck to him, then."

Hamit stiffened. "My lady?"

She sighed, looking again at her watch.. This was one reason she despised having servants underfoot, especially Fesh. With Lectris and Mariet she didn't have to guard her tongue so much. Lectris generally didn't know what she was talking about, and Mariet would only laugh with her.

"A little joke, Hamit. I was only amazed that anyone could escape the Cliff at all."

"Oh." He smiled politely. "Yes, it *is* amazing, but I was told this man is a Phoenix agent."

She frowned at that, then turned away. "Hamit, you and your men may return to the estate now. Lectris, Mariet, we must be going."

She stepped onto the pedway, ignoring Hamit's bow and crisp, "Yes, my lady." The 'way carried her down the corridor, away from Hamit, the guards, the crowds beyond the screens. She closed her eyes. Lectris and Mariet rode the 'way behind her; they couldn't see her face.

The icecap retreat. There was no real reason to go directly to Helen. The banquet was four days away, and her mother didn't need her to help with the preparations. Social affairs were Lady Galia's forte. Still, she'd probably complain about Adrien's "deserting" her, but Adrien could muster no concern for that. A few days at the retreat was little enough to ask in light of the purpose of the banquet.

She opened her eyes, refreshed even in the decision, then stepped off the 'way and walked down a short side corridor to the private hangar where *Bel* waited. The door opened as she approached.

"Good afternoon, my lady."

She smiled for the two guards flanking the door.

"Hello, Sargent Jeffers." The man on her right was unfamiliar. At her expectant look, he snapped to attention and bowed.

"My lady, Sargent Lors Samsen, at your service."

"Ah, and with flair." Then she frowned slightly, noting the bruised, swollen cut on his lower lip; it was recently acquired. "But I think you should go the the port infirmary and have someone look at that cut."

He blinked. "What cut, my—"

His hand went to his lip, following the direction of her gaze, and he paled, his eyes suddenly glazed. Adrien felt a chill. He was stunned and bewildered, and the reaction seemed genuine. Apparently he hadn't been aware of the cut until she mentioned it, yet it must have been painful.

"Sargent, what happened? Did you fall?"

"I—I must have, my lady."

"Don't you remember?"

"Well, I . . . I'm not sure. But it's nothing, my lady. Please, don't be concerned."

She glanced at Jeffers, who seemed as bewildered as Samsen. Not that it mattered. Some sort of brawl, probably, that they considered none of her business. Still, Samsen's reaction was odd. He seemed so honestly confused. She brought out a reassuring smile.

"Do have it taken care of, Lors." Then her smile came more easily as she looked toward the looming silver ellipse of the *Bel*. "Where's Jamison?" Two mechtechs hovered around the open lock, but the pilot was nowhere to be seen.

Sargent Jeffers said, "Master Jamison is already in the condeck, my lady."

She crossed the hangar, Lectris and Mariet following dutifully. Overhead, the roof panels were drawn back for liftoff, and the low hum of the *Bel*'s nulgrav generators seemed to make itself audible through her feet, rather than her ears. The techs bowed as she approached.

"She's all revved and ready, my lady," one of them said.

"Good, Tim, and high time. Close the lock after us, please. We'll leave as soon as Jamison has clearance."

"Yes, my lady. Have a good trip."

She walked up the sloping ramp with trembling urgency. *Bel* itself was haven enough, and within two hours she'd be at the icecap retreat. But she must remember to 'com Dr. Perralt. He'd be worried about her.

The thud of the closing lock was a welcome sound. *Bel* had only three compartments: the condeck, a tiny bedroom in the rear, and this sitting room, a small space warmed with draped walls and plush carpets, furnished with two couches, a vidicom console, and autospenser. But these comforts didn't interest her. Solitude was all she asked now.

The bedroom door was closed. She frowned at that, but was

distracted by a thump and Lectris's stumbling lurch, then Mariet's laughter.

"There goes old Nimble-foot again."

"Mariet," Adrien said sharply, "you're not always so nimble yourself." A reminder of an admonition she'd made privately to Mariet often enough: Don't tease Lectris.

"I'm sorry, my lady," she said contritely.

"It's Lectris you should apologize to." Adrien paused, watching Lectris lean down to pick up the object he'd stumbled over. A small traveling case. He put it out of the way by one of the couches with no hint of curiosity about it.

The condeck door opened, and Adrien's smile came on automatically as Jamison bowed to her.

"How are you, my lady?"

"I'm well, Jamison. I'm sorry for the delay, but Father and I got somewhat entangled with the Hamids."

He smiled obliquely. "I'm sorry for your sake, my lady. For the delay, that is. Are you ready for liftoff now?"

"More than ready. Oh—is that your suitcase?"

He hesitated, looking toward the couch where she'd pointed, then back at her, frowning uneasily.

"What suitcase, my lady?"

She gazed at him numbly. He had looked directly at it, and now he asked in perfect innocence, "What suitcase?" And Jamison wouldn't play games with her. I'm going mad, she thought, remembering Sargent Samsen's cut lip and nonplused uncertainty. But Mariet saved her from further doubt of her sanity.

"*That* suitcase," she said, wide-eyed. "It's right—"

"Mariet, that's enough." Again Adrien's tone was sharp: Mariet too often took liberties that antagonized the Fesh servants. Then she smiled at Jamison. "I'm sorry to burden you with setting up a new navcomp program, but I've decided to go to the icecap retreat instead of returning to Helen."

He smiled at that. "It's no burden, my lady. I programmed for the retreat, too—just in case. We can leave immediately. I checked Port Control for clearance when I saw you come into the hangar. But perhaps you should be seated during liftoff." He bowed and glanced just once in the direction of the suitcase, still puzzled, then withdrew to the condeck.

"We're going to the retreat, my lady?" Mariet's face was alight with anticipation. She loved going to the retreat because she was mistress *domaine* there.

"Yes, for a day or two." Adrien smiled, thinking how hard it was to be annoyed with Mariet in spite of her teasing Lectris or her brashness with the Fesh.

It would be incomprehensible, even shocking, to most of her peers, but Mariet seemed more a sister to her in some ways than her true sisters. And it was ironic, perhaps, that Mariet even looked more like her than her own sisters, despite the Shang family resemblance between herself and Patricia. Mariet had been chosen as her attendant in part because of the similarity in physical measurements; she also served as her mannequin.

The rising hum of the nulgrav generators roused her. "At any rate, it will give Lectris a chance to work on his rock garden."

He grinned shyly at that. "If the weeds haven't taken it over, my lady."

"In that case, you'll have some time to reclaim it. Now, we'd better get settled for liftoff." She slipped off the fur pelisse and draped it over her arm, wondering if it was the vibrations of the ship or her own trembling she felt. "I'm going into the bedroom to rest. You may use the vidicom and 'spenser if you wish."

They took seats, ready for liftoff. As Adrien turned and touched the doorcon, her gaze strayed to the suitcase. Then she stepped into the bedroom, the door closed behind her, and darkness enveloped her. But she didn't turn on the light. The pelisse slipped unnoticed to the floor, and she leaned back against the door, hands pressed to her face, shivering with the mounting vibrations. *Bel* was escaping the bonds of Pollux.

There were no tears. She was alone in the dark where tears needn't be hidden, yet she had none. It was only fear; she still had to fight the fear sometimes, even when her mind was fixed on the goal and she knew what she must do.

Orin Selasis would wish he'd married Karlis to Candis Hamid before it was over; he'd learn that a daughter of Eliseer is more than a granddaughter of Shang.

There was a shift in the tone of the vibrations: the MAM-An generators warming up. *Bel* would be free soon.

Then she stiffened, eyes wide, staring like the blind into the dark.

A sound. But it was gone. Or perhaps she couldn't hear it

for the generators, or for the pounding of her pulse in her ears.

There. Again. A stirring, and—someone breathing. She wasn't alone in the darkness.

The terror was paralyzing; she ached with it. It took an effort of will to move her hand slowly along the wall to the light control, and the light was as blinding as the dark.

On the floor. A strange, dark shape, like a shadow, no face; that was a shadow, too, behind a face-screen. He lay on his side, right hand curled limply near his head. The hand was ungloved; flesh and blood.

Call Lectris, you fool.

But she only stared at this apparition, and perhaps she didn't call for help because she was wondering again about her sanity.

No. This apparition, however irrational in itself, might explain Samsen's and Jamison's strange reactions. What had Hamit said? An escapee from the Cliff; *a Phoenix agent.* Conditioning. That's what they called it; a kind of hypnotic control over the mind, over perception and memory.

Lectris—for the God's sake, call Lectris.

Still she ignored the dictates of cautious reason and approached the sprawled shadow-form slowly. She couldn't hear his breathing now. Was he dead? She wondered at the pang of regret she felt at that, then the relief when she knelt beside him and he stirred, pulling in a shuddering breath. The man was ill; dreadfully ill. Her mouth tightened. She knew something of the treatment given prisoners in the Cliff.

Then again she froze, staring fixedly at his hand. A fine, gold chain was entwined in the long-boned fingers. And a disk of gold. Her hand moved to the medallion, no conscious mental impetus guiding it.

A baying wolf. On the other side would be a lamb.

She turned it over.

"Holy God . . ."

She spoke the words aloud, but she didn't hear them. He moved, the chain slipped from his fingers, leaving the medallion in her hand. He turned onto his back with a long, rasping sigh, the pace of his breathing quickening. Her hand went to his throat, searching out the 'screen ring. She drew back when she touched his skin. It was hot; his pulse was pounding. Then she fumbled at his collar, driven to find the ring, to turn it off, to see his face—

The shadowy haze vanished.

I'm going mad; it was conviction now.

She was laughing. It was odd, though, with the tears blurring her vision. She shook with laughter, and at first didn't realize the choking sound wasn't in her own throat.

The sound chilled her to silence. He was fighting for breath, fighting for life, his body racked with spasms of coughing. He couldn't breath—

"Lectris! Mariet! Come here!"

She heard the door open, Lectris tumbling in, Mariet's chirping cries, but she didn't look up. She was trying to lift his shoulders, to get his head up so he could breathe.

"Lectris, help me!"

Without a word, with only a faint, bewildered frown, Lectris knelt and lifted the man's shoulders, propping his body against his own, something gentle and solicitous in his attitude. Adrien was loosening his collar, her movements deliberate, her mind clear; there was no time for shock.

"Mariet, stop screeching. The oxymask in the emergency kit by the condeck door—bring it to me."

"B-but, my *lady*—"

"Don't argue with me. And hurry!"

The coughing had stopped, but not the desperate straining for breath. Yet he was conscious. At least his eyes were open, turned on her. Dark eyes that should be blue. That *were* blue. She couldn't speak; she could only smooth the black hair back from his burning forehead and watch his eyes close again.

"Here it is, my lady—the oxymask."

She took the mask from Mariet without seeing her, connected the tubes and set the pressure, then strapped it in place and switched on the pump. Her hands were steady, her concentration intense, but when she pushed his sleeve back to take his pulse, she began trembling again. Bandages. Shock cuffs.

The Cliff. It was called "interrogation."

Mariet's voice seemed to come from a great distance.

"My lady, who—who is this man? Do you know him?"

Had he changed so much? Did the dark lenses, the unnatural gauntness of his face, confuse her to that degree? Or was it simply that Mariet's mind balked at recognizing this sick, desperate fugitive—this living ghost—as the Lord Alexand?

Adrien held his nerveless hand in hers, every contour, every bone and muscle, achingly familiar.

"Yes," she said softly. "Yes, Mariet. I know him."

2.

Castor's days weren't so short at this latitude in the summer, but they still ended abruptly. The ochre hills on the horizon held a frosting of light, but the starry sky was black.

Dr. Lile Perralt had been a guest in Adrien's icecap retreat on many occasions; he was one of the few people she allowed here. Sometimes, he knew, she invited him because she thought he needed the rest and solitude it afforded, although she always had a plausible excuse that had nothing to do with his needs. And sometimes her needs were the reason offered, with total honesty.

Loren Eliseer had commissioned the building of the retreat as a solace for his daughter's grief nearly five years ago and let her oversee its design and construction, and Perralt had always particularly admired him for that. She needed it then, both the place of retreat and the distraction provided by the planning and building. It became a very personal expression ultimately, and she was fortunate in having a sympathetic architech. Now it was a shining islet on the edge of the northern icecap, 2,500 kilometers north of Leda, well beyond the encroachment of any human habitation, approached through the rugged gap between the Troyan and New Andean Mountains. A two-leveled structure of white marlite, an airy circle enclosing a courtyard graced by arched arcades, every room looking inward into the court on one side, and on the other, outward to the icecap or the Barrens, with the atmobubbles enclosing a landing area on the south, and a pool and garden area on the north.

Lile Perralt sat in a chair by the windowall in his bedroom staring out at the ghostly white patterns marking the edge of the icecap. A long-range transceiver rested in one hand, but he wasn't ready to use it yet. He sat motionless, breathing slowly, waiting for the pain in his chest to abate. He'd found it necessary to triple his usual daily dosage of medication, but that wasn't surprising. He was only glad it was still effective. The time would come when it wouldn't be. He was a physician and recognized that, and he knew he should talk to Ben Venturi about his heart.

116

Not yet. After the wedding, perhaps. He couldn't leave Adrien before that, especially not after today.

He took a long breath and let it out slowly. A tragedy, the Selasid marriage, but it was too late to stop it now. Both he and Kahn Telman had tried to make Loren Eliseer realize what an error it would be, Kahn on an economic and political plane, himself on a personal one. But Eliseer believed he had his back to the wall, and perhaps he did.

Perralt had his own reasons to regard it as a tragedy. He opposed the marriage because he loved Adrien like the daughter he never had. He had attended her birth and come to love her wholeheartedly before she was a year old. He watched her grow from a gamin of a child to an exquisitely lovely young woman, saw her quick mind flower, watched her fall in love with the promise of a happy marriage before her, only to have the promise crushed a few months short of realization. And it was "Dr. Lile" who was at her side through the long nights after that, not Lady Galia, or Lord Loren, although her father offered what comfort he could. But Adrien never wept in her parents' presence.

And now this extraordinary young woman was about to be chained for the rest of her life to a man known for his insensitivity, even cruelty. The prospect of the Selasid marriage was enough of a burden for her, but now this—a tantalizing hope.

Perralt had assumed until today that the Society's opposition to the marriage stemmed from the fact that it would align Eliseer with Selasis and weaken Eliseer. But now he realized there was more to it.

He pressed his fingers to his throat, counting the pulse beats. Still erratic, but the pain was almost gone.

How could she be so calm? It still seemed incomprehensible.

When his aircar had arrived, she was waiting for him. She led him through the portico into the central courtyard and told him calmly, with almost no hint of emotion, that the Lord Alexand wasn't dead, that he was alive and lying in one of the bedrooms here in the retreat, desperately ill. She wouldn't have told Perralt anything if it weren't for that, nor asked him to come here, and she wouldn't tell him how this ghost came to her. She only told him that Alexand was a fugitive from the SSB, an escapee from the Cliff.

That should have alerted him; escapes from the Cliff were rare, and Ben had called only hours ago. But Perralt had been too overwhelmed by this resurrection, and the questions and implications in it. And too preoccupied with the constricting pain in his chest. He had to take one of his pills, telling Adrien it was for his nerves. She didn't believe that, but she didn't challenge it; she never did.

She led him to the nulgrav lift, then along the balcony, coolly explaining that she'd used the *Bel*'s emergency oxymask, that she'd kept Alexand hidden in the bedroom compartment, and that when *Bel* landed at the retreat, Lectris had carried him inside before Jamison realized he'd had an extra passenger, then she'd sent the pilot on to Leda.

In the bedroom, he found his patient covered with a thermblanket, his face obscured by the oxymask. Perralt approached the bed prepared for one kind of shock, but not for a double shock, and for a time he thought it might be too much for his aging heart.

His first thought when he removed the oxymask was so naïvely, irrationally logical: *Adrien's wrong. This isn't the Lord Alexand. This is First Commander Alex Ransom.*

Only later did he wonder why he had never made the connection between Alexand and Alex Ransom. Of course, he'd only seen Ransom's face in a few vidicom transmissions from Fina, and that had been at least two years after Alexand's "death."

Certain responses become reflexive for a doctor, and Perralt was grateful for them. The labored breathing, rapid pulse, and high fever triggered automatic responses in the physician that gave the man—and the spy—time to get his balance. He sent Adrien away on the pretext that he needed to attend his patient alone and, to his relief, she didn't question that or object.

His patient turned to him, half conscious, fumbling for words. "Doctor, I . . . couldn't warn you . . ."

It had seemed ironic even then. A warning equal to the full scope of this shock was impossible.

His patient slept now under Adrien's watchful eye. He would recover quickly enough. He had exacerbated the viral infection acquired at the Cliff with an overdose of drenaline, and fortunately he'd stayed coherent long enough to explain that. In the two-hour delay at the Leda IP port, the injection Dr. Radek gave him had worn off. He had taken a drenaline tablet out of desperation and in defiance of Radek's warning, hoping it would keep him on his feet a while longer. He was unconscious within a minute of taking it.

Perralt sighed with the resigned forbearance of physicians for the willfulness of their patients, then looked at his watch, and picked up the transceiver. Ben would be frantic. It was four hours past Ransom's scheduled arrival time in Helen.

Alex Ransom would be safe here for three days. He'd be safe with Adrien under any circumstances, and Perralt had taken the precaution of conditioning Lectris and Mariet, checking the building, and particularly the bedroom, for monitors, and installing jamblers. But what would happen after those three days? It was Adrien's future that concerned him; Adrien who would soon be Karlis Selasis's Promised.

It seemed unfair. She didn't deserve any more anxiety or grief, and if Lord Alexand still loved her, why would he inflict it on her? He'd given her grief enough.

Perralt switched on the transceiver. It wasn't for him to pass judgment; there was too much he didn't know. Only Adrien could judge this.

A blur of static, then a voice emerged from the speaker. "Venturi on line."

"This is Lile Perralt. Are you clear, Ben?"

3.

The worst was over. Alexand awoke knowing he was on his way to recovery and there was no danger now of relapse. The illness seemed of endless duration in his mind; time at the Cliff was an equivocal thing.

He knew he wasn't alone, but for some time he lay still, eyes closed, feeling the enveloping warmth of the thermblanket and the soft texture of the sheets, smelling the subtle scents of fine cloth and rich woods. He'd never realized they had unique odors before these years in the plasex, plasment environment of Fina.

And another fragrance, light and sweet, that called up Terran springs. He remembered that perfume. Its name was Primaraude. Adrien was his visitor.

He opened his eyes, searching for her in the dim light. Castor was in its night, and a glance at the clock on the bedside table told him he'd been asleep at least eight hours.

He looked to his right across the shadowed room. The wall was broken by two glassed bays rising from the floor and curving to meet the chambered ceiling. The bay on the left showed tongues of the icecap, pale streaks against the darkness; the black sky was spangled with stars that didn't waver. The white ice streaks, the glitter of stars, served to delineate a dark silhouette. He made no sound, no movement that might distract her from the bleak white-on-black landscape.

Through the long hours while he waited for her in the *Bel*, he had tried to put words together in his mind, words to explain himself and why he came to her now. A futile endeavor. First, because he hadn't had a chance to voice those words. Second, because words weren't enough.

He gazed at the shadow against the stars, his mind straining at adjusting to a kind of temporal displacement. It was as if he'd fallen into a chasm opening into the past and wakened to find himself mentally exactly where he'd been nearly five years ago.

No. He hadn't slipped backward. The truth was in a different kind of temporal shift. The unfathomable time-link binding him and Adrien had survived the interweavings of events and years and surfaced in the future, the *now* that was the future for Adrien and Alexand.

A marriage of destiny.

He closed his eyes, hearing the ominous rattle of locks and thinking of another marriage that could be destined only by the hellish spirts of Nether Dark.

This marriage must be stopped. The words echoed in his mind with the brazen clangor of futility, an ultimatum made impotent by hopelessness.

A soft rustling sound, leaves in a wind; Adrien moving toward him. He listened, savoring that scent of some remembered spring, the fear dissolving like shadows in sunlight. Hope still lived as long as Adrien lived.

He opened his eyes. Adrien sat down beside him, a faint smile modeling the fine contours of her mouth, her eyes shadowed ellipses in the soft light.

He had dreamed of that face. It had never been part of the nightmares; it was relegated to a subtler form of mental agony, one he had never consciously recognized. Images that were only ineffably beautiful, the pain coming upon wakening to realize they were lost. Terran things, all but one: the whisper of eucalypt leaves, the cool earth scent of spring rain, the dapple cloud shadowed contours of green hills, the clean silence of windless snows. And Adrien Eliseer.

Neither of them spoke. There were implications in this encounter, decisions only sensed, not yet comprehended, that must be understood.

But not now.

It was enough to understand that dusky-eyed, luminescent face, to realize there was no recrimination, no bitterness in those somber eyes. To realize that in some sense she hadn't relinquished hope, either, in spite of his death. She still wore the symbol of that life vow on her hand.

He took her hand in his, remembering all the subtle, delicate nuances of it: ivory and velvet. And remembering the night he'd put this ring on her other hand. Then he pushed her silk black hair away from her face, watching her eyes close, the dark lashes drawing shadows across her cheeks. There would be no secrets between them. Her faith deserved enlightenment.

The second parting would come soon enough.

He saw the silver glint of tears on her cheeks and heard the soft intake of breath as their lips touched, and he wondered how he could forget the fragile texture of her mouth, why it came as a surprise that so much could be said without words.

4.

Alexand moved with even strokes through the water, pausing to catch his breath when he reached the rim of the circular pool, looking up through the sheen of the atmobubble to the blue-black sky. The air was tropically warm; this 'bubble let more ultraviolet through than the one over the main part of the retreat. Even the plants here were tropical; Terran, most of them, but a few were Polluxian.

He took a deep breath; there was only a hint of an ache. Then he pushed away from the side of the pool, keeping the rhythm of his strokes slow, enjoying the physical freedom as he never had before the Cliff, luxuriating in the flow of warm currents against his skin. When he reached the other side, he turned and crossed back to his starting point.

Adrien was waiting for him there.

He didn't see her until he started to launch himself across the pool again. He came to an abrupt halt and reached for the rim, hearing her laughter as the splashing died. She knelt by the pool, smiling down at him, her hair caught in a narrow chaplet, falling free over her shoulders. The rose hue of her gown cast warm lights on her face.

"I didn't expect to see *you* up so early," she said. "Dr. Lile won't be happy to find you gamboling in the pool when you should be in bed."

Alexand laughed, resting his folded arms on the rim of the pool.

"Has he complained?"

"He isn't awake yet."

"Then we'll worry about that later." He pulled himself up into a sitting position on the rim. "There's a towel on the table over there . . ."

She went to the table and tossed the towel to him as she returned. He dried his face, then came to his feet. Her hand was ready when he swayed with the too-sudden movement. He laughed as he tied the towel around his waist.

"I guess I'm not used to the gravity level yet."

One eyebrow came up. "Or maybe you shouldn't be out of bed yet."

He paused, feeling already a bittersweet regret that wasn't yet mordant because for the moment she was still here. He leaned down to kiss her, his eyes closing. When he drew away from her, he studied her a moment, then smiled.

"I've gotten you all wet."

"I'll dry under this 'bubble in a short time." She sighed, touching the bandages on his wrists. "Alex, how are you feeling? Really?"

He kissed her lightly to distract her from the bandages.

"I took a reading with Dr. Perralt's biomonitor, and all systems are functioning properly."

"Still, you should be resting."

"Adrien, in three days I'll be on my own again. I won't regain my strength lying in bed."

"No. I suppose not." Her eyes were briefly downcast, then she looked up with a quick smile. "Get yourself dry and covered before you get a chill, and I'll have Mariet bring some breakfast."

Adrien took out her pocketcom and spoke into it while he

gave himself a cursory drying, then pulled on a robe, and sank into one of the lounge chairs, reveling in the warmth on his sun-starved skin.

"I hope you slept again last night, Alex. I should feel guilty for keeping Dr. Lile's patient awake so long." She sat down on the lounge beside him, laughing softly. "But I don't."

"It was I who kept us both awake. I slept again; very well, in fact. Did you?"

"Not really. I couldn't make my eyes stay closed. Haven't you ever had a dream so lovely you didn't want to wake up and find it gone? That's what last night was like, except in reverse."

He felt his smile slip away. It would all be gone soon. That awareness stood like a shadow behind their every word.

"Alexand..." Her fingers were light against his lips. "You're thinking future tense. I can feel it."

"I can't ignore the future."

"Neither can you do anything about it at the moment. Joy in the present tense, love. Remember? Three days. That's a miracle."

He smiled at her, watching the sun-glints in her hair.

"More than a miracle."

"A Rightness. That's what Malaki would call it." She took a deep breath, her eyes veiled with remembrance. "He told me about the Brother. And about Saint Richard the Lamb. The Bonds showed great perception in making Rich a saint. I haven't talked to Malaki for some time; I must go see him when I get back to—" She stopped, and it was more than the awareness of their impending separation.

The marriage. The Selasid marriage. She hadn't once mentioned it, and it was more a shadow than the separation.

"Adrien..."

Her hand tightened on his and she smiled. "What a luxury to have hours and days when I never imagined having even minutes."

The subject of the marriage was closed for now. He nodded and pulled her into his arms.

"A luxury, indeed."

She settled comfortably into his embrace, her head on his shoulder.

"But, Alex, I won't indulge myself to the point of depriving you of rest." She frowned briefly, then, "Thank the God for

Dr. Lile. I suppose I shouldn't have brought him here, but you were so ill."

"Don't worry about that." He felt a little uneasy. Perralt's double identity was one thing he'd withheld from her, but only because he wanted to talk to Perralt and Ben first. He intended to tell her; he would need a line of communication with her in the future.

And there was something he intended to discuss with Erica. Why had his conditioning failed in so many areas with Adrien? They were general and nonspecific areas, to be sure, but he had been surprised at how much he could tell her before the conditioned restraints went into effect. Perhaps it was because in his mind she was so much a part of him, of his life and hopes, she was in a sense a part of the Phoenix. Rich, he knew, would have understood.

Adrien was still frowning; she seemed distracted.

"Dr. Lile would never betray you, Alex. You needn't be concerned about that. Still, I wouldn't have involved him if I hadn't been so worried about you. I'm sorry I had to . . . burden him with it."

Alexand's eyes narrowed. "What do you mean?"

"I'm afraid he's ill. His heart, I think, but he won't talk about it, especially now that he knows about—" She stopped. The marriage again.

"I'm sorry if he *is* ill." And he was wondering if Ben knew about it. Probably not."

She called up a smile. "Well, Dr. Lile is an excellent physician; he'll take good care of himself. Perhaps you'd like to go up to the roof and see my view."

He didn't comment on the change of subject. "Adrien, I'd like to do whatever you'd like, and it doesn't really matter what it is."

She laughed, then looked toward the retreat. "Whatever we do, I'm going to see that you get some breakfast first. Here comes Mariet."

"It isn't as elegant as your viewpoint pavilion in Concordia," Adrien said as they stepped out of the lift.

Your viewpoint pavilion. It seemed so alien, both the memory and the possessive pronoun. He walked with her across the roof, absorbing the sunlight as he did her presence. When she reached the bench against the railing, she rested one knee on it, looking eastward, a smile curving her lips.

"I suppose you have to be born to views like this to love them."

Alexand looked out over the stark vista, senses straining with the equivocal readings of distance, the clarity of the atmosphere, the strong contrasts between light and shadow, the nearness of the horizon.

It was a landscape divided. To the right, a desert whose glaring ochres were softened with a haze of green-tinged gray—the pygmy forests, also called the Marching Forests because they migrated constantly with the melting and freezing of the icecap, dependent on its precious moisture. None of the plants were more than a meter in height, many nearly microscopic. The dry gray-green faded toward the south, the yellow ground rolling toward the horizon and a range of naked hills whose origin in the upthrust of a fault block was clearly evident in this land where erosion was limited to the workings of wind and the slow grinding of extreme temperatures.

The Barrens. This was the temperate zone of Castor. Girdling the equator was the real desert, the Midhar, where no form of life survived. The furious winds were all that moved there, and the sands driven by them. Alexand knew of the Midhar only vicariously, and it was enough to adjust his senses to the Barrens now. And the icecap.

The left half of this view was a startling contrast to the right: an expanse of white vanishing over the close horizon, reflecting the sunlight in a brutal glare. Between the icecap and the Barrens was a pied joining, fingers of ice laced with patches of ochre and olive gray.

This land offered no green welcome to human beings as Pollux did. Castor was one vast, indifferent wilderness that suffered a man to survive unprotected on its surface for a matter of minutes in its temperate zones, or seconds in its polar and equatorial zones.

Yet there was beauty here. Perhaps it was because he was seeing it with Adrien. She respected this dry-hued land, and didn't despise it because it didn't welcome her.

"Sometimes we have auroras," she said, looking up at the star-dusted morning sky. "Even in the daytime you can see them, but at night they're beyond description. In the winter I'm entirely surrounded by ice, and the reflections—it's like being immersed in a sea of color."

He smiled, enjoying her rapt pleasure as much as the images she called up.

"I'd like to see that. Perhaps one day I will."

She looked at him soberly. "I hope so. Alex, you look pale. Are you—"

"I'm all right." He sat down on the bench, turning to face her when she seated herself beside him. He was feeling the draining weariness peculiar to the aftermath of illness, and the lighter gravity level only accentuated it, giving him a disconcerting sensation of lightheadedness. "I'll rest, Adrien, but allow me a little more time to enjoy the sun before I consign my body to that bed."

"I get the feeling you don't like that bed."

"Oh, it's beautifully comfortable. Maybe that's the problem. I'm not used to such comfort."

"Alex, do you miss the old life?"

He gave her a crooked smile. "You mean the comfortable beds?"

"No, that's not what I mean."

He tilted his head back to look up into the dark sky.

"I don't miss it, and I have no regrets, except for the pain I've caused others. I hope I can justify that."

"You will," she said flatly. "Do you think you and your father will ever come to terms again?"

He paused, then, "I don't know. I hope so for many reasons, some of them entirely personal."

"They say he's changed a great deal."

"Yes, he's changed. I haven't been out of touch with the old life, Adrien. Our intelligence system is excellent." He studied the patterns in the mosaic pavement. "Do you know the Lady Olivet?"

"Yes. Only on a social plane, really, although she and your father have both been very kind to me. I met your half sister last year. Alexandra." Adrien smiled to herself. "She's a pretty child; she laughs so much."

"And Justin?"

"I haven't been to Concordia since Justin came along. Alex, Olivet is a gracious and sensitive young woman. I think she's made your father very happy."

He smiled at that assurance that went so directly to the real question behind his oblique inquiries.

"I'm happy for his sake, then."

"And I'm happy for that." Then she turned to gaze out over the arid landscape, a tension underlying her composure now. He waited silently, knowing what must come next.

"Alexand, there's one matter both of us would prefer to ignore, but it must be dealt with." She paused, her eyes opaque. "The Selasid marriage."

There was no beauty in the landscape now, only a promise of death. He read contempt in her eyes, knowing it was for Karlis, read resignation, and behind it, dread. It was the dread that made his hand tighten on the railing.

She looked around at him, her hand closing over his. "Alex, don't blame yourself for this."

"I can't ignore the fact that I made it possible."

"You did what you had to do—as I must. We're both products of the same school, burdened from infancy with obligations and taught that failure to meet them is tantamount to treason. You found it necessary to turn to a kind of treason, just as Rich did, but still, you're acting on the imperatives of duty, and so must I. You can't betray the Phoenix, and I can't betray my father or the House."

He wondered how she kept her voice so level, and wondered if he'd ever entirely understand the paradox she was. He turned his hand, enclosing hers in his.

"I know that, Adrien, but the marriage isn't a fact yet. There's still time."

"Yes, and still hope. I assume the Phoenix has tried to stop it."

"Yes, of course."

"But with no success, and that's understandable. Alex, Father's desperate; Selasis has him backed to the edge. Besides, it's unlikely I'll be offered another scion of a Directorate House. I think I've succeeded in alienating all the available scions."

"You had help with some of them."

Her brows came up. "The Phoenix? Well, that should teach me humility. I thought I'd managed it all on my own."

He smiled fleetingly. "You didn't need *much* help."

She laughed, but it faded as she turned toward the serrated horizon.

"Ironic, isn't it? You and I are already husband and wife *legally*. The only problem is you're also legally dead."

His mouth tightened. "Or legally a traitor."

She shrugged. "That detail will be taken care of when you're resurrected, I'm sure, and when you are, the Woolf-Eliseer Contracts of Marriage should take legal precedence over . . . any subsequent contracts. Tell me, when the Phoenix was calculating means of dealing with this marriage, what did they think *I'd* do about it?"

"We couldn't calculate that, but no one expected you to betray your father by trying to escape the marriage."

"I've never even considered that. But you've forced me into a drastic change of course by being alive. I found myself in a very unique position, and I intended to take full advantage of it."

He felt a constriction in his throat, remembering that wry laughter from other years, knowing it always masked grave purpose. "How was your position unique?"

"In two ways. First, I'd be the wife of Orin Selasis's *sole* heir. Second, I didn't care whether I lived or died. There's freedom in that. No courage; it doesn't take courage to risk something you don't care about. But the result is much the same, and in a way I'm sorry to lose that freedom. It was in my power to bring the House of Selasis to an ignominious end, with all the sons-in-law clawing over the remains."

He raised an eyebrow. "How did you plan to accomplish that?"

"Very simply. I planned to kill Karlis." She gave Alexand an oblique smile. "But not all at once, and not in such a way that I could be held responsible for it. Orin wouldn't limit his revenge to me. He'd make Father and the House suffer, too. That was the most difficult part. My first thought was simply to carry a gun—or perhaps a knife would be more fitting—and use it at the first opportunity, but I realized that for Father's sake I'd have to be more subtle." Her eyes were obdurate as stone, her smile chill as the dark sky. Alexand could only gaze at her helplessly, waiting for her to go on.

"I did some research on poisons, and, oddly enough, the best possibility came—in all innocence, of course—from the gentle Malaki. He warned me of a Polluxian plant called 'death hemus' that mimics the true hemus. It's a cumulative poison. The University memfiles tell me it's also virtually undetectable, and the symptoms are so close to hypertensive stroke, it's unlikely anyone would look for it. Of course, after Karlis's demise Orin might still try to get an heir of me— he probably keeps a sperm reserve for Karlis, even if the Board of Succession frowns on it—but I was prepared to die before I bore any heir to Karlis, however conceived, and even if Orin made a prisoner of me, I'd still have one escape, the ultimate escape of death."

Alexand turned away. It was intolerable to hear her speak so casually of her death. But none of this was unexpected or surprising. Still, it was some time before he trusted his voice enough to speak.

"This is why I had to come to you now. I knew you wouldn't accept this marriage passively. I didn't know exactly what you might do, but I knew you'd do something. And I didn't know if it would make any difference to you that I was alive, or that there was a faint hope for my resurrection, but I had to tell you. You had to know."

She closed her eyes, but not before he saw the glint of tears held behind her lashes.

"Oh, Alexand, did you really think it would make no difference? It changes everything. You've saved my life in a sense. I'll not die willingly now, not for any reason."

I'll not die *willingly*. He took little comfort in that qualification. He knew her and the Selasids too well.

"Adrien, I can't tolerate even the thought of the grief I made you suffer, and I don't think I could survive what I inflicted on you."

A mute sadness was reflected in her eyes. "I know, and I don't think I could survive it twice. And yet . . ." She took a deep breath before she went on. "Alex, I must ask a pledge of you."

He hesitated, then, "What pledge, Adrien?"

"I hope you don't expect me to sit like the fairy-tale princess in her tower, wringing her hands while you, or the Phoenix, fight the dragon. I won't be relegated to that role. I'll take part in the battles that will determine my fate—*our* fate—in any way I can. This is the pledge I ask of you, Alexand: trust me; give me the freedom to take any course, and any risks, I feel necessary. Don't try to stop me or limit me out of fear for my life."

He couldn't meet her eyes; he was numb and aching. The price of this pledge would be paid in fear. But there was no decision to be made. Adrien Eliseer wouldn't be confined even if he asked it of her; the wind wouldn't be caged.

"Adrien," he said softly, "let me think of you as a princess. Don't deny me that. But I won't relegate you to a safe tower, not even if it were in my power to do so."

She pressed his hand. "Thank you, love."

"For what? Recognizing a truth? Call it a pledge if you will, but, please, give me at least some hint of what you intend to do outside your tower."

"I intend to keep myself free, that's all. Free to honor the Woolf-Eliseer contracts when you're resurrected."

"But *how*, Adrien?"

"I can't answer that now, Alex. I have no idea what I'll do—what I *can* do. The only honorable way out is the cloisters, really, but it's too late for that. I may have to go through with the wedding; the ceremony. That's for Father."

"No, I won't—we'll stop it somehow before it comes to that."

"You'll try, I know, but I can't believe it would go this far if there were any way the Phoenix *could* stop it."

He stared bleakly into the white glare of the icecap. "We've tried everything short of assassination."

"And the Phoenix balks at that?"

"Yes. We've never resorted to that and never will for both pragmatic and ethical reasons." He paused, then, "The Phoenix balks at it."

"And you?"

"I don't know."

"Alex, look at me."

Her sharp tone brought his head around abruptly. Her eyes were fixed on him uncompromisingly.

"You are a member of the Phoenix and one of its leaders; you hope to be its representative in the Concord one day. If assassination is unacceptable to the Phoenix, then it must also be unacceptable to you, or you betray your cause. And if you betray the Phoenix, you betray Rich and, in a sense, me. You'll make a mockery of everything you've sacrificed and all the grief I've suffered. You can't do that; you couldn't live with it. Nor could I."

Alexand thought of Ben Venturi, who would find it so hard to accept his decision to come into Adrien's life again, to make her a part of his life. He could only wish that Ben could hear this and see the determination in her eyes.

He touched her hair, warm with the sun. "Karlis is safe

from me. You have my word."

She nodded, then, "Trust me, please; trust me to find a way to keep myself free if you can't stop this marriage. And even if I must go through with the wedding, I promise you this, Alexand: Karlis will never have me as his bride."

He stared at her numbly. If the wedding took place, how could she possibly keep herself free, how could she avoid surrendering herself to Karlis without risking death?

"Alex . . ." For a moment he saw fear in her eyes, and he wasn't prepared for that. He took her in his arms, feeling the tension in her body slowly relax. Her need for reassurance was paradoxically comforting, perhaps because she seemed to find reassurance in him; he had so little to offer her.

He kissed her forehead, whispering her name, then his lips moved along the velvet curve of her cheek to her mouth, and perhaps they were both at a vulnerable point. He closed his eyes against an unexpected vertigo.

Finally, it was Adrien who made an end of it, kept it from becoming a beginning. She rested her head on his shoulder with a long sigh.

"We'll talk of it no more. I won't waste this miraculous time thinking of the Selasids, and especially not Karlis. If he knew, he'd be fairly gloating."

Alexand laughed. "I wouldn't give him the satisfaction, even if he isn't aware of it."

Three days. A miracle, indeed; and a Rightness.

5.

The only sound in the room was the music on the speakers, the languid Auguste *Andante Sinfonia*. Alexand stood in one of the glassed bays in his bedroom, looking out at the stark landscape he'd learned to see as beautiful through the eyes of Adrien Eliseer. In the twilight, the crescent of Pollux shed a blue light on the icefields under a sky spangled with unwavering stars. Alpha Centauri B was out of his line of sight, but its light etched the crests of the hills to the south.

Adrien was with Lile Perralt now, and the doctor's illness must now be regarded as an undeniable fact. Still, he insisted it was only indigestion, and Alexand understood that. Ben would take him off active duty immediately if he knew about it. Perhaps it was an error not to warn Ben, but that was Perralt's decision.

Alexand looked down at his watch and closed his eyes.

Eight hours. Three days had dwindled to eight hours.

And it was time for the call. He went to the bed where his suitcase lay open and took out the microwave transceiver, then returned to the alcove, and as he set the frequency, wondered where he'd be when he made the next call.

On his first attempt, he got a no-answer signal. He frowned at that, then reset the frequency. This time the answer came after only one buzz.

"Radek on line."

"Erica, how's the weather?"

A warm laugh, poignantly distant, but immeasurably welcome; he hadn't talked to her since he left Fina.

"I'm clear, Alex. Oh, it's good to hear your voice. How are you feeling?"

"I'm fine, Erica; recovered. What about Ben? I got a no-answer signal when I tried to call him."

There was a brief hesitation that alerted him. "He's all right, but he's in Leda now."

He despised the limitations of audio transmission; he wanted to see her face, to find the source of that hesitation.

"On SSB business?"

"No, Phoenix business. Or loyal opposition business. It's Val Severin. She disappeared sometime in the early hours of this morning."

The minor cadences of the *Andante* marked the time as he stared out into the pied, chill, blue-hued landscape.

"Disappeared? What—didn't Ben have her under surveillance?"

"Of course, but once she went to her apartment for the night, he had to depend on monitors; his agents couldn't stand around the halls without attracting attention. Unfortunately, the monitors tell us nothing. She slipped out very quietly sometime after midnight and went straight to the MT room. We didn't find out until this morning that she had herself transed to one of our permanent terminals in Leda; the Hender's apartment. She told them she was on a special assignment, and that's the last anyone has seen of her."

Anger coalesced within him, and like the recurrence of a

chronic pain after a period of cessation, it seemed all the harder to bear.

"Erica, if Predis—"

"Whatever happened, I don't think he had anything to do with it. Ben slipped a monitor past him today, and he's as frantic as we are to find her. He thinks we've hidden her away, and that worries him since she knows a little too much for his peace of mind."

Alex paused, his initial relief shading to anxiety. "Then she left on her own initiative? Why, Erica? And where would she go?"

"I don't know. She talked privately with Rob Hendrick yesterday evening; the first time since the poisoning incident. We couldn't monitor that conversation, but I can guess what happened. As for where she'd go, I have no idea. She isn't with any of the members in Leda. Ben's checking all her friends and relatives from her pre-Phoenix days and watching the Conpol and SSB arrosters." Her long sigh was clearly audible. "It was probably a panic reaction, and her only thought was to get away from Fina and Rob. It's anybody's guess where she might end up. The Outside, most likely."

He frowned at that. There was no need to remind Erica of Val's chances of survival in the Outside.

"Erica, I'm . . . sorry."

"So am I, but we haven't given up hope yet, and Ben will find her if it's humanly possible."

"I know, but keep me informed."

"I will. But what about you? Are you leaving for Helen today?"

"Early in the morning, Helen ST. That's in eight hours. I'm taking Perralt's aircar; it's an Eliseer 'car with House Physician in large letters over the House crest. That will get me through the city locks with no questions asked, and it has an autonav system. I'll arrive in Helen during the morning workshift change, then I can send the 'car back to the retreat on automatic return."

"Thank the God for Dr. Perralt. I've been grateful he was in the House of Eliseer more than once, but never more than now. Your contacts in Helen are set up again?"

"Yes. Ben has Vandyne primed and waiting for me."

There was a long pause, and he almost expected her next question, casual, yet still guarded.

"How did Lady Adrien react to finding you alive?"

He laughed softly. "With extraordinary equanimity."

"I suppose it was . . . quite a shock for her."

An understatement, and Erica knew it. Alexand understood her cautious tone, but he found words coming hard.

"Yes, but she seems impervious to shock."

"Alex, has she changed?"

"Some things seem immune to change."

A quiet laugh. "I'm glad you finally recognized that. I wish I could talk to you. I mean, face to face."

"So do I. Perhaps we can—soon."

"I hope so, and maybe it's the mother hen in me, but I'm glad about Adrien for your sake. I hope it doesn't make more grief for you, and it could. Still, I'm glad."

For a moment he could find no words, except, "You're extraordinary, Erica." Then he added, "I didn't discuss this with Ben or explain my change of plans in Leda. He didn't seem . . . interested in discussing it."

"Yes, I know. Alex, it . . . it doesn't make sense to him, you know. I mean, you and Adrien. He's never allowed himself personal involvements of that sort. But give him some time."

"All right, Erica. Has Ben had any news about Andreas since yesterday?"

"No, and in this case no news is good news, to a point. There's still no hint of a trial or execution yet."

"What about Predis?"

"He's busy making up lost ground. You shook him badly with the FO assembly."

"He hasn't made any moves against you or Ben?"

"Not yet. He's even let up on the gossip campaigns while he's working at his recovery."

"I guess that means your bargain is still in force." He paused, knowing there was nothing more to be said, but reluctant to give up even this tenuous contact. "Tell Ben everything's under control here, and I'll report tomorrow at about the same time."

"I'll tell him. Alex, be careful, please. Ben hasn't a franchise on worrying, you know."

"There's enough to go around. Erica, I'm . . . glad we had a chance to talk."

"So am I. Now, get some rest."

"All right, *Doctor* Radek. Good night."

Her voice seemed to fade away. "Good night, Alex."

6.

Her eyes were accustomed to the darkness, and the milky blue light of Pollux seemed bright. Her bare feet sank into the warm, silencing carpet, and the fabric of her robe was too gossamer to make a sound even as her movement set it fluttering against her body.

And yet he was awake. Perhaps he hadn't slept at all. Adrien hadn't even attempted sleep; she'd been waiting in the private darkness of her room counting minutes. And calculating days.

It would be close; tomorrow or the next day would be better, but he'd be gone.

Her shadow fell across his face. She knew he was awake, but he hadn't moved, nor had the slow rhythm of his breathing changed. She realized she should speak, should identify this intruder in the room, but no words came.

He lay with his head turned away from her, the covers thrown back, cleanly naked and outwardly relaxed, and she smiled to herself.

A beautiful creature this was, long-boned, tawny-skinned. Lithe as a cat; a leopard; radiating that same contained animal energy, a hoarded power to be expended with effortless efficiency and unaware grace. The weeks at the Cliff had left their mark in a stringent leanness, but that only seemed to refine the grace.

And what would the Lady Galia say to such thoughts?

Adrien felt the tears burning in her eyes. The Lady Galia would be shocked. To regard a young man as an object of beauty and grace? It bordered on sensuality, and in her mind that translated immorality. Only *second*-class Elite thought in sensual terms, and they, like Lady Galia, would reduce the essence of this vital creature to what they found between his thighs.

But the true measures of grace lay in the rigors of years, the terrible strictures of discipline and experience, that formed those subtle contours of flesh and muscle and bone. And the true meaning of sensuality was *of* the senses, and the senses were rooted in the mind.

The medallion gleamed with every breath. The wolf was

135

uppermost, the lamb toward his heart.

A male child it must be; his name would be Richard.

She watched the glint of the medallion, feeling paradoxically alone, even knowing he was awake and wondering whose shadow was cast across his face.

Alexand, how far does your courage and faith go?

She wouldn't test it by telling him the full scope of her intentions, the sum of her calculation of days, the sum of her hope. Even then, she wondered if he might not turn her away out of fear for her.

He moved, only the turning of his head toward her, yet she was startled.

"Adrien?"

"Yes, Alexand."

He sat up, his eyes fixed anxiously on her face.

"Adrien, what's wrong?"

I'm afraid, she thought; afraid to find out you love me too much or too little, afraid you won't give me what I must have to deny anyone else a claim on me.

"Nothing's wrong, love. Nothing."

She sat down beside him, watching him relax against the headboard, his eyes still fixed on her face. She could read the quickening pulse beat in his throat, and wondered if she would have to put it into words, or if she could. The silence stretched on, and finally he looked down at her hand.

The ring was on her left hand.

His eyes flashed up to hers, the question waiting there, but he didn't speak or even move; nothing but the faint cadences of breath through his parted lips.

"Alexand, don't you understand?"

Still a hesitation, then he reached out and pushed her hair back over her shoulder, but he didn't touch her skin.

"Yes," he said softly. "Yes, I understand."

But he was still afraid.

She waited as the silence expanded, reading the thoughts behind his eyes, hooded, strangely dark. He'd made a pledge that he wouldn't try to confine her to the safe tower of passivity, and he meant to keep it, but it wasn't so easy to put aside his fear.

He would understand that it wasn't impulse or simple need that brought her here tonight. She was here because she'd promised him she'd never be a bride to Karlis Selasis, and this was part of the means to that end.

But he would also understand the potential repercussions if the Selasid marriage couldn't be stopped, if Karlis found his bride had lost her treasured virginity somewhere between Leda and the wedding. It was this danger that constrained him; he wouldn't believe she'd take the risks inherent in the sum of her purpose. This danger was enough in itself, and in asking him to be a party to something that would make her so vulnerable, she asked much of his courage.

But he'd made a pledge.

The smile that shadowed his lips was poignantly sad.

"The Rule of Priority. Calculations. Even in this, little one?"

"Yes. Even in this."

Still he didn't move for some time. Then a hint of irony came into his smile. He leaned toward her until his mouth was nearly touching hers, her face cupped in his hands.

"I could almost muster a little pity," he said, laughter hidden in every word. "Pity poor Karlis, losing his bride to Lord Alexand, nearly five years dead."

Bravado, those words and that laughter. She went into his arms, laughing because she was so close to tears. An act of faith; a gift of love.

"Devious Selaneen." Still the undercurrent of laughter in his voice. "Where's the steel in you? Where do you hide it?"

There was no steel in her now. She pressed her cheek into the comfortable curved juncture of his neck and shoulder and silently asked to be something less than steel for once in her life, and for a time he only held her, recognizing her need for simple comfort.

But gradually, by the nuances of his voice, the gentle, evocative pressures of his hands and lips, he shifted the focus of her need. She acquiesced to that subtle manipulation, savoring and sifting sensations, recognizing and welcoming it. Her eyes were closed, shutting out everything but Alexand. Her flesh recorded his every movement, every breath and heartbeat; recorded the pause as he unfastened her robe and pushed it back over her shoulders, making that small act gently ceremonious.

She let the robe slip from her arms to the floor, watching him now, again aware of that unconscious, contained grace, studying the contours of muscle and bone under her fingers as her hands moved up his arms and across his shoulders. She knew he found grace in her, too; she was intensely cognizant of her own body as he apprehended it; she wanted to stretch herself, pulling every muscle tight, making long, taut curves.

But now his mouth pressed to hers, his arms closed around her, and her breath caught, then came in short, shallow respirations, echoed in the sound of his ragged breath.

It asked strength, a kiss so unequivocal; one that made a beginning, that wasn't subject to the restraints that had always bound them. Her mouth was open to his, a vertiginous, suffocating darkness closing in on her. She thought she was falling, but he was only pulling her down into the bed with him, an unexpected shock in the feel of his body against the length of hers. And he was laughing, a soft, warm sound, a sound she would remember, she knew that even now, and part of the laughter was her own.

Take joy in me, love, and in my body, the vessel for all I am, for all I feel and think, for all my love and hope.

For a time she could still laugh, giving herself up to learning mental and physical states for which she had no verbal vocabulary, and Alexand yielded himself to a similar revelation in the sensations she elicited in him. An energy exchange that fed on itself.

Too fast, she thought numbly, it was happening too fast, and she wondered if that would make any difference. Naive and ignorant as a child in some ways. But they still had hours before them; half the night.

A shivering tension radiated along her legs and within her upward as if it were transmitted through her bones along the double curve of her spine. Her perception was blurring. No—focusing. A warmth like fever on her skin, her body racked with random tensions that she knew weren't born solely within her body. She was presciently aware of everything happening within his body, and conscious of her movements as if they were his, her breath coming faster with his, his heart pounding with hers, and finally welcoming the invasion of cogent, rigid flesh that would be, must be, a part of her, as the child she would carry would be a part of him.

Alexand, it must be.

All constraint dissolved in an exalting satisfaction rooted in nerves and muscles, barely reaching the level of consciousness. Something alien within her body, yet she surrendered herself to it, to an insentient, impelling will, testing second by second the limits of physical capacity, and second by second exceeding them. And yet, in the end, there was a sense of triumph rather than surrender, possession rather than submission.

It must be.

Half the night, she thought in the languid aftermath, a sweet, nerveless exhaustion loosening every muscle. He kissed her gently, but she didn't open her eyes, only holding his mouth against hers for a long time.

"Adrien, never doubt I love you."

His voice was a murmuring whisper. She looked up at his face so close to hers, the milky light and shadows soft upon it.

"Alexand, I never have. I never will."

PART 4: EXILE

●II●II●II●II●II●II●II●II●II●II●II●II●II●II●II●II●II●II●II●II●II●II●II●

PHOENIX MEMFILES: DEPT HUMAN SCIENCES: BASIC SCHOOL
            (HS/BS)
SUBFILE: LECTURE. BASIC SCHOOL 22 FEBUAR 3252
                    GUEST LECTURER: RICHARD LAMB
                    SUBJECT: POST-DISASTERS HISTORY:
                    PANTERRAN CONFEDERATION (2903–3104)
DOC LOC #819/219–1253/1812–1648–2223252

In speaking of the Golden Age of the PanTerran Confederation, I've emphasized the lack of change in governmental and social structures during and since that period, but I don't want to give the impression that they've been frozen in place all this time. There were certain practices and customs pertaining in the Golden Age that are very different from those pertaining today. Some of the most telling are associated with the scientific and technological explosion that occurred during the period.

For instance, consider the first Lunar expedition. Unlike the post-Mankeen extrasolar explorations, which were sponsored by the Concord, the Lunar expedition was organized and financed by the House of Selasis in a coalition with Ivanoi, Galinin, and Daro. (The latter two merged a few years later when the first beamed-power satellites were put into orbit.) Selasis at that time was a new House founded on franchises for rocket-propulsion systems, and its alliance with Galinin and Daro, who both held power franchises, is understandable in light of the potential of beamed solar power. Ivanoi, with its rare metals franchises, was one of the wealthiest Houses in the Confederation and had a strong interest in reaching the potential treasures of ore on Luna.

So, here we have two fundamental premises in Confederation technological development. It was funded and organized by Houses, not by the Confederation, and often entailed joint efforts between several Houses. Those sometimes resulted in House mergers, which tended to balance

141

numerically the new Houses emerging, usually as offshoots (Cognate Houses) of established Houses, based on newly developed devices, processes, or services. Another premise hinted at here is that of speculation.

A spirit of speculation was necessary to fund and encourage technological and scientific development, and during this period House interactions and attitudes toward franchises tended to promote speculation. It took various forms, and sometimes its motivation wasn't entirely profit oriented. As a case in point, there's the laser, which was reinvented (it was, of course, one of the many inventions we owe to the twentieth century) in 3047 in the House of Cobar Wale, which was the franchised weaponer of the Confederation, and therefore one of its most powerful Houses. Lord Vincent Wale financed the development of the laser as a weapon with the intention of setting up his second born, Willem, with his own House based on laser franchises. I wonder if in later years Vincent didn't regret his benevolence. Apparently he regarded the laser as a rather limited device of war and no more, but he lived to see his own House collapse into bankruptcy while Willem, as First Lord of the new House of Corelis, grew rich and increasingly powerful, constantly discovering new uses and markets for that "limited" device.

Occasionally a Fesh benefited from this budding process, and Fredric Cadmon is an example. He developed the MAM-An generator for the House of Badir, working from the principles delineated by Ela Tolstyne in her *Treatise on Matter/Anti-Matter Interactions*—and I'll get back to her later. At any rate, Cadmon, a Fesh scientist, with the backing of Tristan Badir, was awarded a Lordship and the franchises for electrical field screens, another project he was instrumental in developing.

Generally, however, Houses speculated on an idea with nothing more in mind than its potential profits. All the industrial Houses had extensive research facilities and eagerly sought gifted people for them. The competition for the gifted was fierce, and the Fesh benefited immeasurably from it. The Guild system, whose origins predate Pilgram, came into its own, as did the University system established by Paul Adalay; its science departments became a prime source of techs. (That term first came into common use during this period, along with University Board of Standards tech grade ratings.) Allegiance shifts of promising scientists and techs could always be arranged. There were also frequent allegiance shifts from one House to another, and in many cases these shifts were literally bought. In the same way franchises were also bought and sold between Houses, which is indicative of the flexibility in the franchise system. The Lords of the Franchise Board inevitably became extremely powerful, and their practices increasingly underhanded until the Board Reform Resolution formulated by Benedic Daro Galinin, the first Galinin Lord elected to the Chairmanship. (Benedic also established the Civil Standards Code of 3065 and the famous Galinin Rule protecting Bond religious practices.) The Reform Resolution established the revolving membership we have now on boards manned by Elite, and guaranteed that no Lord would remain on any board more than five years.

Speculation was generally the prerogative of the Elite; they had the resources and the power for it and stood to benefit from it. There was one Fesh, however, who profited rather spectacularly on a speculative gambit, and not only made himself wealthy, but a First Lord—the last transmutation of the kind, in fact. That was Orabu Drakon, regarded by historians and even many scientists as the greatest physicist of all time. He was also a very pragmatic man, unlike most of his academic peers. In that regard it's tempting to draw a comparison between Drakon and Ela Tolstyne, and I won't resist the temptation.

Tolstyne was that rarity in Post-Disasters history, a woman of notable accomplishment in her own right. Patriarchy is another part of our feudal heritage we haven't yet escaped. She was born into the Confederation and her interests and talents inevitably led to her assignment to the University, and she was too brilliant to be relegated to the lower echelons where most women are confined in both bureaucratic and guild hierarchies. She also found a mentor and patron in Orabu Drakon, who served as lector in the University in Victoria for ten years.

Tolstyne was, incidentally, a very handsome woman, and apparently her male peers found that dismaying, as if a woman of intellectual brilliance had no right to be beautiful. There is a story—or perhaps it's only a legend—that Lord Tristan Badir's second born, Stevan, was deeply in love with her and wanted to marry her, but Tristan, who made Frederic Cadmon a Lord, wasn't generous enough to make Ela Tolstyne a Lady if it meant letting his son marry a Fesh. Obviously, the fact that Cadmon developed the MAM-An generator from her theories didn't sway him. But Tristan Badir didn't long enjoy the profits of Tolstyne's genius. His House was forced into a merger with Selasis in 3093 that was achieved by nefarious, even brutal, means. Lord Gidion Selasis wanted full control of the MAM-An generators that powered his ships, and like later Selasid Lords, he wasn't a man to let anything stand in his way.

At any rate, Tolstyne's *Treatise on Matter/Anti-Matter Interactions* made possible the MAM-An generator and drive, and that in turn made possible the near-light speeds necessary to SynchShift. Her work also made nulgrav possible, and it was a one-time student of hers, Domic Peresky, who seized upon one interaction of matter and anti-matter, repulsion, to design the first nulgrav mechanisms, much to the delight—and profit—of his Lord, Robert Hild Robek.

Orabu Drakon, like Peresky, was in Tolstyne's debt, and to his credit, he always recognized that debt publicly. Synchronal metathesis was only a mathematical abstraction without MAM-An. She undoubtedly appreciated this recognition, but it had little real effect on her life. She continued in a research professorship for thirty years at the University in Victoria after the publication of her *Treatise*. It was then, at the age of fifty-eight, that she entered a Sisters of Faith convent—*not* immediately after her frustrated, and perhaps apocryphal, love affair with Stevan Badir, as some vididramatists would have it. She died eleven years later, her passing unheralded, the only ceremony marking the interment of her ashes a funeral canta in the convent chapel.

Drakon's career and life ended five years later with an Estate funeral attended by all the Directors as well as most of the Court of Lords, and the eulogy was given by the Chairman, Benedic Galinin.

But Orabu Drakon was a pragmatic—and audacious—man.

He looked the part of the scientist-genius—at least, the general preconception of it. He was lean, as if physically consumed by his genius, with aristocratic features and a lofty forehead. The extant imagraphs of him remind me of Andreas Riis, although their racial heritage is quite different. Drakon was born in Victoria, allieged Confederation—like Tolstyne—but he was of Sudafrikan, and thus negroid, stock, but fortunately for him in that period, it was more obvious in his forename than in his appearance. He was also, from all reports, a man of great wit and charm, and early accounts note, presciently, his "gentlemanly" bearing.

This gentlemanly genius was not satisfied, as Tolstyne was, to let his work be his reward. He recognized the practical potential of his Theory from the beginning, and deliberately withheld its publication for several years after it was formulated. No doubt the delay was due in part to his recognition of the importance of Tolstyne's work in relation to his. In fact, he didn't publish his Theory until after Cadmon produced the first MAM-An generator in 3057, and even then, before making his Theory available to the public—and Lords—at large, he went first to Lord Benedic Galinin and outlined its potentials. Then, with Galinin backing him and overseeing the negotiations, he approached Gidion Selasis, who had a franchised right to any developments pertaining to extraplanetary transport. Drakon offered Selasis a bargain: SynchShift, the ultimate leap to the stars, in exchange for a Lordship and the energy franchises in the first habitable extrasolar system discovered. That meant a concession on Galinin's part—those energy franchises would otherwise be his—but he made it graciously, and saw to it that Selasis kept his part of the bargain, which was to petition the Directorate to recognize the new House of Drakonis with Orabu Drakon as First Lord, as well as financing—liberally—the new House for fifty years. The first Drakonis Estate—it was actually only a residence, but a palatial one—was in Victoria until that habitable extrasolar system was discovered and the Home Estate was established in Danae on Perseus.

In 3078 the first SynchShift ship was launched toward our nearest stellar neighbors, and in that same year Drakon married the Lady Rondal, daughter of Simon Ussher Peladeen, who shared Drakon's high hopes for the colonization of Centauri, and with this marriage made himself a partner in that great venture. Drakon was fifty-three at the time, and I've always wondered why he hadn't married earlier. Was he simply too consumed with his work in his youth, or did he even then recognize the importance of keeping himself free for a House marriage should he achieve his metamorphosis into Lordship?

The marriage was blessed with two sons and two daughters. None of the subsequent Drakonis Lords have shown anything like his genius, but they have all been remarkably astute men, all noted for their wit and charm, and all exceptionally pragmatic.

CHAPTER XI: Januar 3258

●┤●├●┤●├●┤●├●┤●├●┤●├●┤●├●┤●├●┤●├●┤●├●┤●├●┤●├●┤●├●┤●├●┤●├●

1.

Alex Ransom left the transit plaza, riding a crowded pedway toward the Planetary Transystem terminal where the Hild Robek cock-and-serpent crest was displayed over the entry mall. Above him through the soaring escarpments of the buildings, the webs of elevated pedways, the glinting streams of aircars, he could see fragments of Castor's indigo sky. The height of the buildings still amazed him, and his body hadn't entirely adjusted to the lighter gravity.

The morning work shift would begin soon, and he was using the crowds. At the terminal he crossed to another 'way, attracting not even a disinterested glance from the people riding it: Fesh, mainly, with the closed faces typical of city dwellers. The 'way took him into the heart of the terminal, toward the giant subtrain shafts that gave access to the underground sections of Helen where the industrial complexes were located, and where at the deepest levels the Outsider's district flourished. The meeting with Vandyne would take place somewhere in the Outside.

He left the 'way and crossed to a row of call booths, grateful for the cessation of sound when he stepped into one of them and switched on the S/V screens. He put his suitcase on the floor and fed a half 'cord bill into the slot. The screen and controls activated, but before he punched the 'com seq, he attached a jambler to the speaker. When he punched the numbers, he turned and looked out into the terminal, watching the Conpol patrol officers lounging around the ramps.

"Harv Vandyne on line."

There was no visual image, and that surprised him; he had

no way of making a VP ident here. His visual screen was on, and he felt peculiarly exposed.

"You must be busy, Fer Vandyne."

"I have plenty of time."

Alex paused. He couldn't be sure of the voice, but the code response was right.

"You're clear at your end, Fer Vandyne?"

"Yes, Commander. Where are you?"

"That doesn't matter. I won't be here long."

A brief hesitation, then, "No, of course not. Sir, are you all right? We were concerned about the delay."

"Yes, I'm all right, and the delay was unavoidable, but we can't talk on screen. Where am I to meet you?"

"There's a float in the Outside; it's called the Tamborin. Level D-3, on a 'way corner; 47 NS and 115 EW. I'll reserve a pod in the name of Charles Harris."

"What time?"

"I can be there in an hour."

"Very well, Fer Vandyne. One hour."

It was always night in the Outside wherever it might be, a night made garish by flashing, glittering signs, crude but imaginative masterworks of light and color designed to draw the Insiders to the floats, serallios, gambling casinos, and other quasi-legal or illicit attractions.

Alex stood in the shadows of a recessed doorway. A private entrance, apparently; no lights advertised its existence. He was suspended on a tridemensional continuum of light, color, and sound, an illusion typical of an illusory world; the levels seemed to go on indefinitely above and beneath him. He studied the gaudy facade of the Tamborin across the 'way junction with its huge, projected images of barely clad dancers moving with jerking, jarring color shifts; ampspeakers shrieked music to blend with the blaring sound from competitive businesses. The people moving along the 'ways seemed curiously unreal against the surge of color and sound, living shadows, most of them face-screened as he was.

He was late for his meeting with Vandyne, but purposely so. He watched the 'way-level entrance of the Tamborin, studying the crowds, wishing hè had an Outsider's nose for Poles and Shads, and regretting that he had no direct means of contacting Jael; his nose would be useful now.

The focus of his attention shifted abruptly.

He felt the man's presence first, and his left hand came up, ready to snap the X^1 into his palm. He made no other movement except to turn his head toward the man.

An Outsider. No face-screen, eyes with the sheen of tensteel; a tough, ageless face set in a squint of cynical indifference. He stood perhaps two meters away, but now he moved closer until only an armsbreadth separated them.

Still Alex didn't move, but every muscle was tensed.

"Hey!" The Outsider's voice was a husky whisper. "You eyeing out for Vandyne?"

Alex felt the hard beat of his pulse. This man wasn't Phoenix; he was exactly what he seemed, and Vandyne's name on his lips did nothing to reassure him. He made no response, watching the man, waiting.

The Outsider frowned, menace behind his annoyance.

"Listen, tooky, I ast you a question. You want Vandyne, I can line you in on him."

Alex asked levelly, "Did I say I wanted anyone?"

"What the hell's your gim? You slippin' the Poles?" He paused and, when Alex didn't answer, added conspiratorially, "Hey, I can maybe give you a door. You got the passkey? Double-deuce 'cords, friend. That's all it takes."

Alex watched the shadowy figures passing, wondering if the Outsider had accomplices nearby.

"How much will it cost to line me in on Vandyne?"

A low, sardonic laugh. "No tax on that, tooky." And his arm shot out, his hand locked on Alex's neck.

Alex twisted free, snapped the gun into his hand, vaguely aware of a sharp prick at the back of his neck, but he didn't understand it until he felt himself falling.

The lights went out around him, the sounds blurred into a roaring wail that died in black silence.

2.

A burning smell, sweet and rich: tobacco. Music at low volume; minor key, a heavy, insistent rhythm. His eyes were open, but they refused to focus. He waited, gathering sensory impressions. Wherever he was, it wasn't an SSB DC.

He lay cushioned in some beautifully buoyant material, his eyes registering fragments of color that gradually coalesced into a dome of glass or plasex, a glowing mosaic of stylized floral patterns. His gaze shifted slowly downward; slowly, because his head was pounding and even the movement of his eyes set them aching, too. He lost his focus, and when he recovered it, wondered if he were actually conscious or simply dreaming. Or hallucinating.

It was a small, circular room of profligate opulence, teeming with exuberant colors, textures, and patterns. The walls were lined with fine tapestries and brocaded draperies of silk velveen in an abundance of patterns and hues, at intervals drawn back in swashes to display art pieces in ornate niches. Fanciful sconces held lights refracted in crystal starbursts, and each piece of furniture was a masterpiece of whimsy and craftsmanship, cast metal or carved wood, filigreed with exotic floral designs and beasts mythical and real. The chairs and couches were upholstered in a potpourri of colors and patterns, piled with plump cushions; the floor was rich with Ganistan carpets whose cost Alex could guess, and it was unnerving to see them layered one on the other with such abandon.

The man who lounged in the huge, cushioned chair in the center of the room, his feet propped on a footstool supported by bronze mermaids, seemed so much a part of his milieu that Alex didn't even see him at first. It was a leisurely puff of smoke sent out from a jeweled cigar holder that brought him into focus.

A rotund jinni of a man ballooning under brocaded and furred robes befitting an elder Lord, a jowled face marked with negroid characteristics: full lips, flared nostrils, black, heavy-lidded, somnolent eyes, curly gray hair carefully coifed. He returned Alex's scrutiny with a bemused smile, the cigar holder balanced precisely in one pudgy, beringed hand, and at length Alex realized this wasn't a figment of his imagination.

Alex was lying on a couch as richly figured as the rest of the furniture, his head cushioned with pillows in a manner indicating some consideration. He started to rise, then groaned at the pounding ache in his head.

"Ah. He wakes at last." The man reached for an intercom on the table beside him. "Yuba, isn't my son here yet?"

Alex couldn't hear the reply. He concentrated on levering himself into a sitting position, then paused to recover, cradling his head in his hands.

"You must forgive us the headache, Commander, but you might have suffered more than an aching skull."

Alex looked up, trying to make sense of the man as well as his words.

"Who should I thank for this lesser of evils?"

The jinni-man only grinned, displaying in a brief flash a set of gleaming solid gold teeth.

"All in good time. However, I'd advise you to move slowly for a while. Ah—" He turned as a segment of drapery slid back and with it the door behind. "Here comes one with your answers."

Alex rose abruptly, staring at the man entering the room.

"Jael!"

But now he regretted the sudden movement as the pain in his head closed in. He swayed, grateful for the ready arms that eased him back onto the couch. When his vision cleared, Jael was bending over him solicitously. And his eyes hadn't deceived him; it *was* Jael, the Outsider. He straightened and went behind the couch out of Alex's line of sight. When he returned, he had a glass of water in one hand and an enameled pill vial in the other."

"Here, take one of these, Commander. It's only a mild analgesic."

Alex downed a tablet, then leaned back. "Thank you."

Jael nodded, turning to the man in the chair.

"How long has he been conscious?"

"A matter of minutes; no more."

"Good. Commander, I'm sorry this was—"

"Holy God, Jael, will you stop calling me Commander?" He pressed his hands to his head. "It sounds so damned pompous."

Jael laughed. "You lay the lines, brother. I don't suppose you've had a proper intro with my old Ser yet." He gestured toward the man ensconced in the chair. "Alex, meet my father, Amik."

Alex shifted his gaze distractedly. Amik the Thief, master of the Brotherhood, the Lord of Thieves. It could only be *that* Amik.

The man puffed out a cloud of smoke, golden teeth glinting in a sly smile.

"Ah, yes, Commander, Amik the Thief."

And Jael's father. It seemed ironic somehow.

Finally, Alex laughed. "Yes, I've . . . heard of you. Well,

now that we're properly introduced, perhaps you'll dispense with the 'Commander,' too, and perhaps one of you will tell me why or how I'm—wherever I am."

Amik flicked the ash from his cigar into a platinade mini-syntegrator on the table.

"You're in my HQ, Alex, at my son's behest. It seems he was concerned for your safety and found it necessary to look to me and the Brothers for reasons that aren't entirely clear to me." He gave Jael a sidelong glance. "And I assume will never be clarified."

Jael ignored that blunted barb and said to Alex, "I'm short on time now; there's an SI staff meeting up soon and I can't slip it. I'll have more info after that, anyway, but Vandyne got himself pinned. He's dead."

Alex stared at him, then glanced questioningly at Amik.

"It's all right," Jael assured him. "The old Ser's conditioned just short of a full TAB. I don't usually make him incluse on Phoenix business, but I was up to the edge on this gim."

"I trust your judgment, Jael. What about Vandyne? How and when did he die?"

"'Car accident—the planned kind—about four hours ago."

"I see." Alex rubbed his eyes wearily, feeling the familiar anger as he thought of his blind conversation with "Vandyne."

"You were put up, brother. I still don't know the whole story. I didn't find out about the pin until an hour ago, and it didn't come through the local SI."

"Where did it come from?"

"Vandyne's wife. They came into the Phoenix together twenty years when. Anyway, she saw something was out of joint and took it on her own to 'com me, and that got me a little hackled about you. I knew you were due today, but that's all. I tapped the Phoenix in-lines to the Shads and found out they were planning a catch at the Tamborin, and since we use it for a meet, I thought it might be you they had their nets out for. Time was running close, and finding you on the 'ways wasn't a one-man play, so I had to ring in the old Ser." He frowned, obviously less than pleased at that. "He sent the hounds out, but it was a sticky gim. All we could tell the Brothers was to find an Insider eyeing for Vandyne in or around the Tamborin."

"One of the Brothers was quite successful. And fast."

Alex rubbed the back of his neck, then tensed, searching vainly for what wasn't there.

Amik laughed, one hand moving lazily to the table. "Is this what you're looking for?" he asked, dangling the medallion on its chain. Then he tossed it to him, his movements surprisingly deft. Alex caught it and fastened it around his neck, asking no questions.

"A lovely piece of work," Amik commented, smiling benignly. "Interesting symbolism, the wolf and the lamb."

Jael took a step toward him, his face taut with anger. "Father, who made the pickup?"

"Gamor. Don't worry; I searched him thoroughly. He also took your gun, Alex. I have it here. And your suitcase." He reached down on the other side of his chair and pushed the case into view. "The locks are apparently untouched. I don't think Gamor had time to open it."

Jael's anger hadn't abated. "Damn it, I laid edict! I'll have the price in Gamor's blood for this!"

Amik only smiled patiently. "I took care of it, Jael. Personally. But, Alex, I owe you an apology. The Brothers are too often creatures of habit."

"No apology is necessary. I owe you my life."

"You owe *me* nothing. My son owes me, and you owe *him*. That debt you can settle between yourselves."

Alex looked up at Jael. "All I can offer now is thanks. Perhaps the day will come when I can settle it."

"There's no debt between brothers." Then, with a glance at his watch, "Alex, I'll have to ex out now; this is one gather I won't miss. I'll leave you in the old Ser's hands until I get back, and maybe I should lay you a warning."

Amik's eyes widened innocently. "Ah, Jael, you'll give your friend the wrong impression."

Jael sent his father a wry smile. "He's a gentleman born; he might be in too deep with you."

Alex laughed and said, "I think I can hold my own."

"Fortune, then." Jael paused regarding Alex soberly. "I don't know the lay of your course, brother, but I told you once I'm on stand-by. It still holds. But we'll line that out later. Father, remember, I call this man friend and brother."

Amik laughed, waving him on his way. "Go with! He's safe as a babe in his mother's arms."

The drapes slid back with the door, then closed after him, and Amik bestirred himself to rise from the depths of his chair with a grunting effort.

"Alex, my son has made me forget myself as a host. May

I offer you some sustenance?"

"Thank you, no." He was still feeling the drug, even though the headache was easing.

"Later, then. Your appetite will return." Amik went to a table glittering with an assortment of crystal decanters and glasses. "And here's balm to bring it back."

Alex wasn't convinced he was ready for any form of balm, but when Amik brought him a minuscule, stemmed glass filled with a pale yellow liquid, he accepted it with a polite smile. It was a heavy-beaded liqueur; the bouquet and flavor were familiar, but its name was lost to him. Elise Woolf, he remembered, had served it only on special occasions and always in small glasses such as this exquisite cut crystal.

Amik sank into his chair, then sipped from his glass, his jowled face almost cherubic with a gratified smile.

"Ah. This, my friend, is a rarity. A Medit bragnac produced only in a certain area near Marsay."

That jarred the memory. Alex nodded absently. "Marsay Cabray, isn't it?"

"You're acquainted with it?" Amik raised an eyebrow, adding archly, "You are, indeed, a gentleman born, then. Marsay Cabray is generally reserved for Lords, and the like."

Alex hesitated, then, "'And the like' covers a lot of ground."

Amik laughed. "True enough. Well, I've assumed we'll be enjoying your company for the night, at least. Suitable quarters have been prepared for you. You're welcome to stay as long as you wish, of course."

"Thank you, Amik." His gaze moved around the windowless room. "May I ask where I am?"

"Of course you may ask, and I'll even answer that particular inquiry. You're presently under the Outside in Helen. This is my prime HQ."

"And the prime HQ of the Brotherhood?" Then Alex quickly added, "Forgive my curiosity. I don't expect you to answer *that* inquiry."

Amik's eyes had gone hard and wary at the question, but now he shrugged and offered a crooked smile.

"You're surprised that the Brotherhood, which is so ubiquitous in the Two Systems, should have its central HQ on an out-of-the-way planet like Castor? Conpol would be, too, and it hasn't always been this way. Only since *I* became master of the Brotherhood. I was born here; I know the ground. Besides, I find Castor's gravity more considerate of my bulk at this point in my life." Then he noted, "That wasn't as careless a revelation as it might seem, to admit that this is my prime HQ. You are, in fact, six hundred meters beneath the surface at the heart of a veritable labyrinth. It would be virtually impossible for you to lead or direct anyone through it. And, incidentally, I'd advise you against trying to find your way out of it."

Alex looked up at the glass dome with its semblance of sunlight shining through the bright mosaic.

"I hadn't intended to do so, Amik."

"Don't mistake me, you're a guest here and under no constraint. That advise is for your own safety. Even if you reached the upper levels, that would only take you into the Outside where you're a stranger and quite vulnerable. The Shads have put you on the fugitive lists with a price on your head, and as I said, the Brothers are creatures of habit. You'll have to be very circumspect in our halls; the face-screen always, and I wouldn't suggest you wander about alone. At this point, no one has seen your face, nor does anyone know you're here. I will, of course, lay edict, but the Brothers occasionally ignore my edicts as did Gamor, who is no longer capable of passing on or utilizing that information."

Alex felt a brief chill. He had no doubt of the unfortunate Gamor's fate; his greed had cost him his life, the "price in his blood" Jael had promised to exact, and which Amik had taken care of, as he put it, personally.

Alex sipped at his bragnac, his eye drawn to the gold-scrolled knife sheath nearly lost in brocaded folds at Amik's waist. The knife was part of any male Outsider's standard garb, and for Amik it was probably a symbol of authority. It was also, Alex realized, a functional weapon that had undoubtedly been many times put to the fundamental purpose for which it was designed.

Amik was studying him, eyes glinting with amusement.

"If you think I might give you over to Gamor's fate, Alex, or be tempted by your headprice myself, ease your mind. My son called you friend and brother under blood edict. You're quite safe from me. You can also ease your mind on what Jael has told me about you or the Phoenix. My son is annoyingly close-mouthed. He's made me a stranger in that part of his life." Amik frowned irritably. "But perhaps a mere father should be grateful to be told anything at all."

"Perhaps Jael felt a mere father deserved to know anything he was free to divulge."

"Ah. And perhaps he realized *this* mere father might become suspicious of his secretive activities and cause him a great deal of trouble. *Now* he has my very mind under cuff. Besides, he knew I might guess him out; I wasn't totally ignorant of the Phoenix even before he joined it."

Alex concentrated on his bragnac, wondering at that offhand statement. But he didn't pursue it.

"Well, Amik, it's a father's lot, so they say, to put up with the choices of his wayward children, no matter how foolish they may seem."

Amik laughed. "So they say, and in answer to the question you didn't quite ask, I don't oppose his choice of the Phoenix. Jael takes his own way, and I don't cross his lines. If I disagree with his choice, it's only because I'm too old and cynical to consider it anything but a waste of time. But he's young and still susceptible to idealism. I almost envy him that. I can't remember ever being susceptible to that particular weakness."

"You contradict yourself by admitting envy, and Jael didn't acquire that 'weakness' unaided. Your son's qualities speak well of his father, Amik."

"His qualities speak more of his mother, friend, if the truth were known. She was a rare woman."

There was a veiled look in his eyes and something Alex recognized as grief, and that aroused his curiosity; it seemed so inimical to the Lord of Thieves.

"I can well believe that, Amik. Jael didn't talk about her at any length, of course, when he was in—" He hesitated, stopped from speaking the word "Fina" by the momentary memory blocking of his conditioning. "—when Jael and I first met, but it was obvious she was important in molding him."

"Very important." Amik regarded him through a cloud of smoke with an oblique smile. "If you want to know about his mother, I'll tell you. I've told few people about her." He paused, lost in thought, then sighed. "But I'll tell you because Jael calls you friend and brother, and it's too late to go against her now. She's ten years dead. But before her death, if it had been known she lived, the price on that one's head would've made *my* headprice look paltry."

"What was her crime that her head was so valuable to the Concord?"

"Her name was her only crime." Amik puffed at his cigar, then, "First, you must understand that Jael's good looks aren't solely his heritage from his mother. In my youth I was considered the epitome of masculine grace." He sighed, then with a shrug, "But that went the way of youth. At any rate, Jael's mother found merit in me; she held this old thief dear, however strange it may seem."

"Should it seem strange?"

"It always did to me. She didn't need to take me as husband. I'd have kept her safe all her life and asked nothing in return, and she knew it, but she held me dear enough to be my wife and bear my son. Strange! My friend, it's something to wonder at, and I never stopped wondering."

Alex was wondering now at Amik the Thief, his hooded eyes veiled with tears. A man who could put a greedy Brother to death without a hint of remorse, yet still grieved a wife years dead. Alex could think of nothing to say that wouldn't seem banal; he waited silently for Amik to continue.

"We had only the one child, and perhaps we did him no service to bring him into this life to be first born of the Lord of Thieves. But she wanted a child, my child, and Jael was the joy of her last years. I don't know his destiny now, but he's her son. He'll make his way."

"I've no doubt of that. Who was she, Amik?"

He gazed into his glass, smiling secretively.

"Jael's mother was the Lady Manir Kalister Peladeen."

Alex was stunned to silence, and Amik's rumbling laugh was indicative of satisfaction.

"So. Now you understand why I say it was something to wonder at. The wife of Elor, the last Lord of Peladeen. That one bore Jael, my son."

Alex had himself under control, outwardly at least. He was still willing to concede his curiosity to Amik, but not its intensity now.

"Then the Concord has deluded itself in thinking that Manir Peladeen died with Lord Elor."

"The Concord had deluded itself on many things, my friend, but is it written in the histories that the body of the Lady Manir was ever found?"

"No, nor that of her son. I mean, Elor Peladeen's son."

"Do you think she'd have dared let it be known she lived when the Purge began? All the Peladeen were slaughtered after the Fall. That's what I meant about her headprice if the Concord knew she was alive."

Alex took time to sip the Marsay Cabray. "How is it she came to you for protection?"

"She didn't come to me by intent, actually. But I'll tell you that story if you like." He paused, looking at Alex inquiringly. "You find this incredible, my friend?"

He smiled. "I wouldn't doubt your word, Amik."

"Ah. Well, no matter. It's true, and I have proof of it, but you may believe it or not, as you will. At any rate, Elor Peladeen's last battle was fought in Helen, as you know. The night Confleet invaded the city, the Brothers and I were going about our business—one man's disaster is another's good fortune, of course—and I happened to be near the Peladeen estate; the Eliseer Estate now. There was a great deal of confusion; explosions, fires, soldiers flooding the city. *I* didn't find the Lady Manir; two of the Brothers brought her to me. She had at least ten thousand 'cords on her in jewelry in clear sight—not that she had any idea of its worth—yet the Brothers didn't touch it. That should give you an idea of the kind of woman she was. Anyone else would've been quickly done and the jewelry taken, but she backed them to the edge. Of course, the child had something to do with it, although usually even *that* wouldn't make the Brothers pause."

Alex turned his glass to catch the light. "What child?"

"Her child. Peladeen's first born. He was little more than a baby; only two years old, I think. The God knows how long she'd carried him about in all the confusion." He loosed a long sigh. "Perhaps that's why she touched my heart so, that boy. And the look in her eyes. I've been to Terra—anonymously, of course—and toured Lord Galinin's zoological preserve. Have you ever seen a lioness with her cubs?"

Alex nodded, but the image in his mind was the quiet hands of Honoria Ivanoi on the day of her widowing.

"Yes, I know what you mean, Amik."

"A mother protecting her babes; such courage exists nowhere else in nature. The Lady Manir had that look, and this old thief . . ." He laughed ruefully. "I couldn't bring myself to touch a hair of her head. Not only that, I laid edict to the

Brothers for her; blood edict. I loved her from that moment, which isn't so surprising. The only surprising thing was that she came to care for me in time."

Alex asked, "Amik, what about the boy? That was their only son, wasn't it? Predis?"

"Yes, I think that was his name. He was dead. When she was brought to me, he was already dead and growing cold."

Alex felt a tightness in his throat, and he was thinking of the man who called himself Predis Ussher, who claimed Peladeen as his birthright.

"He was already dead? Are you sure it was her son?"

"Would a mother be unsure? *I* wouldn't have known the boy, but she did, and she wasn't confused or hysterical—not that one."

"Did she know the boy was dead?"

"At first, she refused to recognize it. Then—it was quite sudden, too—she accepted it."

"What happened to—I mean . . ."

"We buried him, Manir and I. Nothing would do, in the midst of an armed invasion, but that I should help her bury her son. And do you know *where* he was buried? The gardens!" He shook his head as if he didn't believe it himself. "The gardens of the Peladeen estate. With Confleet soldiers pouring in, the walls collapsing from the fires and bombing, the Lady wouldn't be satisfied until her son was laid to rest on House ground; Peladeen ground. That's what the Lady wished, and that's how it was done. Then I brought her here and I promised I'd keep her safe all her life. In time, I suppose the Concord might have granted her amnesty, and I wouldn't have stopped her if she wanted to take that risk. But she stayed with me and five years later took me as her husband, and finally, nearly twelve years later, she bore our son."

Again, Alex could think of no suitable comment; he waited through a short silence until, at length, Amik's golden, jinni grin flashed on again.

"So. Whether you believe me or not, my friend, you must admit it makes a good tale. And it *is* true. Even an old thief wouldn't dream up something so utterly unlikely."

Alex hesitated, then, "Amik, you said you had proof. If I should ever ask for that proof, would you let me see it?"

Amik studied him intently, eyes narrowed to slits.

"It would depend on your purpose. But you've piqued my

curiosity. Why should you be interested in the proof of my little story?"

"I'm interested in many things, and incidentally, I believe every word of it."

"Do you, now? Well, I'm flattered that you take such faith in this old thief."

Alex tipped up his glass, sending him a slanted smile. "I have absolute faith in you, Amik, and it's only strengthened by the fact that I have access to information that supports your story."

Amik laughed heartily. "And what would that be?"

"Jael. He's too much an anomaly as an Outsider. I was never satisfied with his rationale for choosing the Phoenix. I was also curious about his entroit into the Society. Manir Peladeen knew about the Phoenix. We have correspondence from Lord Elor in our memfiles verifying that. He regarded the Phoenix as the hope for civilization and his own immortality. I doubt Lady Manir felt less strongly, or that she'd fail to pass on her hopes and knowledge to her son."

Amik only smiled benignly. "It *would* seem reasonable. Well, I'm glad you found my tale enlightening, but now—" He looked at his watch, then began maneuvering himself out of his chair, "—I regret to say I have certain business matters I must tend to. I hope you'll forgive me for ending our conversation so abruptly."

"It's for me to ask your forbearance for taking so much of your time, Amik." He rose, cautiously, relieved to find the aftereffects of the drug almost entirely gone.

Amik brought Alex's gun and suitcase to him. "Your cloak and 'screen ring are there on the chair behind you." He waited until Alex had the laser secured in its sleeve holster, his cloak on, and face-screen activated, then nodded. "I'll 'com Yuba and have him show you to your suite."

"Thank you—for all your generosity."

Amik shrugged as he reached for the intercom. "I told you, you're—"

"Jael's guest. Yes, you told me. But like it or not, Amik, you'll have to accept my thanks. There's no debt in gratitude."

Amik eyed him speculatively, then laughed. "We'll speak of that another time."

3.

Alex leaned back, idly surveying the lavishly furnished guest suite, which was only a little less flamboyant in décor than Amik's salon, and included a similar colored dome backed with artificial light. He put his wineglass down by his empty plate with a sigh of purely physical satisfaction, a sensation he indulged for the moment.

He might as well. Jael refused to dishonor the chef's handiwork by detracting from it with any but the lightest conversation. But, at length, he tossed the linett napkin down on a table glittering, even in the ruins of the "small supper," with platinade, crystal, and gold-embellished porceleen, and asked, "Well, brother, enough?"

"Jael, *enough* would hardly describe that meal. I haven't eaten so well since . . ."

Jael, dark eyes intent, only smiled. "Since before you saw Fina, I'll lay. Caffay? Or some brandy?"

"Caffay, please."

Jael reached for the intercom near his plate. "Hebra, caffay for my guest and myself." Then he rose and moved to an armchair and relaxed against the vclveen cushions. "Your face-screen, brother."

Alex touched the switch on his 'screen ring as he sank into the chair across a small side table from Jael. The table was Sinasian, he guessed; austere, yet intricately carved, and as rare as it was old. It occurred to him that Jael would adapt very easily to the Elite world; he lived as well as any Lord both in terms of creature comforts and cultural advantages. He even dressed like a Lord on his own ground, with boots and brocaded doublet, although the cut of his clothes leaned to the rakish— and to Outside standards—and the sheathed knife was always ready at his side.

The door opened, and a young woman entered carrying a tray laden with porceleen cups and a gold-inlaid pot. She gave Jael a brief, polite smile as she put the tray on the side table and poured the steaming black brew into the cups.

Jael said, "You can take the dining table now, Hebra. And remember, I give it to you to see to my guest's comfort. I call this man friend and brother—under blood edict."

She pulled her breath in sharply at that, then with a nod gave Alex that same polite smile.

"I'll be on ready any time he 'coms." She activated the nulgrav control and guided the table out the door.

Alex turned off his face-screen and reached for his cup. "Now that we've done justice to your chef's artistry, perhaps you'll tell me about the SI meeting."

Jael nodded. "The whole thing was on script to the last word, Alex, including a gimmy eulogy for Vandyne that would bring tears to a carraminx's eye. Ian Temple takes over the top seat in SI here, and Ussher pulls the strings on him."

"Was anything said about me?"

"Not a glim, and I didn't put it up to Temple. I wasn't supposed to know about your coming on scene."

"What about you, Jael, with Vandyne *off* scene?"

He shrugged and sipped at his caffay unconcernedly. "I'm in clear, brother. Upped to number three man—according to script. They'll keep their blades sheathed with me; I'm not casting any shadows over them now, and anyway, they aren't sure where I toe up. So maybe I let them think I'm with the tooth-gimmer. I'm a good ear in where I sit, and I don't intend to toss that."

Alex commented levelly, "You seem to be well lined in on the situation with Ussher."

Jael's hooded eyes flickered with hidden amusement. "You mean this under-cloak face-off you've got on? I told you once I read the tooth-gimmer, and I'm good at addition. So I've been adding up the signs past what Harv told me. Of course, it wasn't so hard to tally since I know who you are."

There was no doubt what he meant by that, and Alex finally had to laugh.

"How did you find out?"

"The old Outsider's nose, mostly," he said, touching his nose with a sly smile. "The old Ser must have tallied it, too."

Alex frowned at that. "What did he say?"

"Nothing to me. It's what he said to you. You said he told you that spin about my mother. He *never* spills that to strangers—or anyone."

"Why should knowing my identity induce him to spill it?"

"The old Ser plays every side. Maybe he thought someday you'd have the weight to—well, if you knew I carried some blue Elite blood..." He put his cup aside, frowning uncomfortably. "My mother had this...dream. Something about exhuming the house of Peladeen."

"With you as First Lord?"

"One on, brother. The son of the Lord of Thieves. She made a tape, a death testament, addressed to Galinin 'or his successor,' no less. She laid it out that I was the rightful heir to Peladeen, since I was her only living son. There are precedents—or so she said—for matriarchal succession, and she carried a little Peladeen blood herself. I guess—damn, it's for a laugh, really, digging up the House of Peladeen with *me* in the top seat. But she meant it true."

Alex stared at him, then his annoyance drove him to rise and begin pacing, arms folded across his chest.

"For a laugh! Holy God, Jael, you have a claim to the First Lordship of Peladeen and you didn't tell anyone in Fina about it? You're another candidate for Phase I!"

He replied a little stiffly, "I've got that tallied, brother, but you're a hell of a lot better candidate than I am, and I had *that* tallied, too. And there's a kind of conditioning that doesn't take Phoenix training; the kind you learn from the time you can make words, and you know if you spill, someone you love is going to die. My mother's life hung on the shadow of a word. So I didn't talk about her. Not even after she died."

Alex sighed. "Nor even under Level 3 conditioning, according to Erica. But, Jael, that little 'spin' your father told me does more than establish your claim to Peladeen."

Jael's gaze was direct. "If you're going to call me down because I didn't hand you the blade to cut *Lord* Predis's claim out from under him, just sit on it. When I came on scene, *you* were available for Phase I. You didn't need a blade. Then, in one month's time, the whole stat got turned inside out. The tooth-gimmer's on top, and you've got a hand and a foot tied behind you—I can tally that one, too. Bring this face-off out into the open, and the Phoenix will split down the middle and crumble into that much Midhar sand. The old Ser's spin gives you a blade, but can you use it? And will it hold? You can't *prove* Predis Ussher Peladeen is buried in the Eliseer Estate unless you dig up the grounds. So do you want to take the chance that Ussher can't turn your blade into a lie? That's his gim, Alex, and he's good at it—turning truth into lies, and lies into truth."

Alex looked up into the shining, multicolored dome, feeling the weight of six hundred meters of earth above it. He wondered if he'd ever again live where he could look out a window and see the sky. Any sky.

He said dully, "You're right, Jael. But your claim may still be vital if I ever do have the leverage to help you make good on it." Jael was on the verge of protesting and Alex added, "If I achieve my resurrection, I'll need you, and not as the first born of the Lord of Thieves. You may have to accept the role of Lord of Peladeen, and even the role of focus for Phase I if I fail."

Jael didn't answer immediately, but at length he nodded. "All right, brother, you call it. I can play any gim you name if I have to, and probably a few you've never thought of." He took a moment for his caffay, frowning slightly. "But there's one thing I'd like to know about Ussher. How did he gim the Council so well in the beginning? I mean, they wouldn't even consider running the gant with him unless they thought he had a solid claim to Peladeen."

Alex nodded and returned to his chair. "His claim couldn't be *dis*proved, Jael, and the Council was satisfied with that; they had to be. According to his story, he was saved during the Fall by a Fesh nurse—I don't even know her name—but she *was* a nurse for Predis Peladeen. After the Fall, Ussher said she claimed him as her own child, and no records survived of her marrying or having a child of her own. Ussher also had some jewelry known to belong to Manir Peladeen, and he came up with a few verifiable childhood memories." He paused, then with a bitter laugh, "Now it's obvious where the truth lies: He *was* the nurse's son. The jewelry—she could have stolen it, or Manir might have given it to her. The memories could come from the nurse, too, and it's even conceivable that she knew something about the Phoenix. If Manir trusted her, she might have told her something about it, or maybe she just had sharp ears. Who knows?"

"The tooth-gimmer does." Jael picked up his cup, sipped sparingly, then put it down with an air of resolve. "Well, brother, that's all for the bygone. For the now, we've got a few problems to lay out. You're safe here—at least, a little safer than up in the Inside—but I doubt you want to retire here."

"Retirement—here or anywhere—is definitely not what I had in mind. I'm sure you've tallied my reasons for leaving Fina. I was an open target for Ussher there. But I have a purpose beyond preserving my life—Andreas Riis. I left Fina with only a vague plan of working with loyal members in the Helen chapter to make sure an MT is available—and out of Ussher's reach—when Ben finds out where Andreas is being held, but that rather naive scheme is out now. Ussher has too strong a foothold here, and I can't risk any more lives; I already have Vandyne on my conscience. I have no choice now but to go into total exile. That gives Ussher free rein in Fina, but if we can rescue Andreas before Ussher gets too deeply entrenched, we have a chance of cutting him down without ripping the Phoenix apart."

Jael nodded. "There's the LR-MT to count in, too. How close was Riis on that?"

Alex's jaw tightened. He said bitterly, "Within touching distance. That's what precipitated the sudden reversal of the 'stat' in Fina."

"That puts a light on everything. Alex, even if Ben homes in on Riis, cutting him loose is going to be one hell of a shivvy gim."

"I know. I need an HQ. I'll have to equip it with everything we'll need to free Andreas. An MT, of course, and communication and monitoring systems. And I want to pull Lyden and Bruce out of Fina and set them up with the equipment they need to keep working on the LR-MT."

Jael objected, "But they'd need a comp system."

"Only shielded inputs to one."

"So. You have any particular system in mind?"

Alex laughed. "Of course. Your father's. I can't believe the Lord of Thieves runs his far-flung empire without an adequate computer system."

Jael leaned back, the tips of his fingers pressed together, no hint of amusement in his slanted eyes.

"Alex, you'd better scan one thing straight. Just because *I* opted for the Phoenix doesn't mean you can hold the old Ser to friend. If I hadn't laid edict for you, he'd give you over to the Shads without a quiver."

"Yes, but your father is a businessman; he deals in goods and services. Is he so particular about whom he does business with that he'd refuse to deal with me?"

"Not as long as he can nudge the price enough to pull the kind of profit margins he's used to."

Alex nodded and, finding immobility intolerable, again rose and began pacing.

"Amik will demand quantity, if my mode of exchange is money, or quality, if I can fire his imagination with goods otherwise unavailable to him. The Phoenix has means of larceny open to it even the Brotherhood can't rival. We can also offer items he can't find anywhere except in Fina."

Jael turned palms up, shoulders rising in a shrug. "You can catch his eye, brother, but I'll lay you a warning. The tax on his goods and services is high, and he's an old hand at haggle gims."

"I'll have to take my chances at that." Alex turned to face Jael, brows drawn. "The biggest problem is a space to set up my HQ; one that's as safe as possible from the SSB and preferably out of the Brother's way. Some of the necessary equipment I can get from Fina through Ben and Erica. Like an MT." He frowned as he resumed his pacing. "I may have to pirate one of the Corvets when Barret and M'Kim get them outfitted with MTs. Under any circumstances, I'll need at least three Falcons."

"Three Fal——that means hangar space, too."

"Yes, and living space for the crews and techs; I'll have to bring in some loyals from Fina. And a habitation system as well as basics like water, a food supply, and a power source."

Jael's cup came down into its saucer with a clatter. "Alex, you're talking about *money*. Maybe into millions when you throw in a few Falcons."

Alex nodded, unaware of the tense fisting of his hands.

"Yes, and I'm talking about maintaining the LR-MT research program, because, whatever happens in Fina, we can't bargain with the Concord without that. I'm talking about making sure we have the means to free Andreas when Ben finds him. Jael, I'm talking about the survival of the Phoenix. I *will* have my HQ, and I *will* free Andreas. If I do nothing else for the Phoenix, I'll bring Andreas back to Fina. I'll bring him back if it costs my life."

"Brother, don't ask fate like that."

His anxious, solemn tone surprised Alex and called up a short laugh.

"Don't worry, Jael, I intend to live." An image flashed out of memory. Adrien. Only hours ago. "I intend to live."

"That's good news. I don't like laying my stakes on a low card. All right, you'll have your HQ. I'm not playing quiv on you, but even if you can pay the old Ser's tax, you're asking him to come over with a hell of a lot all at once."

"Who would be more likely to come over with it? And who else can I ask? I doubt the equipment will be much of a problem, or the Falcons; he has a larger fleet than the Phoenix. But what about the space?"

Jael considered the question with narrowed eyes. "You'll need a lot of space—*safe* space—in one parcel, especially if you expect to hangar any lifters. You don't find that under any rock you kick."

"I know you don't. So, where does the Brotherhood hangar *its* fleet?"

"Oh . . . here and there. The Poles never find more than three lifters in any one hide. Mostly we use natural caves or abandoned mine shafts. Anything out of sight or scan. On Terra and Pollux we had underwater hides long before the Phoenix came on to it. Wait—" His eyes went to intent slits. "I think I know a place . . ." Then, after what seemed to Alex a long silence, he nodded. "Yes, it'll pass. A natural cave—or caves, I guess. It's a series of old volcanic tubes. The old Ser called it the Cave of Springs. There are some hot springs in the lower levels. It's about eight hundred kilometers south of Helen on the edge of the Midhar. No sign of life anywhere near, human or otherwise."

Alex felt his pulse quickening. "What about access? Eight hundred kilometers surface travel makes for a high security risk. I don't know about delivery of the equipment, but you and I will have to do a certain amount of commuting unless you expect us to camp in the Midhar until the habitat sytems are functional."

"You said you want to live, friend, and so do I. But you won't have to worry about that much surface travel. You're sitting in the middle of a true-weight historical site, you know."

Alex went back to his chair, finding his patience tried by this apparent diversion.

"Historical in what sense?"

"The oldest part of Helen. Old mine shafts and underground warehouses. Rare earths and metals. That's what made this spot so nice in the beginning. The mines moved out into the Barrens when the lodes gave out here, but the shafts were left where they lay, and by now nobody upside remembers they were ever here. There's one shaft that takes south and comes up not more than two hundred kilometers north of the Cave of Springs."

"Two hundred kilometers?" Alex found himself smiling. "That lowers the security risk."

"That's one reason the old Ser liked it. He was going to put a hangar there, but he eyed in on another hide he liked better. One thing, Poler patrols are skimp over the Midhar. They don't think anything they should worry about could survive there, so they just give it a quick scan now and then. Of course, you have the Obsats up there to hold in mind, but they're tied to a steady schedule."

"Ben can get the information we'll need on the satellites as well as the patrol schedules." His fingers began drumming silently against the cushioned arms of his chair. "We can set up infrared and VF screens to protect the surface access from observation, and once we get an MT installed, we won't have to worry about surface movement at all except for the ships. You said there are springs there? Is the water drinkable?"

"I think so. Maybe a little heavy on minerals. They're hot springs."

"That might solve some of the power problems. How do the temperatures run inside the caves? Will we need heating or cooling equipment?"

"I've never been there, but my guess is it'd be more livable than the surface."

"That isn't saying much. Jael, I want to see the Cave of Springs."

"Now?"

"Yes."

Jael sighed and came to his feet. "I guess any time's right. Come on, we'll pick up some surface suits on the way. Don't forget your face-screen."

At the door, Alex stopped him with a hand on his arm.

"Jael, you understand you're my second-in-command now."

He hesitated, then laughed, an ironic cast in it.

"That sounds like it should rate me at least a couple of solid gold stars."

"There aren't any stars in exile. Jael, I mean it. Second-in-command and heir apparent. If anything happens to me before we find Andreas . . ."

Jael pressed the doorcon. "Brother, you're asking fate again. I'll play out the gim somehow. Hold that in faith. Now, come on. It's a long jaunt to the Cave of Springs."

4.

This morning the newscasts had been full of last night's banquet at the Eliseer Estate. That the Lady Adrien, after mourning her first Promised so long, was at last to be married seemed a source of oddly personal satisfaction to the society 'casters, inspiring them to bubbling flights of speculation about the wedding, which would take place in two and a half months, on 3 Avril. By entrenched tradition, it would be in Helen, the bride's home.

Strange that he could think of that now.

No, not so strange; it was difficult to think of anything else. Alex turned, forcing his thoughts into focus on Amik.

They were alone in the Lord of Thieves' sanctum, Alex wandering the room, vaguely noting the sculptures and other art objects, while Amik, ensconced in his deep-cushioned chair, pored over a sheet of vellum, his frown becoming more marked with every passing second.

At length, he pursed his lips and gave Alex a long scrutiny.

"My dear Alex, you're quite mad. You realize that, I hope? This list—" He tapped the sheet with one hand, then tossed it on the table beside him. "If I didn't know you, my friend, I'd say foolishness, but I give you the benefit of the doubt. Madness!"

Alex picked up a small figure of black wood carved in a primitive style he couldn't identify.

"Madness? Have I overestimated the Brotherhood to that degree? Is it madness to assume the items on that list are available to you by one means or another? I should think that would be the only question. An input into your computer system presents no problems, nor does a temporary work force of thirty or forty men, and I'm willing to accept the security risks involved in using the Brothers. The Cave of Springs? You aren't using it. Why shouldn't you let it turn a profit for you?"

"And the Falcons?" Amik put in, eyebrows arching up. "*Three* Falcons, with maintenance equipment? Madness!"

"Conpol estimates your fleet at four hundred Falcons. I can't believe renting out three of them for a while would put a noticeable strain on your striking power."

Amik paused to place a cigar in the jeweled holder and puffed it alight.

"Renting out? Am I to understand you don't wish to buy the Falcons outright?"

Alex turned his attention to a jade statuette. "If I have use of your ships, I can acquire more on my own from Confleet. But on the other items—except for the construction equipment—I'm talking about outright purchase."

"And the Cave of Springs? Are you talking rent or purchase there?"

"Purchase." He looked around at Amik. "Of course, I *could* question your right to sell *or* rent that piece of property, but being a practical man, I'll grant that."

Amik's golden teeth flashed in a brief smile, then he reached for the vellum and again studied the list, occasionally sending out a puff of smoke to hang like a halo around his head before it dissipated.

"Well, perhaps it isn't entirely madness, Alex, although it borders on it, you'll have to admit that."

"Amik, my entire life borders on madness. At the moment, my only concern is whether you can supply my needs."

"I should think you'd be a little concerned about whether you can *afford* to have me supply these needs. The price of madness of this sort is generally rather high."

"Especially when I'm in a seller's market? Well, I realize it's unlikely I can offer anything in exchange that you need, but I do have something in mind you may want; something I doubt even the most audacious of the Brothers could acquire for you."

Amik's black eyes gleamed behind the studied skepticism. "What could you offer me that the Brothers are incapable of acquiring?"

Alex seemed to hesitate over his answer, then choosing the only uncushioned chair available, sat down and looked directly at Amik.

"First, can you fulfill your part of the bargain?"

Amik smiled faintly at that. "Yes, I can fulfill my part. But—" He pointed the cigar holder in emphasis. "—you said you'd take full responsibility for your security with the Brothers provided for your work force. That I leave to you. I'll lay edict, but I can't guarantee their silence."

"I have means of insuring that. Now, do I understand you— you can supply the equipment and a work crew of forty men?"

"The list reads *thirty* to forty men."

"Of course. And the input to your compsystem? A security-shielded input?"

"As long as my techs oversee the installation of the inter-conn."

Alex frowned, then, "Agreed—*if* I retain the right to subject them to conditioning *after* they report to you, and you're sat-isfied the shields are reciprocal."

"Mm...oh, very well. I'll agree to that."

"And that leaves the Cave of Springs and the Falcons, which are obviously available. Not madness at all, is it? In fact, it seems entirely feasible."

"Oh, indeed, *my* part of the bargain is feasible enough. What about *your* part?"

Alex shrugged. "That depends on the value you set on it. Give me a price."

Amik sent out a languid stream of smoke from his cigar.

"One and a half million 'cords. And that doesn't include the rent on the Falcons. We'll work that out later."

Alex raised an eyebrow. He had some idea of the market value of the items on the list, and Amik was allowing himself, conservatively, a fifty percent profit margin. But Alex was only relieved it wasn't a hundred percent.

"Well, that gives us a starting point," he conceded.

"Then will you test my patience further? What is it you intend to offer in return?"

Alex rose and reached into his shirt pocket. "Do you have a holojector here?"

Amik regarded him suspiciously, then pulled himself to his feet. "Yes, of course." He crossed to the wall on his right and reached behind the drapes; they opened with a soft hum to reveal an impressive comconsole complete with monitoring screens and compconsole.

Alex inserted a spool into the holojector, taking his time about adjusting the image before he finally moved aside. "This is what I'm offering, Amik."

The object in the 'jector chamber called forth a gasp from the Lord of Thieves, and that in turn a smile from Alex.

It was half sculpture, half jewel; a golden egg twenty centimeters in height, mounted on a tripod of gold and platinum, the whole structure accented with jewels set in gold-petaled blossoms. As Amik watched in frank amazement, the egg broke into vertical segments, opening like a flower to reveal a lining of *pavé* aquamarines and diamonds, and out of the egg, a swan, exquisitely modeled in gold of many shades, emerged, spread its perfectly detailed wings and arched its smoothly segmented neck, then curved its head under the folding wings and sank back into the shell as the segments closed around it, leaving no trace of a seam in the surface.

Amik stared, a childlike enchantment beguiling his dark features into a smile, and Alex said casually, "The piece has a musical mechanism, but we were unable to record it. Sao Kuno's *Reflections:* the theme from the andante."

Amik didn't seem to hear him. With a long sigh, he said, "The Zarist Egg of the Ivanoi." Then he frowned, looking up at Alex sharply. "At least an excellent copy."

Alex only laughed at that. "Amik, you don't bother with copies; nothing in this room is an imitation or copy. And that isn't a copy. It *is* the Zarist Egg of the Ivanoi. It was created three hundred years ago by Polenic in the style of the Zarist eggs made in the nineteenth century by Fabergé. None of those survived the Disasters, of course. Polenic designed three of these eggs for the fifth Lord Ivanoi, and of them, only this one survived the Mankeen Revolt. It was given by the Ivanoi to the Lord Galinin on his marriage to Lady Camma Nordreth; Galinin in turn gave it to his eldest daughter, Elise, on her marriage to Lord Woolf."

Amik looked around at him, a subtle glint in his eyes only briefly taking shape as a smile.

"Am I to understand that you're in possession of this object?"

"I have access to it."

"If the Ivanoi Egg were indeed missing, I'm sure it wouldn't be kept secret. I've heard nothing to suggest it isn't still safe in the Woolf Estate museum."

"At the moment, it *is* still safe. Amik, the Phoenix doesn't often resort to larceny, but we have the means to do a very good job of it. If you and I strike a bargain, the Egg will be in your hands within a few days, and you have my word—it *will* be the original. Now, I assume you have an idea of the worth of this little ornament?"

Amik grinned wryly. "Some."

"It's valued in the Archives at two million 'cords. Its beauty and rarity can't actually be calculated, of course. At any rate, this is what I'm offering as my part of the bargain, but only if your part includes free use of the Falcons for an indefinite period of time."

"So. You *will* insist on haggling. But surely you realize that larceny has the unfortunate effect of tainting an object and thereby lowering its monetary value." His eyes strayed briefly to the Egg. "Use of the Falcons for six months with the understanding that they'll be returned to me in perfect condition."

"Six months?" Alex frowned. "All right, but with another understanding that if I still need them after that time, I can have them for . . . five thousand 'cords a month."

"Each?"

"No. Altogether."

"Altogether? Alex, for the three, I thought I'd be doing you a kind of turn by offering them for *ten* thousand."

"Now *you're* showing symptoms of madness. Whatever the taint on the Egg, I'm still offering more than your initial asking price for the other items."

"Well, that depends on the depth of the taint, but perhaps we can compromise. Seventy-five hundred."

"Six thousand. No more."

"But, my friend, those ships will be a dead loss to me in your possession, and I *do* have expenses in my business. Staggering expenses. Seven thousand 'cords. No less."

"I sympathize, Amik, but existence is in itself an expensive undertaking. Sixty-five hundred, then."

"Sixty-seven fifty," he rejoined firmly.

Alex seemed to consider the sum, but it was Amik's tone and attitude he was assessing. Finally, he nodded.

"Very well. Sixty-seven fifty. And the rest of the terms are agreeable? The equipment, the computer input, the Cave of Springs, and a temporary work force of forty men?"

"I prefer the other figure. Thirty men."

"Compromise again? Thirty-five?"

The Lord of Thieves laughed. "No, by the God! Forty it will be. I won't have it said I lay too close a bargain."

"Who would ever say that of you, Amik? We're in agreement then?"

"Agreed." Amik extended a hand to seal the bargain.

And with that handshake, Alex allowed himself an inward sigh of relief. "When can I start on the Cave of Springs? When will the equipment be available?"

"The total will take some time to ... uh, acquire, but the construction machinery and your work force will be available as soon as the Ivanoi Egg is in this room in actuality, not just in image. Your impatience might serve to get it to me all the sooner." He gave the Egg one last look, then turned off the holojector and closed the drape. "Now, would you share some bragnac with me to toast the bargain?"

Recognizing this as part of the ritual, Alex nodded. "Thank you, Amik. That would be a pleasure." He sat down at one end of a couch, and while Amik poured Marsay Cabray with obvious anticipation, he waited, trying to keep his thoughts in rein, to think ahead to the Cave of Springs, not ahead to a wedding.

Perralt should be calling Ben this afternoon. A tenuous and indirect link—what could be said through two people?—but for now it must suffice. He roused himself and called up a smile as he took the tiny glass Amik offered.

Then Amik sank into his chair with a sigh and lifted his glass in a salute. "Fortune, brother."

Alex echoed the gesture. "Fortune, Amik."

They both lapsed into silence while they sipped the bragnac, Amik's eyes closed in delectation. But a moment later, they snapped open and fixed on the console beside him on the table, his attention called to it by a soft chime. He irritably touched a button.

"What is it, Yuba?"

Alex could hear the responding voice only indistinctly. Names, undoubtedly Outsiders; someone awaiting audience with the Lord of Thieves.

"The oval room, Yuba," he replied curtly. "Tell them to

wait for me there." Then he cut him off.

"Amik, we can continue this another time if—"

"No, no, I won't rush Marsay Cabray for anyone." He took time to savor another sip, which apparently restored his good humor. "It's not a matter of imminent importance, anyway. A preliminary TacComm meeting, so to speak. One must plan ahead. Good planning is ninety percent of the battle, so they say."

Alex raised an eyebrow, surprised at Amik's casually revelatory tone; it seemed to invite inquiry.

"Is the Brotherhood about to embark on a war, Amik? That seems a highly unprofitable venture."

He laughed at that. "Indeed. Not a war; only a campaign of sorts." He held his glass to catch the light, smiling to himself. "In exactly seventy-seven days Helen will be host to a veritable horde of Elite, along with their ranks of servants and techs, not to mention the Broadcasting Guild contingents. A cornucopia, my friend, and don't think the merchanters up in the Inside aren't designing their own campaigns on that flow of 'cords. It behooves me, as Lord of the Brotherhood, to see that some of those 'cords flow into *our* coffers, does it not?"

Alex was hard put not to stare at him, and the only question in his mind was *why*? The occasion of the arrival of those Elite hordes was the wedding of Karlis Selasis and Adrien Eliseer.

Amik knew his identity; this couldn't conceivably be inadvertant or purposeless. Was it simply a flaunting of that knowledge or a sardonic testing? No doubt Amik enjoyed playing games, but games of such a sadistic nature?

Amik seemed blithely lost in contemplation of the golden contents of his glass. Alex wasn't deceived. He said evenly, "You'd be derelict in your duty *not* to take advantage of this cornucopia, Amik."

"Exactly, and I'd be especially derelict not to relieve Lord Bane-Eye in particular of some of his bounty. That's what the Brothers call Orin Selasis. They think the patch hides an eye capable of malevolent power. I call him Lord Cyclops."

There *was* a purpose in this. Selasis hadn't been introduced randomly.

"Very apt, Amik. Why do you have such an antipathy for Lord Orin—other than his complaints to the Directorate about your depredations on his ships?"

"Oh, my dear Alex, that's to be expected, not despised."

Then his eyes hardened into cold, black slits. "He's a man totally devoid of honor. A man who hasn't the faintest conception of it on any level. His word is so much sand in the wind. And a short-sighted man, our Lord Cyclops, with a tendency to excess. I suppose you find that amusing—the Lord of Thieves, surrounded by indulgences, casting stones of contempt at a man born to his comforts."

"I recognize the infinite variations in excess."

Amik's furred robes quivered with a rumbling laugh, but after a moment that faded to be replaced by a slight frown and a long, studied sigh.

"I find I have mixed feelings about this wedding. I can't regret the promise of replenishing the Brotherhood's coffers, but on the other hand, I am, whether you believe it or not, a sentimental man. It seems unfortunate that a young woman of Lady Adrien's caliber should be married to Karlis Selasis, a contemptible smug who inherited none of his father's audacity, but all his taste for excess."

Perhaps it *was* sadism. To Alex, in his stunned bewilderment, that seemed the only answer. Anger enabled him to maintain self-control; he wouldn't give Amik the satisfaction of the slightest discernible reaction. He remained outwardly relaxed, his expression one of polite agreement, but not relaxed enough to trust his voice.

Amik went on casually, "I got the impression from Jael— by inference and guess, be assured, not from anything he actually said—that the Phoenix also regrets this marriage."

Alex held on to his anger and the cold self-control it afforded him.

"The Phoenix shares your antipathy for Selasis, Amik. We consider the marriage a disastrous union in terms of its effect on the balance of power in the Concord, and the future of Centauri."

"Well, it *would* tend to put Centauri in Orin's pocket. I suppose the Phoenix has tried to circumvent this union."

"Of course, and obviously without success."

Amik nodded, idly tipping up his glass. "If this dilemma were mine, I'd take the obvious solution. After all, a marriage can't take place without a groom. But I gather the Phoenix balks at taking the obvious solution in matters of this sort."

Alex said tightly, "It balks at assassination."

"Ah. A gentlemanly attitude, and honorable. Now, you

know I honor honor, but I recognize it as an expensive virtue."
His smile was enigmatic, yet equivocally pensive. "Strange,
isn't it, that in the history of crimes and deception attributable
to Selasis, no weapon can be found to put an end to his history.
But, of course, he's a devious man."

"Lord Orin leaves no tracks. At least, none that can be
proven to be his."

"And you must have identifiable tracks, since you're too
honorable, or too much a gentleman, to simply fell the beast
before it leaves more tracks."

There was no sarcasm in that; it seemed only a recognition
of existing limits. Alex was again perplexed by the direction
of the conversation, and that blunted his anger.

"Identifying the beast with its tracks is one way to fell it."

"Ah. Well, fortune in that, my friend. Now, if *I* were
seeking a weapon against Selasis in this gentlemanly manner,
I'd look into *recent* Selasis history." A weighted pause, then,
"I'd take a close look at Karlis's illness of last year."

Alex's silence now was only a product of surprise, which
sent him delving futilely into memory in pursuit of any reference to a recent illness suffered by Karlis Selasis. Ben and
Erica had never failed to give him all available information on
the Directorate Lords, and particularly on the Selasids. Karlis
had suffered an illness SI didn't know about? It seemed impossible.

Then his eyes narrowed. Still no memory of an illness, but
something about an absence, a trip of some sort. . . .

He was on his feet, pacing, no longer concerned about
withholding his reactions. Whatever Amik's intentions, Alex
realized now they weren't sadistic.

Karlis had been away from Concordia a full month. That
had been soon after Janeel Shang Selasis's death, and the public
rationale was grief. The Phoenix had taken the more cynical
view that Orin simply wanted Karlis out of sight so his evident
lack of grief wouldn't become an embarrassment.

A month—where? One of the private House retreats. . . .

Alex turned to face Amik. "The Lima retreat. Karlis spent
a month there after his first—Janeel Shang's death. And he
was *ill?*"

Amik sent out two spaced puffs of smoke, smiling beatifically.

"Extremely. But don't be chagrined that you didn't know

about it. As you say, Orin leaves no tracks, and the main reason is that he has Bruno Hawkwood to cover them. Now, there's a remarkable man. The Master of Shadows. You've heard that appellation? Yes. Perhaps the Concord is fortunate Bruno wasn't born into Orin's place, because *he* is a truly dangerous man. Religion. I never trust a religious man. And I know something about the Order of Gamaliel. That's why I mistrust Bruno. It gives him admirable self-discipline, yet deprives him of conscience with that fatalistic molly-doddle. 'Whatever is must be, because it is ordained to be by being.' Pah!"

Alex managed a fleeting smile. "And you say Hawkwood was assigned to cover the tracks of Karlis's illness?"

"Indeed. The moment it was discovered, Karlis was entrusted to Bruno's loving care."

Alex went to the one uncushioned chair and forced himself to sit quietly in it. "What kind of illness required Hawkwood's 'loving care'?"

"Yes, that's the point, isn't it? And I must admit I didn't learn the entire story until after the fact, so to speak. Now, Karlis, as I've noted, has his father's tendencies to excess, much to the delight of some of my associates in Concordia. Inevitably, one of his excesses is . . . pleasures of the flesh, shall we say. I can't simply say *women*: his tastes are too catholic. He also has a tendency to carelessness." Amik took a long pull on his cigar, looking directly at Alex, who waited, motionless and intent.

"Well, my friend, Karlis's illness was in the nature of a venereal disease, and an extremely virulent strain. He recovered, obviously, although that was for a time in grave doubt, but he didn't come through the experience unscathed." Amik couldn't resist a slight pause for effect. "Karlis Selasis, sole heir to the First Lordship of Badir Selasis is . . . impotent. And more. He's sterile."

Alex came to his feet, too stunned to move further, and it seemed that behind his eyes, his brain had suddenly been reduced to a gelid mass incapable of coherent function.

"Holy God . . ." That he could speak at all seemed only raw reflex. "Are you sure? How do you know?"

"My agents in the House could tell me very little, actually, although I *was* aware that Karlis was ill before he was whisked away to Lima, but the Lima retreat was sealed without a crack. Karlis, however, needed a doctor, and one of the house physicians was chosen, although for the records he was assigned to the Pars estate. Dr. Levit Monig. Now, the good doctor wasn't a stupid man, and once he diagnosed the disease and its effects he realized he was in a very precarious position. Our Lord Cyclops isn't one to trust people, particularly not someone possessed of knowledge that could destroy him. The Board of Succession wouldn't pass off sterility of the sole heir if it were brought to their attention. So Dr. Monig saw Karlis through the worst of his illness, then somehow—I'm not exactly sure how, and it was a remarkable feat—escaped the retreat and managed to reach the city of Lima, where he fled into the Outside."

Alex nodded. "Then that's how you learned about him?"

"Yes. Bruno Hawkwood made it known in the Outside that Monig was worth five thousand 'cords to Orin, and when the Brotherhood clanhead in Lima found him, his first thought was to collect the reward. Monig, however, had filled his medical case with loose valuables before he left the retreat, and it was enough to offset the temptation of the headprice. The Brothers are inclined to avoid dealings with Bruno unless absolutely necessary. When the clanhead heard Monig's story, he immediately notified me, and I invited the doctor to come to Helen as my guest."

"He's here, then? Amik, I must talk to him! A tape—if I could get his testimony on tape . . ."

It was the slow, solemn shaking of Amik's head that stopped him. He asked the question because it had to be asked, but he had already read the answer in Amik's face.

"Where is he?"

"In the Heavenly Realm, if you believe in such things. He's dead, Alex. He wasn't a young man, and he suffered from chronic hypertension. The circumstances of his escape naturally enough put a great deal of strain on him. The very day he was to be brought here, he suffered a stroke. We maintain infirmaries in every clan HQ, but his situation was beyond human remedy."

Alex, stood with his hands clenched at his sides. "But isn't there—the clanhead, didn't he record anything Monig said? For the God's sake, he must have realized . . ." But Amik was again shaking his head in somber silence, and Alex turned away, aching in every muscle, body chilled, it seemed, to the bone.

A weapon against Selasis that came like a gift from the

God, made impotent—that word! The cruel irony in it now—because there was no proof, nothing to present to the Board of Succession, to force an investigation, to force the physical examination that would provide the proof.

Hearsay evidence from a Brotherhood clanhead? That would never even reach the Board. Monig's death? That proved nothing, and undoubtedly was on record as having occurred in Pars.

Karlis was sterile, yet that didn't stop Orin Selasis from arranging a marriage for him. Selasis *would* have an heir, and genetically it might be Karlis's; it wasn't unusual for Lords to maintain sperm reserves. The Board of Succession would under no circumstances accept "unnatural conception," but the risk of discovery was too remote to curtail the practice. And if this marriage couldn't be stopped—

The weapon was Karlis's sterility, and yet, unless it could be used, it was also Adrien's death warrant. If this marriage couldn't be stopped, there was no way she could avoid learning the deadly secret that Monig had recognized as his own death warrant. Selasis would let her live holding that secret only until she provided an heir.

And if shè tried to reveal the secret before she gave birth to an heir? She would be discouraged from that by any means imaginable to a dishonorable Lord and his conscienceless minion, but if all else failed, she would be disposed of, and another wife found for Karlis.

A voice reached him finally from a long distance; from a few meters away; now and here, in this room.

"Alex, if I had the proof, I'd give it over to you willingly. No tax on that, brother. But the proof was snatched from my hands, and all I can offer is knowledge. Still, in the right circumstances, knowledge is as powerful as proof."

The words seemed blurred at first, although Alex understood them. But only two loomed into comprehension. *I offer . . .*

That was the purpose of this involuted game of Amik's. A gift. No tax, brother. The gift of knowledge.

Alex turned slowly and looked down at the Lord of Thieves, cushioned and swathed in silks, brocades, and furs, all bought with the profits of illegal and even corrupt and corrupting enterprises, and at his waist, in its fancifully embellished sheath, the knife that symbolized his Lordship by the very fact that it had not always remained clean.

And yet—*I offer*...

Alex said softly, "Thank you, Amik."

"I told you, the debt is between you and Jael. I take no part—"

"No, Amik, this one is between you and me. Now, you have people waiting for you. I can't ask you to delay that longer." He didn't add that, for himself, he could no longer delay some time to be alone.

As Amik maneuvered his bulk out of the chair, Alex went to the table by the couch where he'd left his glass, found a swallow of bragnac left in it, and turned, lifting it in a salute.

"Fortune, brother."

Amik laughed, then said pointedly, "Thank you."

5.

"Good evening, Dr. Radek."

"Hello, Maya. Good to see you up and about after that virus siege."

The woman smiled pleasantly, but didn't break step.

"Thank you. It's good to *be* up." That ended the conversation; they were past each other now.

Erica continued down the corridor, crowded as the section dining hall disgorged its sated throngs. Two months ago, she'd have stopped to talk to Maya Bezain. A thesis had just been published at the University in Leda on anxiety translation processes, a subject of particular interest to both of them. But, except for pleasantries in passing, they didn't talk openly now. Maya was a loyal, and Erica didn't want to call Predis Ussher's attention to her. He kept both Erica and Ben under constant surveillance, and one object was to identify loyal members. Anyone seen too often in their company was suspect, and that was why the only conversations Erica indulged in outside her work, or in the strictest privacy, were with those members she knew to be uncommitted, or those she knew to be Ussher converts. And that was why she passed by old friends in the dining halls and sat down to eat with the "safe" uncommitted or converts.

It didn't make for pleasant meals, but she refused the alternative of eating in her apartment. She found the company people chose to keep as informative as Ussher did, and probably more so. The loyals had learned to choose their company carefully to protect each other, but the converts tended to group together with increasing exclusivity.

She stepped into a crowded lift shaft, found an empty handloop, and exchanged brief smiles with its occupants as she floated to Level 12. The corridor was empty as she approached HS 1, except for the person following her. She didn't turn to see who it was, but she could hear the footsteps.

Then her step faltered, but only briefly. A faint shock against the skin at her waist like a silent buzz.

Someone was in her office or apartment.

The warning sensor was attached to the waistband of her slacsuit, and like the X^1 in the springsheath on her wrist, she never left HS 1 without it.

She glanced at her watch: 19:10. It would be Ben.

The lights were on in the work room, a signal that assured her it *was* Ben whose presence set off the contact alarm. She locked the 'screens behind her with a lectrikey, then turned on the vis-screen by the door and watched her follower pass. He would turn at the next cross-corridor and wait there out of sight. John Renz, comtech, Communications. He wasn't new to this duty.

She crossed to the office door, pressed her thumb to the lock, and waited the necessary ten seconds to be sure the security mechanisms were disengaged. The office was lighted, too, but it was empty. She locked the door and reset the sec-system, then repeated the entrance procedure at her apartment door. At this point the knotting resentment always threatened to slip out of control, and she had to concentrate on every move. She lived in an armed fortress, even though no crenellated battlements were visible; it was a pattern of living and thinking that was all bitterly alien to her.

Ben was waiting for her just inside the door. Erica turned with a sigh to the final locking and sec-system reset, and Ben smiled.

"I'm finally getting you trained. How are you, Erica?"

He was still in SSB black, and it emphasized the shadows ringing his eyes, the pallor that seemed so unnatural on his ruddy skin.

She said, "I'm fine, Ben, and I won't ask how you are. That way you won't have to tell me you slept like the Blessed—

whenever it was you last slept—and the ulcers haven't given you a twinge for days."

She went to the comconsole, tried two music bands, and settled for the quieter selection on the third. The music wasn't for confusing possible monitors; with Ben here she knew this room was safe. Habit; she always turned on a music band when she came into the apartment, and she wondered as she reached into the cabinet above the console for the brandy bottle if this weren't also becoming a habit.

It would never become a dangerous one. Ben brought the brandy from Leda, and he seldom had time to waste on such trivial errands.

"Will you have some, Ben?"

"Yes, thanks."

It probably wasn't good for his ulcers, but then what was? She poured a small amount into two plasex cups, frowning in annoyance. Brandy deserved crystal. Lately, she found herself resenting inconsequential things like this, resenting the three styleless slacsuits that constituted her wardrobe, the sterility of the prefab, modular furniture, and the processed, vitamin/protein-enriched, tasteless meals.

She handed Ben one of the cups. "Any news?"

In their personal code, that question had only one meaning: Any news of Andreas?

"No. We're still checking classification numbers and trying to trace SSB psychocontrollers."

She expected that negative response. If there *had* been news, he wouldn't have waited so long to tell her. The next inquiry was fast assuming the same ritualistic character.

"Any news about Val?"

He tasted his brandy, but without savoring it.

"Nothing. We've about exhausted all the Concord sources; DCs, hospitals, Guild centers. She didn't have an ident card, so she couldn't have gone off planet; without an ident, she couldn't get a ticket to anywhere."

"The Outside, Ben. That's the last resort, and that's probably where she is." *If* she's alive. Neither of them put that into words.

Ben nodded. "Alex said he'd talk to Jael about the protocol for enlisting the Brotherhood hounds. That's about the only hope if she's in the Outside."

"You talked to Alex?"

"Just signed off a few minutes ago, and to answer your first question, he's fine; safe and well."

Erica laughed and sat down at one end of the couch. "Then what's the answer to my next question? How did he fare in his bargaining session with Amik?"

Ben showed a little animation at that, and even a hint of the old off-balance smile.

"With flags flying. He got everything he asked for, including three Falcons free for six months—he got it all, Erica."

She tilted her head back against the cushions, smiling, savoring the heady and unfamiliar sensation of success.

"Thank the God. When will he have the equipment?"

"When Amik has the Ivanoi Egg, and that's set up with Fenn Lacroy and the loyals in the Concordia chapter. Alex gave Fenn all the information he'll need about the museum alarm systems and made recordings of the code words for the voice locks. They'll still work; nobody bothers to change voice codes for the dead."

"Does Alex have any idea how long it will take to get his HQ operational?"

"Two months, but he plans to take up full-time residence in two weeks."

"In a cave. Poor Alex. He has a tendency to claustrophobia. But he shouldn't have to tolerate it too long. One of these leads on Andreas *has* to pay off soon."

Ben only nodded as he tossed down the rest of his brandy; he put the cup on the console counter, then sat down in a chair near her.

"Erica, there's more. Amik told Alex another one of his stories today. This one was about Karlis Selasis."

She refrained from downing her brandy in one nerving swallow like Ben, although she had the feeling she might need it. Ben recounted the story in flat, matter-of-fact tones as she was sure Alex had told it to him. At first, she was too numb with shock to move, then she found herself on her feet, pacing. Just like Alex. The music became nerve-wracking. She went to the console and turned it off. Ben finished his account in a pressing silence.

She asked tightly, "Is it true, Ben?"

His elbows were propped on his knees, and his big hands moved, palms up, then fell limp again.

"Nothing we know about Karlis's stay in Lima refutes it. Alex believes it. He called this a gift from Amik. I can't quite swallow that, but he's right about one thing. Knowledge isn't proof, but it's better than ignorance."

At that, she was hard put not to weep. She didn't doubt it was very close to an exact quote. So tantalizing, this knowledge—was it better than ignorance for Alex?

"Will the knowledge alone stop this marriage, Ben?"

His head came up, eyes narrowed. "I don't know, but eventually it could destroy Selasis. Sooner or later we'll find a chink in his armor, and we'll have that blade ready to ram in."

"That doesn't answer my question."

He rose and went to the console counter to pour more brandy into his cup. She thought of his ulcers, but said nothing, nodding when he offered her a refill.

"Erica, we'll use this . . . knowledge in every way we can to stop the marriage; you know that."

"What *can* you do with it?"

"The old gossip ploy. Get the rumors circulating in Elite circles. Supposedly they'll come from the Outside, and we'll feed it out in bits so every few days there'll be a new piece of the story to be passed around. They'll love it in the Elite."

"But any concrete action must come from Loren Eliseer."

"Yes. All we can do is fire up the rumors and hope we produce enough smoke to make Eliseer think he's justified in asking for a Board of Succession investigation before he trusts his daughter to the Selasids. We can make Orin more uncomfortable by hinting that Monig left some sort of death testament, but in the end it'll depend on Eliseer."

"And if he doesn't have the courage to risk his House on a rumor? If this marriage does take place, Adrien will be in a very dangerous position."

He went back to his chair, shoulders set tensely. "Don't you think I know that? We've got agents in the House. We'll protect her as best we can, but Adrien Eliseer isn't our only problem right now."

"Ben, don't you think I know *that?*" She smiled as he looked up at her, relieved to see him relax slightly.

"Sorry, Erica, I'm just . . ."

"Worried," she finished for him, "and if you weren't, *I'd* be worried about you. And one of the things you're worried about is Alex's relationship with Adrien, isn't it?"

He sagged back, staring unhappily into his cup. "I guess so. I just don't understand why, after nearly five years, he decided to revive an old . . . romance. Whatever you want to call it."

"I'd never call it that, and the reasons for reviving it at this particular time are obvious."

"But, Erica, we all *had* personal lives and people we loved, but we gave them up when we joined the Phoenix. That's part of the entrance requirements, and every member knows it."

"Ben, he knows it, too, but..." She paused, searching for words. "For one thing, he met Adrien when they were both little more than children, and it's a generally accepted principle in psychology that relationships established in childhood or early adolescence tend to create strong and enduring bonds. Their backgrounds and personality matrices are so similar and complementary, it was almost inevitable that the bonds became permanent."

"All right," Ben interposed impatiently, "I didn't say giving her up would be easy, but—"

"What I'm saying, Ben, is that it's impossible. I'm sure Alex didn't realize that when he joined us, but I can tell you this: Adrien is as much a part of him psychically as his right arm is physically."

"So where does that leave us?"

"Where we always were. There's one thing you must keep in mind. We call him and think of him as Alex Ransom, but Alex Ransom's value to the Phoenix is limited to his leadership potential and his Confleet training. The man on whom all the plans and hopes of the Phoenix depend *isn't* Alex Ransom. Our hopes are built on the Lord Alexand."

Ben studied her, and it seemed the scrutiny was a long one, but she sat it out. At length, his taut posture relaxed and he nodded acceptance.

"Erica, you always have a way of putting things straight."

"Psychic splints are my specialty. And now I think you should worry about getting some sleep. When do you have to be back at the Cliff?"

"07:00 tomorrow morning, but I have to be in my office here by 03:00. Well, that gives me about six hours." He rose and started for the door, glancing in passing at the brandy bottle. "I guess I'd better pick up another bottle tomorrow while I'm in Leda."

He'd been saying that for the past week, but she didn't remind him. She went with him to the door and waited while he opened the locks.

"Good night, Ben." Then she added wearily, "Don't worry, I'll raise the drawbridges after you."

6.

Amik's summons was a source of annoyance, and a time-consuming one with the two hundred-kilometer 'car flight and the long passage via airscooter through the labyrinths of mine shafts. Alex had almost forgotten to activate his face-screen when he arrived at the shafts lock and met the Brotherhood "blade" sent by Amik to act as his guard and guide, and now his annoyance lengthened his stride as he moved through the arched corridors toward Amik's sanctum.

A matter of some interest, the Lord of Thieves had said, and refused to amplify that engimatic statement. Amik enjoyed his little games.

But Alex was in no mood for games. He had only three loyal Phoenix techs to oversee the work at the Cave of Springs. The Brothers Amik had assigned him were conditioned, but it still made him uncomfortable to be away when Jael wasn't there to supervise them, and he was in the Inside today on assignment for the Helen chapter.

Alex wiped a hand across his forehead, and it came away streaked with grime. The work crew was enlarging one of the chambers in the Cave for the hangar. The dust was full of bitter reminders; the Kasai Orongo mines. He wondered how long he could live in a place that continually called up such memories.

He was expected. The blade stopped in Amik's anteroom, where Yuba glanced up from his desk and casually waved Alex through. Within the sanctum he paused, undecided whether to laugh or swear, finding Amik, as usual, at ease in his lush chair, filling the air with the sweet scent of his tobacco, golden teeth revealed in a languid smile. In the background, a Gariletti *Sarbande* cast its sinuous strains.

But Amik wasn't alone.

At first Alex didn't recognize the young woman who was sitting on one of the couches, tense, wary, and, despite her obvious effort to hide it, frightened. She wore a filmy, tawdry costume designed to enhance her physical attributes in the most blatant manner, and her face was marked with the remains of heavy cosmetics that spoiled her clear skin.

187

It was Valentin Severin, and for a moment Alex was overwhelmed with the old anger, yet behind the fear and degradation in her eyes there was still a spark of defiance. When he saw no hint of recognition, he realized his face-screen was still on. He switched it off and saw her eyes widen, defiance—and fear—dissolving in bewilderment.

"Alex? Is it—oh, dear God . . . Alex—" She rose, started to come to him, then broke into tears, which seemed to anger her and add to her confusion. He eased her back down onto the couch and accepted the linett handkerchief Amik offered with only a brief nod of acknowledgment.

"Val, you're safe here." He pulled her clenched hands away from her face and gently wiped away the ugly smears of cosmetics with her tears. "It's all over."

She recovered faster than he expected, finally taking the handkerchief to finish the job herself, frowning at the dirtied cloth.

"I'm all right, Alex. Oh, I'm sorry, I never . . . cry." Then, with a glance at Amik, "But what are you—I mean . . ."

"What am I doing in this den of thieves? I'll explain that later." He straightened, noting the glint of laughter behind Amik's hooded eyes.

"My friend, I hope you're duly impressed. To find such a one as this is like finding a single grain of sand in the Midhar. And yet . . ." He made a little flourish toward Val with his cigar holder. "You asked, and I have delivered."

"And I'm sure it will cost me dearly. Where did you find her?"

"In Leda; in the Outside. She had been taken . . . ah, shall we say, under the wing of an associate of mine."

Val glared at him. "Under the wing! That slimy—"

"I'm duly impressed," Alex cut in, "with your efficiency, Amik."

"Ah! I should hope so. It was no easy task—" He stopped as the door slid open, his initial frown quickly restored to a smile. "Jael, you got my message."

Jael didn't answer, stopped in his tracks inside the door, his dark eyes fixed on Val. And Val, again taken by surprise, could only stare blankly at him.

Jael asked curtly of Amik, "Where was she?"

"The young woman's past adventures seem a matter of extraordinary interest." He puffed at his cigar, regarding his son with patient amusement. "Leda, Jael."

He glanced at her filmy costume, his voice betraying his angry disgust.

"In one of Powlo's serallios?"

"In his main serallio, as a matter of fact. He was quite taken with her and very reluctant to part with her."

"I'm sure he was." Jael approached Val, but with uncharacteristic hesitancy. "Val, I'm sorry. If you were . . . harmed in any way . . ."

She blinked at him, still bewildered, then looked down at her clasped hands, cheeks flaming.

"No, I wasn't . . . I'm all right."

Alex studied Jael curiously. Val had obviously made a lasting impression on him in Fina. Then he glanced at his watch.

"Amik, I must get back to the Cave. I'm not only impressed, but grateful to you for finding Val, and—"

"Well, my friend, gratitude is always appreciated, but, you understand, some effort was involved . . ."

"And I'll be responsible," Alex assured him, "for any expenses incurred in the search. You have my word."

Amik's glance went to the curtained niche where the Ivanoi Egg now resided in shining splendor.

"And I value your word, my friend." Then his eyes slid across to Val, his lips curled in a faint smile. "However, I'm not sure I'll accept your recompense. I find myself taken with the fair Ferra, too. I always had a weakness for green eyes and blonde hair. Ah, yes, I can understand Powlo's reluctance to part with her, and I'm not sure *I* will."

Val was white, more with anger than fear, and that seemed to add to Amik's amusement until Jael stepped in, his eyes cold and stone-hard, to cut his game short.

"Father, you do yourself—and me—down with this gim. Now, one off, the 'fair Ferra' is uppercaste in all but birth, and she'll be treated as such. I lay edict for her; blood edict. I call her friend and sister." A slight pause; Amik's eyebrows lifted. "And there'll be no gaffing at Alex's expense. Powlo owed up on you, to the neck, and there was no tax for you on the gim."

Amik only laughed at that, a response that confounded Val; she didn't know Amik's penchant for games or understand that Jael's revelatory anger was the object of this one.

"So. Run short by my own kith." Then, with a long sigh, "But, so be it. Alex, take your pretty lostling, and your gratitude will be recompense enough, apparently, since my son has developed such a taste for honesty." Then Amik looked at Val with an engaging smile. "Forgive an old dodder his foolishness, my dear. Valentin. A lovely name, and a lovely young woman. Now—" He put on a frown for Alex and Jael. "Go with! I have no more time to waste on lessons in honesty at my son's hands."

Jael sent him a brief, annoyed look, then offered his arm to Val. "Alex, where shall I take her?"

"The Cave. But first you might get her some more practical clothing. Are you off duty with the chapter now?"

"Yes. For a few hours, anyway."

"Then you can escort us to the shafts lock. I'll wait for you here."

Val went with Jael without hesitation, but cast a questioning look back at Alex before the door closed behind them.

Amik was smiling faintly through a veil of smoke.

"It seems my son is full of secrets. Apparently he and the Ferra have met before. Alex, will you take supper with me tonight?"

"Thank you, no. I have too much work at the Cave."

Amik sighed gustily. "My friend, you've hardly come up for air these last ten days. It isn't healthy or reasonable."

"But necessary," Alex laughed. "Amik, thanks for finding the 'lostling.' Again, I'm indebted to you."

"From the look of it, Jael's the one most indebted."

"Then this one is between you and Jael."

Amik nodded, smiling wryly. "So it seems."

7.

Alex set the doorway shock screens as he left the small, rock-hewn bedroom. He set them for Val's protection, not to imprison her there. The sleeping rooms were cut into the walls of the large natural chamber that presently served as a dormitory for the Brotherhood workers. But Val wouldn't be leaving her room soon. When he left her, she was already succumbing to the inevitable reaction and exhaustion.

He found himself smiling, and there was reason enough for it. Val Severin would recover, and Predis Ussher would find an ally turned into an enemy. And this was one problem that had resolved itself positively. In that it was unique.

He paused outside his own sleeping room and looked down

the tunnel connecting this chamber with the next—the chamber that would house the comcenter. It would be functional in three weeks, and within six weeks his HQ in exile would be self-sufficient and independent of Amik and the Brothers, and that would be another occasion of profound satisfaction. '

It would be especially satisfying to be rid of the Brotherhood work crew, hard, wary-eyed men who prowled the chambers like wolves and, even when stripped all but naked against the daytime heat, never removed the knives sheathed at their sides. But they were hard workers, especially under Jael's sharp eye, and they were not only conditioned, but Jael had laid blood edict for the "Insiders" supervising them. There had been no discipline problems, except for a few brawls among themselves, and the knives had never been drawn.

Still, Alex wouldn't be sorry to see them gone.

He went into his room and set the doorscreens, then stripped off his shirt and unfastened the X^1 sleeve sheath. The shirt was soaked with perspiration, and even without it he felt no cooler. Yet in a few hours, in the Midhar night, he would be uncomfortably cold. But, as Jael had promised, it was more livable here than on the surface; there his blood would literally boil at noon and freeze at midnight.

This room—he found himself thinking of it as his cell— was larger than the one assigned Val, but only because it housed a bank of monitoring screens and a comconsole. His hand moved across the controls, and six screens activated, showing him different parts of the cave.

In the hangar, where Jael was supervising the bulk of the Brotherhood crew, blasting lasers threw up dense clouds of dust; the men, wearing filter masks, moved like faceless wraiths through a hellish and bitterly connotative scene. But the work was going well; the inner locks for the surface ship access tunnel could be installed tomorrow.

Another screen showed less violent activity: the comcenter, a cavern thirty meters in diameter that would be the heart of the COS HQ. Already it had been reduced to that initialed shorthand. Ten Brothers were at work here under the aegis of three face-screened men—Phoenix comtechs, defectors from Ussher's Phoenix—and, in time, this chamber would be comparable to the Fina comcenter, if on a smaller scale.

Alex frowned and looked at his watch. Ben would be in Leda now, but Erica was on stand-by. He put on a transceiver headset, then set the call seq on the microwave console. There was still no visual image, and these disembodied conversations were an added irritant.

"Radek on line."

"How's the weather?" he asked.

"I'm clear, Alex. How are you?"

"Hot and dusty, but otherwise very well."

"How's the installation going?"

"On schedule on every front. My next major hurdle is an MT."

"Ben's been working on that. M'Kim has most of the raw materials for the MTs for the Corvets. He's already set up an assembly area, so we'll just purloin what you need. Ben thought it would be safer to trans an MT to you piece by piece than for you to try to capture one of the Corvets. The components are small; they can be hidden or disguised very easily."

"We'll work out the details later." He shifted the images on one screen to the surface and the glaring, barren vista of the Midhar. On the southern horizon, a procession of black, volcanic cones rose stark against the yellow sands. "Erica, I have some good news for you. Valentin Severin is here at the COS."

"*Val?* Oh, thank the God! Is she all right, Alex? Where *was* she? How did you—"

"Give me a chance, Erica," he put in, laughing. "She's exhausted and probably a little malnourished, but otherwise unharmed. Amik's hounds found her in Leda in the main ser-allio of one of the Brothers; Powlo, in fact. But the hounds reached her before Powlo introduced her to his line. Anyway, she has no illusions now about the great lover, Hendrick, or about Ussher."

"No, I'm sure she doesn't. I'd like to talk to her."

"She's sleeping now, and she needs it. I'll have her call you tomorrow. I think she'll be just as anxious to talk to you." He turned from the screens and sat down on the narrow bed, nerving himself to ask the question. He knew the answer, but some stubborn compulsion always drove him to ask it. "Any news on Andreas?"

Her long sigh was as much expected as the answer.

"No. Nothing new."

Alex stared at the black stone across the narrow width of the room. "Well, they haven't announced his execution. He's still alive, Erica. Any field reports I should know about?"

"Yes, but there's something else that's come up in the last hour. We've only had fragmentary reports so far. You'd better turn on your PubliCom screen; there should be some reports on the newscasts soon. There's been an uprising in the Ivanoi mine complex on Ganymede. We anticipated something of the sort there, you know, and the uprising itself was relatively limited, but the 'bubble systems were at least partially incapacitated. We don't know yet if there was a total failure or how long it lasted."

If it was more than thirty seconds on Ganymede, it didn't matter, not even if it was a partial failure. Jupiter's radiation belts would make even that lethal. And if there had been a total failure—

He sat stunned and silent, skin crawling with an irrational chill. For those who lived outside the protective atmospheres of Terra or Pollux, it was a fear as basic as the infantile fear of falling: fear of the loss of those artificial wombs that closed out the ravenous, frigid vacuum of space.

"Any idea of the casualties?" he asked dully.

"Not yet, but if the 'bubbles were totally knocked out, the fatalities can't be less than fifty thousand."

"Fifty thous——Holy God!" He ran his hands through his hair distractedly. He couldn't translate that number into comprehensible terms.

It was perhaps inevitable that one of these uprisings would turn into a real disaster in the vacuum colonies. It would also be a disaster for the liberals on the Directorate, a disaster for all Bonds, for the Concord. He went to the comconsole and turned on the PubliCom screen, leaving the sound off, watching a clown in a suit of flashing lights entertaining the children of the worlds with skillfully inept acrobatics. No news bulletin yet.

"Erica, keep me up to date on this, and get me any information you can on what triggered the uprising. There was only one strong Shepherd in the Ganymede compounds, old Matheus; he died six months ago, and I didn't have much confidence in his successor. And as soon as the COS HQ is operational, the Brother will have to go on tour again."

"I know. I've been correlating field reports, and I can pinpoint the compounds that need attention first. I'll get that in a tape capsule tomorrow and send it to you. I have two other reports almost ready, too. One is a general stat report on the ROM, and the other—"

"The ROM?" He stared at the flashing clown, finding a dark irony in its antics.

"Oh, I guess that was one of the things that came to a head

while you were vacationing at the Cliff. ROM stands for Rights of Man, an extremist liberal student organization headed by a young agitator we've been watching for some time, Damon Kamp. It's a small group, but adept at attracting attention, and that tends to polarize liberal and conservative factions in the Fesh. I have another report for you, too; the Court of Lords is drafting a resolution censuring Galinin. Their main complaint is taxes and 'general disorder,' and it's indicative of reactionary tendencies among the Elite."

Alex turned away from the silenced clown and sagged down on the bed again, frowning at his begrimed hands.

"I suppose the Court *doesn't* have anything better to do, but Galinin hardly deserves that. Anything else important?"

"Yes. The report you've very carefully refrained from asking about—the progress of the rumor campaign against Selasis."

There was a container of water and a cup on the table by the bed. No dispensers here at the Cave of Springs, only a stringently rationed liter of water. He poured out half a cup, annoyed to find his hand so unsteady.

"Is it working, Erica?"

"Well, the story is making the rounds, and as Ben predicted, the Elite love it. In fact, some incredible embellishments have been added along the way. Both Orin and Karlis are privately livid, but publicly aloof. Karlis, of course, doesn't manage that as well as his father. Last night he went storming into some of his old haunts in the Outside in Concordia threatening to have the entire Outside district shut down if the rumors weren't stopped and the culprits guilty of spreading them turned over to him personally. A PubliCom news team caught him in action at one float. The story went out on the evening newscasts in Concordia."

"What about Eliseer? Has Ben heard from Perralt?"

"This morning. He'll fill you in when he gets back from Leda. He only had time to give me the highlights. The rumors have definitely reached Lord Loren, though. Perralt went out on a limb to talk to him about it, and Eliseer *is* worried, Alex. He even asked Perralt's medical opinion—if sterility could result from any known type of venereal infection. Perralt assured him it was possible, of course, and quoted medical confreres on a recent outbreak in Concordia of a particularly virulent strain."

Alex took a swallow of water, wincing at the bitter, mineral taste of it. It seemed to catch in his throat.

"Did Eliseer give Perralt any hint of what he might do?"

"No. Perralt said he wouldn't hazard a guess at what his final decision will be."

Alex looked up at the stone walls. "Erica, I *must* have a direct line of communication with Perralt. I don't ask or expect it with Adrien; it's too risky, I know, and I know Perralt is in SI and responsible first to Ben, but I would hope Ben has enough faith in me to realize I won't abuse the . . . privilege." He drained the cup and put it down, aware that he was betraying himself with that irritable tone. "Be grateful for small luxuries, Erica, like pure water."

She laughed at that. "I gather you've slipped back into the stone age temporarily. Alex, have you talked to Ben about a direct line to Perralt?"

He rose and returned to the comconsole. "Well . . . no."

"Then I think you should."

"You've softened him up for it, I assume? All right, Erica, I'll talk to him. Now, what's the situation there?"

"The same. Both sides are still working at covert levels; nothing's out in the open yet."

"What about this war of nerves you were talking about last week?"

"I've come up with a tentative program, but I'll need some recordings from you. I have a series of statements for you to tape, then Ben will plant some microspeakers. The timing will be important. Ideally, no one should be present except Predis when the speakers activate, but there should be witnesses close enough to catch his reaction."

Alex smiled coldly. "Send me the scripts. I'll give them the best dramatic rendering I can manage. What about Lyden and Bruce? Are they ready to leave Fina when I get set up here?"

"Yes, they're ready and willing any time—" She stopped, and Alex saw the reason before him on the vidicom. The dancing clown was abruptly displaced by a sober newscaster, and superimposed over his image were the red-limned words, SPECIAL NEWS BULLETIN.

Alex reached for the sound control.

"All right, Erica, we'll finish this later." After the disaster, he thought grimly; the latest disaster.

PHOENIX MEMFILES: DEPT HUMAN SCIENCES: BASIC SCHOOL
(HS/BS)
SUBFILE: LECTURE, BASIC SCHOOL 29 FEBUAR 3252
            GUEST LECTURER: RICHARD LAMB
            SUBJECT: POST–DISASTERS HISTORY:
            PANTERRAN CONFEDERATION (2903–3104)
DOC LOC #819/219–1253/1812–1648–2923252

One question should be asked in considering the Golden
Age of the PanTerran Confederation—or even in considering the post-Mankeen Concord—and that is, What happened to the promised leap to the stars? Why have we leapt
no further than to Centauri, our nearest stellar neighbor?

One answer is inherent in the Confederation's method
of funding and organizing exploratory expeditions. As I've
noted, that was left to individual Houses or coalitions of
Houses, and it was done in the spirit of speculation, in the
hope of making a profit on an investment. Exploration for
its own sake tends to be highly unprofitable, although it
must be said to the credit of the Confederation Lords that
many of them did invest in such nonprofit investigations
in the sciences. However, with his fiscal survival at stake,
a Lord might invest a small percentage of his revenues in
a venture with little hope of future return, but he won't
invest a large percentage unless he's very sure of a return,
and stellar exploration is an expensive undertaking. The
manufacture and "fueling" of MAM-An generators alone
is a major fiscal factor, and the greater the distance involved, the greater the cost. Sometimes I think we tend to
forget that SynchShift doesn't eliminate distance, or the
energy requisite to moving a body across it; it only elimi-
nates—or, rather, modifies—the time factor.

Still, the Lords of the Confederation did invest very
heavily in the leap to the stars, although more money and
effort went into colonizing Centauri, as well as further development of the established Solar System colonies. In
3079, just after the discovery of the Twin Planets, when

196

enthusiasm for extrasolar exploration was running high, a coalition of three hundred Houses pooled their resources to finance a series of voyages beyond Centauri, the last of which lifted off in Febuar of 3104, only three months before the fateful meeting of dissident Lords in Lionar Mankeen's Mosk Estate.

By that time, however, the number of Lords in the stellar coalition had dropped to 140, and the loss of enthusiasm wasn't due entirely to the disruptive effects of Mankeen's impending revolution. It was a natural result of disappointment. When the first reports came in from Alpha Centauri A describing planets that were not only inhabitable as vacuum colonies, but one so much like Terra that people could walk about on it sans vacuum suits in perfect comfort, the Lords of the Confederation—ignoring the negative evidence of Proxima and Alpha Centauri B—concluded that the existence of such planets in any solar system must be the rule and not the exception. Those Terrene planets were important not only as future sites of colonization, or for what they might produce themselves—without the expense of habitat systems—but as in-system backup and supply bases for vacuum colonies, which would lower the cost of resource exploitation considerably.

However, such Terrene planets proved to be the exception in our stellar neighborhood, although, if you could take a galactic average, that probably wouldn't be the case. The Confederation coalition's first ventures beyond Centauri, to Barnard's star and Lalande, were total disappointments. The former offered only three gaseous giants, protosuns larger than Jupiter with even more extensive radiation belts, and the latter nothing at all in the shape of planets. The coalition gamely dug deeper into its collective coffers and built more advanced and powerful MAM-An generators and sent another expedition to Sirius, and there met with some success in the first four planets of Sirius A. But they found no watery Terrene planets, only small images of Mercury and Mars. Still, the initial surveys indicated huge lodes of ores of many kinds, and Ivanoi, Cameroodo, and Shang established outposts on all of Sirius A's inner planets.

The coalition pressed on, although at that point, in 3091, their numbers were already reduced to 180. The House of Mankeen, by the way, was one of the early members of the coalition, but dropped out in 3089 when Lionar Mankeen became First Lord. Whatever his vision of the future of humankind, it did not include the leap to the stars, and it was his contention that the stellar expeditions were immorally wasteful and that their only purpose was to make the Lords wealthier and more powerful, while the Fesh and Bonds languished in servitude and slavery. The Fesh and Bonds were indeed languishing, but it's difficult to establish a direct correlation between their plight and the stellar expeditions.

At any rate, more expeditions were sent out, to Epsilon Eridani, 61 Cygni A, and Procyon A. It was only in the Procyon system that more exploitable planets were found, and again, they would have to be vacuum colonies. No new Terras were discovered. They *are* out there; you have only to talk with any of our astronomers to be assured of that, and perhaps one day with the long-range MT to facilitate exploration, they will be found. But that's for the future.

The Golden Age of the Confederation ended abruptly in 3104, and for sixteen years all its resources were consumed in a brutal civil war that not only precluded further stellar exploration, but forced a wholesale retreat from every extraterrestrial colony (except Pollux, of course), and sometimes that took the form of abandonment rather than retreat. An estimated two million lives were lost in vacuum colonies because their supply lines were severed and they had no means of evacuation.

The Mankeen Revolt put the stars out of reach for a long time. The Confederation metamorphosed into the Concord during the Revolt, and in a sense we can be grateful that so much power was concentrated in the Houses, especially those holding Directorate seats and thus the reins of command. They brought the power structure through the holocaust virtually unscathed, as I've noted before. In fact, it emerged as a stronger and even more stubbornly immutable structure; that was a key stabilizing factor and probably all that averted a third dark age, whatever its subsequent results.

After Mankeen, the Concord's resources were for many years solely invested in the process of recovery; there was nothing left for new stellar voyages, nor any interest in such undertakings. The Concord couldn't even spare any concern for Centauri, where over three million people lived. The recovery period took the better part of a century, the terminal date generally given as 3200, when the last Solar colony was reestablished—Shang's mine complexes on

Charon. That was just fifty-two years ago, and eight years later the Concord was again at war, this time with the Peladeen Republic. That lasted only two years, but like all wars it was costly and totally engaged the Concord's resources.

Finally, in 3218, humankind once more turned its eyes to the stars, but the spirit of speculation no longer impelled Lords to seek profits beyond the Two Systems. The new Sirius A, Procyon A, and the Kruger 60A and B, Van Maanen's star, and Altair expeditions—and there were ten altogether—were sponsored by the Concord and paid for out of Concord taxes, and it was only with Concord assistance that the Sirius A outposts were reestablished by the Houses that originally planted them, and Cameroodo established outposts on Procyon A One and Two. All of them have since been abandoned as unprofitable. Now our only stake in the stars beyond Centauri consists of research stations under the aegis of the University on Sirius A One and Procyon A One.

The quietus was dealt the Concord's stellar explorations by the disastrous Altair expedition in 3241 when the ship *Felicity* and her crew of fifty disappeared. No one knows what happened; SynchCom transmissions simply ceased after a routine check-in. A Confleet Corsair sent to find *Felicity*—after a delay of a month while the rescue ship was fitted with suitably powerful MAM-An generators—reported no sign of *Felicity* anywhere near her last known position, then itself vanished from human ken.

A daunting experience, granted, but it doesn't explain why the Concord stopped reaching for the stars. A more realistic explanation is simply that the quest proved unprofitable. At least that's been the reason offered by the Directorate majority each time they voted down tax levies for further stellar explorations. Yet, despite the high-transportation costs, mining of various ores on the planets where outposts had been established promised to be very lucrative once the initial investment was recovered. But apparently the Lords didn't feel they could afford to wait for long-term profits, and perhaps that's because too many have suffered declining revenues as a result of the increasing incidence of Bond uprisings, either through direct losses, or rocketing taxes, or the resulting economic recession now endemic in the Concord.

But the real explanation for the Concord's failure to rise

to the challenge of the stars is a pervading indifference to it. A year ago, on the tenth anniversary of *Felicity's* voyage, I expected to see something commemorating the event on vidicom; perhaps some retrospective documentary, or at least a passing reference on the newscasts. But there was nothing. It was as if the *Felicity* had never existed.

An ominous index, that indifference. Any civilization that turns its back on its frontiers is in grave danger, and the Concord can claim no golden age for that reason. The arts have flourished, to be sure, particularly in the last twenty years, which is in part a response to affluent patronage, and there is evident in the arts an innovative spirit that offers some hope, even if it springs from a limited segment of the Fesh, not the rulers of our civilization. But there has been no correlative innovative spirit in science since Mankeen, and that is a result of the Concord's indifference to its frontiers.

Not indifference; it's more than that.

Fear.

We always come back to that. More precisely, fear of change. Change has come to be equated solely with destruction and with loss of power by those now in possession of it. That's the real reason the Concord turns its back on its frontiers, that it refuses to look out to the stars in hope of reaching them. Such an accomplishment would inevitably create change, and there's no way to predict the nature or scope of it. The Concord—or, rather, its Lords, and only they have the power to make such decisions—would rather forfeit the rich potentials in stellar exploration than accept the concomitant changes that would inevitably result.

If the Phoenix is successful, if we do achieve Phase I, that must be one of our primary goals: to turn the Concord's eyes once again to the stars.

CHAPTER XII: March 3258

●||●||●||●||●||●||●||●||●||●||●||●||●||●||●||●||●||●||●||●||●||●||●||●||●||●||

1.

"Why can't you go to the Lord Galinin?" Adrien didn't look at her father as she asked the question; her gaze was fixed on the electroharp in her lap. In the sun-lighted room, the soft tones sang plaintively from under her fingers.

"Galinin!" Eliseer paced the salon restlessly. "Adrien, there's no *proof*. Nothing but rumor. And Dr. Perralt heard of an outbreak of a virulent type of—well, something like the rumors suggest. But that *proves* nothing."

Lady Galia looked up from her tribroidery frame, the incessant movement of her hands never stopping, her black eyes turned impatiently on Adrien.

"It *can't* be more than a rumor. Lord Orin wouldn't be so foolish as to try to hide it if Karlis *is* . . ." She averted her eyes modestly. "If he *has* been . . . permanently affected by some illness."

Adrien struck a minor chord. "Wouldn't he, Mother?"

"Of course not! How would Karlis provide an heir!"

"Well, certainly not personally." She watched her own hands, and the flash of the ruby and sapphire ring; still on her right hand. It should be on her left. The other ring, sapphire and emerald for Badir Selasis, was in her bedroom; she only wore it for public appearances.

Lady Galia was staring at her. "Adrien, what *are* you suggesting?"

"*I'd* provide the heir, Mother." She looked up and laughed at her shocked expression. "I'd be impregnated by artificial insemination. Of course, the Board of Succession disapproves of it, but I can't believe that would discourage Selasis from keeping a sperm reserve for—"

"Adrien!" Galia Eliseer's face was crimson.

"Oh, really, Mother, open your eyes."

Lord Loren turned abruptly. "Adrien, I won't tolerate this disrespect for your mother."

That cut deep. He had never used that chiding tone with her, and it gave her a profound sense of loneliness. And how was she to tolerate her mother's disrespect for *her*? Her prim ignorance, her complacent myopia?

Adrien looked down at the 'harp, her fingers seeking the threads of a melody in a minor key. She was thinking of Harlequin. Blind Harlequin, who had taught her this melody long ago in Concordia in those halcyon days when Alexand had first been her Promised. Harlequin was dead now; he had followed his Lady to the grave.

"Father, you, at least, should be able to look at this with open eyes. If the rumors *are* true, do you think Orin Selasis would admit defeat so easily?" She stopped mid-phrase, cutting the sound off with the flat of her hand. "His first born and *only* male heir impotent and sterile."

"Adrien!" Again, the shocked protest from Lady Galia.

"It's the *words* that disturb you, isn't it, Mother?— not the truth behind them. You don't like to think about that. But *I* must think about it, just as I've thought about how Janeel became pregnant again after she was warned a second birth might kill her. And it *did* kill her. I must consider Lord Orin's present dilemma and how he'll solve it. I'll bear Karlis an heir, however the conception is managed, but think about my position once that child is born. I'll *know* it wasn't naturally conceived; I'll know Karlis's dreadful secret. And you can plan your mourning wardrobe now. If Selasis runs true to form, I'll die in childbirth, like Janeel." She put the 'harp aside and rose to go to the windowall and stare out into the garden. "But you always looked good in black, Mother."

Adrien heard the scrape of the chair, Lady Galia's gown rustling.

"Loren, for the God's sake, *talk* to her!" Then the explosive sigh. "*I* can't. 'Zion knows I've tried."

Then Eliseer's voice, placating, but distracted, "All right, Galia, I'll talk to her. Don't be upset."

"Upset!" When she talks so—so blatantly of..." Another sigh. Adrien waited for the next words. "Loren, I have a throbbing headache. I'm going to my suite."

"I'm sorry, dear. You'd better call Dr. Perralt."

The rustle of her gown again. "I think I will." Her retreating steps, and finally the door closed on a silent room.

It might have been empty for the sound of it, but Adrien could sense her father behind her, watching her. She stared out into the garden; a garden full of Terran flowers, solace for Lady Galia. It reminded Adrien of Concordia, of the rose garden, of Alexand. She pressed her hand to her waist.

She knew the truth existing within her. She would need confirmation, but in her mind there was no doubt. It made all her arguments a lie, in a sense; she would mother no heir for Karlis. But the lie was only in the reason for her jeopardy, not in the jeopardy itself.

3 Avril. Less than a month before the wedding.

Alexand had tried to stop it. The Elite were in turmoil with the rumors. She believed them because Dr. Lile assured her Alexand did, and for a time she took hope that the marriage might be stopped, that she might avoid the more dangerous course—both for herself and the House— that the marriage would force her to.

But that hope died now. Her father wouldn't ask for a Board of Succession inquiry. The galling irony of it was that the truth that inquiry would reveal would destroy Bakdir Selasis and free her, and her father—the Concord itself—of that ever present threat. Yet because it was wrapped in rumor, it wouldn't even stop this marriage.

She took a deep breath, composing herself as she turned to face her father. And she wanted to weep. He looked suddenly old, all the vigor drained from him, the quiet self-confidence vanished. He had made so many good decisions during his tenure as First Lord of Camine Eliseer, it seemed unfair that this decision was costing him so dearly.

He said stiffly. "It was never my intention to make you unhappy, Adrien. You know that."

She watched him as he moved to the windowall, taking up a position a few paces from her; he seemed reluctant to come too close.

"I know, Father, and I'm well aware of the advantages this

union seems to offer the House. And I know the consequences if you attempt to renege on the contracts. I understand your position entirely."

"Yes, I suppose you do. You've always been very astute in political matters. Perhaps that makes it easier for you to understand—" He hesitated, staring blindly into the garden. "—to understand that I can't make a serious accusation against Karlis Selasis on the basis of a rumor."

Adrien nodded, a bitter smile shadowing her mouth.

"It seems ironic that Selasis could demand medical confirmation of my virginity, yet you can't demand similar confirmation of Karlis's virility."

"Adrien, for the God's sake!"

"Do the frank words disturb you, too? They're not ladylike, I suppose."

He clasped his hands behind his back, but even there they wouldn't stay still.

"It's a matter of ... of custom. One doesn't challenge a Lord's virility without very good reason."

"Especially not Orin Selasis's first born."

"Under no circumstances would such a challenge be made lightly, and no one challenges Selasis on *any* ground unless they're very sure of themselves. Look at Gorimbo and L'Ancel. They challenged him on matters relating to his franchises, something far less important and personal to him, and both are broken men, Lords only in name, if even that. L'Ancel's wife committed suicide within a year, his son disappeared without a trace; into the Outside, they say. And Gorimbo—his nephew, Orongo reluctantly pays the cost of maintaining him in a mental hospital. Adrien, don't you see, don't you understand what I'd be risking on the basis of a rumor that might not be true?"

"Won't you consider talking privately with Galinin?"

"I'm sure he's already heard the rumor, and if he thought there was any substance to it, he'd initiate a Board inquiry without *my* prompting."

"Wouldn't it be as logical to assume he's waiting for you to make the first move?"

"Why should the Chairman wait for *me* to move first?"

Because you have a daughter about to be wed to this monstrous eunuch. She didn't voice the answer; it was too much an accusation. Instead, she turned and walked slowly back to her chair. She didn't sit down, but stood silently, brushing her fingers over the strings of the 'harp.

She heard his footsteps moving hesitantly toward her.

"I don't want you to think I'm balking out of—of stubbornness. I have no choice, Adrien; no choice at all."

For him it was true. She felt very much alone now.

"All right, Father." She turned to face him. "I understand your position. Now I want you to understand mine."

"Your—what do you mean?"

"Simply this: I won't jeopardize you or the House by personally challenging Karlis's virility, nor will I make any attempt to avoid the wedding, or embarrass the House in any way. For your sake, the wedding *will* take place."

He stared at her in stark bewilderment. "Adrien, what in all the worlds are you—"

"You may choose to believe Karlis still capable of siring an heir, but I don't, and I intend to take what measures I deem necessary to save my life. I'll do nothing until after the wedding, and even then I'll take every precaution to make sure Lord Orin realizes I'm acting independently, without your consent or knowledge. I intend to make myself the focus of his wrath, not Eliseer."

"What are you thinking of? Holy God, have you gone mad?"

"Is it madness to want to live? Father, I *will* do what I must to save my life, but I want to assure you that in doing so, I'll protect Eliseer in every way I can."

"But what do you mean? What do you intend to do?"

"I won't tell you."

"If you're worried about monitors here—"

"I'm not. I'd be glad for Lord Orin in particular to monitor this conversation. I want him to know that whatever I do, it will be entirely on my own initiative. You'll have no part in it, and no control over it."

"Adrien . . . *please* . . ."

She looked at him, and she could feel no resentment or anger. He was caught in a dead end, suffering unfathomed agonies of doubt and fear. She took his hand and, out of the depths of her own fear, called up a smile.

"That's all, Father. I only wanted to warn you."

He didn't understand, not any part of it. She read that in his uncertain frown as he looked down at her hand, at the ring.

"Oh, Adrien, if only . . ."

"Don't dwell on 'if onlys.' Remember, you're Lord of Camine Eliseer first. After that, you're my father. And I love you."

He took her in his arms, holding her as if she were a child in need of comfort, but she knew he was more in need of comfort than she.

"Adrien, no man could be more blessed in his daughter than I am."

2.

Sister Thea had left the convent of Saint Petra's of Ellay only twice in her seventy years. The first occasion wasn't literally a departure; she was born outside the convent. No one knew where, or how she came to be left a few days later on the altar of the lock chapel. The Sisters of Faith didn't question such deliverances; they were too common.

The second occasion was a true departure. On her fiftieth birthday, she voyaged across the light years to the Cathedron of Concordia where the Reverend Eparch and High Bishop ordained her Sister Supra of Saint Petra's. That was twenty years ago, and she'd never had any inclination to venture beyond the locks of Saint Petra's again. What she wished to know of the outside world was available in book- and textapes or on vidicom, and she watched the newscasts and educational programs conscientiously. She sent her charges into that world regularly, and it was her responsibility to prepare them for it.

Now Sister Thea stood at the oriel window in her study, taking advantage of a break in her afternoon schedule. From this window high in the cloister, she looked out over the children's play court, the school, the dormitories, the hospital—except for the cloister, the largest building in the convent—the clusters of residences for Church Bonds and Fesh, the warehouses and maintenance buildings, and beyond them the farm plots, squared out with green hedgerows and interspersed with wooded glades. The flora was almost entirely Terran; the first trees had been planted at the convent's founding and had flourished and grown to majestic maturity. That it was a microcosm of Terra had come home to her only on her one short visit to the mother planet.

Beyond this green microcosm and its protective 'bubbles, she could see a stretch of horizon and the Barrens, stark in the slanting rays of the late afternoon sun. The pygmy forests had moved north, she noted, in their annual migration, leaving the low hills around Saint Petra's naked. No sign of human existence was visible from the convent, although it was only an hour's flight over the shoulder of Mount Dema to the south to the town of Oriban.

The languid quiet of the afternoon was broken with a sound so melodious, and so expected, it only made her smile and look down into the play court. The sound was the chiming of the hour from the triple spires of the cloister chapel. It was followed by a rush of footsteps and laughing shouts as the children plunged pell mell into the court for the afternoon play period.

The chapel chimes had shaped time in the convent for nearly two centuries. The chapel was the oldest structure here, nearly as old as human history on Castor, and built of white marlite in contrast to the pinkish stone of all the other buildings, the stone quarried at the foot of Mount Dema.

The Sisters of Faith maintained three convents on Castor; one in Helen, another in Tremper in the southern hemisphere, but Saint Petra's was the largest and the oldest, and Sister Thea knew—through vidicom and imagraphs—that none of them were graced with any buildings so solemnly beautiful as the cloister chapel of Saint Petra's of Ellay. Yet for her, the real heart of the convent was below her—the children laughing, dancing out the age-old rituals of their games.

The Sisters of Faith served the unwanted children of the worlds and, when necessary, their mothers. That was why the hospital was the second largest structure in the convent. It was a maternity hospital.

Many of the children below, whose laughter seemed to rise like bubbles to her window, were born in that hospital. They were officially classified as orphans and would eventually leave Saint Petra's to be allieged to the Concord or Church. As Fesh. There was no way of knowing the class of most of these children's parents, although the majority of them were probably Fesh. Still, a few no doubt were Bond, and a few Elite. The Church compromised by allieging all of them as Fesh, which Thea had always considered fair. Some of these children—like herself and so many of the Sisters who were teachers, doctors, nurses, and surrogate mothers—would stay.

A good sound, she was thinking; laughter is a good sound.

At length, she turned from the window, crossed to her desk, and eased into the straight-backed chair. As she looked down at her appointment schedule, a sigh escaped her.

"New patient. Anonymous. 13:10."

It was almost time. She pushed the veil back over her koyf, which was stretching, even breaking, the rule. The Sisters of Faith was a secret Order, the veils as distinctive as their blue habits. The veils were not to be lifted except in private encounters between Sisters if it were considered absolutely necessary, and then only within the walls of the cloister. But the patients she met in this room were anxious enough already; she didn't think the forgiving spirit of the Holy Mezion would be offended if she spared them the necessity of dealing with yet another veiled, faceless figure.

The door chime sounded, and Thea pursed her lips. She always felt a certain uneasiness at this point, wondering what the new patient would be like, what she would be hoping for, what her decisions would be.

"Come in, Sister."

Sister Camila, tall, spare, engulfed in her blue habit, entered first, then stood aside and turned to the young woman following her.

"This way, please."

She was face-screened—so many of them were—slender and small, her carriage erect, making her seem taller than she actually was. She wore a casual slacsuit with a short cape. The clothes were of good quality; upper-class Fesh. No jewelry, no House badge, nothing to identify her, and this was also the rule, rather than the exception. Thea was briefly attracted to her hands—small and well tended. They'd seen no manual work.

Thea smiled and gestured to the chair across the desk. "Please, sit down with me, if you will."

She moved to the chair with a purposeful stride that was surprising—most covered that space very hesitantly—and when she was seated, folded her hands in apparent calm.

Thea said, "That will be all, Sister Camila, thank you." She waited until the door closed, then turned to the young woman. "I'm Sister Thea, Supra of Saint Petra's. I won't ask your name, my dear. It's your privilege to tell me or withhold it as you wish."

"Thank you, Sister. For the present, I'll withhold it."

A confident voice; unafraid. Thea touched a button on her desk console, and the medical report appeared on the screen. The mother was in good health; complications were unlikely. The pregnancy was in its second month. Sex of child, male. No—sex of *children*. Thea tried not to frown as she read the final notation: "The patient is carrying twins; identical."

Somehow that made it harder. *Two* lives. . . .

She switched off the screen and looked up at the young woman. This was another moment she approached with some trepidation—informing the patient of her pregnancy, knowing she would be waiting for the answer to a question that could drastically alter her life. But this one seemed so calm; she seemed to know the answer already.

Thea began, "I have the results of your examination. It's my hope that what I have to tell you will be considered good news, but I know it can't always be so. In any case, the Sisters of Faith will serve you in every way we can. You are pregnant, my dear. The pregnancy is in its second month."

A long sigh; it was difficult to guess whether it indicated relief or despair, yet it seemed nearer relief.

Then she leaned forward. "Sister, can you tell me the sex of the child?"

That was one question Thea had never been asked at this stage. Her sparse brows came up.

"Why, yes. The sex is male. The chemohormonal analyses are quite dependable."

Again a sigh, and it was unmistakably one of relief. "For me, Sister, that's good news indeed."

Thea smiled with unexpected pleasure. "There's something else you must know. According to the report, you're carrying twins. Identical twins."

A silence, then a hesitant, "Twins? Are you sure?"

"Yes. Those tests are also quite dependable."

She laughed, and the sound was as free as the laughter of the children in the courtyard outside.

"Twins," she repeated softly. "It runs in the family." And, again, that laughter. "*Two* sons. A double blessing."

A blessing. This young woman *was* extraordinary.

"Then perhaps you've answered my next question already. Do you wish to bear these children?"

"Yes, of course I do."

"And after they're born?"

"I won't give them up, if that's what you mean."

"I see. I'm pleased, of course, but in all fairness, I must warn you that—"

"Thank you, but I need no warnings. Nothing short of death could part me from my children."

The determination in her tone was chilling, as if the possibility of death was more than a figure of speech.

"Well, then, we have only to work out certain details concerning your medical requirements and any other needs the Order is qualified to meet."

"Sister, my needs will be great, and only you and your Order can meet them."

There was no mistaking the chill quality in her tone now, and Thea felt a fleeting, but very tangible, fear.

"I...don't think I understand..."

"I know, and I'll explain in part, at least, if you'll bear with me. First, I've done some research on your Order. I've learned, for instance, that you're bound by vows of silence if any supplicant asks it of you. Personal vows that include your Sisters as well as anyone outside the Order. I also know you're bound to protect any mother or child who comes to you, no matter who they may be, or how great the danger to the Sisters. And you will offer sanctuary to any supplicant against any threat, whatever it might be, even if it comes from the highest officials of the Concord."

Thea nodded, aware that her heart was pumping too fast, a sensation that at her age she could only regard with alarm.

"All of that is true. Sanctuary is an ancient and honored tradition of the Church."

The young woman went on in the same level tone, "I've also made inquiries about you. It's easy to take a vow, but to keep it is another matter. I'm told you keep your vows."

"I...I always have, and I should hope nothing would ever stop me from keeping them. These are life vows we take upon entering the Order. We break them at the risk of our immortal souls."

There was a brief silence, then she said softly, "I know about life vows, Sister. I made one that I intend to keep, but I can't do it without your help. I came to Saint Petra's of all the Faith convents because of what I've been told about you. I've come as a supplicant, and I'll hold you to your vow of silence and protection for me and my children—above all, for my children. I've come to ask sanctuary."

Thea was still mystified, but she didn't hesitate.

"Santuary is yours, if you ask it."

The young woman leaned back, her hands resting on the arms of the chair. But there was a ring on her left hand now. At first, Thea's attention was drawn to it only because she was sure it hadn't been there before. Then she stared at it with unintentional directness. An Elite betrothal ring; the stones were ruby and sapphire. And she felt that chill again as she had when the young woman promised to die before being parted from her children.

Thea touched the first two fingers of her right hand to her forehead, then her heart, and repeated the promise, more as a reminder to herself than as an assurance.

"Sanctuary is yours."

3.

The Phoenix contingent at the Cave of Springs had expanded to thirteen. The physicists, James Lyden and Caris Bruce, had disappeared from Fina two days before, and were presently setting up their laboratory in another part of the cave. The remaining defectors were also from Fina: two comtechs and three MT techs. Within two weeks, the COS HQ would be fully manned with a staff of thirty-four, including the Falcon crews.

A square chamber had been cut into one wall of the com-center, and Alex watched with profound satisfaction as the techs completed the installation of the matter transmitter—the link to Fina and the means of freeing Andreas. When he was found.

It was exactly three months today since Andreas's arrest, and Ben still didn't know where he was being held. But he was convinced Andreas hadn't been transferred to the Solar System, and if he were on Castor, or anywhere in the Centauri System, they would be ready now.

Alex found the face-screens increasingly annoying: Of the Phoenix members, only Jael went without one. It was like dealing with automatons. Or perhaps it was only a reminder of the faceless acolytes at the rituals in the Cliff. Still, as long as the Brothers were here, the 'screens were necessary.

Alex turned at the sound of footsteps; Jael emerging from the passage leading down to the hangar cavern. His tirelessness was a source of amazement. He still kept up his duties with the Helen chapter and, whenever he was free, he was at the COS HQ. But neither of them had wasted much time sleeping the last two months.

Jael stopped to watch the installation of the MT. "When will it be on line, Alex?"

"Dr. Lind said he can check it out in the morning."

That was morning TST. It was morning now in the Midhar above them, and the temperature was rising in the cave. The Brothers helping with the installation were already stripped to the waist.

"Alex, I just 'commed the old Ser. He says the Falcons are ready for deliv. After dark upside; ten hours."

"Good. I sent Ben a crew list; he's double-checking them. I considered all of them loyals, but I can't be sure after three months away from FO. Ben agrees with me on Vic Blayn, though, so Leftant Commander Blayn will become First Commander of the exile FO. I'm not sure whether that's a promotion or a demotion."

Jael said with a wry smile, "If he's the right ilk, he'll take it like a new star on his shoulder. Did you talk to the old Ser about an MT terminal in his HQ?"

"Not yet. I'll see him tomorrow, and I might as well broach it then. We need access to Helen, and we can't look to any of the chapter terminals there, which means I'll be in a seller's market again." He stopped, alerted when one of the Brothers paused for a long look.

Val Severin was coming out of the tunnel into the sleeping quarters, moving with an air of intent purposefulness, but moving, naturally enough, like a woman. She wore a face-screen, and the borrowed slacsuit was dusty and ill-fitting, but Val had never had to work at attracting a man's eye.

"Banic!" Jael was also aware of the Brother's wandering attention. "You don't rate half a 'cord standing around like a dodder."

Banic gave Jael a quick glance and returned to his work.

"Hello, Alex—Jael." Val's voice conveyed the smile lost behind her 'screen. "We've finished setting up the bath areas.

Thank the God for the hot springs. At least we'll have *hot* water. You know, when you give up this place as an HQ, Alex, you should make a health spa of it. That water has enough mineral content to cure anything."

Alex glanced at Jael. "Maybe I'll sell it back to Amik for that purpose—at a tidy profit, of course."

"Fortune on the profit, brother. Any problems, Val?"

"No, but we're almost ready to set up the S/V screen partitions. I just wanted to locate the equipment."

Alex pointed to an opening into a smaller chamber. "In our future conference room. I'll have them brought in to you."

She waved the offer aside. "I have plenty of strong backs available. Thanks." Then, as she started back to the tunnel, "I may need Lennis or Jao to check the circuitry."

Jael frowned as he watched her go. "Step light, Val."

Alex doubted she actually heard that quiet admonition, and he was thinking that there were some advantages to the face-screens; he could study Jael's expression of solicitous concern quite openly without his awareness.

Finally, Jael turned his attention to the MT chamber. "Alex, maybe I can slip in a word with the old Ser on that MT terminal. It'll give him the quivs having a permanent Insider dig on his ground."

"You don't think it'll give me a few quivs having a Phoenix dig on Outsider ground? All right, why don't you sit in on the haggling. For one thing, you can suggest a spot for it, preferably near the accesses—"

A cry of alarm brought him up short. His eyes moved in a quick arc, searching its source. Jael had already guessed it: the passageway to the sleeping quarters.

Alex pelted toward the tunnel, but Jael was ahead of him, the knife flashing from its sheath, while Alex snapped the X¹ from its sleeve holster into his left hand. Val was halfway down the eight-meter length of the passage, struggling with a hulking man twice her weight; one of the Brothers, and his intentions were clearly amorous.

Alex paused at the tunnel entrance. Val's face-screen was off, and her expression was one of impatient anger, not fear; the man was in for a surprise. And this was a Brotherhood affair. He raised his gun so that the twenty Brothers gathered at the other end of the passage could see it, and waited.

"Ibo!" Jael's shout got no response from the Brother. Val had gone into action.

Her arms were pinned but her legs were free, and a quick upward thrust of her knee doubled the Outsider with a hoarse shout of agony. Then, with her hands free, she delivered a hatchet-like blow over the kidneys, and swinging back from that, momentum calculated to the microsecond, snapped a kick to the face, just under the chin. Had it been a little harder, it would have broken his neck. As it was, Ibo found himself, in less than five seconds, rolling in moaning helplessness on the floor. Jael stood over him, eyes slitted, stone-black. He glanced only once at Val.

"Ibo!" The name low, taut, cracking in the rock-bound space. "You unmothered nuch—*stand up!*"

Val pressed back against the wall, and she felt more fear now at what she read in Jael's eyes than she had when the Brother began pawing her.

Ibo lurched to his knees, groaning with the effort, and went white when he looked up into Jael's face. His mouth moved, but produced only spongy, garbled grunts. Jael stood motionless; he didn't even seem to blink, as Ibo pulled himself to his feet in jerking stages, finally making words of the choked noises.

"J-Jael . . . I—I didn' mean . . . brother, gimme a *say*, f' the God's sake!"

"I laid edict," Jael pronounced coldly, the long blade of his knife catching the distant lights. "I called this woman friend and sister. Blood edict, Ibo."

Blood edict. Val suddenly realized what he meant by those words. They had only seemed picturesque before. She tried to protest, but her voice failed her. One end of the tunnel was crowded with half-naked men; the Brothers, unmoved and unconcerned. Only curious. Alex stood at the other end, a gun in one hand, but he raised the other hand, palm down, a gesture that told her not to interfere.

A sudden movement brought her attention back to Ibo with a spinning wrench. The sheath at his side was empty, the knife in his hand, driving toward Jael. She was only a meter away and focused intently on them, but she couldn't be sure exactly what happened. Ibo's knife seemed to find its mark. In the grappling of their bodies, she heard a wretching cry, and thought in a moment of horror it might be Jael's. Yet when they separated, it was Ibo's knife that clattered to the floor, fell gleaming and clean at her feet, and it was Ibo who sprawled at Jael's feet.

And it was Jael's knife that was buried to the hilt in Ibo's heart.

Val stared at the knife, and only when she heard a buzz of comment and low-pitched laughter did she realize she was trembling. She looked up at the Brothers, at their callous, smirking faces, and she was suddenly angry.

"All of you have assignments—get back to work!"

That crisp order was met with calculating silence, and she saw their eyes shift from her to Jael.

But he seemed unaware of their attention as he leaned down with leisurely unconcern, pulled his knife from its grisly sheath, and wiped the blade on Ibo's pants. When he straightened, he looked up at the waiting Brothers and frowned irritably, as if he were surprised.

"What the hell's gone down with you gutless—Go with! You heard the Ferra. Back to work. Except you, Heber." He glanced at Val. "I'll need Heber for a short job, if you don't mind."

This was all for her benefit, she realized, and took her cue. "Heber," she said coolly, "you're excused until Jael is through with you."

The man stepped forward a little warily, and, as if that were a signal, the rest of the Brothers turned away with a murmur of comment to go back to their work. Jael returned his knife to its silver-embossed sheath as Heber approached.

"Take Ibo upside and dig him in, Heber. Get a surface suit at the hangar lock. When it's done, report to the Ferra for work."

Heber leaned down and lifted Ibo's body to his shoulder carrying the burden as indifferently as he might a rock.

"This sister's quick, Jael. A straight blade."

Jael didn't smile. "Hold that thought in, brother." Then as Heber moved off down the passageway, "Val, I'm sorry."

She looked around at Jael, and it was hard to believe this was the same man who had called Ibo to account; his dark eyes reflected only regret now. But it was for her, not for Ibo. She wondered why that didn't bother her more, that he could kill so easily. But Jael was born to that; it was a requisite to survival in his world.

The only thing that amazed her was that he was also capable of devotion to a cause as abstract and hopeless as the Phoenix, that he could speak well and knowledgeably on almost any subject from politics to music, that he had the bearing and manners, in spite of his Outsider colloquialisms, of a born gentleman, and that he was capable of this concern for her feelings.

She glanced toward the sleeping quarters where the Brothers were already hard at work. "Thanks for reestablishing my authority."

"You did all right for your own." He paused, searching her face. "Heber called you a straight blade. From him, that's a compliment."

"What does it mean?"

"It implies courage. And...cômpetence, I suppose."

Competence.

She closed her eyes, swallowing hard, seeing that knife hilt-deep in Ibo's heart, placed with extraordinary precision. They would call Jael a straight blade, too.

"Val..." A short, regretful sigh, then, "I was afraid something like this would come down finally."

"I know. I've been very careful, but—" She shrugged uncomfortably. "Anyway, you had no choice about Ibo. He'd have killed you."

Jael's gaze was direct, yet it still seemed masked.

"No. He wouldn't have killed me. I could've taken Ibo down without the blade. He called me on a blood edict, Val." He paused, watching her. "I suppose that rubs wrong, but blood edicts are seldom called."

She nodded numbly. "I can understand that."

"Then maybe you can also understand why I had to—" He took a deep breath, looking down the tunnel toward the com-center. "No, I don't expect that to square up for you."

She stared at him, realizing with a dull shock that it mattered to him whether she understood; it mattered a great deal.

"Jael, I'd be less than honest to say it didn't bother me to see someone killed right in front of me, but I know the Brotherhood isn't bound by laws that would suit the average Fesh. I understand."

He looked around at her, testing the veracity of that with the instincts bred into him. For a long while, he didn't move. Then he leaned close and kissed her gently.

When he drew away, he laughed and said, "I'm asking fate, after seeing you pull a man down."

"You seem to be upright."

He studied her with a hint of a smile that was more apparent in his eyes than his lips. Then he nodded, as if the matter were resolved and in that sense finished.

"Val, you have your 'com on touch?"

She felt for it in her pants pocket and nodded. "Yes."

"Keep it on emergency alarm, and next time hit that first. Don't you wear a gun?" He took her right hand and pushed the sleeve back from the spring sheath, then looked up at her with a resigned sigh.

"Jael, I just . . . didn't have time to use it."

He laughed. "You had time; it just never came into your head. But your way was better." He pulled her sleeve down but didn't release her hand. "I don't see any more face-offs here, but if something *does* come down, don't step slow. The Brothers came up in a hard school; hold back, and it might mean your life, and I'm not sure I could bear under wearing black for you."

She was close to tears, and the only words she could think of were, "Thank you."

"Go with, sister." He gave her hand a quick squeeze, then turned and walked away down the passage toward the com-center. "Fortune, Val."

She smiled to herself, watching him.

"Fortune . . . brother."

4.

Predis Ussher strode down the corridor, reveling in the press of bodies and voices around him. He clasped the hands stretched out to him, giving each man or woman a smile, meeting each pair of eyes directly. He took in their words as dry earth absorbs rain. He was earth—no, he was a wind. He was a wind sweeping the waters, shaping their masses with the invisible waves of his own power.

It had been good. FO's Hangar 1, the only place in Fina large enough for that jubilant crowd. The words had come right; he felt them welling from within him, from the source of that exhilaration, the potent source of power. Halfway through, he gave up the memorized speech and let the words come free, trusting the power within him.

. . . the long gestation draws to an end, and the time of

parturition is near. Not a birth, my friends, but a rebirth. We will all take part, we will all be witness to a miracle, the miracle of rebirth, the rebirth of freedom in Centauri! The Phoenix will rise from the ashes of disaster; the Phoenix will be born again, and its talons will strike into the flesh and hearts of the slave masters. The Phoenix will take under its soaring wings all those bound in the cruel chains of slavery, will cast off those chains, and the unshackled masses will rise on the wings of the Phoenix into the light of freedom! The Republic of the Peladeen will be born again and the slave masters cast out! Our time is near! The Phoenix will live again. . . .

It had been good. As he worked his way toward the lifts the echo of the sound was still in his ears—cheers from thousands of straining throats, a sound like the rush of surf pounding at the walls of the hangar cavern. He was the wind, whipping that sea to storm intensity, a storm of joy and hope and faith.

They believed.

That was what counted. Riis and his endless ex seqs. The old prophets said faith could move mountains, but you couldn't build faith out of computers, and computers never moved anything.

When at length he reached the lift that took him up to the Communications section, he left most of the crowds behind, and he felt some of his exuberance slip away. There were still some who doubted; less than three thousand had come to this meeting, fewer than the first. Still, that was enough. In time, there would be more; in time, there would be no doubters.

Radek. She fostered doubt; she radiated it as he radiated promise. She had only to pass in a hall, to enter a room, and a pall of doubt spread like some heavy, noxious gas. She'd been at the meeting, standing near the comcenter deck, but her presence never suggested support; she was only there to watch him. Without a word, she made that clear. To watch; to analyze; to dissect his psyche with those penetrating, emotionless, tensteel eyes.

She must be dealt with, and Venturi, too. All in good time.

They thought he was blackmailed into impotence with those microspeakers. Well, perhaps they were right for the time being. It would at least confuse the members to hear about—what did Radek call it? The Ransom Alternative.

But the time would come when the name of Ransom would

be so despised, he wouldn't dare set foot in Fina, much less offer himself as a candidate for Phase I. The time would come when Phase I would be meaningless, when the Phoenix burst from its rocky tomb and made the entire Centauri System its own, when the Peladeen Republic again ruled Centauri as it was destined to do.

He turned into the anteroom outside his office, too preoccupied to be consciously aware of his surroundings.

"Fer Ussher?"

His secretary, Caren Regon. She was standing by her desk, her plain features transformed and glowing, and he felt his exhilaration returning. *She* believed. Her eyes were wide with awe, and it was for him. She believed, and there were plenty more like her.

Her cheeks colored self-consciously. "I—I don't know how to tell you how . . . moved I was by what you said at the meeting. We're so lucky to have you. I mean, with Dr. Riis and Commander Ransom gone. I don't know what would happen to us—to the Phoenix—if it weren't for you."

Riis and Ransom. Would they never forget? But Ussher held on to his smile.

"Thank you, Ferra, but I'm only doing my small part for our cause; the cause of freedom." He pressed the lock by his office door, then said as the screens clicked off, "Ferra Regon, I'd like to see the requisition sheets from Dr. Tomas, please."

"I'll bring them in to you. Just a moment."

While she called up the file, he left the doorscreens off and went to his desk, humming to himself.

They'd forget. Riis and Ransom would become only dim memories. They'd forget, and they'd believe. And those who didn't—well, they could only be regarded as traitors to the cause. He studied his appointment list. Hendrick. He must talk to Rob about the new laser modifications.

The quiet, sourceless voice triggered a cold shock of adrenaline that was literally paralyzing.

"Elor Peladeen commanded a force comparable to a thousand Corsair TCs, five thousand Corvets, and nearly ten thousand Falcons. . . ."

That voice. He needed no identification. It was the voice that haunted his nightmares. *Ransom.*

". . . Peladeen was battling the Concord when it was at approximately half its present level in armament and manpower. . . ."

A speaker! Another microspeaker—where was it? He stared around the empty room, his face a mask of chagrin and rage.

"...Predis, how do you propose to drive the Concord out of Centauri with the paltry resources at your command, when Peladeen with his vast fleets failed?".

"Stop it!"

The cry came from his throat unexpectedly, reverberating in the quiet; he wasn't even aware of it. He was on his feet searching, tossing aside piles of vellum, sending a forgotten cup of coffee flying in an explosive spray.

"...and remember, Predis, I still live, and Andreas Riis still lives...."

It was here—it had to be here! Somewhere close—God, it seemed to be inside his head! He spilled out the contents of the drawers with shaking hands.

"...Andreas Riis lives, and he will return to Fina when the true faithful of the Phoenix free him. He *will* return. Think on that, my Lord Peladeen...."

He swept the desktop clean in one violent movement. "Damn you! Damn you!"

Ransom! He'd pay for this! He'd pay—

"Fer Ussher?"

And Venturi. He was in on this; he *had* to be. A microspeaker. Where the hell *was* it? He'd pay, too, and Radek. They'd *all* pay—

"Fer Ussher, what's wrong?"

He froze, suddenly aware of the silence in the room, aware that the voice had stopped, aware of the debris that littered the floor, and, most of all, aware of Caren Regon standing in the doorway, a sheaf of transcript film in her hand, staring at him incredulously.

"Didn't you *hear* it? That voice, damn it! You must've heard it. *His* voice."

Her eyes went wider. "Voice? I don't understand."

"Just now—you *had* to hear it!"

"I—I was outside. I didn't hear anything, except..." She paused, gazing distractedly at the littered floor.

Ussher's eyes narrowed, and the seed of suspicion took root in his mind.

"Except *what*, Ferra Regon?"

She was trembling; it was evident even from this distance. Why was she so nervous?

"Except...*your* voice."

Of course, he was thinking, looking at her as if he'd never seen her before. And, in a way, he hadn't. He hadn't seen her for what she was, hadn't recognized her as the most obvious suspect. All the monitors and microspeakers that had been planted in the office—it never occurred to him to suspect Caren Regon, the faithful secretary, the staunch supporter, the *believer*.

"Now I understand," he said coldly. "Of course you didn't hear it. That's part of the plan, isn't it?"

The transcript films slipped out of her hands and scattered silently on the carpeted floor.

"Fer Ussher, what do you mean?"

"You're *part* of it! I should've known. But I trusted you, Ferra. I *trusted* you!"

"I don't know what you're talking about. Please—"

"Don't you?" He laughed bitterly. "Is this one of Radek's plots to make me think I'm going mad? Oh, she'd like that. She'd love to get at me, to get a my *mind*. But it won't work!"

"Oh, Holy God . . ." She was frightened now; he could see that. "I *don't* know what you're talking about, Fer Ussher. Please believe me!"

He stiffened, every muscle taut. He'd been so intent on her he'd forgotten the open doorway, and now he saw a cluster of curious faces at the anteroom door. He forced his features into a semblance of calm, sinking into his chair, gripping the arms to control the shaking of his hands. The effort of keeping his voice level made his throat ache.

"Ferra Regon, I won't discuss it further. You'll be transferred to another subdepartment tomorrow; one where you'll be quite useless to your friends."

"*What* friends? Fer Ussher, what have I *done?*"

"Keep your voice down! Go get your desk cleared out. You'll be notified of your new assignment tomorrow morning. You're dismissed for the rest of the day."

For a long time she didn't move, and her hopeless, even accusing gaze, was strangely distrubing. But he knew that was part of the plan, too; Radek's plan. But it hadn't worked. It had only succeeded in revealing their agent.

"I said you're *dismissed*, Ferra Regon!"

She moved finally, turning to the door, only nodding silently when he added, "Tell Alan Isaks I want to see him in five minutes. And close the doorscreens."

She looked back at him once before the screens went on,

but he was already busy restoring order to his desk.

Five minutes. He gathered transcripts, tapes, memo sheets off the floor and stuffed them with no concern for order into drawers. Alan Isaks. Yes, he'd be the best choice. It should have been done long before. He should have known better than to trust a woman in such a vital position. Isaks was a Second Gen; his mother was one of Rob Hendrick's stattechs, and if Rob wasn't letting his ego get out of hand again, she harbored a secret affection for him.

He went to the door to pick up the transcripts Regon had dropped, consigned them to a desk drawer, then arranged the intercom and reading screens on top of the desk. The door chime sounded. He pulled his chair up to the desk and sat down, taking a long breath while he composed his smile. Not too much; just enough to put Isaks at ease. He reached for the intercom.

"Come in." Then, when a dark, sober-eyed young man came hesitantly into the room, "Ah, Alan, how are you?"

"I'm fine, Fer Ussher. Was there some . . . problem?"

"Yes, Alan, there *was* a problem. You see, Ferra Regon— well, I'm afraid she's been under a great deal of strain lately. Perhaps I'm to blame for that. I've been so busy, I didn't realize how much I was asking of her." He hesitated just long enough before adding, "She . . . she's ill." Then, lowering his voice slightly, "Alan, you may have heard part of our . . . well, a little disagreement in here. Now, I wouldn't want anyone to think badly of Ferra Regon. She served the Phoenix and me to the best of her ability for nearly ten years. However, in all fairness to her, and out of concern for her well-being, I was forced to ask her to transfer to another position where she won't be subject to such severe pressures." He paused for another long sigh. "I'm afraid she didn't take the decision well."

Isaks was frowning, still puzzled. "Was that what—" Then, perhaps thinking he was overstepping himself, "I—well, naturally, I asked her what was wrong. I mean, we've been working together for four years. All she said was something about . . . voices. It didn't make much sense."

Ussher frowned. "Voices? Oh, dear, perhaps it's worse than I thought. Unfortunate. Really unfortunate. Well, that's not why I asked to see you. Ferra Regon's departure leaves a void, of course, and I was hoping you'd be willing to fill it."

Isaks flushed with pleasure. "I'd be honored to try, and perhaps—well, I hope I'll be able to handle the pressure. Maybe it comes easier for Second Gens."

"Yes, I think it does. You're born to the dream. In that, you're very lucky. Of course, I'm not a Second Gen, but I know what the dream means to young people like you. In a sense, *I* was *born* to it, too." He smiled enigmatically, then looked at his watch. "Alan, you'll need some time to finish up any work you have pending. Perhaps by tomorrow morning you'll be ready to go at your new job full rev."

Isaks pulled his shoulders back and came very near to saluting. Ussher smiled privately at that.

"I'll be ready."

"Very good. Thank you, Alan."

Ussher waited for the click of the doorscreens, then squeezed his eyes shut, fists pressed to his temples. His head was pounding.

Damn them! Damn them all!

But he'd pulled out of this one. It looked bad for a while, but Isaks would pass the word. Caren Regon would come out of this looking like a hysterical neurotic, and no one would take anything she said seriously. Voices, indeed.

Voices. The aching in his head intensified. *Think on that, my Lord Peladeen. . . .*

Ransom considered that amusing; Ransom looking down his long, high-born nose, curling his Elite lip in contempt—

He wouldn't laugh at the Lord Peladeen in the end!

The microspeaker. It must be found. Now. Before it activated again, before that voice—

Ussher jerked out his pocketcom and set the 'com seq with shaking fingers. Three buzzes. Where the hell was Hendrick?

"Hello?"

"Rob, get up to my office!"

A brief hesitation. "Predis, what's—"

"Damn it, get up here—now!"

"All right, I'm on my way."

Ussher snapped the 'com shut, then pressed his hands to his aching head.

They'd pay. They'd *all* pay.

PHOENIX MEMFILES: DEPT HUMAN SCIENCES:
SOCIOTHEOLOGY (HS/STh)
SUBFILE: LAMB, RICHARD: PERSONAL NOTES
6 MARCH 3252
DOC LOC #819/19208-1812-1614-633252

I have before me a copy of what is purported to be the last imagraph taken of Lionar Mankeen. It shows him standing alone on a balcony at his Ruskasian Estate; in the background are the foreboding ramparts of the Ural Mountains. There is nothing in the imagraph suggesting the ruin of the city that had borne the House name, nothing of the ruin of the vaunted League military machine, nothing of the ruin of cities shattered and abandoned on the planets and satellites of two stellar systems.

The ruin is only in his eyes, and the face caught in this imagraph in a moment when he no doubt thought himself alone, only aware of the person—and his or her identity is unknown—who took the imagraph in time to turn to see the lens, that face is one that forever haunts the memory.

He was fifty-five at the time. A handsome man by any standard, tall and graceful, his long red hair a beacon of confidence. He wore the uniform of the League military command, and even in this private moment the high collar is closed, not a snap or seam out of place.

But in his eyes everything is out of place. The ruin is there, the bewilderment, regret, resentment, despair—the whole spectrum of defeat.

Lionar Mankeen from this balcony at the feet of some of Terra's most ancient mountains looks back at sixteen years, the prime years of his life, of civil war. In those years he has seen war reduce a stellar civilization to savage vestiges of its former grandeur, seen it retreat, step by

224

bloody step, to the mother planet, seen it sink to the edge of a dark age, seen even the tactics of war sink to a nearly medieval level.

He has seen nearly half the Lords who signed the League Charter with him killed, their Estates confiscated or destroyed, seen half the surviving League Lords turn against him and crawl—in one case, Lord Modo, literally—to the Concord begging clemency. He has seen his wife and two of his sons leave him to seek sanctuary of her House, Lesellen, a Concord House. He has survived an attempt on his life by his son-in-law, Aldred Berstine. He has seen Mankeen Bonds, in irrational terror, attack the Estate garrison and strip the city of its defenses just before the final Concord assault. And that must have been the cruelest blow; the emancipation of Bonds was one of the primary objectives of his rebellion. And he has seen the Confederation transmuted into an institution even more rigid and tyrannous under the goad of his struggle to make it more flexible and humane. He has seen his attempts to make the world into which he was born a better place only succeed in making the world he was about to leave a broken ruin occupied by death and terror.

He was a proud, even an arrogant, man, and in view of the terrible legacy he left—almost a billion lives destroyed and a civilization very nearly so, and the heritage of fear that congealed the doctrines of the Confederation into the dogmas of the Concord—it's hard to forgive him, even knowing his intent was diametrically opposed to the results. He wanted, in the words of the League Charter, "to force the Confederation to recognize the rights of individuals to determine their own destinies." His fatal fallacy is in the words, "to force." That was his arrogance speaking.

Yet, looking into his face in this imagraph, into those eyes shadowed with monumental defeat, I can't hold any of it against him, against the man. I can only pity him.

It was probably only a few hours after this imagraph was taken that Mankeen with his daughter, Irena, his second son, Leo—the only one of his three sons who stayed with him to the last—and three other League Lords and some of their families, as well as the First Commander of the League's armed forces, Scott Cormoroi, lifted off in one of the last vessels of the League fleet still intact. They were tracked by Confleet ships, and it was reported that their trajectory took them directly into the Sun. An epic self-immolation, and fitting for a man who once described himself as a modern Saint Ichrus.

There was a rumored epilogue, a story that was widely believed by his remaining partisans—those who survived the Mankeen Purge. It can be found now only in a few obscure contemporary histories. The story is that Mankeen and his handful of loyal followers struck out toward the Sun only to deceive their Confleet pursuers, that in fact the ship accelerated into SynchShift just within the orbit of Mercury, bound ultimately for Sirius A or another of the nearer stars in the hope of finding a planet suitable for human habitation where they might live, and where their heirs would create the new order Mankeen had envisioned.

A pretty story, but it ignores the fact that stellar expeditions had discovered no such viable Eden orbiting any star within thirteen light years, and the fact that the MAM-An generators in Mankeen's ship weren't sufficiently powerful to take him more than a light year beyond Centauri.

And, looking into the eyes of the face in this imagraph, I can't believe Lionar Mankeen's intended destination was anywhere but the heart of the Sun.

CHAPTER XIII: Avril 3258

●I●I●I●I●I●I●I●I●I●I●I●I●I●I●I●I●I●I●I●I●I●I●I●I●I●I●I●I●II

1.

Alex stared at the black hull of the Falcon and the triangle-flame motif above the port vanes with the name *Phoenix One*. It had amused him to name his three-ship fleet and emblazon the Phoenix symbol on them. It had amused him three weeks ago, but nothing amused him now.

"Dr. Lind, Ben can trans most of the components from Fina. The standard components I'll have to get from Amik. Again. Is it feasible?"

The MT tech shrugged. "There's no reason it wouldn't be, but it'll crowd things a bit on a Falcon."

"Look it over and see what your space requirements will be. Tear out whatever you have to. You should have Commander Blayn and some of the crews to help with the work. I'll send him down." He turned to the sloping ramp that led up to the comcenter. "Ben said he could start transing the components whenever you're ready for them."

Lind frowned slightly, wondering at the commander's tense mood. But it wasn't surprising; there was still no news about Dr. Riis, and he'd been in SSB hands nearly five months.

"We can start degutting this thing today, Commander. Tell Ben to go ahead with the shipment."

Alex nodded and began climbing the ramp; it felt like a mountain. It was hard to concentrate on the smallest tásk, yet all day he'd been desperately grasping at small tasks, at anything to keep his mind occupied. When he emerged into the comcenter, he stopped, frowning. Most of the staff was gathered at the PubliCom screen, watching in apparent fascination.

Didn't they have anything better to do than stand around watching that damned screen?

But his resentment didn't take verbal form. It died as suddenly as it was born. What else did they have to do that was so important? Wait for news of Andreas?

Operating the COS HQ didn't take up their every waking moment now that the installations were complete. There was work enough: full-time monitoring of the perimeter; monitoring of all vidicom and microwave frequencies, PubliCom, Confleet, Conpol, SSB, and Phoenix bands. There was also a certain amount of maintenance work and the mundane problems of tending the personal needs of thirty-four people. There were incompleted projects, such as the MT for the *One*, and an improved VF camouflage screen over the surface access. There were lines of investigation to pursue on Andreas, and there was the physics lab, although Lyden and Bruce seldom required assistance except occasionally from the comptechs. There was work enough to stave off restlessness and boredom—and hopelessness—but not so much that he could reasonably ask them to give up this brief diversion.

That's all it was to most of them: a diversion.

The wedding of Lord Karlis Badir Selasis and Lady Adrien Camine Eliseer.

He could hear the tinny, blurred voices, the hollow chords of the orchestral organ in the cathedron of Helen, the cheering of the crowds. He remembered the crowds that gathered in the Plaza in Concordia for Concord Day. He had always wondered why they cheered.

But they were cheering now in Helen. Half the Houses in the Court of Lords were represented, and Helen was proudly, ecstatically overwhelmed with the influx. The high-pitched voice of the female newscaster rasped over the cheers and music, the jubilant Talmach *Recessional*.

"...the couple will be emerging from the cathedron—oh, yes, there they are! The Lord Karlis..." The words faded in and out under the onslaught of background sound. "...the Lady Galia, wearing a pink satinet gown with brocaded...Lord Loren is shaking the groom's hand now...certainly agree that Lady Adrien is the most exquisite bride ever seen...gown is made of true Sinasian silk, a gift from her grandfather, Lord Sato Shang...embroidered in silver, shiffine panels and veil, koyf brocaded with pearls...long sleeves, with a high-waisted bodice, also decorated with pearls. . . ."

Pearls. She always had an affinity for pearls.

Alex was startled at the sound of soft laughter from one of the women near the vidicom.

"'Zion, Sinasian silk and pearls. You could run Fina for a month on the price of that little outfit."

"At least." Another voice; he couldn't see whose. "Looks like a fancy maternity dress."

A murmur of laughter in this cavern room melding with the cheering of the crowds; there was something ironic in that. Something bitterly ironic in the fact that he was here in this rock-held cave, and Adrien was only kilometers away in Helen, the bride of Karlis Selasis. The 'caster bubbled on, and he listened only because he couldn't force himself to move out of reach of that voice.

". . . guests for the ceremony. Oh, and there's Lord Phillip DeKoven Woolf and Lady Olivet. She's stunning in a gown of pale green velveen with tucking across the bodice . . . necklace of matched aquamarines, a gift from her lord husband on the birth of their son, Justin. . . . Lord Phillip is—uh, striking in a formal suit of black with gold brocade and a sable-trimmed cloak. . . ."

Alex almost smiled. No one but the Lord Phillip Woolf would wear black to this wedding. Adrien would appreciate the connotations in it.

". . . the Lady Selasis seems to have fallen! She's . . . no, she's getting into the 'car. The Eliseer House physician is talking with her. Was that—yes, Dr. Lile Perralt . . . switch now to Emly Hargrove in the plaza near the Eliseer 'car. Emly?"

Another voice, shrill against the louder crowd sounds.

"Thank you, Jenett. Well, apparently the new Lady Selasis fainted, but she seems recovered now. The 'car is lifting off to lead the procession to the Estate . . . festivities tonight at the ball, including a symphalight concert designed and conducted by Master Korim Jasik . . . appearance of the Concordia Cor d'Ballet with . . ."

"Alex?"

He frowned. Someone standing beside him. For how long, he didn't know.

"Yes, Jael?"

"Perralt's sent no word yet?"

"No. Nothing today, and he had nothing to tell me yesterday."

"The show's past finale. Alex, I'm off line upside now. Anything I can do here?"

"What? Oh. No, I don't think so. We're starting on the MT for the *One*. I came up to... to find Vic Blayn."

Jael nodded. "He's on the comp checking out some tac seqs. You go down to the hangar; I'll send Vic around."

Alex turned to retrace his steps down the ramp, and Jael watched him until he reached the bottom, wondering what kept his back so ramrod straight.

But, then, Alex Ransom came up in a hard school.

2.

It was an endless gauntlet of faces, of jeweled hands pawing familiarly at her, of grinning mouths offering—again and again—congratulations.

Congratulations.

These haughty, self-proud Lords and Ladies knew the Selasids, and only a few didn't loathe and fear them. Condolences would be more appropriate, and all of them knew it.

The wide, arched entry was only meters away; beyond that was the columned portico and the broad stairway, decked with heady garlands of roses. At the foot of the stairway, the gleaming Faeton-limos would be waiting. They would also be garlanded with roses. The Lady Galia had chosen roses, the traditional symbol of matrimony, as her decorative theme and imported them by the millions of blooms from Terra.

The last ceremony, this leavetaking, the last appearance of the nuptial couple with their families. Then the cavalcade of rose-decked 'cars to the InterPlan port where Lord Orin's private ship waited for the voyage to Concordia. Adrien choked back her nausea, wondering if the ship would also be filled with roses, wondering, again, how her mother could have chosen roses, if she'd forgotten that morning in the rose garden at the Woolf Estate so many years ago.

Beyond the portico, beyond the stairway, beyond the 'cars, the other crowd waited; the other crowd that filled the Estate plaza, tens of thousands of grinning, cheering, laughing Bonds and Fesh. Yet, given a choice, she would face that crowd willingly rather than this pompous, patronizing mob. The Elite. The rulers of the Concord. The aggregate din of their voices, their raspinq laughter, made the very air oppressive.

"You're trembling, Adrien." Karlis, his hand on her arm, guiding her through this tiresome, bitter gauntlet, leaning close to her ear to make that cold observation.

"Don't be concerned, Karlis. I'm quite recovered now. My lady . . . my lord, thank you." This in response to yet another inane expression of congratulations.

The faces and words were blurring, her breath was coming too fast; she was suffocating in meaningless rustlings of words and cacophonous slitherings of silk and satinet, her eyes incapable of focus, recording only a coruscating montage of haloed flashes and shimmers of light.

Congratulations . . . again and again. . . .

Lord Orin hovered behind the nuptial pair, a huge, impending shadow. She was intensely aware of him, even though he was behind her, more aware of him than of Karlis, whose classic, spoiled profile was ever at the edge of her vision, whose mannered responses echoed hers, whose perfume was as cloying as the pervading scent of roses, as repugnant as the feel of his hand on her arm. But Orin Selasis she saw in her mind's eye, an ominous, chilling presence swathed in furred robes of silent velveen, gliding with that curiously light step, his single eye constantly moving, recording every face and gesture.

There would be nothing but smiles and congratulations for her from this crowd.

She heard her own voice, as distant and meaningless as those around her, making the expected responses. But she would not smile. Let them blame it on the "illness" that made her faint three times on this wedding day, the illness that was feigned and purposeful, but still too nearly real.

And only one thought was clear in her mind now, clear as the polished shaft of a knife blade.

Lile Perralt wasn't here. She hadn't seen him since he left her suite half an hour ago.

Yet he had promised to go with her to the IP port, had insisted upon it. She wouldn't hold it against him if he didn't keep that promise; it would be a relief to her. But she knew him too well, knew he wouldn't break that promise unless he were incapable of carrying it out. A few minutes, he'd said. He'd go to his apartment to make the call to Alexand, then come back to her suite.

Another grinning couple. Lazar Hamid and Lady Falda. Adrien's words of thanks were cold and short.

Dr. Lile. . . .

She was close to tears, remembering his waxen face and the physical pain he tried so hard to conceal.

Perhaps she'd asked too much of him, or too much of his ailing heart, but he was her only contact with Alexand. She had no choice but to tell him the truth she carried within her, to tell him her plans. She had delayed this long out of concern for his heart, and out of fear for what Alexand might do. It was too late now for Alexand to try to stop her or put himself in jeopardy for her. She had his pledge, and perhaps she was showing a lack of faith, but she knew it would be virtually impossible for him to stand idly by while she attempted this escape alone once he learned she was carrying his sons.

But he *must* know. He must know about the twins, about her plans, about where she was going. And Perralt had promised her Alexand *would* know.

She didn't send anyone to the doctor's apartment to ask about him; she didn't know what was involved in making the call to Alexand, and wouldn't risk anyone discovering him in the process. She had waited in her suite, delaying until she could delay no longer, leaving it with the hope that if he missed her there, he would come here to the entry salon. But he wasn't here.

She held one last hope. Perhaps in the face of this crowd he took another exit and would be waiting at the 'car. She knew it was unlikely, she knew something was wrong, but to enable her to walk this endless gauntlet without screaming, she held on to that hope.

Alexand must know. If Dr. Lile didn't—or couldn't—deliver her message . . .

She was only dimly aware of the next face that materialized before her. A young woman with fair skin as flawless as alabaster, hair the color of white wine, eyes the blue of Polluxian skies, deep and leaning toward lavender. Adrien knew that face, but at first all that registered was that she wasn't smiling. Her smile came only after Adrien recognized her, a pensive smile, for her alone. The Lady Olivet Omer Woolf.

"Adrien, the Holy God be with you and watch over you."

It occurred to Adrien how unfortunate it was that Lady Olivet would always be compared to Lord Woolf's first wife; to live up to Elise Galinin Woolf was an impossibility. But this young woman—only a year older than Adrien—had met the challenge. She met it by ignoring it, by being herself—gracious, serene, devoted to her husband and children. And honest, Adrien thought; honest and capable of empathy.

"Thank you, my lady," she said softly, letting her tone carry the message beyond her words, as Olivet's had carried her understanding in words even Selasis couldn't fault.

Her eyes moved to Lady Olivet's right almost reluctantly. She had been aware of the lean, black-garbed figure from the moment she recognized Olivet, yet she found it difficult to look at him. It wasn't Lord Woolf himself who inspired that reluctance. The one even remotely pleasurable aspect of this day of meaningless ceremonies and hypocrisies was seeing the Lord Phillip DeKoven Woolf dressed head to toe, elegantly sardonic, in black.

Alexand...

He looked too much like Alexand, and in this context, the reminder was nearly intolerable.

He seemed to understand that. He offered his hand silently, and he hadn't been smiling, either; not for Orin Selasis. His smile now was for Adrien, and Karlis might not have existed for any hint of awareness he showed.

"Adrien, we both had other visions of this day, but if our hopes were crushed, our friendship needn't share their fate."

"My lord, I hope you know how much I've treasured your friendship."

Karlis's hand tightened painfully on her arm.

"Come on, Adrien, the 'cars are—"

One searing glance from Woolf silenced him. Adrien was still aware of Selasis hovering behind her, but for the moment she felt no fear.

Woolf said, "Lady Olivet and I would be pleased to have you visit us, and we hope it will be often, since you'll be in Concordia." Then he stiffened slightly; he had recognized the ring on her right hand. Alexand's ring.

His eyes flashed up, meeting hers with an ironic smile. "We'll look forward to seeing you in Concordia. And, Adrien, if I can be of assistance to you in *any* way, don't hesitate to call on me."

She felt Karlis's grip tighten on her arm again. Under those polite words was a promise, an offer of help. Of all this high-born, jeweled-and-brocaded assembly, Phillip Woolf was the only one who dared offer her aid, the only one who openly recognized the fact that she might need it.

"My lord . . . thank you."

It seemed so inadequate, but she was incapable of saying more, and it wasn't Karlis's impatience that drew her away with an abruptness she could only hope the Woolfs would forgive. It was the threat of tears, the icy paralysis stealing along her nerves.

The entryway . . . a few meters, a few steps. . . .

And Dr. Lile—*where was he?*

At the 'car, she told herself, moving past the last few grinning faces without even acknowledging them. Dr. Lile would be at the 'car.

The family was already waiting on the columned portico. Lord Loren smiling woodenly, Lady Galia flushed and radiant with triumph. The twins, Galen and Renay, growing so fast, Adrien thought wistfully, both tall and fair-haired like their father, with that quiet confidence in their bearing that he had nearly lost. Patricia next, another daughter of Shang, very conscious of her fragile, dark beauty, but at the moment trying unsuccessfully to hide her boredom, or perhaps it was envy. And Annia. Little Annia, constrained in her ruffled dress and the bandeau of rosebuds that held her blonde hair in unaccustomed confinement.

As Adrien and Karlis stepped out onto the portico, the night sky exploded with starbursts of fireworks, trumpeters lining the steps loosed shimmering fanfares, and the plaza reverberated with thundering cheers. The neural shock left her shuddering, and she didn't at first hear Annia calling her name as she ran toward her.

"Annia?" She knelt and took her small hands. "Too much noise, love?"

Annia shook her head, her voice pitched high against the onslaught. "I *like* the noise. Are you going to be all well?"

"Of course." Adrien smiled as she straightened the bandeau. "I always told you I was tough, didn't I?"

She grinned at that. "Like a belnong!" Then, turning sober, "I'll miss you. When are you coming home again?"

"Soon, love, soon." She pulled her into her arms; Annia mustn't see her tears. "And I'll miss *you* very much."

"Are you cold, Adrien? How come you're shivering?"

"I . . . don't know, Annia."

But she did know.

She was looking over her sister's golden head down into the cordoned area where the rose-decked 'cars waited.

Lile Perralt wasn't there.

And she knew she would never see him again.

3.

The rock seemed to exude a damp chill; it was deep night in the Midhar. Alex paced the comcenter, arms folded, shoulders hunched. The thermogenerators were on, but the chill still gripped his legs and hands.

Night in the Midhar, night in Helen, and early evening here in the Cave of Springs. The comcenter was quiet, most of the staff at supper in the sleeping chamber, where one end of the cavern was periodically converted into a dining hall. Only Val Severin and three comtechs manned the monitors. Jael was on the microwave console.

Alex stopped his pacing, realizing it was distracting to the others. He forced himself to stand in one place, to look at the screens and scanners, to interpret the signals on them; forced himself not to think about Helen or about what was happening there.

He frowned irritably, staring at Jael's back. Jael didn't have to be here now; he should be having supper with the rest of the staff. Or sleeping. He would be on duty with the Helen chapter in less than five hours.

But the annoyance dissipated. Jael was here for the same reason he was. Rather, he was here because he understood why Alex was here, and he was manning the microwave console so that Alex wouldn't have to suffer through the numberless extraneous messages coming in while waiting for the one message. The one that might never come.

Alex couldn't stay still. He began pacing again, aware of Val's questioning glance, and aware that he was serving no purpose here. He should go to his room. Or to the hangar. Not that he'd serve any purpose there, either.

"Alex!" It was Jael. "Kahn Telman on line from the Eliseer Estate."

"Telman?" Not Perralt? Alex crossed to the console in a few long strides and reached for a headset. "Stay on, Jael. Ransom on line, Kahn. Have you talked to Perralt?"

"Not since early this morning. Commander, something's happened. Lile—Dr. Perralt is dead."

The dull, breath-stopping, solar plexus blow; it was fear and shock, and even grief all in one.

"Oh, God, no. . . . How? What happened?"

"I'm not sure, but I think he died of . . . of natural causes."

"His heart?"

"Yes, sir. I think so."

"When did it happen?" He reached out to turn on the PubliCom screen, but left the audio off.

"I don't know exactly, but it must've been within the last hour. He was . . . he was still warm."

Alex felt the strain in Telman's voice. The vidicom showed the crowds at the IP port dispersing, one shot homing in on the Eliseer family. Adrien wasn't with them.

"Kahn, give me the whole story."

"Yes, sir. Well, I knew Lile wasn't feeling too well. He told me that when I talked to him this morning. He didn't say much; we only had a few minutes. But he was worried about Lady Adrien. He—he was genuinely fond of her."

"Yes," Alex said softly, "I know."

"He said he was sure she had some sort of plan. She told him all along she would go through with the wedding, but after that—well, he didn't know. But she refused to let him go to Concordia with her. I thought that was odd."

A new image on the screen, an overview of the IP port, the vidicam zooming in on one ship, already airborne, as its lights disappeared into the background of dim stars. Alex realized sickly that it was all over; the newlyweds had departed, bound for the bride's new home; for Concordia.

"Did he tell you anything else, Kahn?"

"Only that he had no idea exactly what she intended to do. She kept putting him off, telling him he'd know when the time comes.'"

When the time comes. . . .

Alex stood numbed, his breathing slow and shallow, his eyes fixed on the grinning face of the female 'caster on the screen, bubbling with practiced enthusiasm.

"And that's all?"

"That's all he could tell me this morning, but she was—well, apparently ill today. I suppose you know about that."

"What was wrong?"

The image on the screen changed. Recaps of the wedding ceremony. His hand moved jerkily to turn it off.

"I'm not sure anything was really wrong, Commander. I mean, Lady Adrien never fainted in her life. But she had three fainting spells today, all very public. Maybe they were real. I could understand that on *this* day."

"But you think she may have faked the fainting?"

"Yes, sir. The last faint was at the ball, and she was carried out with that one. Lile was with her, of course. She was taken to her bedroom, and she didn't come out until it was time to leave for the IP port. Her father was there part of the time, but I know Lile was alone with her for at least twenty minutes. I wondered if that wasn't the reason for the fainting spell, to have some time alone with him."

Alex rested his palms on the console counter, recognizing the quivering within him as panic, fighting doggedly to keep it under control. On some level he was conscious of Jael beside him, listening to the same disembodied voice, and a few meters away, Val Severin, watching him, the scanners forgotten.

"All right, Kahn. Go on."

"I went to the entry salon and watched the big exit. Everything went off as expected, except Lile wasn't there. That bothered me because I couldn't imagine him not going to the port with her, especially when she'd been ill, and at that point I'm not sure it was faked; she looked a little shaky. In fact, she fainted again as she was boarding the ship and was taken straight to her cabin."

Alex frowned, wondering why that sounded an alarm in his mind.

"Who was going to Concordia with her? There must have been someone from the Eliseer household."

"Only Mariet. I guess she didn't *want* anyone else to go with her."

Alex tried to make sense of that, and perhaps it was simple enough: she didn't want to put anyone else in jeopardy with her.

"What about Lectris?"

Telman hesitated. "Well, Lectris is a question mark all around. He got a leave to visit a sister in Cuprin about five days ago, and he hasn't returned. I don't know how long his leave was, or if he was supposed to return before the wedding."

"Are you *sure* he didn't board the ship with her?"

"Yes, sir. I'm sure."

Alex pulled in a deep breath, working at the overwhelmingly difficult process of ordering his thoughts.

"We'll find out about Lectris later. Get back to Perralt."

"Well, when Lady Adrien left the Estate without Lile, I thought I'd better check on him. The crowd slowed me down, but I got to his apartment as soon as I could, and..." He stopped, the words choked off.

They had been friends, Alex thought, fellow spies in the Eliseer Estate for over a quarter of a century. A man shouldn't have to talk about the source of his grief so soon.

"Kahn, I'm sorry, but I must know what happened."

"Yes, I... understand." His voice was dulled with the effort of control. "Lile's door was locked, but it's keyed for me. When I went in he... was lying on the floor by his desk. No signs of violence. I'm sure it was his heart. I went over the apartment with a montector and checked his alarm system. Everything was square. And he had his transceiver in his hand. That hadn't been disturbed."

"His... transceiver? Did you notice the frequency setting?"

"Yes, sir. It was on the COS HQ band."

When the time comes.

Above him, the black stone turned, closing in; he shut his eyes against it.

The time had come. The princess had emerged from her tower, sword in hand, to meet the dragon, and trusted Perralt to convey her battle plans to her prince, her timid, timorous prince hiding in his stony keep.

And if those plans included a plea for help, if she were depending on him to help her fend off the dragon—

The message was sealed where no power could reach it.

No. He wasn't thinking; the panic was getting out of control. There were Phoenix agents in the Selasid Concordia Estate; a new contact could be set up as soon as she arrived.

"Kahn, how long has it been since you... found him?"

"At least half an hour. I had to search his apartment and dispose of his Phoenix equipment."

"Have you notified anyone at the Estate?"

"No, I thought I should check with you or Ben first."

"Use your own judgment. Do you know if we have any agents on the Selasid ship?"

"I don't think so."

His jaw muscles tensed. "Damn. Do you have the Selasid agents in Eliseer identified?"

"Yes."

"I want them watched closely; every move they make, every contact, every call."

"We already have them covered fairly well, but we can tighten the cover. Will you be calling Ben about... about Lile?" There was a silent plea under that toneless inquiry.

"You needn't call him. I'll take care of it. If he needs more information, he can contact you later."

"Thank you, Commander."

"Keep me posted. If I'm not available, talk to Jael." He paused, searching for words, finding none adequate. "Kahn, I'm sorry about Dr. Perralt—for your sake."

Telman didn't answer immediately, and when he did, his voice was thick and tight.

"So am I."

Alex slowly removed the headset, only vaguely aware of Val and the comtechs at their stations; aware in the same vague manner that Jael had put aside his headset and was watching him. His strongest awareness at the moment was of the stone walls and ceiling, of the megatons of rock borne on that irregular, light-swallowing dome. Black as night. Black as death.

Perhaps it was only the combination of seemingly unrelated facts: Adrien's refusal to let Perralt go with her—her only Phoenix contact. Lectris granted a leave five days before the wedding, a leave from which he apparently hadn't returned; Lectris who would die to save or avenge his Lady. And the fainting spells, the last one at the ship, sending her immediately to her cabin.

Perhaps that anomaly birthed the conviction. He knew her strength, knew that steel-boned Selaneen capable of bearing even this terrifying day without giving way. And perhaps it was that linked-twin akinness, the same nearly telepathic communication he had shared with Rich.

He said to Jael, "Adrien isn't going to Concordia."

"She isn't . . . brother, are you—how do you know that?"

The question roused him. He didn't *know* it. But explaining why he was sure of it was beyond him now; he could only shake his head, grateful that Jael asked no further questions, or offered any expression of sympathy.

"Jael, try to pick up any transmissions from the Selasid ship. I'll be in my cell—my room. I have to call Ben and let him know about Perralt."

"I'll 'com you if anything comes down."

Alex nodded and started for the passageway; his footsteps echoed against the black stone.

Val rose and went to Jael, her hand seeking his. "What did he mean?" she asked. "If Lady Adrien doesn't go to Concordia, where *will* she go?"

"The God knows, Val. *We* don't. Not now."

4.

Karlis Selasis looked out over the humming expanse of Concordia, gilded in the clear morning light, the new sun flashing from tens of thousands of windows, but his eyes were aching from a sleepless night, and he was hardly aware of the scene. He listened to the sweet tones of the claripipes, molten and slow as honey, and his frustration was approaching an explosive point. He turned and frowned into the green shadows of the solarium.

He despised this room, and his father knew it. A damn jungle, rife with the cloying odors of exotic, suffocatingly lush verdure. There were even flocks of jewel-bright parakeets in its fan-vaulted, glass-domed heights. He could never tolerate the proximity of birds.

"Father, for the God's sake—"

But Orin Selasis, from the depths of his green-cushioned chair, waved him to silence without a word, without so much as a glance, his hand, once in motion, taking up the languid rhythm of the claripipes.

Karlis went to a chair near the windowall and slumped into it, his fair features suffused with a deep flush.

His father didn't have to treat him like a stinking Bond. Not in *front* of a Bond. He didn't have to show that—that *contempt*.

There was no other word for it, and it had become increasingly
manifest since . . .

Karlis's mouth tightened against the quivering of his lips.
It wasn't fair, when a man needed a father, needed *someone*
to show a little understanding. Did he think it was easy bearing
up under this, did he think it didn't tear him up inside?

Damn that Outsider whore! It must have been that one, what
did she call herself? Why couldn't he remember? They had
drugged him. They must have. But if he ever found that girl . . .

He lapsed into black fantasies, elaborating on details of
vengeance formulated in previous fantasies. It was all that was
left him.

Impotent.

The very word made his stomach turn. The other part of
it wasn't so bad; his father had always insisted on maintaining
a sperm reserve, and to hell with what the Board of Succession
thought of "unnatural" conception. But *impotent*—that was
intolerable.

He shifted in his chair, the subtle cadences of the claripipes
as cloying in his ears as the scents of bizarre and fecund plants
in his nostrils. He turned his attention, and frustrated anger,
on the source of the dulcet melody that seemed so engrossing
to Orin Selasis.

The boy was perhaps fourteen; a Bond, but skilled enough
at the 'pipes. He sat cross-legged on a green velveen cushion
by Selasis's footstool. A well formed boy, Karlis had to admit,
nicely muscled, smooth, fair skin, blond hair curling around
his face, blue eyes shadowed with long lashes. He was naked
except for the lamé trunks and the gold chains looped around
his shoulders, and oblivious to everything beyond the instrument at his lips.

This was no time for pretty Bond boys.

But seeing his father's single eye half closed; his faint smile
of absorbed pleasure, Karlis waited in resentful silence. Perhaps it was to be admired, this ability to seem so totally at
ease in the face of disaster. But something *must* be done. His
hands knotted into fists as his frustration found a new focus.

That black-eyed bitch! To walk out on Karlis Selasis on
their wedding day—it was incomprehensible.

And no doubt she thought herself very clever, playing on
his sympathies. *I'll be all right, Karlis . . . just let me rest until
after liftoff.* No, she didn't need anyone to stay with her. Only
Mariet.

Then that seeming afterthought. *Oh, Mariet, I've lost the pills Dr. Perralt gave me. They must be in the 'car.*

And after liftoff...

Gone. Vanished into vacuum.

The cabin empty except for the rings on the bedside table, the betrothal and wedding rings. And the tape spool; Adrien's parting gift. It might as well have been a bomb.

A final rising scale and a fillip of a slide recalled his attention. At long last the piece was finished. The boy lowered the 'pipes and looked up at Selasis.

"Ah, Lalic, nicely done." He leaned forward, smiling obliquely as he cupped Lalic's chin in his hand and tilted his face up, his thumb moving slowly across his smooth cheek.

Lalic only looked back at him, blue eyes expressionless, the pupils reduced to black points, and Selasis's massive body quaked with soft laughter.

"Oh, yes, very pretty...the song." Then he leaned back with a wave of dismissal. "You may go."

The boy obediently came to his feet and bowed, first to Selasis, then to Karlis.

"Good day, my lords."

Karlis watched him walk to the double doors, bare feet soft on the marblex floor, wait for Selasis to press a button on the table console by his chair, and when the doors opened, walk on, eyes straight ahead.

Karlis turned abruptly to Selasis. "Damn it, Father, how can—"

"Karlis, if you're thinking of commenting on the way I choose to use my time, I'd advise against it. I'd also advise you to control your tendency to panic."

Karlis bit back a caustic reply, contenting himself with a cool, "I think we should at least discuss the matter."

"Discuss it? You and I? I'd prefer to waste my time on a bit of music. There's no *discussing* to be done. There are a number of decisions to be made and carried out, most of which I've already attended to. At the moment, we're waiting for Master Hawkwood. He was busy with another matter in Coben when I called him last night, but he should be here in a few minutes."

Karlis frowned. Bruno Hawkwood. At least something was being done, but Hawkwood was such a strange man...

"Don't pout, Karlis," Selasis said curtly. "Holy God, that

Eliseer girl has more pluck than you do."

"Pluck? I can think of more appropriate terms."

"Can you? Try *courage*. And don't balk at that. You must always recognize the capabilities of your opponent, or you enter the circle blindfolded, and we're already entering this circle with one hand shackled." He fixed his single eye on his son, and Karlis was hard put not to flinch. Then he turned away, making no attempt to conceal his disgust as he muttered, "Damn it, how many times did I tell you to stay out of those Outsider serallios? And don't try to tell me that isn't where you picked up that—that disease!"

"Dr. Monig said it could've been—"

"Dr. Monig said a great deal too much, apparently. I have one disaster stepping on the heels of the next, and you—" He sagged back in his chair, and in profile there seemed something peculiarly·sharklike in the sleek curves of forehead and hair, in the drawn line of his mouth. "We'll be damned lucky to pull out of this with the House intact, Karlis, but take this as an oath—I *will* pull out of it! A few may fall by the wayside, but I won't see the House brought down by a conniving wench like Adrien Eliseer!"

Karlis smiled with grim satisfaction; here, at least, he was still on common ground with his father.

"She's got a lesson coming, and I'd damn well like to give it to her personally—and whoever's in this with her. She couldn't have engineered this—this disappearing act by herself."

"Don't underestimate her. Who do you think engineered her disappearance? Loren Eliseer?"

"He must have. Or Woolf. He's part of this. You heard what he said to her yesterday—'If I can be of assistance to you in *any* way...' Damn him! And he had the gall to wear black. Black at a wedding!"

Selasis sighed ponderously. "The God help me, I've been given an idiot for an heir. With Adrien Eliseer, I might have gotten an heir worthy of...but that's counting birds flown. Karlis, we can't be sure of Loren Eliseer yet, but there's one thing we *can* be sure of: Woolf is *not* involved. If he were that concerned about Adrien, he'd have backed Eliseer in a challenge to your virility *before* the wedding. He wouldn't risk getting found out in a subterfuge so dangerous and desperate as this."

Karlis subsided, his eyes narrowing. "What about Eliseer? It's even more of a risk for him."

"Yes, and that makes me wonder if Adrien wasn't telling the truth about him. He didn't have the courage to demand a Board of Succession investigation when the rumors were running rampant, why would he take this even more dangerous course—" He stopped at the sound of the door chime and turned on the vis-screen on the table console. "Well, perhaps Bruno can find the answer to that. Here he is."

Karlis turned to the opening doors a little uneasily. Hawkwood didn't like this room, either, so his father had told him. The Master of Shadows was uncomfortable in a room where the artificial jungle made so many hiding places.

Selasis smiled almost cordially as Hawkwood entered. "Ah, my dear Bruno, you're looking well. Coben's climate apparently agreed with you."

Hawkwood didn't smile; he seldom did. He was dressed in dark brown, as he always seemed to be, with silent, soft-soled shoes, and no jewelry except a narrow wedding band and a gold medallion in the shape of a seven-spoked wheel. Tall, lean to the point of emaciation, eyes of a pale, tawny brown set in a long, narrow face whose skull-like contours were emphasized by a head shaved clean, its curved planes catching the light like molded bronze.

A religious fetish. Hawkwood belonged to the Order of Gamaliel. Karlis had only the vaguest idea what that meant, and he regarded that shaven head with distaste. What kind of religion asked a man to disfigure himself like that?

Hawkwood inclined his head to Selasis in what for him sufficed for a bow.

"Yes, my lord, Coben's climate is agreeable. The matter of interest to you there was concluded successfully a few hours ago. Would you like a report now?"

Selasis waved a hand irritably. "No, I'll take your word on the success of the conclusion. Right now, I have a matter of far greater interest to deal with."

Hawkwood drew up a chair, seating himself without asking leave, and Karlis's uneasiness turned to impatience. Hawkwood hadn't even bothered to acknowledge his presence.

"Good morning, Bruno," he said caustically.

Hawkwood's amber eyes shifted in his direction. "Good morning, Lord Karlis." Then he was silent, as if waiting for Karlis to come to a point.

He blurted, "Father told you enough about what happened. Do you really think this scheme is entirely Adrien's?"

"At this time, I can't say. I haven't enough information yet."

"But you think she's capable of carrying off something like this—managing to disappear into nothing—without help?"

Hawkwood studied him with that unblinking, dispassionate gaze that stirred the centers of rage in Karlis's mind.

"I think the Lady Adrien is capable of it; that doesn't mean it was actually accomplished without help."

Selasis turned his single eye on Karlis in a cold and unmistakable warning, then while Karlis sank into sullen silence, addressed himself to Hawkwood.

"I know my account was sketchy, Bruno, but so was my information at the time. Master Ranes, your second-in-command, performed admirably in your absence, by the way."

Karlis smiled at that. It was a barb and a reminder, but that was more evident in his father's tone than in any reaction it got from Hawkwood. He only nodded, as if the information came as no surprise to him.

"Master Ranes is an able man. Can you tell me more about Lady Adrien's actual method of escape?"

Selasis raised an eyebrow. "Escape? I prefer to call it a flight. Yes, I can tell you exactly what happened. The Lady Adrien was apparently ill on her wedding day; she did a great deal of fainting, and the last occasion was when she boarded my ship. She was taken directly to the cabin prepared for the newlyweds. Karlis and I accompanied her, and by the time she arrived, she had regained consciousness."

"Did you call a physician, my lord?"

"We had none on board, and the Lady professed to be recovering and nobly insisted we not delay our departure."

"It was an act," Karlis declared angrily. "The fainting, all the gasping and trembling—an *act!*"

Selasis sighed. "Of course it was, Karlis, but a very convincing one, you must admit. Even I was convinced, Bruno, and when she asked to be left alone to rest until after liftoff, I wasn't at all suspicious."

"You had no reason to be, my lord. She *was* left alone, then?"

"Yes, except for her attendant; a Bond girl. Adrien seemed strangely attached to her. I left her then, and Karlis followed soon after. We were only a few minutes short of liftoff. However, just before Karlis departed, she realized she'd left some pills given her by the Eliseer family physician in the 'car." Then, with a withering glance at his son, "Wasn't that it, Karlis?"

His face burned as Hawkwood's tawny eyes turned on him.

"Yes," he admitted truculently, "pills, and since she was so *sick*, I offered to send someone after them, but she said Mariet could go; she'd know where to look. And so—"

"And so," Selasis said, taking up the narrative, "Karlis 'commed the guard at the lock and advised him that an Eliseer Bondmaid would be leaving the ship on a short errand. The liftoff lights were already on, so Karlis retired to another cabin, content to spend his wedding night under a psychimax mask, which, thanks to his recent adventures in the Outside, was all he—"

"Father!" Karlis surged to his feet, his hands fisted. "Damn it, you don't have to—"

"All right, Karlis, all right!" He took a long breath, then when Karlis slumped back into his chair to glare at him in seething silence, he turned to Hawkwood, who observed this brief clash as he might an encounter between two ants simultaneously discovering a single crumb.

"The guard at the lock," Selasis continued, his tone only a little less caustic, "didn't notice that there were *two* Eliseer Bondmaids on Adrien's errand—not one, as Karlis had told him. He waved them through without a thought, nor did he stop to think when he closed the lock for liftoff, that neither of them had returned. Admittedly, there was a great deal of confusion in the last minutes before liftoff, and there were Eliseer Bonds all around the ship. They'd been allowed at the port to see the Lady off. Eliseer is incredibly lax with his Bonds. But that didn't excuse the guard's blindness." He paused, smiling coldly. "I thought it fitting that he should learn the price of metaphorical blindness with literal blindness."

Hawkwood made no comment, seeming to record that piece of information as a fact, but one of no immediate interest.

"When did you discover Lady Adrien's absence?"

"At least half an hour after liftoff. *I* discovered it. Karlis was . . . resting. She left her wedding and betrothal rings and the tape I told you about. It's fortunate, of course, that I found it before anyone else."

"From what you told me of its contents, it *is* fortunate. May I hear it in its entirety?"

Selasis reached into one of the pockets of his robe and handed him a tape spool. Hawkwood took a tiny audio speaker from his tunic and inserted the spool after examining it closely, then for the space of two minutes sat motionless, listening. He showed no hint of emotion; nothing but cold, intent concentration. Karlis wouldn't have been surprised if, having heard the message once, he recited it verbatim.

Karlis couldn't recite it, but he knew the general purport all too well. First, an assertion that Adrien was aware of Karlis's "physical incapacity," as she put it, and with her cousin Janeel's fate in mind, had planned this escape to avoid a similar fate for herself. Then a declaration that she was acting entirely independently of her father, that he knew nothing of her intentions before or after the fact. And last, a warning. She had proof of what she referred to with caustic nicety as Karlis's "condition" in the form of a taped death testament made by Dr. Levit Monig in Lima on 5 May '57. If Selasis harmed her, her father, her family, or her House in any way, she would see that the testament was brought to the attention of the Board of Succession, as well as the Chairman of the Directorate. She would leave it to them to judge whether it was more reprehensible for her to escape this marriage, or for Selasis to enter into the contracts knowing Karlis was both impotent and sterile. No euphemisms then.

Karlis stirred restlessly, his frustration mounting again, and finally Hawkwood removed the speaker from his ear and returned the tape to Selasis.

"A remarkable young woman, my lord."

"Granted, Bruno. What do you think of her message? Could she conceivably make good her threats?"

Hawkwood's shoulders came up in a scant shrug.

"Her use of Dr. Monig's name, the location, and the date suggest she can. I know Monig died two days after his escape from the Lima retreat, and that was the exact date. I find that information particularly puzzling because it could only come from the Outside, but I know of no Outside source available to her. To my knowledge, she doesn't frequent Outside entertainments, nor does anyone close to her."

"But she didn't pull all that out of nothing, Bruno, and I doubt it came to her in a vision. To *my* knowledge, she's not prone to religious ecstasies."

Another barb; Selasis had little patience with Hawkwood's religious orthodoxy, and Karlis relished the flicker of disapproval in those pale, unblinking eyes.

"No, my lord," Hawkwood replied levelly, "she pulled it out of the Outside, obviously, and her source will have to be identified. However, there's one thing that makes me think it may be a bluff. If she does have this proof, why didn't she make it available to her father so he could initiate a Board of Succession investigation before the wedding?"

Selasis's eyes flashed. "That occurred to me, Bruno. Damn it, it *must* be a bluff."

"It *may* be. However, it's possible that she's not actually in possession of the death testament at this time, but could gain access to it in the future—*if* it exists, and we can't assume it doesn't. I'll put my agents in the Outside to work on that immediately."

"Monetary incentives are unlimited in this matter, Bruno. I'd empty my coffers to—" He frowned at the sound of the door chime, checked the vis-screen, then said into the intercom, "Dr. Lazet, I'll see you in a few minutes."

Karlis frowned at the closed doors. Lazet's chief claim to fame, and his exorbitant salary, was his skill as a plastic surgeon.

Selasis made no reference to the interruption as he went on. "Another thing, Bruno, I want to know if Loren Eliseer is involved in this scheme of Adrien's. And if he *is*—" His hands curled into powerful fists, but after a moment relaxed. "One mustn't anticipate. That stretches the Writ of Destiny, doesn't it, Bruno?"

Another barb, but Hawkwood only said calmly, "No, my lord, it leads one off a True Path into the thorns of Chaos."

Selasis laughed softly. "No doubt. At any rate, Eliseer isn't my primary concern. *Adrien* is. Find her, Bruno. I'm helpless, entirely at her mercy, until she's found, and if she expected me to tolerate this sort of blackmail, she made an error. I won't have this knife at my back, and the only way to be rid of it, is to be rid of her. *Find* her, Bruno!"

"If it can be done, my lord, I will do it. And I'll pursue the investigation personally. I plan to leave for Helen by midday."

"That's gratifying. But until you *do* find her, I have something of a problem. I'm not ready to announce to the worlds that Karlis's bride slipped away from him on their wedding night. Under other circumstances, I'd simply announce her death, but I can't do that when she might suddenly come back to life—with Monig's death testament in her hand. So the Lady Adrien must be kept alive in the bosom of her new husband's family until you find her, and I can *safely* announce her death."

Hawkwood even smiled by a millimeter. "I see. Dr. Lazet has been entrusted with this life-preserving mission, then?"

Karlis didn't see, and it annoyed him, that air of conspiracy between them. But he didn't ask any questions.

"So he has, Bruno," Selasis replied. Then, after a thoughtful pause, "What about Lazet? I've never found it necessary to trust him with anything so critical before."

"He can be trusted. He's presently taking ten milligrams of eladane a day simply to avoid withdrawal symptoms, which are, I understand, quite painful." Then, perhaps anticipating Selasis, he added, "But with Dr. Monig's escape in mind, I'll watch Lazet closely. His addiction, of course, gives me an advantage I didn't have with Monig."

Selasis smiled. "I've never known you to make the same error twice, Bruno. I hope you continue to maintain that record." Then he pressed a button on the console. "Dr. Lazet, you may come in, and bring the girl."

Karlis frowned toward the doors as they opened. He only glanced at Lazet, whose round, flaccid face displayed a little less euphoria than usual. It was the young woman following him who occupied Karlis's full attention.

A Bond, dressed in shapeless pants and tabard so dirty the House colors were nearly unidentifiable, she shuffled behind Lazet, head down, sending darting glances from under a mat of unkempt dark hair. Karlis's lip curled. Lazet might at least have bathed her before bringing her here.

Both Hawkwood and Selasis studied the girl with an intentness that made no sense to Karlis. Finally, when the doctor was two meters from Selasis's chair, he stopped and bowed deeply, then with a quarter turn, bowed again to Karlis. The girl emulated him nervously, adding a bow for Hawkwood. Her dark eyes shifted constantly from him to her Lords, then to Lazet, but under the evident fear was a peculiarly avid glint, and Karlis thought disgustedly that Lazet had best watch any loose valuables on his person.

Selasis said pleasantly, "Well, Dr. Lazet, I see you've found a candidate."

"An *excellent* candidate, my lord. I was amazed to find such a good one so quickly." He turned and prodded the girl a few steps closer. "You see, my lord, height and weight are nearly perfect. She's only six centimeters taller, and a kilo heavier. And the facial structure—" He pushed the girl's matted hair back from her face with one hand, the other grasping her chin, turning her head from side to side. "It's *beautiful*, my lord. No epicanthic fold, of course, but that's a simple matter. The zygomatic arch is a bit wide, but the worst problems—the nose and upper lip—are easily remedied surgically. Hair and eye color are even a close match." He took her hands and turned them over with a fastidious frown. "As for her hands . . . well, perhaps that can be remedied cosmetically. Try to picture—stand up straight, Elda—picture her with her hair properly coiffed, brows trimmed, hands manicured, and suitable clothing, of course."

Selasis tilted his head, still examining the girl.

"So, Doctor, you're satisfied that the metamorphosis is feasible."

"Oh, my lord, indeed I am."

"Yes. Have you talked to her?"

Lazet's mouth sagged open. "About—about the—uh, metamorphosis, my lord? No, of course not. I thought—"

"Rightly so. I simply wondered if you'd formed some opinion of her *mental* suitability. She seems alert enough."

The girl's eyes narrowed as she looked from one to the other, and since Lazet's admonition, she kept her back almost *proudly* straight.

The question of her mental suitability, however, seemed to be more than Lazet could handle.

"Well, yes, my lord, she's . . . alert, I suppose. . . ."

Before Selasis could clarify the question or express his obvious annoyance, Bruno Hawkwood rose and walked silently toward the girl. She drew back, her eyes inky pools of apprehension, but he stopped a pace away, his slight smile conveying a cordiality Karlis found incredible.

"What's your name, girl?" Hawkwood asked, almost gently.

"Elda," she replied, still uncertain, but assured enough to try to meet Hawkwood's eye, if only briefly. "Elda Ternin, sirra."

"Ah. A pretty name. Tell me, Elda, have you ever dreamed of being a Lady?" Then, noting her shocked glance at Selasis, "It's all right. Dreams aren't deeds, you know."

Finding only expectant approval on her Lord's face, she laughed nervously, casting a sidelong glance at Hawkwood.

"Oh . . . there was times I dreamed things like—like that when I was little. When I first went to the big Plaza on a Corcord Day and saw all the fine Lords and Ladies. But children—well, they say even kittens and puppies dreams."

Hawkwood smiled understandingly. "So they say, and children always like to make games of their dreams. You have a nice voice, Elda; a soft voice. When you were a little girl, did you and other children ever play at being Lords and Ladies? Ah—of course, you did. What Lady did you like best to play?"

Hawkwood had her thoroughly charmed now. That avid glint Karlis had recognized earlier was even more obvious, and there was a hint of coquetry in her shy smile.

"You'll laugh, sirra, and . . . and my lords." Then, seeing Hawkwood's and Selasis's encouraging smiles, she admitted, "I—I always liked to pretend I was the most beautiful Lady I ever saw on a Concord Day. She was . . . I mean, the Lady Elise."

Selasis's mouth twitched, and Karlis almost laughed, too. Phillip Woolf should be here. But Hawkwood didn't share their amusement. He nodded to the girl agreeably.

"She was indeed lovely, Elda, and I'm sure you played the Lady better than any of the other children. Do you remember how the Lady Elise walked? I always thought her so graceful in the way she walked. Remember how she crossed to the first tier of steps on her lord husband's arm, then she'd turn and smile and wave to the crowd, with the lights flashing in her hair and on all her shining jewels."

The girl was entranced, eyes moist and unfocused.

"Oh, yes, sirra, and the pretty gowns she wore, silk and satinet and fur. I never even touched fur . . ."

Nor silk and satinet, Karlis thought irritably, then he stared at Hawkwood. After a quick look around the room, Hawkwood went to a table by one of the windowalls and pulled the cloth off, and now he returned to the girl, still smiling. And that cloth—brocaded Sanseret silk, the rare peacock pattern, fringed with pure gold thread—the man had gone mad! He was actually draping that cloth around the Bond's shoulders, laughing lightly when she tried to put him off.

Karlis looked at his father and got another shock. Not only was Selasis offering no protest himself, he shook his head at

Karlis in a clear warning not to interfere. At least Lazet hadn't slipped over the edge into this incredible insanity; his gaping mouth served as a reminder to Karlis to close his own.

"Look, Elda—silk as fine as any Lady ever wore. No, don't be afraid." For the first time there was a hint of threat in Hawkwood's voice, and it stopped the girl's frantic protests; but he was still smiling, and the hint was so subtle, it only calmed her, rather than making her afraid. "Now, Elda, show us how you used to play the Lady Elise. Remember how she looked on Concord Day? Remember how she walked? Show me how she walked in all her silks and furs."

"You—you're making mock of me, sirra." Still, that misty enchantment was back in her eyes, and Karlis winced as her grimy fingers stroked the silk.

Hawkwood said, "You're afraid we'll laugh? Well, Elda, if you should provide your Lord a little amusement, is that so bad?"

Karlis saw his father actually smile encouragingly at that cue, and the girl laughed and tossed her head back.

"Well, when I saw the Lady Elise in the big Plaza, she held her head up so high . . . like this, and she'd lift up her silk skirt just a little in front, and she'd smile . . . oh, she seemed to shine all by herself!"

And as Karlis watched in stunned disbelief, Elda lifted her chin and began walking toward the door, every step a ludicrous swoop, the cloth dragging behind her, one hand raised, no doubt on her "lord husband's" arm, while she grinned at imaginary crowds. When she reached the door, she turned, swept her "train" around behind her, and retraced her steps with the same swooping gait, and finally climaxed this grotesque parody with a *formal* curtsy to Selasis.

Hawkwood seemed delighted, and Selasis smiled beatifically as the Bond straightened.

"Very good, my girl," he said, giving Hawkwood an almost imperceptible nod.

"Elda, I think you're possessed of untapped talents. I'll talk with you soon about them. But for now—Lazet, take her to the minimum security section and tell Master Ranes to make her comfortable."

"Uh . . . yes, Master Hawkwood." He was still bewildered, but the direct order seemed to reestablish his equilibrium. In reverse ratio, it shook the girl's, and she was suddenly embarrassed and afraid. She pulled the silk cloth off and tried to fold it, and Karlis groaned inwardly at the mauling of the delicate brocade.

"You may keep it for a while, Elda," Hawkwood reassured her. "I want you to get used to the feel of silk. Lazet, I'll need to talk to you later, so keep yourself available."

"Yes, of course, sirra. Ah . . . my lords, good day."

When at length he and the girl had concluded their nervous bowings and shuffled out of the room, and the doors finally closed on them, Selasis loosed a long sigh.

"Oh, Bruno, a Sanseret silk?" Karlis waited with some anticipation for the dressing down Hawkwood so thoroughly deserved for the desecration of a rare work of art, but he was due for another shock. His father looked up at Hawkwood and actually laughed.

"But an effective demonstration. A signpost to a True Path, wouldn't you say, finding a girl like that—one with the physical characteristics Lazet found so inspiring, and enough intelligence and imagination to show promise as an actress."

Hawkwood returned to his chair, sober, contained; himself again.

"It may be a signpost, my lord. At any rate, the metamorphosis, as you termed it, is entirely feasible. She'll need training, of course. Mistra Radin, I think. She can also be trusted. She has two daughters of whom she's inordinately fond, both dancers in the Concordia Cor d'Ballet."

Selasis grunted. "And dancers are so vulnerable to injuries. Well, the outward aspects of the metamorphosis will be simple enough, but all the surgery, cosmetics, costuming, and training won't make that girl convincing in close contacts with friends or family. You will, of course, make available all the information you can garner on Lady Adrien's personal life, but that won't—"

"Father!" Karlis rose, staring at the two of them, the full import of this charade having at last come home to him. "You're going to let that girl act as a—a stand-in for . . . Adrien?"

"Of course, Karlis. What did you think this was all about?"

"But she's—she's a *Bond!*"

"What would you suggest? That I use a Fesh? Or should I delve into the Outside and dredge up one of your—" He stopped, venting a weary sigh. "Never mind. It will only be temporary, but it's imperative that no one suspect your new bride has fled her groom. That must be obvious to you."

Karlis sagged back into his chair. "Yes, I suppose—but it seems like a hell of a risk . . ."

"It *is* a hell of a risk, and she can only successfully manage it at a distance, so to speak, or in very brief appearances." Selasis turned to Hawkwood. "To reduce the number of public appearance for the 'Lady,' we must invent a plausible and perhaps lingering illness. Adrien laid the groundwork for that herself with those fainting spells yesterday. My greatest concern, of course, is her family."

Hawkwood nodded, the light moving on the bronzed contours of his head.

"But an ordinary illness might induce them to come to Concordia to offer personal solicitude. Perhaps this illness should be more *mental* than physical, and she's laid the groundwork for that, too. Her reluctance to enter this marriage, her nearly obsessive attachment to the Lord Alexand. I'm told she wore his betrothal ring yesterday; in fact, she's worn it continuously since his death. Hardly normal behavior. A state of chronic, or even manic, depression shouldn't seem unreasonable to her family or anyone else."

Selasis smiled almost warmly. "Yes, very good, Bruno. I can get clinical evidence, of course. That psychologist at the University—what's his name?"

"Lassily," Hawkwood supplied. "Bern Lassily."

"And a mental illness will serve very nicely to explain any inconsistency in her behavior."

"Perhaps, my lord, Lady Adrien might go so far as to refuse to see or talk to her family, especially her father. Dr. Lassily could insist that they refrain from forcing their attentions on her until—well, for as long as necessary."

Selasis nodded decisively. "Excellent, Bruno. Well, I have no choice but to attempt the subterfuge. Karlis and his new bride will leave for the Lima retreat in a few hours. A nuptial trip, for public consumption. Dr. Lazet and Mistra Radin will accompany them, of course, although that *won't* be made public, and I'm depending on you to make sure it doesn't become public. I'll let it be known within a week that Lady Adrien isn't well, and their stay in Lima will be prolonged to give her more opportunity for rest, etc. And Lassily—before you leave Concordia, Bruno, you must make the necessary arrangements with Lassily, and the less he knows, the better."

"He'll only know that *you* say Lady Adrien is suffering a mental disorder. He's too . . . indebted to you, my lord, to question your judgment publicly or privately. He'll lend his name to the 'treatment' in any way you wish."

"Good. But be sure of him, Bruno. And keep in mind that this subterfuge can't be maintained indefinitely. I want Adrien found, and found *soon*."

"She'll be found as soon as possible, as soon as is Written. My lord, have you any idea where she might go for refuge?"

"How in the God's name should *I* know?"

"And you, Lord Karlis? Anything she might have said— some passing remark, perhaps?"

"Well . . . no. I didn't really know Adrien too well. But she has this private retreat somewhere on Castor. Her father built it for her a few years ago."

"Yes, to solace her after Lord Alexand's death. She won't be there."

"What makes you so damn sure?" Why did Hawkwood have to keep harping on Alexand Woolf and Adrien?

"It's too obvious, and it would be much too easy to find her there." Hawkwood rose, turning to Selasis. "There aren't many places a Lord's daughter can hide. Unless she does have help from her father or someone in a similar position, her choices will be limited."

"My time is also limited," Selasis noted coldly.

"Yes, of course. I think her source of information in the Outside is a logical line to follow; that source might also provide her a refuge. Then there's the obvious alternative of the cloisters. Now, if you'll excuse me, I have a great deal to do before I lift off for Helen."

Selasis nodded, then let him take five steps toward the door before he stopped him with a quiet, "Oh, by the way, Bruno . . ."

Karlis took some satisfaction in the tense set of Hawkwood's shoulders as he turned.

"Yes, my lord?"

"Give my regards to your lovely wife, Margreta, and my apologies for sending you off on another assignment without even a day's respite."

Hawkwood said coolly, "I'll convey your message, my lord."

"I understand she's been quite ill."

"Yes, she has."

"Rather a rare disease; a malignant brain tumor affecting the optic nerve, isn't it? I've been told the doctors you've seen haven't had much success treating it."

Hawkwood didn't move a muscle. "That's true, my lord."

"Most unfortunate. Margreta's a charming young woman. But perhaps . . . that is, if all goes well in the next few weeks, I could put in a word for you at the University Research Hospital. They always have such a long waiting list."

Hawkwood's cold gaze bordered on hatred. But only bordered. A self-contained man, Karlis was thinking; probably part of his religious training. Gamaliel. Fanatics, no doubt. Cultists.

Hawkwood lifted his chin a scant centimeter. "A word from you, my lord, would be helpful, of course."

"At any rate, you needn't worry about Margreta during your absence. I'll make it a point to keep a close eye on her. You can count on that, Bruno." Then he waved a hand in dismissal, and Hawkwood bent in a mockery of a bow, first to Selasis, then to Karlis.

"My lords . . . good day."

When the doors closed behind him, Karlis pulled in a deep breath, then rose and went to the windowall.

"I don't trust him."

"Nor do I, Karlis, but you shouldn't expect to trust anyone. I suppose you find him a little too independent."

"Independent! I'd say he could use a lesson or two in respect at Master Garo's hands."

"That would be futile and only succeed in killing him, and I find Bruno very useful. No, Karlis, you must learn to suit the tool to the victim."

"So you use his wife as a tool?"

Selasis smiled approvingly. "Exactly."

"Still, he's short on respect. What's this religious Order he belongs to, this Gamaliel business?"

"A rather limited cult; limited mainly, I'm sure, by their pessimistic view of life. They're fatalists; every event, past, present, and future, is recorded in the Writ of Destiny, every man's fate predetermined, and nothing can change it. Something like that. Suits them for this type of work. It relieves them of the sting of conscience without making sadists of them. And, above all, Karlis, never trust a sadist; they're too self-concerned." He paused for a short, mocking laugh. "But, of course, it's difficult for any human being to be a *true* fatalist. Bruno made the error some years ago of falling in love, and we must be grateful for that. Without that leash on Bruno, his fatalism would be a double-edged blade; he'd shift allegiance or accept death without a second thought, regarding either as simply one more event written indelibly by Fate."

"Strange. What about his wife? What's she like?"

That called up a laugh and a slanted glance.

"You're wondering what kind of woman would marry a man like Bruno? Actually, Margreta's quite attractive in a pale sort of way. Ethereal, you might say. I understand she was chronically ill as a child. She was allieged Concord and went into Conmed as a medtech. Her specialty was crippled and retarded children. It seems Margreta has an odd sympathy for the halt and lame." Then, with an abrupt change of mood, he frowned at his watch and pushed himself up out of his chair. "I have work to do, and you must get ready."

Karlis blinked. "Ready for what?"

"Weren't you listening? You and your new bride are going to the Lima retreat for a few weeks."

"Why the Lima retreat, for the God's sake?" A pile of stones on a pile of a mountain, full of grim and painful memories. He didn't bring those to his father's attention. "It's a thousand kilometers from anywhere."

"That's why I'm sending you there—you and the future Lady Adrien. And you're not to leave the retreat until I say so. Don't think for a second I won't know if you try to sneak out. I'll see that you're well entertained and quite comfortable. Now hurry. The sooner you're out of Concordia, the better."

Karlis started for the door, but there he paused.

"Father, when Bruno finds Adrien, I want to...to see it done."

"I sympathize, Karlis, but satisfaction must sometimes give way to expediency." Then, with a soft laugh, "But one can always hope the True Path leads to satisfaction."

5.

"Ben, for the God's sake, at least now we *know* she went into the cloisters."

"All right, Alex, but why would she tell *Malaki* what she was going to do?"

Ben Venturi's voice existed as a noncorporeal entity in his ear while Alex paced his room; his cell. The rock seemed a tangible weight on him. It would crush him one day.

"She didn't tell him her plans. She went to him for information; he would be her best source. Church Bonds, Ben; they're a very cohesive group, and they maintain close ties with the Bond Church. We know what Malaki could tell her, and that was the information she was working with, and he said she only asked about convents in the Centauri System."

"But she could get plenty of information on any of the convents, in both Systems, out of the Library or Archives."

Alex took another turn in his confined pacing space. "But she had to know something about the *people* she'd be dealing with, not just facts and statistics."

"All right, but even assuming she stayed in the Centauri System, there's—wait a second; I'm checking the memfiles—let's see, three different female orders, and they all have a string of convents. No—the Order of Holy Writ only has one."

"You can forget Holy Writ. It's a contemplative Order. Malaki calls them the Sisters of Silence. They don't talk to each other except by signs, and entry into the Order is very restricted. Adrien would have a hard time even reaching the convent. It's on the island of Kristas; a supply ship lands there once every three months—and that's all. I checked, and the next ship is scheduled a month from today."

"What about the Sisters of Solace? They have two convents on Pollux and one on Castor."

Alex closed his eyes against the rock. The panic was still

258

waiting, just under the surface of his thoughts, a primordial thing that sapped his energies and demanded constant vigilance to keep in check.

"I doubt she'd go to the Sisters of Solace. All their convents are ruled by a triumvirate of Sister Supras. She'll need co-operation from someone within the convent, logically the Supra, and that would mean tripling the risk. So that narrows the field to the Sisters of Faith. Their convents are ruled by a single Supra."

"Even if you're right, there are still seven Faith convents in the Centauri System."

"Malaki could only give her information on four of them—the three here on Castor, and one in Leda. I think you can ignore that one; she'd have the additional problem of arranging passage to Pollux. But don't discount it entirely."

Ben's long-drawn sigh was audible and expressive. "Look, I'm not scratching the gold on this, but it'll still be next to impossible to find her if she's in *any* of the convents. Those cloisters are no-man's land, and then you have the habits and veils to contend with."

"There's one consolation in that—it will be equally difficult for Hawkwood to find her. But Lectris won't be veiled. If you find Lectris, you'll find Adrien."

"Well, he might be a little easier to spot. Oh—we finally tracked down that sister he was supposed to be visiting in Cuprin. She died five years ago."

"Lectris never went to Cuprin, Ben."

"I just like to tie up loose ends. If he's with Lady Adrien, though, he'll be easier for Hawkwood to spot, too. She must've realized that."

"What was she to do with Lectris and Mariet? Leave them to be abducted by Hawkwood? They're obvious sources of information on Adrien, and if a couple of Bonds disappeared from the Eliseer Estate, who'd call out Conpol? They'd simply be put on the runaway lists, and you can be sure they'd never survive Hawkwood's inquisition."

"So you think Mariet's with her, too?"

"Yes, but Mariet can go into the cloister with her. Lectris can't." He wandered to the comconsole and activated a screen focused on the surface; it was the closest thing he had to a window in this windowless world. "Ben, I talked to Jael, and he's going to deal directly with Amik to put his hounds on the trail of Lectris and Hawkwood."

"But not on Lady Adrien's trail—I hope?"

"No. They'll be told nothing about her. Can you imagine the headprice Selasis will have on her? The Brothers aren't up to resisting that kind of temptation."

"And Amik? How much is he being told?"

Alex stared at the screen, the endless dunes stark against the black night sky, the sand moving in slow waves in the double shadows cast by Alpha Centauri B and Pollux.

"Ben, the old thief doesn't have to be *told* anything. There isn't much he hasn't figured out for himself already. But he's a man of honor, in his own way, and Jael knows the rules. He won't expose Adrien to any danger from the Brotherhood."

"Well, thank the God for Jael. We'd be in a hell of a mess without him—*and* his old Ser."

"I know. And I'm convinced Jael *is* Manir Peladeen's son. That's an alternative we must keep in mind."

There was a short silence, then Ben said warily, "Maybe, although the Directors might not be too impressed with his *paternal* lineage, but I guess with enough pressure they could be encouraged to overlook that. Alex, the Ransom Alternative is still our best choice. Why are you worrying about other alternatives?"

He wasn't sure of the answer to that, yet the problem of viable alternatives had been much in his thoughts the last two days. Since Adrien's disappearance. He stared at the moving sand, then turned away abruptly.

"Because I'm mortal, I suppose. It's never wise to put all your money on one number." He slumped down on the bed and leaned back to put his shoulders against the chill stone. "Ben, I'm tired. That's all. What about Eliseer?"

Ben laughed humorlessly. "That's a good question. If you mean has he given any outward signs that he knows what happened to his daughter—no. But Erica's been collecting data on him, and she thinks he knows *something*. We're fairly sure he had a message from Lady Adrien. How it got to him, I don't know. Maybe the Bond network. I hope so. Hawkwood won't be so likely to tap into that. Anyway, Eliseer seems to be working from somebody else's script—at least that's Erica's expert opinion—and it's probably Adrien's script. If so, it looks like she wants to keep everything quiet for some reason. When Selasis told Eliseer she was sick, Lady Galia was ready

to go to Concordia, but he squelched that. He told her in so
many words to let well enough alone; he had faith in Orin and
Dr. Lassily."

"How is Selasis explaining Lazet's absence?"

"For public consumption, Lazet is in a Brothers of Benediction sanatorium in Pesh Lahar; a retreat for his health."

"I hope you can keep him in good health when—or if—he
returns from Lima."

"We'll try, but don't count on it."

"I don't count on anything, Ben." He leaned forward, away
from the chill of the rock, and propped his elbows on his knees.
"Do you know who Adrien's stand-in will be?"

"Well, we have a pretty good idea. We've been checking
death lists. About four hours after Selasis and Karlis got back
to Concordia after the wedding, a Bondmaid from one of the
Estate compounds died. But there's no record of cremation or
burial for her, and it's interesting that she matches Lady Adri-
en's physical description almost exactly. Her name is Elda
Ternin."

"The Moon Princess," Alex said wearily, "reigning until
the dark of the moon."

"We'll try to save her. If nothing else, her face will be
damned good evidence when Lazet gets through—" He stopped
and went off mike briefly, then, "Alex, I've got a call coming
in. Anyway, that about covers everything from this end. Anything else I should know about from your end?"

Alex shook his head, then almost laughed. There was no
one in this stone cell to see that movement.

"No, nothing more. Just . . . be careful. Damn, I wish you'd
pull out of the SSB now. You're an open target for Ussher
there."

"I'm well covered, both here and at the Cliff, and I'm only
staying with the SSB until I get a line on Andreas. Then I'll
pull out, I promise you. So, don't worry."

"Sure. The same goes for you."

Ben laughed at that, then turned atypically hesitant. "Alex,
I . . . well, I never was very good with words, but . . . damn
it, we'll *find* her."

Like they'd found Andreas? Alex stared at the black wall.
"Thanks, Ben."

"Later, Alex."

It was curious that the walls seemed to draw closer when

that voice ceased. Alex removed the headset, then sat motionless in the stony silence. Finally, he stretched out on the bed, his arm curved over his eyes to shut out the light. He wondered how long it had been since he'd slept. Over forty-eight hours. Since before the wedding, before—

Adrien, where are you? Where are you?

He felt the thudding of his pulse, and a cold wind breathed on his skin, damp with a feverish sweat; his hands locked in trembling fists. A shadow hovered at the edges of his vision; it was there even in the darkness behind his closed eyes. And a distant rattling, a sinister rustling. Black wings beating in the blackness at their black cage.

Alex, we'll find her. . . .

The Phoenix and the Brotherhood were a potent, if unintentional, alliance, and wherever she was, at least she was out of Orin Selasis's grasp for the moment.

And she would have planned this very carefully.

You're learning, he thought numbly; you're learning the special kind of courage demanded by that pledge of faith made at the edge of the icecap. She would make herself as safe as possible. She wanted to live.

He held on to that thought until the unseen shadow, the throb of black wings finally receded. He had no intention of sleeping; it came suddenly, dropping him into the deep sleep of exhaustion before he realized it was upon him.

PHOENIX MEMFILES: DEPT HUMAN SCIENCES: BASIC SCHOOL
(HS/BS)
SUBFILE: LECTURE, BASIC SCHOOL 7 MARCH 3252
GUEST LECTURER: RICHARD LAMB
SUBJECT: POST-DISASTERS HISTORY:
THE MANKEEN REVOLT (3104–3120)
DOC LOC #819/219–1253/1812–1648–733252

History is, and should be, so much a process of trying
to figure out how we got here from there. A great deal of
verbiage has been expended on trying to figure out how the
Confederation got from the heady heights of the extrasolar
colonization period to the catastrophic nadir of the Mankeen
Revolt in just twenty years. Since historians who wish to
stay on good terms with the Concord can't very well probe
to the real heart of the matter, they tend to focus their
attention on Lionar Mankeen.

He's certainly worthy of attention, since he organized
the first large-scale revolution of Post-Disasters history, and
since he came so close to precipitating a third dark age.

He was born in 3065, the only son of Fedric, the third
Lord Mankeen. The House of Mankeen was a landed House,
one of those established by Ballarat's conquests during the
Wars of Confederation, and the first Mankeen Lord, Andray, was one of the "native" Lords, an existing hold ruler
who chose to accept and fight for the Holy Confederation,
rather than against it, and for his aid to Andrasy in the
Ruskasian campaign, was awarded a First Lordship, land
grants on a vast area west of the Ural Mountains, including
the Volg River drainage, and agrarian franchises for various
grains, primarily wheat. Andray Mankeen built his Home
Estate and a small city bearing the House name on the Kama
River near the Urals, and graciously accepted Bishop Almbert's priest-soldiers and Mezionism, and even built an impressive cathedron in Mankeen.

Obviously, the House was destined to prosper, and it
did. At the death of its third First Lord, Fedric—Lionar's

father—the House had four million people Bonded or allieged to it, and an annual revenue equivalent to half a billion 'cords. Fedric was, from all reports, conscientious, shrewd, likable, and very conservative, so the question arises—how did he get a son like Lionar Mankeen?

Most historians classify Lionar as a sort of genetic rogue, but it isn't necessary to resort to mutation to explain him. First, remember that he was born in 3065 and that his formative experience was in the waning decades of the thirty-first century when the Golden Age was beginning to seem a bit tarnished to some of those living in it, and a strong dissident element was developing among the Fesh. The middle class was at last contemplating the existing order of things and its allegiance to the Lords in particular, and recognizing it as a form of slavery and the Bonds as true slaves. Not all Fesh reached that conclusion, of course. The aware and vocal minority was confined generally to the University and what was even then called "Independent" Fesh.

Concord textapes have little to say about this prevailing dissident mood, and the names of only a handful of outstanding "revolutionists" are recorded in our histories. Foremost among them is Horris VanZyl, psychosociologist at the University in Victoria, who because he persisted in his "subversive and inflammatory" writings and lectures was finally executed as a traitor in 3090.

Another revolutionist whose renown was extraordinarily wide, considering that he was only a Fesh student—sociology, of course, at the University in Paykeen—was Nikoli T'sian. He was assassinated while addressing a student meeting in 3092, and his killer was never apprehended.

Then there was Lessander Forsite, who used the pseudonym "Sander." He wasn't a product of the University, but was allieged Galinin and trained as an executech in the Home Estate in Victoria. He was an electronic gadfly, whose taped treatises were unassailably rational, despite their caustic tone, and widely, if clandestinely, read. When Conpol identified Forsite as the infamous Sander, he seemed doomed to be condemned as a traitor. (Yes, it was called Conpol then, but the "Con" stood for Confederation, not Concord.) Forsite, however, managed to escape, probably into the Outside; illicit tapes continued to be disseminated under the name of Sander, and analysis has shown them to be of the same authorship, but they stopped a few months after the Revolt began, and Sander's ultimate fate is unknown.

Of course, the temper of the times (or the Fesh) doesn't explain why a young *Lord* would be infected with the fever of rebellion, and perhaps such things can never be fully explained, but part of the explanation is that Fedric was a doting and tolerant father. Also, he had a real fondness for the land, for the process of wresting sustenance from it, and a strong rapport with those closest to it, including his Bonds. Fedric did not harbor any thoughts about changing the lot of his Bonds, but he didn't object when his son came into frequent contact with Bonds at an early age, and was obliviously unaware of how telling those childhood encounters were.

Fedric was equally oblivious to the potential effects on Lionar when he hired Lector Clement Troyon as his tutor. Today any serious student of sociology is well acquainted with Troyon. He was one of the few true scientists in his field, and I'm sure he was an excellent teacher. Undoubtedly, he taught his student to think and instilled in him a recognition of the dangers of the status quo and of the need for change. Troyon was not, apparently, successful in teaching the young Lionar that the *means* of change must be cautiously considered.

Another key factor in Lionar's development as a revolutionary was the untimely death of his father.

Lionar was only twenty-five when he became First Lord. Had he been older perhaps the bitter wisdom of experience would have tempered his ambitions, although I'm not really convinced of that. At any rate, in 3090, at that youthful age, he found himself vested with a great deal of power. 3090 was also of the year of his marriage. The bride was Lizbeth, daughter of Tomas Lesellen, Lord of a landed House whose Home Estate was (and still is) in Bonaires. The marriage was not, from all accounts, a union of love, but it produced four children: Feador, born in 3091; Leo, born four years later; then their only daughter, Irena, in 3096; finally, Julian, born in 3098. It's said of Mankeen that he was a loving father, especially to Irena, but fatherhood didn't distract him from his political ambitions.

The Concord refers to his League solely as the *Mankeen* League, as did the Confederation, but Mankeen and his followers called it the Emancipation League. That was his basic intent—to emancipate Bonds and Fesh from allegiance to their Lords, *and* to emancipate Lords from the domination of the Directorate. Unfortunately, the alternatives he proposed were extremely vague. He envisioned an "era in which individuals may seek by choice the level of accomplishment for which their innate ability equips them, without imposed limitations of birth or class." He also proposed "a government whose authority stems from the will of those governed." But in both theory and practice, he seemed incapable of coming to grips with the mechanics of realizing these worthy aims.

For example, one of his first acts upon becoming First Lord was to make the Bonds in his House salaried employees. The result was chaos not only for Fesh overseers, but for the Bonds themselves. Since they were being paid, they were expected to *buy* many of the goods and services that had previously been supplied by the House, yet few Bonds could even count past ten, nor could they judge the monetary value of what they bought, and inevitably some Fesh took advantage of their ignorance to fill their own pockets. Mankeen simultaneously instituted a program for educating his Bonds, but education takes time, and after a year of rampant confusion, he submitted to necessity and modified his Bond salary policy so that they received only a small monetary payment, and basic services and goods were again supplied by the House.

He did not, however, give up the education program, and began campaigning actively among his Fesh in its behalf. He was a very attractive man and a convincing speaker, and during the months he spent traveling from one estate to the next talking with his Fesh, his idealistic ambitions struck a responsive chord among many of them, and their devoted efforts succeeded in making some of his reforms at least partially successful, in spite of their shortcomings. Nor did he exclude the Fesh from the benefits of reform. He instituted a profit-sharing plan that of all his House reforms was the most successful. Mankeen also campaigned, in a sense, among his Bonds during this period, and since no other Lord had ever spent time actually talking with his Bonds or showing personal concern for them, it's natural that they came to regard him as their hero and savior, and ultimately made him one of their saints.

All this brought him under the intent scrutiny of his peers in the Court of Lords, and he welcomed it and enlarged his campaign to seek converts among the Elite. In 3098 he published privately a treatise titled grandiosely, *The Future of Civilization and the Imperative of Emancipation*, which was condemned as subversive by the Board of Censors, but still had wide circulation among upper-class Fesh and the Elite. Most of the latter viewed it with dismay, but some were attracted to its principles. Of course, few Lords were interested in reforms affecting the Fesh and Bonds; they were attracted to the idea of divesting the Directorate of its power. It should be noted that most of Mankeen's Elite converts were Lords of landed Houses who felt themselves increasingly overshadowed by industrial Houses, and with some justification. On the Directorate at that time, there were only three landed Houses. (And there are only two now.) During the years between his ascendancy to the Lordship in 3090 and 3102, Mankeen established a broad base of support in both the Fesh and Elite, and in the latter year he was joined by 135 Houses in flatly refusing to meet the Confederation tax levy for the year.

The ploy stunned the Confederation, but it didn't have quite the results Mankeen hoped for. He hoped that a mass show of dissatisfaction would force the Directorate to recognize the error of its ways and consider his reform demands. He asked for a Directorate audience so he could present those demands himself, but his request was pointedly ignored by Chairman Arman Galinin, Benedic's successor. Instead, Galinin ordered Conpol and Confleet units into the rebellious Houses to take from their granaries, warehouses, and House banks goods or monies equal to the taxes owed, and to remove bodily from their compounds enough Bonds to fill the tax conscript quotas, as well as serving notices on the requisite number of Fesh of allegiance shifts to the Confederation. There was no resistance on the part of the dissident Lords; there wasn't time to organize any meaningful resistance even if they had had the men and weapons for it.

Mankeen was both humiliated and enraged, but far from crushed. In fact, that bold move on Arman Galinin's part was in some ways an error because it incensed so many Lords who had previously been neutral or only slightly sympathetic to Mankeen and drove them into his League. But I wonder what else Galinin could have done? If Mankeen's reform demands had been more reasonable, perhaps Galinin might have considered them; as it was, he couldn't, nor could he tolerate any Houses escaping their tax obligations.

The confrontation taught Mankeen one lesson: that, as

the Bonds put it, "Might makes its own Rightness." He quoted that maxim in a lettape to his friend and supporter, Lord Alric Berstine. Mankeen realized he needed might for his Rightness, but that was easier said than done. Ships and weapons were manufactured and distributed solely by the Houses of Selasis and Corelis, both staunch Confederationists, and it was unlikely they would sell Mankeen or any of his allies so much as a freight tender or handgun.

But the confrontation also polarized opinion among the Fesh, and one of them was in a position to put the requisite might in Mankeen's hands. That was the First Commander of Confleet, Scott Cormoroi. He was one of those individuals the Phoenix would give a Critical Potential rating of one—a person in a crucial position at a crucial time.

CHAPTER XIV: June 3258

●I│●I│●I│●I│●I│●I│●I│●I│●I│●I│●I│●I│●I│●I│●I│●I│●I│●I│●I│●I│●I│●I│●I│●II

1.

Ben Venturi was only half listening; he'd heard it all before. Ussher was going into another oration. The Council meetings were sounding more and more like the weekly "general membership assemblies." The rallies.

Ben sat motionless, eyes shifting from one face to the next, his stomach churning painfully.

It was inconceivable.

The subject under discussion wouldn't even have been broached six months ago. None of the councilors—except Ussher—would have given it serious consideration. Now they were not only considering it, it was accepted as a foregone conclusion, something inevitable and desirable.

War.

Ussher called it a "full-scale military offensive."

He kept referring to the General Plan ex seqs, and a military offensive *was* clearly indicated as the most effective way of forcing the Directorate to the bargaining table, but with his usual selectivity, he ignored the equally clear indications that the offensive must be limited to well defined parameters— which he had already exceeded—and that any attempt at bargaining would be futile without the LR-MT.

But Predis Ussher was getting worried.

With good reason, Ben thought grimly. The enthusiasm of the members wasn't what it used to be; he didn't draw the flocks of avid sycophants every time he appeared in an open gathering, and attendance at the rallies had dropped to a little over a thousand last week. With every passing day, more mem-

269

bers slipped out of his grasp. A few of the disenchanted joined the still covert opposition, but most moved to neutral territory. He was still chairman of the Council, and no overt challenge had been made to his leadership.

Still, Ussher felt the loosening of his hold, and now he was fighting to regain it, to strengthen it. That was the real reason for his war on the Concord. If he promised victory—a word he had introduced into the Phoenix lexicon—and made the promise convincing enough, the members would forgive him anything.

Erica had predicted this. It was a calculated risk in the war of nerves that had been so successful in goading Ussher into behavior that served to disillusion the undecided and even converts without a word from the opposition.

The risk had been calculated, but what couldn't be calculated was the fact that Andreas Riis was still—five and a half months after his arrest—a prisoner of the SSB. Ben felt the abrasive ache of frustration, remembering the thousand dead ends he'd explored in the search, the days and weeks that had become months wasted, spent in futility.

And while he searched for Andreas through the labyrinths of the Conpol-SSB bureaucracy, he and Erica were moving targets, constantly patching the chinks in their defensive armor, Alex Ransom paced his stone cage on Castor, testing the limits of his sanity, the Phoenix was slowly dissolving in the acid of uncertainty, and the Concord was one giant *caldera*, smoldering in its core.

And Predis Ussher was planning a full-scale military offensive.

Ben seethed behind an expressionless facade, studying the intent faces of the other councilors, while Ussher's voice nibbled at his patience with glib banalities and garbled generalities. There should at least be boredom on some of these faces, if not disgust, but Ussher had made believers of them; they looked to him for all their answers. Ben glanced to his right at Erica, her gray eyes cool, detached, fixed on Ussher's face.

That was part of the war of nerves, and she could make it work; she could drive Ussher into a rage without saying a word, never offering a tangible target for attack. But somehow this seemed a peculiarly feminine ploy. Erica could carry it off, but Ben found it increasingly difficult.

He looked up at Ussher, contemplating him with as much detachment as he could muster. The old vibrancy was still there, but it was becoming an equivocal, hectic thing, as if the energy sources was overloading the circuits. Still, Ben couldn't deny the power in the compelling confidence in his voice, his posture and gestures.

He thought of Andreas Riis, quiet, methodical, precise, and kind; gentle to his soul. He didn't have Ussher's energy, nor did he cut as striking a figure, nor could he use words so well. But he had been loved, and he had guided the Phoenix since the chaos of the Fall, and it had never strayed from its purpose in all that time.

Five and a half months. How long would it be before Ussher could truthfully claim Andreas was dead?

The monologue was coming to a climax, and Ben tuned in mentally for the last few words.

". . . break the hold of the Concord on the Centauri System. They can't hope to keep *two* stellar systems in chains. They'll have no *choice* but to free us!"

There was a moment of respectful silence, then John M'Kim leaned forward, frowning. But that indicated no concern for the general direction of Ussher's plans, only for the means.

"Predis, you said you'd outlined a multileveled plan of attack. Perhaps you should enlarge on that."

Ussher had been standing as he delivered his introductory oration, and now he seated himself, his tone businesslike and crisp. It always was with M'Kim.

"Of course, John. First, our operations will be limited to the Centauri System. We won't make the error the Concord has of spreading ourselves too thin. We'll reestablish the Peladeen Republic here, and if in the future it can be expanded to include the whole of humankind, our purposes will be served. But for now we must look to that which is possible, and leave to the future that which is desirable. The heart of the plan is a surprise attack, one of brief duration, to be sure—in fact, no more than six hours total—but all the more devastating for its unexpectedness. Our objectives will be primarily of a military nature. We cannot antagonize the Fesh and Bonds; the innocents. They must look to the Phoenix for leadership when they recognize the failure of the Concord."

Jan Barret asked, "What exactly will our objectives in this attack be?"

"Well, Jan, that's one area in which we'll have to work out details later."

"In general, then."

Ussher hesitated, as if he suspected antagonism in his insistence. But with Barret there never was. Uncertainty, perhaps, but never antagonism.

"In general . . . well, all Confleet bases and arsenals, and as many Conpol and SSB commands as we can hit without undue loss of civilian lives. We'll close all the IP ports and Planetary Transystems terminals, all major factories and smelters supplying war matériel, take over the power plants on the Inner Planets, and, of course, wreak as much havoc as possible with Confleet and Selasid fleets."

Barret frowned. "That's an ambitious program, considering our limited forces."

"Of course it's ambitious," Ussher agreed tolerantly. "Our goals are ambitious; they always have been. To bring freedom to all people. That's why the Phoenix exists. Perhaps we won't achieve all of our objectives, even if repeated offensives become necessary. However, you've already enlarged our military capability tremendously in the last few months, Jan—showing great skill and courage, I might add—and I'm confident that in the next six months, before our 1 Januar deadline, you'll expand FO's striking power even further. Of course, we won't depend solely on standard military tactics; we'll use various methods of sabotage, and there the MT will be particularly telling. An explosive transed into an arsenal is as effective as a propulsion bomb from a Falcon. Don't you agree, Commander Venturi?"

It was a challenge. Sabotage was SI's specialty and Ussher was asking for a declaration of position.

Ben said flatly, "SI never has and never will let the Phoenix down."

Ussher considered that, and judging from the subtle cast of triumph in his smile, apparently took it as a concession. Ben felt the heat in his cheeks and knew it betrayed his annoyance.

"Now, this sort of strategy demands careful planning," Ussher was saying, addressing the other councilors. "Everything must be coordinated to the second. The Concord must think the whole Centauri System is exploding at once, and it must be a total surprise. Let's be honest with ourselves, we *are* relatively limited in our military capabilities. By coordinating a combined strategy of sabotage and open attack, we can give the impression of greater strength than we actually possess, and the element of surprise will further serve to confuse and demoralize the Lords of the Concord."

Ben tried to imagine men like Galinin, Woolf, Camcroodo, or Selasis confused and demoralized, but his attention was drawn to Marien Dyce. She was watching Ussher intently, her sharp eyes reflecting a profound inner excitement. Ben recognized it as something he would see in terrifying repetition in the eyes of the other members in the future.

She asked, "Predis, is this what you meant by a multileveled plan, or is there more to it?"

"There's definitely more to it, Marien. We must look to those we hope to free from enslavement to help us in striking off their chains. We must look to the Fesh and Bonds."

Ben stared at him. Involving Fesh had been hinted at earlier, but not Bonds. Ussher was talking about organized Bond revolt. Ben was stunned, and even more so when he looked around at the other councilors. Not one of them even seemed surprised. Whatever Erica felt was carefully hidden behind her expressionless features.

"Our problem," Ussher continued, "is to find ways to let the Fesh and Bonds know who we are and what our purpose is. Once they understand that, once they realize we're fighting for *their* freedom, that our attack isn't directed against them, but against their masters, they'll fall in behind us. The time is right; they're desperately searching for leadership, for someone to show them how to strike off their chains. We'll *offer* that leadership."

Marien nodded. "Yes, but how can we make our purpose clear to them?"

Again, that warm, tolerant smile. "Very simple. We must shut down the PubliCom System facilities as soon as the offensive begins. Shutting down the Woolf systems will be difficult, of course, but I'm convinced that with careful planning we can do it."

John M'Kim was frowning again, gnawing at feasibility. "That will work very well for getting our message to the Fesh. When the attack begins, they'll turn on their vidicoms immediately to find out what's happening. But what about the Bonds? We can't reach *them* through vidicom."

"You're right, John," Ussher admitted soberly. "We can't reach them through any written means, either, and we haven't enough people to give them the message directly. For the answer to this problem, I've turned to my research staff in Communications. We'll plant microspeakers ahead of time in all the Bond compounds. Then, at the onset of the offensive, we can activate them by radio. It won't be necessary for any of our members to enter the compounds during the offensive."

Ben almost laughed. Ussher had taken a lesson from the microspeakers that had plagued him the last few months. But it was strange that he could speak of this ploy so freely, as if he recognized no relationship between this method of reaching the Bonds and the disembodied voices that had so often sent him into livid rages.

M'Kim seemed satisfied, even impressed. "Yes, that would be quite effective with the Bonds. Voices from the Beyond, and all that."

Erica's quiet voice brought every eye into focus on her.

"I assume, Predis, that you've considered the fact that you'll have to overcome the influence of Saint Richard the Lamb and the Brother?"

Ussher hesitated. He knew it wouldn't be politic to speak too carelessly of Richard Lamb here.

"With all due respect to Richard Lamb, whom we all loved and admired, his influence with the Bonds obviously hasn't succeeded in stopping the uprisings, although it may have limited them to some degree; I'd be the first to give him credit. As for this 'Brother'..." He shrugged expressively. "Well, we know the Bonds are apt to confuse the real world with the...uh, spiritual. But when it comes to a choice between slavery or freedom, the real world will take precedence. It always has."

Ben found that puzzling, too, but only because of the suggestion that the Brother was a figment of Bond imagination. Alex had tried to keep his identity as the Brother secret, but Ben had evidence that Ussher knew about it. Certainly, he knew the Brother wasn't imaginary.

The other councilors were satisfied, and Erica offered no further rebuttal. She never let herself be drawn into an argument.

Ussher was answering a question from Barret now. "After the initial attack, our course of action depends on the Concord's response. It's my conviction that a second offensive won't be necessary; they'll be ready to bargain with us. The Concord is already suffering too many internal stresses; it can't *afford* a war with Centauri."

He was becoming more expansive with every word, and

Ben braced himself for another oration.

"My fellow members, the Concord is disintegrating from within. Consider the events of the last week alone. There was the outbreak in one of the new Special Detention compounds, which were the Concord's only answer to Fesh revolt. Of course, all of us recognized those SD compounds as a dangerous symptom when they were established last year."

Ben's jaw clamped tight. It was Erica Radek who had brought the dangers inherent in the SD compounds to the attention of "all of us."

"To concentrate known extremists and activists is obviously dangerous," Ussher enlightened them, "and this week the Tokio SD compound erupted. Fifty guards were killed or injured as well as a thousand prisoners. And only yesterday Concordia was the site of another highly indicative incident. An explosive device was thrown into a contingent of Directorate Guards—and the Guard stands as a symbol of the Directorate itself in the minds of the people—killing ten outright, wounding another twenty-five. Add to the week's events, the month's events, and the year's events. Add the staggering number of public executions of so-called agitators—that is, anyone who dares take action against tyranny and brutality. And these are Fesh, not Bonds. Bonds are disposed of without so much judicial ceremony. Add the passage of yet another measure to expand Confleet and Conpol. Add the number of minor Houses that have been bankrupted by crushing tax levies and swallowed up by major Houses. Add the economic recession that has crippled entire industries. Add the 120 Bond uprisings requiring Confleet intervention, the hundreds of 'minor' ones quelled by House guards at untold cost in death and suffering. Add the Ganymede uprising, a colossal disaster that took fifty *thousand* lives. Add all these and the hundreds of other indices I haven't even touched on, and you have a picture of an archaic, stiff-necked, feudal system on the verge of *collapse*. My friends, the time is *right* for us. The Concord won't take on the added burden of a war with us—a full-scale revolution—if it's offered an alternative. The Concord *will* come to terms with us!" He rose slowly, and Ben could see the slight trembling of his hands.

"My fellow members, I'm going to make a prediction. A few years ago, none of us would have believed this could come so soon, but history has its own laws of inertia; history is moving faster and faster, and it's moving for *us*. This is my prediction, and I know in my soul I'm right. In half a year's time, the Lord Galinin and the Directors will be meeting with a representative of the Phoenix. The proud Lords who brand us pirates and traitors will be coming to terms with the Phoenix, and by the God, they'll be grateful to give us anything we ask for!"

Ben could never explain what triggered him; he'd listened patiently to rhetoric in the same vein before, heard Ussher twist and select facts, heard him use the name and goals of the Phoenix callously, even heard similar predictions of ultimate victory.

Ben couldn't explain it, and neither could he control it. His chair crashed backward as he came to his feet. Ussher's head snapped around, and Ben was beyond hiding his contempt; it was all he could do to restrain the urge to drive his fist into that mouth that sagged with surprise.

"Predis, you unmothered fool! Who the hell do you think you are?"

Rob Hendrick sprang to his feet, glaring hotly at Ben. "Listen, you have no right to—"

Ben's hands closed. "Hendrick, stay out of this, or so help me, I'll smash that pretty face of yours to a pulp!"

Hendrick sagged back into his chair while Marien Dyce chimed in with a shocked, "Ben, now, really!"

Then M'Kim, "For the God's sake, Ben, calm down! This is no time—"

"Calm down? After that rousing oration? John, don't you realize that speech was supposed to overwhelm us with enthusiasm and confidence?" Ben turned on Ussher, the meeting of their eyes a palpable clash; he almost expected a shower of sparks. "That speech was supposed to make us forget everything the Phoenix stands for and has sacrificed so many lives for. That speech was supposed to make us overlook the fact that, in spite of the Concord's internal problems, it is *still* capable of smashing us in a military confrontation; to overlook the warning in the General Plan ex seqs that bargaining *without* the LR-MT is hopeless. And we're supposed to forget that the Phoenix has worked for over fifty years to *prevent* the Bond revolt Predis is proposing. *My fellow members* . . . is it so easy to forget? Is it so easy to forget the *real* aims of the Phoenix? Is it so easy to forget Andreas Riis and all he stands for? To forget that he's still alive and waiting to be freed?"

"Andreas Riis is dead!"

For a moment Ben could only stare at Ussher, stunned by the terrible conviction in those words. Then his mouth twisted sardonically, shock swept away in renewed anger.

"And what about Alex Ransom, Predis? Is *he* dead, too? You tried hard enough to kill him. You made three tries for him, but you failed on every one!"

Ussher's fist smashed down on the table.

"Ransom *deserted* the Phoenix! He betrayed Riis and deserted! He's a traitor! A deserter!"

He believed every word of it. Ben was silenced again. Perhaps on some level, Ussher still recognized the truth, but now, at this time and place, he believed his own lie with a conviction that would not be shaken, and that conviction was more frightening than all his self-serving ambition.

Ben said softly, "The God help us, Predis, you're *insane*."

The air seemed to vibrate in the sudden silence. No sound, no movement, no one seemed to breathe. Ussher went white, his hair blazing against his pallid skin, his body taut, as if it would snap at the slightest touch.

"Venturi, no one says that to *me!* You'll swallow that one day, I promise you. You'll *choke* on it!"

"If I do, Predis, everyone will know who garroted me."

He turned away and looked down at Erica, vaguely surprised to see a brief, wistful smile where he might have anticipated recrimination for his loss of control.

"I have business in Leda, Erica. I'll be back tonight." He didn't wait for her response, but turned on his heel and strode to the door.

And Predis Ussher's eyes never strayed from him until the doorscreens snapped on after him.

2.

Ben paused at the windowall, looking out at the glittering night vista of Leda; the gibbous Castor made a golden path across the waters of the Pangaean Straits. A beautiful view, and an expensive one, but an SSB major could afford such luxuries. Still, it was a waste of 'cords; he had little time to enjoy it.

He turned and surveyed the bedroom carefully. The "body" was tucked in the bed, set to radiate the proper amount of infrared, as well as sounding alarms and activating hidden vidicoms if its delicate "skin" was touched. The comconsole was programmed to detour all incoming calls to his quarters in Fina or his pocketcom. The sensors that surrounded and filled the apartment were all activated.

He glanced at his watch. Mike Compton would be on the MT now. Before he darkened the windowall, he took a last look out, wondering what the view of Leda would be like after Ussher's full-scale military offensive.

Six months. 1 Januar. A new year.

Ussher *was* insane. It had been foolish to tell him so, but it was true.

True or not, Ben thought irritably as he waved off the lights, it had been an error to lose control. He must talk to Erica tonight. He took out his transceiver as he crossed to the inner wall and felt along the plasment for the faint depression. Then, when a section of the wall slid back silently, he stepped into the chamber behind it and switched on the 'ceiver.

"Mike? Are you clear?" He set the timers on the shock screens and closed the door while he waited for the response.

"Clear, Ben. Ready for trans?"

"Yes, go ahead—"

He froze, every muscle springing taut; his hand flashed to the holster on his hip.

The answer to his first question should have been, "The weather's fine."

He had his laser out when he felt the faint shock of the trans, then he was blinking in the blaze of light in the Fina MT chamber.

There were two of them, face-screened, one turning away from the control console, the other in front of him, between him and the open door into the corridor, an X^2 in his hand.

Ben fired, aiming for the gun, even as he ducked and lunged, head down; the heat of a beam breathed lightly over his shoulder. They hit the floor together, and Ben felt the air crushed out of his lungs. He rolled with his attacker, straining to bring his gun up, his hand exploding in pain as the second man kicked it away.

The corridor—the fire alarms. . . .

He gripped clothing and flesh, fumbled for leverage, and heaved his assailant's body between him and the other man, heard an angry cry of pain.

"You hit me! You hit *me!*"

Ben scrambled to his feet and plunged into the corridor, only to be thrown down as a hurtling body leapt on his back. He tried to turn, to pull the man under him, and took the impact of the fall on his shoulder.

A hand closed over his mouth, stifling his cry at the pain in his left side, a pain so intense, his body jerked in uncontrolled muscular spasms, and he knew he had only a few seconds of consciousness left him. He thrust his elbow back, felt flesh smash against bone; the momentary loosening of his assailant's grip was enough. He twisted free, his right arm snapped down, the X¹ was in his palm, and his finger closed on the firing button.

The hall echoed with screams of agony, but Ben only understood that the threatening shadow had fallen away. He moved the beam in a searing arc upward, toward the ceiling, toward the heat sensors. The fire alarms began shrieking; the very air shivered with the sound as he swayed to his feet and staggered across the hall to put his back to the wall, ready for the next attack.

But there was none. A blurred shadow; a man running into the MT room. Ben held the gun in both hands, the beam hissing until his trembling muscles failed, and the gun fell to the floor.

Shouts and footsteps moving toward him, the sounds dim against the alarms. He felt himself sliding down the wall, one hand at his side, blackened with charred cloth and flesh, and he thought the shrieking was his own. His vision was gone; he wasn't aware of hitting the floor except for the intensification of the pain. The footsteps and voices were close, but he couldn't move.

He wondered if Ussher had sent someone to finish the job.

"Ben! Holy God—somebody call a medsquad!"

Haral Wills . . . thank the God. . . .

"Willie—"

"Don't talk, Ben. We'll have a medsquad here in a few minutes."

"Willie, take care of . . . Erica. . . ."

3.

Alex Ransom walked slowly up the hangar ramp, thinking that he was exchanging one black vault for another—the black vault of space for a vault of stone.

Halfway up the ramp he stopped and looked down into the hangar. It was silent now; the crews and techs had retired for a well earned rest, the flurry of excitement occasioned by their homecoming had died, and the COS HQ staff returned to their duties.

The foray had been productive as well as distracting. His eyes moved over the black hulls of the Falcons. There were four of them now. Capturing the fourth with a meager fleet of three had been no small feat. There was personal satisfaction in that, and more in the knowledge that eventually he could return Amik's ships with no concern for rent or further bargaining.

He looked up at the rock walls and ceiling, knowing he should be in the comcenter. Jael forwarded only high-priority news to him when he was away from the COS HQ; there would be endless minor events and decisions to consider. But he didn't move to answer the imperative of duty; not yet.

It was a paradox that he felt less confined here than in the comcenter which, if smaller, was still more open. The sheened hulls of the Falcons overwhelmed this space, making the chamber seem cramped, and in spite of the helions mounted around the ceiling, making it seem darker. Perhaps these shark-sleek black hulls had a smell of space about them, a residue of voyages in unconfined dimensions of space and time.

Andreas Riis had become a prisoner of the SSB five months and two weeks ago.

It had the weight of eons in it.

And one month and twenty-eight days ago, Adrien had disappeared, for all intents and purposes, into vacuum.

It was beginning to tell on him, these multiple anxieties accruing endlessly over days and weeks and months. It was a medieval torture; an emotional rack.

280

All the exiles felt it. It was a miracle that the thirty-four men and women confined in these rocky chambers could even tolerate each other by now. But there had been no clashes, no flares of temper, no hints of dissatisfaction. They were a select group, separated in the centrifuge of doubt and dissension in Fina. They understood the Phoenix; they knew why they were part of it, and why there were here.

And they had faith. He felt the pull of tension in his shoulders. They had faith in Commander Alex Ransom.

As if to bring that point home, his 'com buzzed, and it both startled and annoyed him. The face in the small screen was Jael's.

"Alex, I'm in the comcenter. You'd better get up here."

A moment of paralysis; fear and doubt. No hope. Jael's tone left no room for that.

"On my way, Jael."

He took the remainder of the ramp in long strides, then crossed the comcenter, acknowledging the greetings of the monitoring crew with only a brief nod, his eyes automatically scanning the screens. Jael was at the microwave console, headset on.

"Yes," he said into his mike, "all right, Erica, but Alex is right here. You'd better line him in."

Alex reached for a headset from the counter and hurriedly hooked it over his ear, signaling Jael to stay on.

"Erica? What's wrong?"

"Oh, Alex . . . thank the God you're back." That voice, farther away than distance, sounding in the hollow of his ear; it had a ragged edge to it now. "It's Ben, Alex, he—"

"Ben? What happened to him?"

"I'll explain, but first, he'll be all right. He was badly hurt, but he'll recover. He has some broken bones in his right hand and a laser wound in his chest. It's serious, but not critical. An ambush was set up for him in the Fina MT terminal."

Alex reached blindly for a chair and sank into it, and it was a moment before he could even speak.

"Erica, I'm coming to Fina. Ussher's going to kill both of you if—"

"If *what?* What do you intend to do—come back to Fina so he can make a clean sweep?" Then her tone softened. "I've been in surgery with Ben for two hours, and I haven't the strength to argue now. Please, just stop and think."

He let his head sink into his hands, closing his eyes. "Are *you* all right?"

"Yes, and Haral Wills is taking over security for both Ben and me. We have loyal medtechs on tap to be with Ben full time."

"I hope Willie's looking out for himself, too."

"He is. Have you talked to Jael since you returned?"

"Not yet."

"He'll fill you in on the Council meeting this afternoon. I gave him the full story a few hours ago. The would-be Lord of Peladeen is about to declare war on the Concord."

It had the leaden feel of inevitability. There was no sudden shock, only enervating numbness.

"When does this war begin?"

"1 Januar, if he sticks to his schedule."

"I'll get the rest from Jael. Tell me about Ben."

"Well, he finally blew up at the Council meeting, and among other things he told Predis he's insane. Since it's so close to the truth, it rankled with him." She hesitated. "I should have warned Ben. Predis was too quiet when he threw that at him; I knew there'd be a strong reaction. I didn't expect anything *this* strong, though. I haven't heard Ben's side of the story yet; he's still unconscious. Mike Compton was on the MT, but he was knocked out, and all he knows is that two men in face-screens came in about half an hour before Ben was due. But, in spite of the odds, Ben managed to kill both his assailants and set off the fire alarms with his laser. Willie was the first to reach him, thank the God. He told me Ben was late and he was on his way to check with Mike when the alarms went off."

"There were no other witnesses?"

"Just Mike, who can only testify that he was knocked out by two men in face-screens. I suppose he was intended to be the scapegoat for Ben's murder. Of course, the alarms pulled quite a crowd after it was all over."

Alex leaned back, absently scanning the screens. "The alarms pulled them to a scene that could be interpreted in a number of ways, Erica."

"I know, but I haven't had a chance to find out how it *is* being interpreted. Predis will probably try to make Ben the villain now; he *did* kill the two men."

"But Compton can establish the fact that they were waiting for him. As soon as possible, we'd better transfer him here to the exile staff. Fina won't be safe for him."

"I know. Well, there's one thing you might call a benefit to come out of all this: Ben's been forced to retire from the SSB. Willie's setting it up. A 'car accident; an explosion, and if the SSB thinks it's sabotage, that will only make Major Venturi a hero in their minds."

There was a huskiness in her voice that was becoming increasingly marked, for her a symptom of exhaustion that Alex had long ago learned to recognize.

"Erica, you'd better get some rest."

"I will, but first there's something else you should know about. Willic just told mc about it a few minutes ago. He had a report from Dal Wood, one of the agents assigned to the search for Lady Adrien. Dal is almost sure he's found Lectris."

Alex's breath caught, his throat constricted on the question. "Where?"

"Saint Petra's of Ellay. It's near—"

"Oriban, yes, I know. You said *almost* sure. No positive ident yet?"

"Not yet. The Bond Dal spotted is wearing a Church tabard; he's a groundskeeper in the children's play court, and that's just outside the cloister. The court is closed to anyone but Church personnel; closed with walls and guarded gates. But Dal will try to get some telelens imagraphs."

"Well, keep . . . keep me posted."

She laughed gently at that tense request.

"Oh, I thought we'd just wait until it was all over, and I'd send you a capsule—"

"Erica, how you're up to making jokes right now, I don't know, but I haven't your . . . guts." Still, he was laughing, and the release of tension was welcome.

"Or my gall? Just remember, Alex, even if we've found Lectris, we haven't found Adrien. I don't doubt she's in Saint Petra's if he's there, but she'll be in the cloister wrapped in about ten meters of blue habit with a veil she doesn't have to lift for anyone. We'll have to get a female agent in as a novice, and that won't be easy. The Sisters are rather exclusive."

"At least we're getting closer, Erica."

"Bruno Hawkwood is undoubtedly getting closer, too. Willie says he's apparently given up his inquiries in the Outside. The cloisters are an obvious alternative."

"He hasn't found her yet; she's still alive. The Moon Princess still reigns in the Selasid Estate. And don't qualify your good news with objections just to force me to take a positive stand against them."

Her laugh was half a sigh. "You're a very difficult man to manipulate. I'm giving it up for now and going to bed. I'll call tomorrow and let you know how Ben's doing. We can discuss the Council meeting then."

"All right, and when Ben's conscious, tell him I wish to hell I'd been there to make the odds more even."

"He did all right by himself. Good night, Alex."

"Good night, and Erica—be careful."

He put the headset down on the counter, mouth drawn into a grim line, then came to his feet. "Jael, let's adjourn to the conference room. I want to hear about this war of Ussher's."

Jael gave a short mirthless laugh.

"Come on. It'll turn your guts, but we might as well get it lined out."

4.

Adrien heard the second pair of soft footsteps on the worn stone and looked up along the shadow-patterned colonnade through the haze of her veil toward the approaching veiled figure. The first pair of footsteps were her own, measured and even. With little conscious effort she had assumed many of the outward characteristics of the nuns in her two months at Saint Petra's. No—nearly two and a half months now. She found herself walking always with that measured step, head bowed, hands thrust into the full sleeves of her blue habit.

She studied the approaching figure, searching for the subtle clues of identity. That had been disturbing at first, these veiled figures wrapped in anonymity, but she'd learned to look for differences in height and weight, posture and step, and trained her ear to voices. Except for Sister Thea, she had seen none of the faces behind these veils.

The nun approaching wasn't a novice; her koyf was blue, not the white of the novice's koyf Adrien wore. Sister Helen. The identifications were coming easier now. Adrien paused when they met and bowed her head respectfully.

"Good morning, Sister Helen."

"Good morning, Sister Iris. How are you feeling today?"

"Very well, thank you."

"Good. Lord bless."

"'Bless, Sister."

Adrien smiled as she listened to Sister Helen's fading footsteps. Her question had been more than an amenity. She was genuinely concerned about Adrien's health. At five months, the pregnancy was becoming obvious in spite of the fullness of her habit. That she was pregnant raised no eyebrows in this cloister; because of its special calling the Order made exceptions unthinkable in others, and Adrien knew she wasn't the first to enter the Order when she was with child. But she would probably be the first to leave it *with* her child. Or children, in this case. At least . . .

She frowned and crossed to the balustrade to look down into the play court through the intricate screen spanning the arched spaces between the columns. It was nearly time for the morning play period; she was waiting for the chimes in the triple spires of the cloister chapel to ring the hour.

The metal of the screen was cool under her fingers. A shaft of sunlight found its way through the leaves of the trees and caught on the gold band on her left hand, the symbol of commitment to the Sisters of Faith. She still wore Alexand's ring on her right hand, but she had to be careful to keep it out of sight. The rules of the Order precluded wearing any jewelry other than the gold band and the chain of white prayer beads.

She would not surrender that ring, rules notwithstanding. Thea had given her a warning, but that was all. She seemed to understand this as she did so many things, purely empathetically.

Adrien's fingers moved along the intertwining patterns of the screen, and she found herself smiling. Vision screens might have been installed to shield the arcade from curious eyes, but Saint Petra's builders had been concerned with more than function. She didn't know what kind of metal the screens were made of; it had a dull, golden patina. She only knew they were wrought by loving, patient hands. Written into the intricate designs were deities and saints, dictums and dogmas, history and parable; an entire ethos.

The screens were nearly two centuries old, and she knew their designers were Terran; the animal and floral motifs were based on Terran forms. She thought of those long-dead artisans whose passion for their god brought them to a newly colonized planet, an inhospitable wilderness. The passion was there in every line of the designs, but she read beyond it and felt the longing homesickness for a warm, green planet reaching out to her across the centuries.

Even the living flora and fauna here were Terran. The patriarchal trees shading the arcade, scenting the air with cool remembrances, gave shelter to bees, butterflies, and other insects she couldn't identify; even to birds and gray, tuft-eared squirrels. She listened to the hidden buzzings and chirpings, knowing that in a few minutes they would be drowned in the pleasant cacophony of children's shouts and laughter, and she was looking forward to it.

Sister Thea had assigned her and Mariet the duty of helping the teachers supervise the morning and afternoon play periods. Adrien had asked for the assignment. It was the only time she left the cloister, and she hesitated at exposing herself even for these short periods, but it had become a necessity for the sake of her sanity. There wasn't enough to occupy her thoughts in the rest of her daily ritual. The lessons, the mandatory periods of prayer and meditation, the religious ceremonies, the everyday chores associated with maintaining this large, cooperative household—none of these demanded enough of her mental energies and time to hold the fear at bay.

She pressed one hand against the swelling curve of her abdomen. These entities existing within her, half formed but intensely living, were an integral part of her consciousness. She was thinking of these fragile beings locked in the warm, protective shell of her body. The cloister was another womb of sorts, a comfortable and safe haven.

But even the womb is a prison as well as a haven.

Two months and ten days.

Her fingers locked in the screen, metal cutting into her flesh. *Dear God, Alexand, find me. Husband and Lord, my Promised, beloved, Alexand, find me. Find me. . . .*

She held on to the screen, trembling, until she had herself under control again, until she put the memories, the fear, the mordant loneliness back into the farthest recesses of her mind. It was more difficult with every passing day, and the long nights were becoming intolerable.

Finally, her hands relaxed on the screen; she looked down into the court, forcing herself to concentrate on what she saw.

Across the court in the school, the children waited in their windowed classrooms. In this section they were five to ten years old, and she found them a source of delight and satisfaction. It pleased her that some had already learned to recognize her and call her by name. Sister Iris. They learned early the secrets of identification.

The courtyard was surrounded by strips of green lawn interspersed with trees and flower beds where a handful of Church Bonds worked at a leisurely pace, tending them with primitive tools that didn't disrupt the contemplative quiet. Lectris was one of those Bonds. She smiled when she saw him, leaning on his hoe almost directly below her. She recognized the risk in bringing him to Saint Petra's with her; his height and bulk were impervious to disguise. But she'd had little choice, and now she found his presence a source of comfort. There was also a very pragmatic comfort in the fact that he carried a concealed gun, and on her twice-daily sojourns outside the cloister, he was always near her.

She heard a light laugh; a novice had joined Lectris. She was also waiting for the play period to begin; waiting for Adrien. Mariet. No—Sister Betha. Strange, it was harder to think of Mariet as Sister Betha than to think of herself as Sister Iris.

Mariet had chosen the name herself, after Saint Betha, she told Adrien, guardian of lost children. It had become bitterly appropriate, the "lost" part. But the thought didn't call up the usual smothering anxiety now, and she attributed that to her little brother and sister below. She had always thought of them in those terms to some degree, but now it seemed even more fitting.

A week before the wedding, Adrien had taken them to a secluded spot in the Estate gardens and told them her plans, or what she felt they must know. They'd both been afraid, but neither hesitated, showing a childlike faith in her that almost made her weep. She told these two what she dared not even hint at with her family, and, as with Malaki, she felt no concern. They wouldn't freely divulge anything she said if she asked a pledge of silence, and no one was likely to force them to betray her. At least not before the fact. But she couldn't risk leaving them behind, knowing Bruno Hawkwood to be a thorough and conscienceless man.

She felt a chill and forced that thought back, too.

There was so much for which to be grateful. For one thing, that the cloisters were such anomalously democratic institutions. There were no class bars; anyone could enter the Order, Elite, Fesh, or Bond, if they met with the Supra's approval. Bonds seldom applied, Sister Thea had told her; there had been more Elite applicants than Bond in her tenure here. But Bonds weren't turned away simply because of their class. "The Holy Mezion calls all children His own," Thea quoted in explanation.

Adrien suspected Saint Petra's was more democratic than most convents because of Thea, and she was something else to be grateful for. Not only did she accept a supplicant whose very presence endangered everyone around her, but she graciously made a place for Lectris and assigned "Sister Betha" the room next to Adrien's.

Lectris and Mariet were laughing. Adrien could hear their voices, but not the words. If she thought of them as brother and sister, she knew they thought of each other in the same way and perhaps to a greater degree. Mariet still teased Lectris, although she had to restrain the bantering here, and Lectris tolerated and looked after her exactly as he would a wayward little sister.

At length Adrien turned, pulling her shoulders back, aware of a dull ache in the small of her back. No doubt it would get worse in time. She tucked her hands into her sleeves and started toward the nulgrav lift at the end of the arcade, but the sound of hurried footsteps stopped her.

Sister Thea. Adrien waited, wondering at her purposeful pace, and, when Thea reached her and raised her veil, wondering at the uncertain frown deepening the lines in her forehead. Thea glanced warily up and down the colonnade.

"Sister Iris, I'm glad I found you alone."

Adrien pushed back her own veil. "Is something wrong?"

"I'm not sure. Perhaps I'm worrying over nothing. A young woman came to me today seeking entrance into the Order. I've dealt with many applicants in my time here, and I suppose I've developed a sort of sixth sense about them, and with your safety to consider, I've been especially—well, suspicious lately."

Adrien nodded. "And this young woman?"

"She . . . didn't seem to have the right attitude. It's hard to explain, but even the applicants I know wouldn't be happy here still have certain attitudes. They must be inclined to strong religious convictions or they wouldn't seek entry. This girl didn't have the right . . . feeling about her, although she was well versed in doctrine—more so than most—and answered all my questions freely, and I asked quite a lot."

"Did her answers satisfy you?"

Thea shook her head, her frown more marked.

"No, that's why I finally tested her with a lie. She told me she'd talked to Frer Jamed at the cathedron in Helen. As it happens, I know the Frer." She glanced at Adrien and added, "Through lettapes, mostly, although he has visited the convent. At any rate, I asked the young woman if Frer Jamed had recovered from the illness that made him limp so badly, and she said he had. I then asked if he still used a cane, and she said, 'Yes, but only occasionally.'"

Adrien asked tensely, "And what was the truth?"

"Frer Jamed never had an illness that made him limp, nor did he ever use a cane. I don't know why she lied, but I know she did. That's why I denied her entrance. It may have nothing to do with you, and I don't wish to alarm you, but I thought I should tell you about it."

Adrien nodded absently. "Thank you, Sister."

Thea was silent a moment, watching her; then she turned to look down into the play court.

"It's nearly time for the morning play period. I'm so happy you enjoy working with the children. Sister Marain says you've been a great help to the teachers."

Adrien roused herself and smiled. "I'm glad, but I've been helped if anyone has."

"A mutual blessing, then. My dear, are you feeling well?"

"Yes, I am. I had my weekly examination yesterday, and all three of us are in excellent health."

"I know about your state of health; the reports always come to my desk." She sighed. "I suppose I'm worried about your state of mind, but unfortunately I seem to be quite helpless there."

"No, Sister, that isn't true." Adrien reached out for Thea's hand. "You've been so kind and done so much for me, I can never repay you."

Thea smiled. "Don't be concerned about repaying *me*. Your gratitude belongs to the Holy Mezion and the All-God. Give your thanks to Him in whatever manner satisfies you." She reached up to pull her veil down. "Now, I must be about my business. Remember, my door is always open. Lord Bless, Sister."

"Lord Bless."

Adrien lowered her own veil, watching Thea walking away through the patterns of light and shadow. The sweet tones of the chapel chimes sounded, and she knew that within seconds the court would be alive with the rush of running feet and childish laughter. But for a moment she didn't move.

She was thinking of the applicant Thea had turned away, a young woman who lied to her. The lie might have been motivated by some personal quirk; she might have been entirely innocent of malign intent. But Adrien trusted Thea's instincts. The woman might also have been seeking entry to the convent for one reason: to find the Lady Adrien Eliseer.

She started down the colonnade; her hands, locked together under her sleeves, were cold.

The young woman might have been sent by Selasis, and that was frightening enough, but another possibility was equally unnerving: she might also have been sent by the Phoenix; by Alexand. But there was no way to be sure.

She quickened her step, looking down into the courtyard, filled now with exuberant children. Thank the God for the children, for these brief interims of distraction.

Alexand . . .

She was almost running, as if she could flee the ever present shadow of fear.

Alexand, find me. . . .

PHOENIX MEMFILES: DEPT HUMAN SCIENCES: BASIC SCHOOL
(HS/BS)
SUBFILE: LECTURE, BASIC SCHOOL 14 MARCH 3252
GUEST LECTURER: RICHARD LAMB
SUBJECT: POST-DISASTERS HISTORY:
THE MANKEEN REVOLT (3104–3120)
DOC LOC #819/219–1253/1812–1648–1433252

Unlike Pilgram and Ballarat, Lionar Mankeen did not
have a Colona or Almbert, which no doubt contributed to
his downfall. The Orthodox Church stood solidly opposed
to him, and it was the Archon, Bishop Nicolas III, who first
called Mankeen the "Heretic Lord." Nicolas also passed
a blanket excommunication edict on anyone who worked
or fought in his behalf, and although this had little effect
on Elite partisans—who were generally more concerned
with their fortunes in this world than in the next—it did
have a great impact on the Fesh and explains in part why
a majority of them remained loyal to the Confederation.

But Mankeen had a formidable ally of another kind, a
military mastermind, First Commander of Confleet, Scott
Cormoroi.

The question arises, inevitably, why would a man of
mature years (Cormoroi was fifty-seven at the beginning of
the Revolt) and a history of distinguished service to the
Confederation, which had won him not only the respect of
his peers and subordinates, but numerous decorations and
the highest rank possible in Confleet—why would such a
man turn traitor to the Confederation and lend his talents
to the cause of rebellion? Obviously he wasn't as happy in
his work as he was successful at it, and the roots of his
dissatisfaction go back to his youth.

Scott Cormoroi was born into the house of Albin Reeswyck, his father a ranking tech in Reeswyck's research
department. Cormoroi's brilliance was evident in childhood,
and his parents went to great lengths to procure educational

opportunities for him. Thus at sixteen he was enrolled in the University in Norleans on a House studies grant. By the time he was twenty, he had a doctorate in biochemistry, a tech rating of eight, and a guild degree of one. It was at that point in his scientific career that he was conscripted in a tax levy to Confleet.

Needless to say, he wasn't happy about it, but made the best of it and did very well as a soldier, working his way up through the ranks to the top in a little more than twenty years. No doubt he found it relatively easy, considering his intelligence index. Confleet was at that time—as it is today—more a policing than a military force, but it didn't have to sink to making war on Bonds. Its main adversary was the Outsider pirate clans that preyed on interplanetary shipping—as they do today. Cormoroi learned everything Confleet could teach him about the principles of military strategy, approaching it as someone else might chess or calculus, and he added a great deal in tactical theory. He also reorganized Confleet on every level and made it a highly efficient organization, and thus unique among Confederation bureaucracies. Cormoroi was also notably sympathetic with the men in his command, since most of them were, like him, conscripts; only a quarter of Confleet's personnel at that time were volunteers or born Confederation. He went to the Directorate on many occasions to make personal appeals for higher salaries for his men, for improved and better organized facilities for dealing with battleline injuries, for increased pensions for both the disabled and the retired. He also made promotion more accessible to non-Academy personnel, set up grievance boards to which a 'Fleeter could apply anonymously without fear of reprisals from his immediate superiors, and was prone to frequent unannounced visits to even the most remote Confleet bases to see for himself what conditions were on them. It's also said of Cormoroi that he was a strict disciplinarian, but scrupulously fair in his judgments.

A paragon of commanders, it would seem, and it isn't surprising that the loyalty of his troops was such that he could with confidence offer Lionar Mankeen half of Confleet, men and machines, and *more* than half its officers.

Less than a month after the debacle of the tax rebellion of 3102, Cormoroi met secretly with Mankeen and made exactly that offer. They weren't strangers. During Mankeen's Age of Rights tour of duty with Confleet (that custom was initiated by Ballarat during the Wars of Confederation) he was assigned as an aide in Cormoroi's office, and although their relationship wasn't close, the potential for the strong friendship that eventually grew between them was already there.

Mankeen and Cormoroi made their fateful alliance, and a week later there was another secret meeting at which Mankeen presented Cormoroi to twenty of his staunchest Elite allies. On the strength of Cormoroi's offer of a fleet-army—one that would simultaneously deprive the Confederation of half its armed forces—the Emancipation League began to take on solidarity.

Some accounts—notably Alric Berstine's in *The Mankeen League from Within*—tell us that Mankeen and some of his more hotheaded Lordly allies were ready to declare open war immediately, but it was Cormoroi who persuaded him to accept a more cautious and reasonable course. There followed nearly two years of covert preparation and organization, both in the ranks of Mankeen's League and in Confleet. The process was carried out with an amazingly successful degree of secrecy. At one time there were reports, some of which reached the Chairman, Arman Galinin, that a conspiracy might be forming in Confleet, but no proof was discovered, and Cormoroi was never once suspected of being involved in any way.

There was more awareness and concern for the burgeoning Elite conspiracy, but since none of the suspected Lords took any action that could be regarded as unlawful or subversive, Galinin was helpless to stop the formation of the rebellious conspiracy. In fact, it's questionable whether he was actually fully aware of the scope of the conspiracy or how imminent a threat it was. He had already induced the Directors to forgive and forget the tax rebellion. The guilty Lords had been brought to heel and the taxes paid, however unwillingly, and the following year the levies were met without the necessity of armed persuasion. Galinin no doubt hoped the rebellion had been nipped in the bud.

He was disabused of that fallacy when in May of 3104 he learned of the meeting of 302 First Lords—nearly a third of the Court of Lords—at the Mankeen estate in Mosk where, after three days of deliberation, the Lords signed the Charter of the Emancipation League.

Galinin called it the Mankeen League, its signatories traitors, and after reading a copy of the Charter—which was sent to him by Mankeen to serve as a declaration of intent and war—ordered Confleet to mobilize and, in conjunction with local Compol units, to take by force the treasonous Lords and confiscate their holdings.

Confleet mobilized, of course, but not in the anticipated manner. Scott Cormoroi had made meticulous preparations for this day, feeling out the leanings of his officers and as far as possible his troops, transferring those he called "loyal" (and the Confederation called "rebel") to strategic positions, concentrating them in five of Confleet's ten wings. Galinin's mobilization order didn't even reach most of the Confederationist officers, and the orders received by the rebels implemented a detailed plan that deployed a quarter of the ships to protective guard on League Lord holdings, another quarter to hidden bases in the Ural Mountains where they were kept in reserve, while the remaining half was deployed to attack Confleet bases on every inhabited planet and satellite in the Two Systems. The Mankeen Revolt was under way, and Arman Galinin found himself with only half his armed forces, and those in total disarray, without a commander or even a firm chain of command.

It should be noted that the rebel officers had orders from Cormoroi to explain to their men exactly what was happening before any hostilities occurred, and any who didn't wish to take part in the revolt were left behind at their bases. It should also be noted that only ten percent of the 'Fleeters in the five rebel wings took that alternative.

CHAPTER XV: Augus 3258

●||●||●||●||●||●||●||●||●||●||●||●||●||●||●||●||●||●||●||●||●||●||●||●||●||●||●||●||●||●||●||●||●||●||●||●H

1.

"Ah! The wanderer returns!" Amik went so far as to move his feet from the plush footstool, flourishing the smoking wand of his cigar holder. "Jael—bragnac for your weary commander. The Marsay Cabray."

Alex laughed, but it wasn't at Amik's welcome. It was his own sense of irony at the contrast between this exotic sanctum of Amik's and the spare Bond chapels where he'd spent most of the last two weeks. He'd returned within the hour from a tour of Shepherds in the Solar System.

Jael had left a message at the COS HQ: "Val and I having supper with the old Ser. Trans in when you can."

Alex had known what to expect; Amik lived up to his title of Lord of Thieves in every sense. On one side of the room the drapes were drawn to reveal a circular dining room, the table set with platinade, graced with fresh flowers and scented tapers. The music was a complex Miskaya *Fuguetta:* that would be Jael's choice. Amik reclined in his usual chair, swathed in brocaded velveen and jeweled chains, his pudgy fingers glittering with rings. Val Severin was sitting near him, radiant in a full-length gown of soft green that complemented her eyes and fair hair, and Jael was richly garbed in dark brown trousers and formal boots, with a brocaded doublet of deep ochre. He looked every centimeter the Lord's first born.

And Alex, in an inelegant and travel-worn slacsuit, felt momentarily out of place. He smiled faintly at that, then took Jael's offered hand, a little surprised at the intensity of his pleasure in seeing him again.

"Jael, how are you?"

"Well enough, brother, and welcome." He handed him a small, stemmed glass. "Here—smooth out the creases."

Alex took the glass, but only inhaled its aroma now.

"Thank you. Amik, I'll always be grateful for your excellent taste. Valentin, you're a delight for weary eyes." He laughed as her cheeks colored prettily.

"If I offer any delight for the eye, you have Jael to thank; he provided the unaccustomed luxury of this gown. But don't worry, Alex, I won't have time to get spoiled. This gathering is a welcoming party for you and a farewell party for me."

Alex raised an eyebrow and glanced at Jael. "A farewell? I came directly from the hanger. You'd better bring me up to date."

Amik interrupted testily, "This was intended to be a civilized evening, my friend, with civilized conversation. If you must muddle the atmosphere with business, at least sit down. I loathe craning my neck."

Alex sank into a chair, commenting drily, "You might save yourself some neck-craning if you could contain your curiosity about our business. So, Jael, what prompts this farewell party?"

Jael took a chair near Val. "You give it over to him, sister. It's yours by rights."

Val sent Amik an uneasy glance; she'd never become accustomed to discussing Phoenix "business" in his presence, despite Jael's assurances that Amik was well conditioned. But when she turned to Alex, a faint smile lighted her eyes.

"Alex, I managed to pass Sister Thea's X-ray eye. I begin my novitiate tomorrow."

He was too tired; he felt his control slipping and laughed with relief because he was close to weeping.

"Oh, Val—thank the God. You're the third agent we've tried to get into Saint Petra's. Congratulations are in order. And a toast." He raised his glass and, when she followed suit, admonished, "Enjoy that. Novices get nothing but curds and flat bread. Something like that."

She laughed. "I hope it isn't that bad."

"So do I, for your sake. Jael, anything on Hawkwood?"

"One of the hounds sniffed him up at the 'train terminal in Tremper, but old Bruno slipped him."

Alex frowned. "Tremper? There's a Faith convent there, too. When was that?"

"Two days ago."

"Damn. He could be anywhere by now."

"I know, but Tremper isn't Saint Petra's, and we have an eye inside now." He glanced at Val. "At least, we will have, unless the old Supra gets an itchy nose."

Alex smiled at her. "Val, Master Jeans would be proud of you. This isn't an easy role."

"Jeans would be astounded. But, Alex, getting into the cloister doesn't mean I'll find Lady Adrien immediately."

Jael nodded. "It won't be a downhill slide. There are nearly three hundred nuns, and they're always veiled, even inside the cloister, and Val will have to step light if she doesn't want to start the Supra's nose itching."

"It may not be quite so overwhelming," Val put in. "We're assuming Lady Adrien went in as a novice, and there are only thirty-five to forty novices." Then, with a sigh, "*Only*, she says. That's better than three hundred, though. Anyway, our— uh, HS chief has put me through an intensive course on Lady Adrien. I know her height and weight, and I've studied all the vidicom film available to get a feel for posture, gestures, that sort of thing, and I've heard every recording of her voice on file and had recognition conditioning on it." She stopped, hesitating a little before she asked, "Alex, is there anything *you* can think of that might help me identify her?"

He let his head fall back into the cushions, wondering how to explain the subtle, intensely personal characteristics that would set Adrien apart. He could find her, despite the veils and habits, if he could get inside those walls.

"I . . . can't help you, Val. Except . . ." He frowned. "She might be wearing a small ring. Two stones: ruby and sapphire."

Val said softly, "Oh." It was Jael who broke the silence that followed.

"There's another problem, Alex. Val will need a way to prove to her she's Phoenix and not one of Bruno's shadow corps. Val's going in under the name of Alexandra, and that might catch her ear, but she needs something Lady Adrien will tie with you, something that could *only* come from you."

Alex was silent, numbed at the necessity of thinking back, of remembering. His hand moved unconsciously to his throat, and finally he opened his collar and unfastened the medallion. Four months ago he'd had three facsimiles made of it, of the side showing the lamb. It was his entroit into the confidence of the Shepherds, and the facsimiles were insurance against loss of the original. But they were in Erica's office in Fina; he'd never used them. He hadn't wanted to subvert the ritual of recognition by using an imitation. The Shepherds might not know the difference, but he would. But now perhaps this golden disk would serve as an entroit for Val into Adrien's confidence.

Alex rose and crossed to Val, offering the medallion in the palm of his hand as he did to the Shepherds.

"Give her this. Tell her it was blessed by a saint."

Val only stared at it at first; she remembered it and knew what saint Alex meant. He pressed it into her hand and returned to his chair, while she fastened the chain around her neck, then slipped the medallion under her bodice, out of sight.

"Be careful, sister," Jael said lightly, "Alex would lose his right arm before that medal."

"I'll be careful. Don't worry."

Alex said, "Be careful for yourself, Val. This venture could put you right in Hawkwood's path." He picked up his glass, glancing over the rim at Amik, who was listening intently, his deceptively somnolent eyes missing nothing. Alex took another swallow of bragnac; he was beginning to feel its effects, made all the more potent by an empty stomach and two weeks with little sleep. Or perhaps it was rekindled hope; a heady sensation.

"Amik, you're a patient host. Bear with us a little longer. Jael, any reports from the Selasid Estate?"

"Nothing new. Lady Selasis is still ill, and Concordia hasn't seen much of her except at a long slant."

"Anything from . . . SI on Andreas?"

"No. He said he was tracking a strong lead, but nothing definite yet."

Alex stared into the golden liquid. Adrien had been missing for four months, but now there was a solid hope for her. Andreas Riis had been missing for eight months and they could still be sure of only on thing: he was alive. The Concord hadn't made a public announcement of successfully breaking the TAB, or of his death, or hinted that a trial and inevitable execution were impending.

Alex looked over at Jael. "Any new developments at the main HQ?"

"Nothing important. I talked to our HS chief today. You can scan the tapes later."

"Then I think that concludes our business. We can turn to

more civilized subjects now, and perhaps a more civilized custom—such as dining. Amik, are you going to let your guests
expire from starvation?"

Amik laughed, grunting as he pulled himself to his feet.

"Never let it be said that a guest in the house of Amik went
hungry. So. We'll retire to the dining room, but with one
stipulation: I won't have my digestion upset with talk of business or problems of any sort."

Alex rose, nodding acquiescence. "You have my word.
Nothing but the most civilized conversation."

"I'll hold that in faith, friend."

Amik's stipulation was met, and for a full two hours the
meal was uninterrupted by anything that might conceivably
upset his digestion. It was only when the attentive servants
were serving the caffay that Alex heard the buzz of his pocketcom.

He shrugged helplessly at Amik's disgruntled sigh.

"My apologies to my gracious host," he said as he rose.
"I hope the interruption will be brief. Excuse me."

Amik waved him away. "Go with! I should be satisfied with
so long a time as this in peace."

Alex put the 'com on hold until he was in the salon with
the drapes pulled between him and the dining room. There was
no image when he flipped the 'com open; the call was probably
from Fina relayed through the COS HQ comcenter.

"Ransom on line."

"Alex, are you clear?" It was Ben Venturi.

"Yes. Where are you?"

"Fina, but I'm transing to the Cave as soon as I can get to
the MT room."

There was an undercurrent of excitement in his voice, and
Alex felt his pulse quicken.

"Ben, what is it?"

"Thank the God and say a couple of prayers that I'm right—
I think I've found Andreas. We'll have to get an agent in for
positive ident, but every piece of information fits. Alex, I'll
stake my life on it. We've *found* him."

"Where—no, wait." He took a deep breath, bringing his
mind and body under tight rein. "Jael and I will meet you at
the COS HQ. Ten minutes."

He didn't wait for Ben's response, but snapped the 'com

shut as he strode to the drapes and pushed them back.

"Jael, we have to get back to the Cave."

Jael rose, black eyes intent, and after a moment a tight smile pulled at his lips.

"Finally," he said.

Alex didn't take time to wonder how Jael read the truth in his face.

Finally, indeed.

2.

Mike Compton was manning the MT console at the COS HQ. He cocked his thumb in the direction of the conference room, and Alex crossed the stone floor, Jael keeping pace with him, both too preoccupied even to scan the monitoring screens. In the conference room, Ben had a portable reading screen set up on the table. He rose, offering a hand, his rugged features home for a smile that seemed a stranger there.

"Alex, how was your research expedition?"

Alex laughed; Ben still referred to his work among the Shepherds as "research."

"It was a propaganda mission, but informative." His smile faded as he studied Ben's face; he still hadn't regained his color or all the weight lost during his recovery from the laser wound. "How are you, Ben?"

"I'm too damned relieved to feel anything but great. Jael, you look fit as a Lord—and dressed for the part."

Jael smiled crookedly as he moved around to study the image on the screen.

"Oh, I'm fit enough, Ben, but I thought I was off the line for the night. What's come down on Andreas?"

Ben seated himself in front of the screen, and Alex, looking over his shoulder, saw an aerial view of what seemed to be a Confleet base. From the landscape and 'bubbles, he guessed it to be on Castor.

Ben said, "If I haven't gone clear over the edge, this is where we'll find Andreas. Pendino. It's a small base; Class C. Damn, there are ten thousand like it in the Two Systems. Pendino's a repair depot, mainly, but they have a small active fleet. It's about twenty-five hundred kilometers northwest of

Helen." His hand went to the controls, and a series of images flickered across the screen until he stopped at a map with Helen in the center. "Here—in the middle of this open patch of the Barrens between the Troyan and Polyon Mountains. The only civilization closer than Helen is a few Eliseer mine complexes in the mountains." Then he switched back to the aerial view of the base. "I'll give somebody credit—a Class C Confleet base is the last place I'd look for Andreas. Almost the last place I *did* look. I didn't expect the SSB masterminds to run the risk; the detention centers are so short on security systems. But it was worth the risk just because we didn't expect it. Besides, keeping him on Castor meant less transportation; they knew our best chance of getting a lead on him was in transit. I think the only reason they moved him off Pollux was to make us think he was on his way to Terra. We almost took that bait, too."

Alex gazed at the screen, the image layered with the images of memory. Andreas Riis with his aesthete's face, his probing eyes, and that pervading gentleness that had been his undoing. Andreas was somewhere in that complex of slab-like buildings and mushroom hangars. At least, he *might* be.

"What led you to Pendino, Ben?"

He leaned back, turning his palms up. "That's a long story, but the key was the psychocontrollers. We knew they'd call in the best to work on Andreas's TAB, so we've been tracing the movements of the top SSB PCs. Of course, they covered their tracks damn well, but we finally caught enough leaks to realize there'd been an unusual number of ranking PCs visiting Pendino in the last eight months, so we took a closer look at it."

Alex shifted his gaze to Ben, almost reluctant to take his eyes from the stark scene.

"But you don't have positive identification yet?"

"No imagraphs or VPs, but I got a look at the DC files— and nearly lost one of our best agents in FleetComm. Anyway, one prisoner hits you right between the eyes. Prisoner number 10-273. Confleet DCs are generally used for 'Fleeter disciplinary problems until they see the error of their ways or sober up. That usually means a few days or weeks at the most. But 10-273 has been in for *eight months*. He was registered *two* days after Andreas was arrested. Then I saw a medical requisition for 10-273 for copadine. It's an anticoagulant: not something the average 'Fleeter would take. Erica says Andreas has used it for years; that or similar drugs. The number 10-273 is interesting, too. Conpol, Confleet, and the SSB all have a code system for classifying their prisoners."

Alex nodded. "The first two numbers are the key, aren't they?"

"Right. All SSB prisoners start with one, Conpol with two, Confleet with three. The second number refers to classifications within each of those categories; the other numbers are codes used by individual DCs. All Phoenix prisoners come under SSB jurisdiction, so 10-273 *begins* well enough with that one, but the number one-*zero* doesn't mean a damn thing. The SSB has no classification for it. Phoenix prisoners are all classified one-*seven*. But they knew we'd be looking for that, and I think to keep from fouling up their computers, they put Andreas in a class by himself."

"Very perceptive of them." Alex stared mesmerized at the screen, and some part of him wanted to laugh aloud, but it was only evident in a slight lift in his voice. "Ben, I can't believe you're wrong—probably because I don't want to—but we'll still need positive ident. Do you have a layout of the DC?"

Ben nodded and flipped through another series of images, then stopped at a floor plan.

"This is Level 1 of the base HQ. It's underground, and most of it's used for storage and maintenance. The water cyclers are up here, power exchange here, equipment storage in this area. He brought the image up and shifted it to put one section in the center of the screen. "This is the base DC."

On the right edge of the screen a corridor ran north and south; from the wider view, Alex knew it was the main access corridor for the entire level. In the center of the screen a hallway branched to the left off the main corridor, forming a horizontal "T." Against the wall of the main corridor, across from the second hall, a square was drawn with the initials MS inscribed in it. Monitoring station.

The side hall led to a large circular area; a smaller circle was drawn just inside the outer perimeter, with radiating lines connecting the two. Alex felt a chill. Even after seven months, the memories of the Cliff were bitterly clear. The spaces enclosed within those lines represented cells. There were twenty of them around the circle.

In the center of the circle was another small square with the initials MS. A guard stationed there could see into every cell, and vidicams within the cells would give him even more detailed readings. Dotted lines crossed the openings of each cell: shock screens. Across the hall leading to the main corridor was another dotted line.

"We have two monitoring stations to contend with," Ben was saying, his blunt finger moving across the screen. "This one in the main corridor, and the one in the DC. The corridor station picks up the signals from the DC station; that gives them backup. The guards at either one of the stations can activate the shock screens on the cells and this one in the hall, and they both have alarm switches. With a lot of luck, you'd have maybe thirty seconds before reinforcements arrived if somebody hit the alarms."

Jael frowned absently at the layout. "What about access from the upper levels?"

Ben pulled back again to show the entire level.

"There are five nulgrav lifts along the main corridor. The closest to the DC is here—that's about fifteen meters south of the corridor monitoring station."

Alex began pacing the room, hands clasped behind his back. "Our first problem is positive identification. *Then* we can worry about access."

Ben nodded. "We'll have to get someone inside the DC. I've dug as deep as I can. There isn't an imagraph or VP ident on prisoner 10-273 in the Pendino files, and definitely no interrogation tapes we could use for VP comparison. The SSB file on Andreas is sealed so tight, I'm not sure if even Galinin could touch it."

"We can't risk sending an agent into the DC. One hint that we're that close and they'd have Andreas out of there before we could do a damn thing about it. We'd be right back where we started."

"I know, Alex, but we can't risk going in without positive ident, either."

"We'll go in once, and only once—when we go in for Andreas." He leaned over Ben's shoulder to reach the controls, pulling the image up until only the DC was visible. "All Confleet bases operate on Terran Standard Time; they have three shift changes a day. There are six men in Pendino who have the answer to our question; six men who see prisoner 10-273 every day." He pointed to each of the two monitoring stations in turn. "I want one out of six. That shouldn't be too difficult."

Ben nodded. "If we can get hold of one of the guards, Erica can work on him and get an ident from imagraphs. Then we send him back to Pendino with memory blocks, and he'll never know he's been aiding and abetting."

Alex turned away from the screen to resume his pacing.

"Nor will the SSB, and we may find the same method useful in freeing Andreas—once we're sure he's there. The guards at those monitoring stations are the keys."

"I hope to hell we can get two nonresistants on the same shift."

Alex shrugged. "Confleet attracts nonresistants, even susceptibles. First, we have to capture just one of those guards."

"Helen is the closest city to Pendino," Jael put in. "A lot of Pendino 'Fleeters spend their leaves there, and most of them end up in the Outside sooner or later. If we can box one of these six in the Outside, he'll be a kid's gim to pull down."

"We'll pull him down," Ben said firmly, "one way or another, but that's a good line to follow up." Then he added, "*If* we don't get tangled up with the Brothers."

"You won't if you let me handle the catch."

"Fine with me." Ben switched off the screen and removed the tape spool. "I'll have to get copies of Pendino's personnel files and leave schedules. That'll take a few days, then maybe we'll have something we can get our teeth into."

Alex paused in his restless pacing. "You'd better go over the personnel files with Erica. She can suggest the best candidates for conditioning, in case we have a choice."

"Alex, I hardly make a move these days without an expert opinion from her. I guess there's nothing more we can do now. I'll get back to Fina and start the wheels turning on the files. By the way, Erica sends her regards, Alex, and she wants a detailed report on your tour. Verbal, and as soon as possible; she says she likes her impressions fresh. Besides, she was jumpy as a cat the whole time you were gone."

"She needn't have been," he said absently, "I was set up for MT trans to *Phoenix One* at any time."

"Well, she worries a lot, especially when you're wandering around Cameroodo or Selasid compounds. She calls them time bombs."

Alex took a quick breath, frowning. "She's right about that. I'll call her as soon as I can. How is she?"

Ben slumped back into his chair, arms folded.

"She's all right, and we haven't had so much as a hard look from Predis lately. He got a negative reaction when he sent his boys after me. I think if everybody wasn't so caught up in the war fever, that would've laid the whole thing wide open. But it's working, Alex, the war fever's working. He had another one of those rallies a couple of days ago and pulled over four thousand members. That's nearly everybody in Fina who wasn't on essential duty. The way they were cheering, you'd think they'd already won his damned war."

Alex nodded, but he didn't feel the old numb rage; they would—might—have Andreas free soon. And the LR-MT.

He turned to Jael. "Have you talked to Lyden or Bruce lately?"

"Lyden. He wants to see you. He says they're on a new tangent and they have some promising read-outs. I think that means they're closer to lining in on the tangent Andreas was taking. As far as I'm concerned, Lyden's in the Beyond. I don't speak the language."

"Neither do I, and talking to him usually doesn't help any. Damn, Andreas was so *close*. Along with everything else, we've lost eight months on the LR-MT, and I doubt we'll have time to make it up."

Ben frowned at him. "What do you mean? Predis?"

Alex hesitated before he answered. "He's only part of it. I told you my tour was informative. Ben, the Concord's going to see some uprisings in the next few months to make the ones in the past look like children's games. Cameroodo. Both the Lamb's and the Brother's influence there is virtually non-existent because the Shepherds are so weak. Lord James likes to keep them in their place. The Toramil compounds are going to explode, and when they do it'll be a real disaster. Like the Ganymede uprising. It's always more dangerous where you have habitat systems."

Neither Ben nor Jael responded to that, and Alex felt the uneasiness in their silence. He looked over at Ben with an oblique smile.

"Sorry. This is no time for gloom-casting when we might have Andreas free soon."

Ben laughed as he came to his feet. "If I got discouraged with a little gloom, I'd have gone over the edge long ago. Jael, tell Val I wish her luck at Saint Petra's. You have her set up for emergency trans?"

"She's well screened on every side. Don't worry." He

smiled faintly. "We almost lost her once. If we lose her on this gim, we can't send the hounds after her. Not into Saint Petra's. Alex, if you don't need me here for a while, I'll go back to the old Ser's for Val. She'll be wondering what's come down."

"Go ahead, and I won't need either of you tonight, so you can both relax."

"Thanks." Jael touched the doorcon and as the screens clicked off turned to Ben. "If we're going to cage one of those guards in the Outside, I'll need a little running time to set it up."

"You'll have it. Alex, get some rest. We may be too busy to sleep the next few weeks."

"I'd give up more than sleep to have Andreas free. That's worth any price asked."

Jael frowned. "Brother, you're asking fate."

"Probably. Ben, thanks for the good news."

"Feels damn good, doesn't it? Later. . . ."

Alex watched Ben cross to the MT, a vigor in his stride that had been absent for a long time.

Hope, Alex thought; that ambivalent blessing.

He walked with Jael as far as the bank of monitors and scanners. Even their tickings and hummings seemed to have a more positive pitch, and the faces of the monitoring crew reflected hopeful anticipation.

"Jael, I'll talk to you and Val in the morning." Then, after Jael had gone on to the MT, Alex turned to one of the comtechs.

"Mistra Rosiv, will you call a general assembly here in the comcenter. I have some news for the staff."

3.

Master Bruno Hawkwood listened to the soft chunking of his hoe, guiding the primitive tool with intent concentration, carefully skirting the clusters of flowers around the base of the tree.

Daffodils. They seemed incongruous on this desert planet, but at Saint Petra's a place had been made for them, a place where Terran things thrived, and in the controlled sunlight enjoyed an eternal spring. The graceful notes of bird songs emerged from the green shadows of the trees, lending a pastoral calm to the afternoon. His hoe moved in rhythmic strokes, turning the soil, cutting out the straying grass. The daffodils had a peculiarly heady fragrance, more like Terran narcissus. It reminded him of Margreta; narcissus was her favorite flower because of that sweet fragrance. With the fading of her vision, she'd learned to cultivate the pleasures of other senses.

The rhythm of his movements faltered. He recognized the danger of this line of thought and called up an epigra, reciting it silently to the steady chunking of his hoe.

> *Holy Lord, mover of stars, move my hand in thy will.*
> *Mover of suns, move my arm.*
> *Mover of worlds, move my body,*
> *Maker of Order, align my thoughts.*
> *Holy Lord, Author of Fate, make my Destiny;*
> *I am thy body, I am thy arm, I am thy hand.*
> *In the name of Gamaliel, sainted of the All-God.*
> *Ahm.*

He finished the thrice-three recitative, feeling the calm moving in his veins, feeling his body—bone, nerve, and muscle—working in harmonic consonance with his mind.

He would be ready. And the day was right; there was a clarity, a stillness in the atmosphere.

It would be today.

Yesterday there was a tension in the air; something that had no reasonable source, but it was there, and he took it as a sign; the time wasn't right.

Today it was right.

27 Augus. Even the numbers were right. Except that it was the *eighth* month. But two was the number of sacred dualism, seven the number of the Wheel of Destiny, and together they totaled the alpha number nine, and eight added to that produced another alpha number, seventeen.

And the time—Terran Standard 14:00, the double seven, and local Castor Standard would be 13:00.

It was right.

He paused to survey his handiwork, the freshly turned earth clean of straggling grass, the clusters of daffodils stripped of dead leaves and blossoms, the buds and fresh blooms smiling around the creased trunk of the tree. There was something to be said for this work; there was satisfaction in it. But he had other work to do, and the Lord Selasis was not a patient man.

Hawkwood leaned on his hoe and opened the collar of his tabard, the white and gold tabard of a Church Bond. He wasn't overly warm. He was only aware that the afternoon play period would begin in a few minutes.

His tawny eyes moved around the courtyard, somnolent in the afternoon sun, the dark pools of tree shadows cool and comfortable. On his right, behind the spaced row of trees, loomed the colonnaded walls of the cloister, screened, shadowed, inaccessible. Across the court was the school, and behind the windowalls, the impatient children, counting the minutes as he was. One end of the court was closed off with a row of low buildings, and behind him, the other end was fenced with a stone wall two meters high. It could be vaulted if necessary, but its gate was open during the day. Normally, a Church Fesh guard lounged there, but he had left his post hurriedly a few minutes ago, his destination the convent infirmary. They would diagnose it as food poisoning.

Hawkwood moved with unhurried steps to the next tree and its girdle of flowers. The pace of life at Saint Petra's was leisurely. He prided himself on his ability to absorb the rhythms of the people around him as well as their mannerisms and accents, and so he moved at a slow, ambling pace that brought him to the next flower bed and ten meters closer to the Bond, Lectris.

A signpost, that Bond.

Hawkwood set to work again, feeling the resistance of the soil transmitted through the hoe and into his arms, but now his eyes shifted as he worked. There were four Bonds in the court tending the plantings, including Lectris. The other three were on the far side by the school.

The hoe sliced into the pinkish soil; it had a rich smell, augmented by the bleeding grass.

Lectris was busy at the foot of the next tree, pausing from time to time to look toward the nulgrav lift. She would be coming down with her novice attendant in a matter of minutes.

Hawkwood thought of the second novice as an attendant out of habit; a Lady is always attended, and one never appeared in this court without the other, and they seldom strayed more than a few meters from each other. But he was satisfied that the attendant wasn't Mariet for the same reason he was satisfied that the other novice *was* the Lady Adrien.

Lectris had been the signpost pointing to these two novices.

When they appeared, he ceased immediately to be a gardener and reverted to what he was trained for— a bodyguard. Hawkwood assured himself that one of the novices was Lady Adrien by planting minicorders in the lift, but VP indent was useless in determining *which* of them was his target. From the discreet distance he was forced to maintain, it was impossible to be sure which was speaking at any given time; the veils precluded that. And they were so nearly the same height, that means of differentiating them was also precluded.

But all things are Written. The means were given him.

Their height might be virtually the same, but the difference in weight was obvious in spite of the loose, shapeless habits; a difference he estimated at ten to twelve kilos. The Lady Adrien's slender figure had always been her hallmark. No doubt her attendant was older, judging from her cautious, somewhat heavy-heeled gait.

The hoe broke the ground in slow, even strokes.

Nearly five months. The Lord Selasis might well grow impatient; it had been a long search. But Selasis knew no one else could have accomplished the task sooner, if at all.

Hawkwood took deep, spaced breaths, savoring the scents of earth and grass and flowers. It was almost time. He stopped and leaned on his hoe, bringing the ring on his right hand close to his mouth. It was a holy medallion ring that raised no eyebrows on a Bond's hand; they were awarded by the Church for devoted service.

His lips barely moved. "Raymon, are you at the lock?"

He bent his head, apparently looking down at the ground, bringing the ring close to his ear.

"Yes, Master Hawkwood. I'm in the 'car; a dark red two-seater with an Order of Benediction insignia."

"A few minutes, Raymon. No more."

Lectris had stopped working entirely. The nulgrav lift was still empty, but Hawkwood trusted the Bond's time sense. He resumed his hoeing, his eyes constantly shifting from Lectris to the lift.

Holy Lord, mover of stars, move my hand in thy will . . .

They were in the lift now, floating slowly downward, but the rhythm of his movements didn't falter, nor did his hoe so much as touch one blossom. His shifting glances were as effective as a direct gaze. He saw the two novices leave the lift.

Mover of suns, move my arm . . .

They were talking together as they approached. He heard a soft laugh, and now Lectris propped his hoe against the tree and walked toward them. Hawkwood kept at his work, watching to see where they would meet.

It was just six meters past the tree where Lectris had left his hoe. Hawkwood scanned the courtyard; its only other occupants were the Bond gardeners. The gate was still clear. The guard's replacement hadn't arrived yet.

Mover of worlds, move my body . . .

Lectris and the two novices were talking; again, a trill of laughter, light on the warm afternoon air.

Hawkwood rested his hoe on his shoulder and ambled toward the next tree and flower bed, the tree where the Bond's hoe was leaning. Lectris had his back to him.

Maker of Order, align my thoughts . . .

He moved with his shambling Bondman's gait, unhurried and unconcerned. The tree would make good cover; there would be a few seconds in which the gun would be exposed. The grass was springy and soft under his feet.

Holy Lord, Author of Fate, make my Destiny . . .

All three of them were looking toward the school. A matter of seconds. The chimes in the cloister chapel would mark the time. He reached the tree, put his hoe aside, and knelt to break off the withered blooms. Only six meters; an easy shot. He worked his way closer to the grooved trunk.

I am thy body . . .

He must aim for the face. If there were a Conpol investigation, he must make sure her identity wouldn't be obvious. And he must watch Lectris. He was probably armed.

The first bell-toned chime sounded.

I am thy arm . . .

He rose, his hand moving to his tabard. As the second tone sounded, his fingers closed on the laser. At the third, across the courtyard, the doors of the school rooms opened.

I am thy hand . . .

The flood of sound didn't distract him. He brought the gun up, elbow braced against the tree.

In the name of Gamaliel, sainted of the All-God . . .

The beam hissed, a clean line straight to the mark. The blue habit billowed; the attendant novice reached out for her, falling under the plunging weight.

Ahm.

The children's carefree shouts became shrieks of alarm, drowning the sonorous tolling of the chimes. Lectris stared at the fallen figure, face contorted with rage and grief. The brute power of the man's agony radiated from him, and Hawkwood hesitated a vital half second, chilled to his soul.

Then the Bond's hand flashed into his tabard, and Hawkwood broke into a run. The gate was still clear, the confusion centered behind him. He heard a strangled roar—Lectris.

"You! You stop! You *killed* her!"

Hawkwood fired over his shoulder; the beam cut across the Bond's leg, and he fell with a hoarse cry. Hawkwood reached the gate, and as he ran thrust his gun into his tabard.

"You—killed her! You killed—"

Hawkwood jerked in a paroxysm of pain, clutching his arm. The Bond—that damned Berserker Bond!

He dodged behind the wall, then ran down a narrow passageway between two buildings and across another open area, only dimly aware of the staring eyes of passersby. Another narrow passage. There was a storage building at the end of it. The door would be open.

The thirteenth chime rang in the distance as he plunged into the darkness and pushed the door shut behind him, grimacing in silent agony, while the shouts and pounding footfalls of pursuit passed.

Maker of Order, align my thoughts . . .

Thrice three he repeated the epigra until the pain was under control and his breathing settled to an even pace.

The wound wasn't serious; he knew that even before he looked at it in the dim light filtering through the high windows. But any laser wound was painful.

At least the Bond had reassured him.

That Berserker's rage reassured him. Lectris would have pursued him if he'd killed any of the nuns at random. The Bond was as highly trained as a guard dog, and pursuit would be an automatic response. But that potent agony was an intensely personal response. It was grief. Grief for his Lady.

There was no doubt in Hawkwood's mind now that he had at last accomplished his mission. He'd found the Lady Adrien, in spite of her cloistered inaccessibility, in spite of the veils. He'd found her. And killed her.

The Lord Selasis could rest easy now.

And perhaps Margreta might . . .

The Writ of Destiny would be revealed in its own time, in its own way.

He went to a shelf, reached under the bottom tier, and pulled out a rolled bundle of clothing, then stripped off his Bondman's garb.

A few minutes later, a monk of the Order of Benediction left the storeroom and walked with measured pace and bent, hooded head to the main lock of Saint Petra's.

4.

"Loren, I'm really worried about Adrien."

Loren Eliseer looked up across the sun-flooded salon. Near the windowall, where she could take advantage of the morning light, Galia sat working at her tribroidery frame. He didn't reply to her comment; not with the Bondmaid hovering nearby, silently attentive to the task of pouring tea.

"Will you have sucros, my lady?"

Galia looked up irritably, then hesitated; the girl wasn't the one who usually served their morning tea.

"No. I never take sucros."

"Yes, my lady. My lord?"

"Five drops."

"Yes, my lord."

The stirring rod clattered in the porceleen cup, a small sound loud in the warm silence.

Sucros to temper the taste of Black Shang tea; an acquired taste, Galia had warned him years ago. He still hadn't fully acquired it. Out of curiosity, he had once computed the cost of keeping Galia supplied with that special blend. Ten 'cords per gram.

Not that it mattered. Galia was Terran, and there was too much about life on Castor that was jarring to Terran senses. The Black Shang was important to her, as was the morning ritual of taking tea with her husband in the roof salon. It never occurred to him to deny her either.

He glanced at his watch with its double set of digits: 06:00 Helen Standard and 15:00 Terran Standard Time. The Bondmaid put one of the cups on the ebony and mother-of-pearl table next to Galia's chair. She only glanced at it, her fingers moving incessantly, weaving the colored strands into airy intricacies. She seemed incapable of sitting with her hands still; they were always occupied at something.

The Bondmaid brought his cup and put it on the table by his chair, but he didn't look up. He was mesmerized by the unceasing movements of Galia's hands, and preoccupied with his own thoughts.

Galia was worried about Adrien.

He felt the now familiar, vague sickness; regret, anxiety, doubt. When will it end? He asked himself the question daily. There was no answer to it, nor to its corollary; How long can I tolerate an intolerable situation without giving way?

It had been two weeks since he'd had one of those ambiguous messages from Adrien. And nearly five months since the wedding.

Patience. She had begged for his patience.

She would have it. He had no choice in that. At least, she would have it as long as—

"Will there by anything else, my lord?"

He glanced up at the Bond. "No, not for me. Galia?"

"That's all." She paused, frowning slightly. "What's your name, girl?"

"Jama, my lady. Karen took sick this morning."

"I see. You may go, Jama."

Eliseer heard the girl's quick footsteps, the door opening and closing, but he was still watching Galia. There was a brittle tightness around her mouth and eyes that had become more marked in the last few months. She *was* worried about Adrien, but she didn't begin to understand what she should be worried about.

She paused to sip tentatively at her tea, then gave a little sigh of annoyance.

"I hope Karen isn't seriously ill. This girl hasn't the faintest idea how to brew tea properly." She put the cup down and her fingers resumed their incessant movements. "But, dear, I really am concerned about Adrien. This . . . this *illness* of hers. I just don't know what to think of it. She's always been such a strong girl."

Eliseer felt the constriction in his throat, wondering who would be monitoring this conversation, wondering how long Adrien thought the ruse could be maintained.

"She's recovering from her illness, Galia. Lord Orin assured us—"

"Oh, yes, I know, and I'm sure she's getting the best of care. But I *do* wish Dr. Perralt hadn't died." There was a hint of reproach in her tone. "I'd feel so much better about Adrien if he were with her in Concordia."

"I'm sure she would, too, and perhaps that contributed to her illness. His death was a terrible shock for her. She was very fond of him."

Eliseer tasted his tea, then almost dropped the cup with the sudden tensing of his muscles, as he stared numbly at the saucer. When he realized he was trembling, he roused himself to get it under control, and looked across at Galia. The shock must have been apparent in his face. But she hadn't noticed; she was too engrossed in her tribroidery.

"I suppose you're right, Loren," she was saying. "I really miss Dr. Perralt myself. I mean, Dr. Hermon is a very capable young man, but he *is* so young."

Eliseer remained silent as she went on to discuss the relative merits of the two physicians. Her monologue was only a vague droning in the background of his thoughts. His whole attention was focused on the white saucer, and on the tiny disk resting in it.

He knew what it was, knew its ultimate source. Another message from Adrien.

Briefly, he considered how it came to be under his cup. The Bondmaid. What was her name? He'd been too preoccupied to listen; he couldn't even remember what she looked like. And it was immaterial. He would make no effort to find out how the tape spool reached him. Adrien had warned him; he couldn't risk—

"Loren?"

Galia was looking at him anxiously; the movements of her fingers had ceased. He got himself in rein and raised the cup to his lips. She wouldn't see the tape spool; Galia didn't look for the unexpected.

"Yes, Galia?"

"You look so pale. Are you feeling well?"

"I'm . . . tired. That's all."

The tense lines in her face softened. "I know, Loren. You've been driving yourself much too hard lately, and you have the trip to Leda tomorrow. I do wish you could put that off for a while."

"I can't, unfortunately, but perhaps after that I can take a little time off."

"I hope so. You mustn't let yourself get so exhausted." She resumed her embroidery as she inquired, "Will you be talking to Lord Lazar about Galen and Coretta?"

"Possibly. I'm not sure yet." He leaned forward to put his cup down and tucked the tape spool into his palm.

"It's really high time you made plans for the boys' marriages, Loren, and Coretta is such a well bred young woman and very attractive."

Eliseer rose and crossed to the comconsole on the wall behind Galia. He managed tó keep his pace slow and his attitude casual as he called up a music list.

"I'll talk to Galen this evening, Galia. I'd like to know how he feels about Coretta before I discuss it with Lazar."

Her brittle laugh made him stiffen.

"Oh, don't worry too much about that. Galen's too young to know how he *really* feels. It's an excellent match. Hamid is one of the oldest Houses in the Court of Lords *and* a Directorate House. And what about Renay? It's time to be thinking of a wife for him, too."

Eliseer reached for an earspeaker; his hands were still trembling slightly.

"Renay will be First Lord, Galia. I won't rush into signing any Contracts of Marriage for him."

"Of course, but I understand Charles Fallor is looking for a suitable match for his youngest daughter, Charla. Are you going to put on some music, dear? Don't make it too loud, please."

He touched out a number sequence, lowering the volume when the music began. Then, as he inserted the tape spool into the earspeaker, he asked, "Do you have a headache?"

She loosed a sigh. "Oh . . . a touch of one. I took something for it. That's one reason I miss Dr. Perralt. Dr. Hermon really doesn't seem to take my headaches seriously, but of course *his* head isn't aching."

Eliseer turned, putting his back to the console as he slipped the 'speaker into his ear. Galia's hands flashed in and out among the colored threads, seemingly independent of her thoughts; the subject of her headaches took her back through Perralt to Adrien, to her *illness*. She always pronounced the word as if it might start crawling down her back.

This message was short. Only a few words. His eyes squeezed shut, and the trembling was almost out of control.

". . . I was thinking this would be a good time—Loren?

Loren, darling, are you all right? You're absolutely white."

He turned his head away and hurriedly slipped the 'speaker out of his ear and into a pocket, then returned to his chair, concentrating on the seemingly insurmountable task of calling up a smile as he seated himself.

"Yes, of course I'm all right, Galia."

"Are you sure?"

He took time to taste his tea; his throat was dry.

"Yes, I'm sure, dear. Now, you were saying . . . ?"

She studied him a moment longer, then her hands resumed their deft, incessant movements.

"Well, Patricia's been invited to the Winter Ball at the Robek Estate next week, and it would be such a wonderful opportunity for her to meet some of the young Sers. After all, she's seventeen. We must be thinking more seriously about *her* future, too, and it would give me a chance to see Adrien. Surely that Dr. Lassily would let me see her—her own *mother*—if I'm right there in Concordia."

He was on the verge of panic, and for a moment he felt lost between roles; he couldn't find himself among them.

"No, Galia, I don't want you to go to Concordia. There's been . . . too much violence there. I don't want you—you and Patricia going there without me, and I can't get free to go with you."

"Violence? Oh, Loren, I'm sure those stories are exaggerated. I mean, if one can't be safe in *Concordia* . . . besides, we'll be staying with the Robek. I'm sure Lord Trevor can provide us adequate protection."

Eliseer closed his eyes, and he wanted to shout, *It doesn't matter; whatever I say doesn't matter*. But the monitors—the ultimate listener behind them would wonder how he knew it didn't matter now whether he gave Galia and Patricia permission to go to Concordia.

He said tightly, "Galia, let me think about it. I'll discuss it with you when I return from Leda."

Her sigh of concession was clearly audible. "Very well, Loren, we'll discuss it later, but please remember Patricia has her heart set on the ball, and this sort of thing is so important at her age—the social contacts. Otherwise, we might have another unmarried matron on our hands as we *almost* did with Adrien."

Eliseer looked at her sharply, but she was intent on her

tribroidery frame; she'd gotten in her last thrust and was satisfied to let the matter rest for now. He picked up his cup and sipped the tea. It was only pallidly warm, its taste flat. He drank it out of habit and to give him something to do with his hands. He watched Galia's hands in their unceasing motions, and he was beginning to understand.

For a long time they sat in silence, the only sound the soft strains of music. He welcomed the silence, and Galia seemed content with it. They were still capable of comfortable silences.

The tension in his shoulders eased with a regretful sigh. Galia should never have had to leave Terra. He had taken her from her green world, from Paykeen's ancient, gracious halls, when she was little more than a girl; taken her to a planet she could only regard as a hostile desert, far removed from her family and the social life she thrived upon. Yet she had carried out her duties as Lady of Eliseer with skill and grace, never expressing her loneliness or homesickness by word or attitude, and she loved him to the degree she was capable of loving anyone.

The next few weeks would be hard for Galia.

You always looked good in black, Mother. . . .

That had been unkind, but he understood it.

He was startled by the buzz of his pocketcom. He pulled it out of his doublet pocket, nearly dropping it as he opened it. Mils Fendro, his personal secretary.

"Yes, Mils?"

"My lord, I'm sorry to disturb you, but there's a priority SynchCom call for you. From Concordia."

So. Here it was. It seemed too soon.

"Concordia? Who's calling?"

"The Lord Orin Selasis. He says it's a personal matter and extremely urgent."

Eliseer rose. "Very well, Mils. I'll take it in my private office." He snapped the 'com shut and started for the door. "Excuse me, Galia. I have an important call."

She frowned questioningly, but didn't look up from her tribroidery frame.

"Did Mils say it was from Lord Orin?"

"Yes. I'll have to hurry; I don't want to keep him waiting." He paused at the door. "It's probably just some business matter. I'll finish my tea with you as soon as I'm through."

"All right, dear. Ask him about Adrien."

He touched the doorcon. "I will."
But he wouldn't have to ask.

5.

27 Augus. The realization of a hope was at hand. Eight months and ten days after his arrest, Andreas Riis might this day be freed.

He was in Pendino. There was no doubt of that now.

It was exactly one hour before liftoff.

Alex Ransom sat at the comconsole in his black cell: 15:00 Terran Standard Time in the Cave of Springs, in Fina, in Concordia, in Pendino.

And 06:00 Helen Standard, midmorning in Castor's twenty-hour day. The temperature was rising in the Cave. He had already donned the black shirt, pants, and boots of his SSB uniform. The black jacket, cloak, gloves, and helmet waited on the bed behind him, along with the X^2 in its black holster and the face-screen ring.

All the console vis-screens were on and focused on the surface: his windows. But he wasn't looking at them. On the counter were three tape spools, and they had occupied him for the last hour; they were as much a part of his preparations for this mission as the uniform.

Yet he eyed them now with a sense of mocking irony. On the eve of battle, a good soldier prepares for the obvious contingencies. These tapes would be heard only in the event of his death or total disability.

He had already replayed two of them. Now he took the last and inserted it into an earspeaker. The tape was addressed to Jael, the voice was his own.

"Jael, seven months ago I appointed you my second-in-command and heir apparent, a dubious honor you'll probably regard as a burden at this point. The following may be considered an advisory command, a contradictory term popular in Confleet. I can't argue from the grave with you or the Exile Council, but I ask that the course of action I outline here be accepted as the only viable alternative.

"I base everything on two incredibly optimistic assumptions: that Andreas will be freed, and that the LR-MT will be available, even if it's still in an experimental stage, to offer the Concord. I have no choice in this, as in so many things, except optimism, since the alternatives are unthinkable.

"With these assumptions understood, I'll proceed.

"Point one. Accept it as a truth; I haven't time to defend it. Predis Ussher cannot be negated as the de facto leader of the Phoenix now—not even if you bring Andreas back to Fina—without precipitating a schism. It's too late; Ussher has built up too much momentum. You can't call a halt to his war effort without splintering the Phoenix any more than an object moving at high speed can be suddenly stopped without disintegrating.

"Point two follows logically. If his military offensive can't be stopped, it must be used. The energies he's set in motion must be directed and controlled. That's the only way you can, as you would put it, pull him down, and the only way you can hope to achieve Phase I. Ussher rationalizes his offensive with the military confrontation indicated in the General Plan ex seqs, and you can use it as such, but only if you control it, and in some areas subvert it entirely.

"First, the appeal to the 'enchained masses' must not reach them. Aborting the preemption of the PubliCom System won't be difficult; SI will be in charge of that mission. The appeal to the Bonds is a far more difficult problem. Some of the microspeakers have already been planted, and although Ben might slow that program to some degree, it isn't entirely under his control. An obvious alternative is preventing the activation of the speakers when the offensive begins, but you can't depend on successful sabotage in Ussher's own department, and that task will, of course, be entrusted to Communications.

"The Bonds must be forewarned.

"Go to the Shepherds. Anyone will be accepted as the Brother's 'acolyte' by presenting the lamb medallion or one of the facsimiles with the words, 'I come in the Name of the Lamb. The Brother sends me.' I suggest the Shepherds simply be given a demonstration with a microspeaker and told that on the day of war, which I've been predicting for some time, a man infested with a Dark Spirit will try to goad their flocks into revolt against their Lords by using similar speakers and hoping they will think them voices from the Beyond. Trust the

Shepherds to convey the warning to their flocks in a manner that will be effective without arousing suspicion among any Fesh who might overhear their sermons.

"Another phase of Ussher's offensive that must be aborted is the attack on the Inner Planets power plants. He calls them a military objective, disregarding the catastrophic effects of a possible power outage on vacuum colonies like Castor or the Inner Planets themselves, while piously mouthing his concern for the 'innocents.' The real objective in this case is Isador Drakonis or, rather, the House of Drakonis.

"Those planets must be protected. You'll have to bargain with Amik for a temporary strike force to augment the exile fleet; five Falcons won't be enough. Yes, I know this means combat engagements with Phoenix ships. And crews.

"The attack on Drakonis betrays an objective of Ussher's campaign he won't openly admit, but which is too obvious for you to overlook. He'll try to destroy the three ruling Houses in Centauri. In light of his real ambition, to force the Concord out of Centauri and make himself its Lord, ridding himself of the present Lords is a logical move. But with the ideals—what's left of them—of the members in mind, he won't admit that objective. He'll simply arrange with some of the convert FO officers for a few 'accidental' strikes on the Estates of the Lords. How better to destroy a House than by destroying its First Lord and his heirs?

"Eliseer, Drakonis, Hamid, and their immediate families must be protected, and I think this can only be done by putting them into protective custody of sorts. Kidnap them and keep them in a safe place until after the offensive.

"Jael, I can hear your laughter at that, Ben's apoplectic protests, Erica's resigned sigh, and Andreas's puzzled, 'But, how?'

"We have agents in every House and we have the MT. It can be done. If you can think of a better way to insure their survival while their Estates are being bombed, I'll no doubt be applauding from the Beyond.

"With these exceptions, his war can be allowed to run its course. Ben and Jan Barret's general strat seqs are beautifully designed and the offensive will, as Ussher promises, shake the Concord to its moldering foundations. It will also shake the Phoenix.

"Ussher professes a distrust of the figures spat out of mindless computers; he doesn't like to look reality in the face unless it agrees with him, and he's induced the members to ignore the unpleasant truths presented by the computers, too. But we've been forced to face those truths, and we've calculated the price the Phoenix will pay for this 'victory.' Ussher is on a collision course with reality, and the inevitable crash will occur on 1 Januar.

"I'm ever mindful of Erica's maxim: to negate a leader, one must first consider his followers. They're riding with him on this collision course. Consider his followers in the aftermath of his offensive.

"Of the Society's fourteen thousand members, a minimum of eleven percent will be killed, injured, or captured. No one in Fina can escape personal loss. Nearly half the Phoenix fleet will be in a few hours' time destroyed, and the hangars will be filled with the wreckage of men and machines. Ussher can assure his followers then that they've shaken the Concord, that they've inflicted a hundred times the damage they've sustained, but I doubt they'll be impressed, because what they'll see when they look around them will bear no resemblance to the triumphant victory he promised them.

"At this nadir of shock and disillusionment, you can and must return to Fina with Andreas. You'll be welcomed then, and no schism will result. Ussher will no longer be a contender for their loyalty, and if you show them that the offensive can be used to achieve Phase I as it was originally delineated, that all their sacrifices weren't in vain, then you can begin to heal the Society's wounds.

"Jael, when you return to Fina, Andreas will be, as he always has been, the spiritual leader of the Phoenix, but you must become its secular leader. You must also take advantage of the period of shock the Concord will suffer in the wake of the offensive to make the initial approach to the bargaining table. The first move is a private meeting with Galinin. By law, the Chairman may unilaterally recognize an enemy envoy, and that will be your entroit into the Directorate Chamber and negotiations with the Directors. With the Ransom Alternative negated by my death or disability, you must fall back on the Peladeen Alternative, but you will take Ussher's place as the future Lord of the resurrected House of Peladeen. You must also assume the burden of representing the Society at the bargaining table. Haggling should be left to experts, and as you are your father's son, no one else in the Phoenix is better qualified.

"So, in the wake of the offensive, you must not only return with Andreas to Fina to reclaim his rightful place in the Phoenix, but immediately afterward embark for Concordia and present yourself to Galinin with the hope of claiming *your* rightful place in the Court of Lords. You'll be armed with a statement of authorization from Andreas, whose name will be familiar to Galinin as the Society's founder, with the Lady Manir Peladeen's death testament—I'm sure your father will surrender it to you for this purpose—and with what might also be called a death testament from me. That's the second tape I'm leaving with you. It's addressed in my handwriting to Galinin, and my voice can be checked for VP ident. This tape includes an offering of sorts, one that can't be included in the package the Phoenix will offer the Directors: an assurance that I know the rumors regarding Karlis Selasis's sterility to be true, even if I can't offer proof. I hope the assurance will be enough to induce Galinin to demand a Board of Succession inquiry. That's another legal prerogative of the Chairman. If he still has any faith in my word, he can relieve himself of a threat that has stymied him for decades, and perhaps as a result he'll look more favorably on you, the Phoenix, and the reforms vital to the survival of the Concord.

"In this tape I've also made a personal appeal to the man who was my grandfather and Rich's, the man who loved us both. I've asked him to recognize the Phoenix as a beneficent power, as we did, and to regard it as a useful ally. Galinin is a skeptic, but an open-minded one. And, Jael, above all, be honest with him; trust him. I've also asked him not only to support your bid for Lordship of Peladeen, but to regard you as an advisor and liaison with the Phoenix. In this way you might achieve a position of influence, if not actual power, that will facilitate the reforms of Phase I. I've also asked Galinin to try to bring Lord Woolf around to a similar understanding. Woolf is still heir to the Chairmanship.

"I'm assuming you'll let Erica, Ben, and Andreas hear this tape since these 'advisory commands' must be considered by the Exile Council. I'll end with thanks to you who were loving friends to Rich and me, whom I came to love as well.

"And to you, Jael, friend and brother...fortune."

Silence spun out from the final word. For the space of a

minute Alex listened to it, watching the veils of sand drifting off yellow dunes against an indigo sky.

Finally, he removed the earspeaker and took out the spool. Under the clear plasex disk on one side he had already written Jael's name. Now he broke off the switch tab on the rim and waited while the edges melted and sealed themselves, then he put it beside the other spools; they were already marked and sealed. The third had Adrien's name on it. He picked it up, wondering when, or if, or under what circumstances that seal would be broken.

6.

Phoenix Four, rechristened CFF *Orion* F-738-2C, had been carefully prepared for her final voyage. Alex could pilot her alone; the ship was almost entirely operated by remote control through radio relays from the COS HQ. Alex and Ben Venturi were the sole occupants of the transformed *Four*, but every effort had been made to conceal the fact. Ben was at the com-console, wearing the SSB uniform with the ease of familiarity. They were entering Pendino as Central Control inspectors, and during the last week rumors of their impending tour of inspection had leaked out in Confleet ranks. They would be expected, if not welcomed.

Four had taken a detour into space from the COS HQ so that it could approach Pendino on a typical entry vector, and now as the ship skimmed Castor's thin atmosphere, the temperature gauges spinning upward as the altitude indicator turned downward, Alex cut back the MAM-An generator and phased to nulgrav, staying on manual control to bring the ship out of orbit sequence and into the automatic landing grid beamed from Pendino. He was bound by an equivocal calm, mind and body functioning at a sustained pitch just below crisis level.

A glance at the navcomp console assured him he was locked in on the grid. He checked his watch: 17:21 TST. They were two minutes ahead of sequence. He relaxed and looked up at the vis-screens. They were approaching from the west and the stark ridges of the Polyon Mountains rose beneath them. Beyond this rampart was an open plateau enveloped in the fog of a Barrens dust storm. He listened to the voices from his headset as the ship sloped downward.

"*Orion* F-738-2C, Pendino Navcomp Center on line. We have you in landing grid."

Then the voice from the COS HQ relayed through *Four*'s comsystem, "Right, Pendino. We are on automatic. Relative ground speed twenty kpm and decelerating. We are moving into a dust storm. Check reception variance, please."

"Your signals are clear, *Orion*. You are two minutes from the field locks."

Another voice now. "Pendino, this is Captain May, *Orion*. Major Ransom and Leftant Bently from SSB Central Control are aboard. Request that you have a 'car on stand-by at the hangar to take them to base HQ immediately upon arrival."

Alex noted the brief pause before the response.

"Uh—yes, sir. A 'car will be ready."

Alex nodded toward the comconsole. "Put me on the Pendino frequency, Ben." He heard the faint click, then said quietly into his mike, "Pendino, this is Major Ransom, SSB CC on line. Inform Commander Paten that I'll expect to talk with him briefly as soon as we've touched down. And tell him we're in a hurry. We have a demanding schedule."

"Yes, sir. I'll inform him immediately."

"Thank you. Out."

Ben switched off the interconn, smiling obliquely. "The old SSB black magic. Strikes fear into the highest-ranked heart."

"For once, I'm grateful."

The storm was falling behind, and on the horizon Alex caught a reflective flash of light. Pendino. The voices went on, dry and monotonous, the yellow, arid plain turned slowly under them.

"*Orion*, will you require maintenance or servicing?"

The voice of "Captain May" answered, "No servicing is necessary. We will remain on stand-by for departure."

"Very good, sir. Your crew won't be disembarking?"

"No. We'll stay aboard on liftoff alert. We have Pendino on visual now."

"Yes, sir. Lock approach, one minute."

The cluster of 'bubbles, slab-shaped buildings, and oblate hangars was visible now. The voices went on, but Alex ceased listening to them; the lock approach would demand no attention on his part. He rose and reached for the helmet in the empty chair beside him.

"You'll have to inspect me, Ben. I'm not used to this uniform."

Ben laughed as he reached for his own helmet. "That's one area where I'm an expert."

Alex adjusted the chin strap as the voices marked off the final approach, then snapped the holstered X^2 on his belt and pulled on the black gloves, pausing to twist the bezel of the ring on his left hand. Ben wore a similar ring; they were equipped with transceivers that put them on open radio transmission to the COS HQ.

"Better sit down, Ben," Alex said, returning to his own chair, his hands resting on the manual controls, "just in case they foul up the autolanding. Here come the locks."

The *Four* slid over the bleak landscape, angling down to ten meters and leveling, finally coming to a full stop within the air lock. Across the flat waste of the field, the huddled buildings and mushroom hangars of Pendino seemed small and unreal, like toys or models, but as the ship moved out of the lock and floated toward them, they loomed into reality.

Alex spoke into his mike. "Commander Blayn?"

"Yes, sir. I can take her from here."

"You're on, Vic." He switched off the mike, then rose and donned his cloak. "Ben, do I pass inspection?"

Ben gave him a close scrutiny. "Yes, except for wearing your gun on your left side. I don't care what Fenn Lacroy taught you, nobody in the SSB shoots left-handed."

Alex laughed as he moved the holster to his right side. "Right-handedness is a prerequisite in the SSB?"

"No, but you damn well have to use a gun with your right hand. Part of the image of anonymity; no observable personal idiosyncrasies allowed." He looked up at the vis-screens. "Efficient bunch. There's our 'car, and that looks like a genuine Confleet major out to meet us."

The *Four* was taxiing to a slow stop in front of the main hangar. Alex went to the comconsole and pressed a button, then spoke into his headset mike.

"Jael, we've touched down. No problems yet. How's your pickup on our personal monitors?"

"Clear, Alex. Switch on the ship's vidicams."

His fingers moved across the controls. "They're on."

"We're pulling good pictures on all of them."

Alex felt a slight jolt as the ship came to a stop. Outside, a cluster of 'Fleeters waited by the 'car.

"Jael, don't hit the destruct switches until all three of us are clear of Pendino, unless someone gets too inquisitive. And close the ship locks as soon—"

"Don't get hackled; we'll see to the lifter. And Alex . . . fortune, brother."

"Thanks." He removed the headset, then looked at Ben. "Jael sends us fortune. We'll need it. Ready?"

He nodded and touched his face-screen ring. "Ready."

Confleet Commander Marvin Paten was nervous.

Alex had no intention of putting him at ease. He strode into the office, ignoring the ineffectual flutterings of the major who escorted them to the HQ, and for the moment ignoring the SSB officer, face-screened as he and Ben were, who stood near Paten's desk. That would be Captain Torenz, assigned to oversee security for prisoner 10-273.

Alex stopped two meters from the desk. "Commander Paten, I'm Major Ransom. This is my aide, Leftant Bently."

Paten was a rank-and-file pro, Alex knew, a few years short of retirement, and not at all pleased with the SSB's attention to Pendino or himself. He had come to his feet when Alex and Ben entered, and now he licked his lips, staring at the dark haze that was all he could see of Alex's face.

"Uh . . . welcome to Pendino, Major. This is . . . a pleasant surprise."

"I doubt it's either pleasant or totally surprising."

Paten looked faintly alarmed. "I don't understand, sir."

"Never mind." Alex purposely omitted the 'sirs' that were his due. He turned now to the SSB officer. "Captain Torenz?"

Torenz came to attention, right hand snapping to his left shoulder in a smart salute.

"Yes, sir."

"Are you the only SSB representative at Pendino?"

"No, sir. At the present time there are also two PC officers attached to the base."

"Where will I find them?"

Torenz glanced at his watch. "I believe they're setting up in the interrogation room, sir. Shall I call them?"

"No, not now. Is the prisoner in interrogation?"

"I . . . not yet. He should be in the DC now."

Alex allowed himself a sigh of relief. This was a risk they'd taken in assuming the role of inspectors. Andreas wasn't due for interrogation today for another two hours; the PCs were rushing the schedule to impress the inspectors with their diligence.

"I'm not interested in interrogation procedures, Captain," he said sharply. "PC isn't my field. Security *is*. Now, Commander, Bently and I will have a look at your DC. You have clearance ident cards for us?"

"Of course, sir. My secretary has them for you. But I thought . . . that is, Captain Torenz assumed you'd want him to escort you—"

"That won't be necessary. I suppose it's too late to ask you not to warn anyone in the DC of our arrival. However, I'll ask you to give them no further warning. I'm not here for a parade inspection."

Paten swallowed, glancing uneasily at Torenz.

"Of course not, sir. I assure you—"

"We won't be long, so if you will, keep yourself available. Captain Torenz, I'll talk to you after I've completed my inspection."

Torenz stiffened, then with a quick salute, "Yes, sir."

Alex answered the salute in a desultory fashion and started for the door.

"But—but, Major . . ."

Alex turned, conveying his annoyance in the stiff set of his shoulders, and Paten fumbled out, "Don't you—uh, need someone to . . . well, guide you, sir?"

"I'm quite familiar with the parts of your HQ of interest to me. Bently, let's get on with it." He turned on his heel and strode out of the room with Ben a pace behind.

His mind and body were still functioning at that sustained pitch, tension reined into concentration. He didn't speak to Ben as they stopped to pick up their clearance cards. There would be no words between them unless it became absolutely necessary; they would be monitored every step of the way. Alex had seen the array of screens behind Paten's desk.

Three of them were focused on the DC.

The reaction of the Confleet personnel to the SSB uniforms was an advantage they were playing on. Their appearance generated a silence wherever they went. The clearance cards served to pass them through every check point, but the uniforms were equally effective. They marched down the quiet corridors, booted feet marking a rhythmic cadence, Alex leading the way, guided by the memorized floor plans, translating the flat images of lines into the three-dimensional reality of halls, doorways, junctions, monitoring stations, nulgrav lifts.

They had calculated that it would take five minutes to make their way from Paten's office to the DC; five minutes in which Paten or Torenz might have second thoughts, and a call to SSB Central Control in Concordia would suffice to unmask the "inspectors." But Torenz was a captain; he'd think twice before questioning a major. So would Paten. At least, an SSB major.

They paused to show their cards to the guard at the lift that took them to Level 1. Alex's eyes were constantly moving behind his face-screen, assessing every detail, searching for discrepancies in expected procedure, while he mentally reexamined the plan, calculating time intervals, extrapolating potential alternatives.

It would be over within minutes. The two guards at the monitoring stations in the DC would be vital, if unwitting, accomplices to Andreas's escape. Both men had had leaves in the last two weeks, both had spent them in Helen, and both had spent part of their leaves in the COS HQ with Erica Radek. Neither would believe that if he were told, but at the right cues, they would respond with carefully programmed responses. They would open the doors for Andreas.

Sargent John Macintire, on the corridor station, was conditioned to go through the usual pass procedures, allowing them to enter the DC, then after activating the hall shock screen, he would fall immediately into a nonreactive trance state.

Sargent Jeremy Ross, on the monitoring station inside the DC, would react similarly. Once Alex and Ben identified themselves, he would turn off all the monitors and all the cell shock screens, then go into a trance state.

The most vital part of Ross's role was switching off the cell shock screens. The hall screen was distant enough to cause no interference in MT transmission, but the cell screens would surround them in an electrical field that would make the MT virtually impotent.

Once the cell screens were off, they would have less than a minute to complete transing; Paten and Torenz would sound the alarms as soon as the monitors went off. But it would be time enough. The MT at the COS HQ was already homed in on the fixes in their boots. The trans would be instantaneous once the order was given.

The corridor monitoring station was only a few meters ahead, looming closer with the long strides that set Alex's cloak whipping around his legs. He didn't so much as glance at Ben, but he trusted his reactions, trusted the almost telepathic rapport existing between them.

Sargent Macintire was at his post.

Alex had the ident card in his hand; he flashed it briefly as Macintire came to his feet and saluted.

"Major Ransom, SSB," Alex said tersely. "This is my aide, Leftant Bently."

"Sargent Macintire, sir. I've been exp——" He stopped, flushing with embarrassment. "I . . . uh, well, I mean—"

"I know exactly what you mean, Sargent. Military grapevines are the fastest form of communication known. I suppose Sargent Ross has also been alerted to our arrival?"

Macintire glanced down the hallway into the DC. "Well, Sargent Ross isn't on duty today, sir. He's in the infirmary on sick call."

Alex was too stunned to respond, and he was grateful for the face-screen. He could feel the blood draining from his face and knew he was beyond controlling his features.

That meant someone else was on the DC station; someone who wasn't conditioned.

His hesitation was brief; the subcrisis mental set still functioned. He felt Ben's accedence to necessity.

"A postleave ailment, no doubt," Alex commented acerbically as he leaned closer to study the monitoring console. At least Macintire was here; his reactions could be depended upon.

There was a vidicom screen for each of the twenty cells, but only five were occupied; the prisoners all seemed to be supine in various stages of stupor, recovery, or boredom. His gaze moved to cell number eleven, but he let it rest there—and on the figure huddled on the bed-ledge, apparently asleep—only momentarily. He felt the acceleration of his pulse, but his tone was cool, almost indifferent.

"I see you have backup controls on the cell shock screens, Sargent."

"Yes, sir. This console is an exact duplicate of the one inside the DC. I can take over any of the DC stations's functions. The cell screens are controlled individually—" He pointed to a row of switches, then at a larger one at the end of the row. "—or this switch turns all of them on or off at once."

Alex took careful note of the position of the latter control. "And the hall screen?"

"Again, either station can control it. We take the precaution of verbal notification by intercom when either of us changes the status on any of the screens."

"Who has access to the DC?"

"No one who can't show me—and the DC guard—a clearance card from Commander Paten, sir."

Alex turned and looked down the hall into the DC. The monitoring station and the guard were clearly visible, but he was looking past it to the open doorway of cell eleven.

"Very good, Sargent. You may clear us for entry into the DC."

"Yes, sir." Macintire sat down and activated the intercom, and at his next words, the man at the DC station turned to look down the hall. "Sargent Kile, I'm passing Major Ransom and Leftant Bently, SSB CC. Hall screen going off."

The voice came through the speakers, curiously remote. "Very well, Sargent."

Alex turned and started down the hall with Ben falling into step beside him. The click of the hall screen reactivating after they passed was the only sound except for the echoing beat of their footfalls. Inside the DC, Alex felt a fleeting chill. White. The walls, the floor, the low ceiling, all white. The distance between the monitoring station and cell eleven was five meters. It seemed a long span.

As they approached, Sargent Kile rose and saluted. A young man, not long out of Confleet training school, Alex judged. The worst possible substitute for Ross. He might still be fired with the zeal of conscientious ambition.

"May I see your clearance card, Major?"

Alex sighed; a zealous youth. But his voice had a cool snap as he presented his card.

"Yes, of course. Leftant Bently, your card. At least we have one man on duty who sticks to security procedures. Sargent Kile, is it?"

He returned the cards and nodded. "Yes, sir."

"Sargent Macintire was explaining your monitoring system. Perhaps you could enlighten me further." Alex leaned over the low railing, locating the shock screen controls, then added, as

if it were an afterthought, "Oh—Bently, you may as well look
in on the prisoner. Sargent, will you open the cell shock screen,
please?"

"Of course, sir." Alert, efficient, nothing slow or sloppy
as he seated himself at the console and touched the switch
marked eleven. Impressive, Alex thought bitterly.

Ben was on his way to the cell, moving at an unhurried
pace. Alex stayed on the side of the station closest to the DC
entrance to draw Kile's attention away from him.

"I understand all signals are relayed from this station to the
sec-comcenter upstairs, Sargent. Does that include pickup from
individual cell monitors?"

Kile glanced up, his hand poised on the intercom switch.
Duty urged him to notify Macintire of a change in the shock
screen status, but an acute awareness of military etiquette and
Alex's supposed rank distracted him.

"Uh . . . yes, sir. It includes both audio and visual on every
cell."

Ben was inside the cell; he'd be ready for trans within
seconds. Alex wasn't concerned with the monitors now. The
shock screens—he had to reach the main control switch.

"Does the sec-comcenter monitor the cells all the time or
on a random basis?"

"On a random basis, sir, but with the two stations here on
full-time monitoring, there's no risk of anyone getting past us."
He looked toward the corridor station uneasily. "Excuse me,
sir, but I'll have to notify Sargent Macintire about the cell
screen."

"Yes, of course. Go ahead."

Alex swallowed at the dryness of his throat and moved a
few steps around the railing, careful to keep his posture relaxed.
The shock screen switch was close, and there was little time
left, but if he could reach that switch without alerting Kile, it
would mean a few extra seconds of reaction time, a few extra
seconds for the trans to be made before the alarms sounded.

"Sargent Macintire," Kile said crisply into the intercom
mike, "cell eleven shock screen off for inspection by Leftant
Bently, SSB CC."

Alex rested his elbows on the railing, his right hand only
half a meter from that vital switch.

There was no response from Macintire, who sat in blank-
eyed oblivion.

Kile frowned irritably. "Sargent Macintire, do you hear me?"

Inside the cell, Ben had Andreas, listless and unresisting, on his feet, supporting him with both arms in a close embrace that would bring him into the MT transmission field. Time was running out; someone in the sec-comcenter or Paten and Torenz would realize something was wrong, that one of the "inspectors" was behaving in a highly unusual manner.

"Sargent Macintire!" Kile's voice had a tight edge, but his attention was still focused on the corridor station.

Alex's hand moved; a casual movement, neither too fast nor too slow, that didn't attract Kile's eye. He reached the switch.

He looked away from Kile only long enough to nod to Ben.

"Mac! For the God's sake, what's wrong?"

Ben's hand was near his face, the brief order spoken too quietly for Alex to hear. Even the rush of air into the vacuum of their disappearance was barely audible.

But Kile was suddenly on his feet. "Hey! What the hell—"

Kile's left hand shot out to the console, and with the shattering scream of alarms, he launched himself across the railing.

Alex tried to sidestep, but Kile was on top of him, bearing him down to a jarring collision with the floor. The alarms drowned out the sounds of the brief struggle, drowned out every conscious awareness except that of passing seconds, and finally Alex rolled free. Under the shriek of alarms he heard the pounding of footsteps from the hall. He stumbled to his feet, lost his balance and fell to his knees. Kile, still on the floor, had his gun out of its holster.

Alex reached for his own gun—at his left side.

And it wasn't there.

The mental adjustment took only a fraction of a second; he aimed for Kile's gun, his arm extended in a tense line. A fraction of a second too late.

The gun was hurled from his hand, the beam seared through flesh and muscle from his knuckles to his shoulder. He staggered blindly to his feet, the floor lurching under him.

"Trans . . ." His voice seemed only a hoarse whisper. Guards were pouring into the DC. He had to stay on his feet, had to—

"Trans—NOW!"

7.

The scream of alarms ceased abruptly; he crumpled against a solid wall.

"Commander! Are you—oh, Holy God...."

The Cave of Springs.

He was slipping into darkness, rocked by pulsing waves of pain. His eyes went out of focus when he looked down at his right arm; his stomach cramped with nausea.

The sleeve hung torn and ragged, cut away by the beam that coursed up his arm. And that arm seemed a piece of horror that was foreign to him; an appendage that might be worn as a macabre, obscene joke. Flesh laid open, seared black, flecked with meaty read, and, at his wrist, the charred bones exposed under the burned tendons.

"Commander, let me help you!"

Dr. Lind. Other faces floated in a gray haze behind him.

"No."

Alex pulled his cloak around him, hiding the arm, that piece of his body that didn't belong to him any more.

But the pain was all his.

He moved haltingly out of the MT chamber into the com-center. He had an illusion of moving under the sea, pushing against the resistance of the water, every sound garbled, every image wavering and pale. And the pain moved with the currents, coming in long waves.

Andreas. He would not surrender until he saw Andreas. Until he was sure. Eight months; he must be sure....

"Brother, hold on to me."

Alex heard the voice and turned to his left, trying to bring his eyes into focus. Jael, asking no questions, slipping his arm around his body, taking his weight, and letting Alex draw strength from him. The waves of pain ebbed enough for him to make sense of what was happening around him.

A homecoming. All the exiles were gathered, laughing, talking, shouting, even weeping, and Andreas Riis was at the heart of it, taking each hand in turn, laughing with them. Erica was at his side, vainly trying to contain the overwhelming press of enthusiasm, caught up in it herself, her cheeks streaked with

333

tears. Ben was in it, too, but his eyes were moving, reflecting only a little of their joy. He shouted to someone, but the words were lost in the jubilation.

Alex knew Ben was looking for him, but he didn't have the strength to call to him. All his remaining energies were concentrated on Andreas, on his facial expressions, on the fragments of his words.

". . . Dr. Lyden! Did you work out the error on the alpha sequence?"

Lyden's answer was lost. Alex strained for Andreas's voice.

". . . always had faith, Erica, even if I couldn't remember what I was having faith in. Ben! So it was you. How long has it been . . . ?"

Jael's voice was close to Alex's ear, yet the words seemed infinitely distant.

"Brother, you pulled the gim, close and clean. Rest easy now."

"No, not . . . yet. Andreas. . . . I must . . . talk to him."

A fear was growing within him; fear for that wound; fear that it might be mortal. Somewhere in the subaqueous world outside himself, there was a cessation in the hectic voices and movements, and Andreas was looming toward him through the milling school of faces.

"Alex, there you are. I wondered . . ."

Jael's hand went out, intercepting Andreas before he could embrace Alex. But Alex saw nothing except Andreas's face, searching every line of it, searching his eyes for the light that had always been hidden in their depths, finding it still there.

"Alex?" His smile faded into anxious query. "Alex, you've been hurt."

"Yes. Andreas, are you . . . are you all right?"

"They were very careful to keep me in good health. As for my mental state—well, I have a great deal to catch up with, and I don't even know where I am. But I'm quite clear, Alex. I'm all right."

"Thank the God . . ." The pain came in a new surge that cut his breath off momentarily.

"Brother, it's done." Jael's voice, quiet but insistent. "Come on, we'll get you to the old Ser's infirmary."

Erica seemed to materialize out of the tidal mists, her gray eyes full of fear now, still wet with tears of joy quenched. Alex was aware of an anxious quiet, the sounds of jubilation silenced, the homecoming spoiled. But it didn't matter. Not even the pain mattered. Andreas was free—

"Commander!" A voice dim in his ears. "'Zion, its—*Commander!*"

The monitors. Only a few meters away. The voice wafted on the currents, carrying an uncomprehended alarm. Something that had nothing to do with Andreas, or himself, or that arm. It was still covered; no one could see it.

Ron Letz at the PubliCom screen. That was the voice Alex heard. His time sense was dysfunctioning; even sound seemed slowed by the miasma in which he was immersed.

He managed to form the words. "What is it, Letz?"

"A special news brief. It's the Lady—"

"You damned fool!" Ben lunging through the crowd, pushing Letz aside; Ben reaching for the controls, turning off the screen.

But not soon enough. In the split-second before it went dark, Alex saw a face on it; recognized it.

Adrien.

For a moment he blacked out, but didn't fall. Adrien. A news brief. *Why?*

"Turn on that screen."

Ben gazing at him in stricken appeal. "Alex, please . . ."

"Turn it *on!*" He started toward the console, but Jael held him back.

"It can wait, brother. For the God's sake—*Alex!*"

He pushed Jael away, teeth clenched against a cry of pain, swayed the few measureless steps to the console. Beyond the quiet in the cavern he heard a sound. A dull thunder; a beating of wings; black wings. His left hand went out, caught the edge of the console counter, and that was all that kept him from falling.

The switch. His right arm wouldn't move. He would fall without his left hand braced on the counter, and his right arm wouldn't move. He would pay any price in agony, but it refused to function.

"Turn it on!" He stared at the black space. *"Jael!"*

Jael was still at his side. His hesitation was brief, even if it seemed endless. Finally, his hand went to the controls. He said nothing.

The image was a blur of color. Alex fought to bring it into focus, finding the effort of simultaneously assimilating the words nearly beyond him.

Concordia. The DeKoven Woolf Estate. He was seeing himself on the screen; himself in that other world, that other time. Adrien was at his side in a gown of gossamer gold, a blue diamond at her throat. The betrothal ball. . . .

It was incomprehensible, as were the next images. The cathedron in Helen. Adrien on Karlis Selasis's arm, walking down the steps to the 'car . . . falling; fainting.

". . . her marriage to Lord Karlis Selasis. The Lady Adrien's tragic death is reported to be a suicide. . . ."

Suicide.

He stared at the screen; a newscaster wearing an expression of earnest concern. The dull thunder was louder now. Black wings beating against steel bars.

". . . according to sources within the House of Badir Selasis, the Lady Adrien's last words were, 'Alexand, wait for me. . . . .' Referring, it is assumed, to the late Lord—"

"No!"

Alex reached for the controls with his left hand and almost fell. Jael caught him, snapped an order to someone. The screen went dark.

Suicide. Wait for me. . . .

That was malicious, sordidly malicious, the product of a malign mind.

He turned, searching the vague blurs for one face, finding it close to him.

"Erica, what . . . what *happened?*"

Unjust, bitterly unjust that he should demand that answer of her. She deserved no part of his grief; she'd already shared too much of it. Perhaps that was why he turned to her now.

"Alex, we're not sure yet. You must understand—"

"When? When . . . did you . . . ?"

"Only a few hours ago. You'd already lifted off for Pendino. We still don't have the full story, and we can't be sure—"

"Val—what did . . ." The pain was pulling at him as if he were in a centrifuge; he could barely hear for the pounding thunder. "What did Val say?"

"One of the novices at Saint Petra's was . . . killed. But the Conpol investigators took the Supra's word on the identification without question. Alex, we don't have positive identification of the victim yet."

Suicide . . . the Lady Adrien's tragic death . . . sources within the House . . .

"But Selasis does, Erica. *Selasis* does! The Moon Princess . . . Elda Ternin—is she alive?"

Erica's eyes clouded, and it seemed a long time before she answered.

"Our agents couldn't save her. It happened too fast."

"She's . . . dead, then."

Erica's voice, aching and tight. "Yes, Elda's dead."

"Adrien is dead." He was surprised he could speak the words, surprised it could be expressed so simply.

"Alex, Selasis might have made a mistake—"

He stared at Erica. Did she think Selasis would order Elda killed if he weren't sure beyond the least doubt?

It was coming. He heard the rasping clamor under the thunder. He pushed away from Jael, away from Erica, and for a span of seconds or hours or days, time had no relevancy, stood swaying in the wind of those unseen wings, looking up into megatons of revolving blackness.

The Lord is my shepherd . . .

Adrien is dead.

And why was it that the image that shaped itself against the blackness wasn't Adrien's face, but Rich's?

He leadeth me beside the still waters . . .

Adrien is dead.

And why was it that the sound of bright laughter he heard wasn't Adrien's, but his mother's? Elise Galinin Woolf with her bronze hair trapping the sunlight.

He restoreth my soul . . .

Adrien is dead.

A death is one bead on a prayer chain; to read each bead is to read every death you have ever known, every death you will ever know.

Yea, though I walk through the valley of the shadow of death . . .

Adrien is dead.

The last bead is your own death.

Adrien is dead.

The pain came in sudden, brutal surges, and it could no longer be called pain. It was agony, and he knew it, knew the look of it; he'd seen enough of it. The shuddering of flesh, the wracking muscular spasms, the gaping mouth, every breath a choked cry. The black angel beat at its cage, smashing its pinions against the steel bars. The locks were shivering to powder. They would not hold.

...my cup runneth over...

A sanna for my passing, my friends. Gentle hands easing him down, whispering voices floating him into darkness. The wind blew chill through the caverns of his skull. He found Rich; found him lying forever locked in a frozen piece of time, like a sea bird, broken and still.

Where was Adrien?

Did she lie somewhere, a Selaneen doll smashed on some obdurate pavement? All he could see was her hand, that ivory hand that seemed born of the imagination of an artisan of a vanished dynasty.

The locks did not hold.

You're free! Damn you—you're free!

He cried out, screamed in terror, but every sound was silenced in vacuum.